IN THE NAM

Dear Dr. Scott – april 2020

The state of our nation, the state of the world will all be OK. And so will we.

I'll bet you read this novel with eyes you didn't have less than three weeks ago.

God bless,
Guy

IN THE NAM

A PILOT'S RECOLLECTION OF DANGEROUS TOP-SECRET MISSIONS AND THEIR IMPACT ON SO MANY LIVES

A VIETNAM WAR NOVEL BY

GUY SEABROOK

Cover Design: Hannah Linder
hannahlinderdesigns.com

Book Design: Denise Maksimowitz

ISBN—13: 978-1-7109-4799-1

Dedication

In honor of the 2.7 million brave men and women who served their country during the war in Vietnam, and their families and loved ones. A staggering 58,220 were killed and 153,000 were wounded. At present, there are 850,000 living Vietnam Veterans.

The story that follows is based on the actual experiences of the author, Guy Seabrook, and other pilots and soldiers as told through the voice of Sam Walker, a fictional character.

Table of Contents

Introduction

I had a name, rank and serial number, but I did not exist. I participated in conversations that never took place. I took direction from high ranking officials who never spoke to me. I executed authorized missions for which no written record exists. I am haunted by real memories that for many years I could not discuss.

I am a war-time pilot with top-secret clearance who returned from the war, but did not live 'to tell ...' Only God knows how I survived 187 treacherous missions, but I have been honor-bound not to divulge these ugly truths, and I believe in living up to my promises. However, I carry each of these missions, in their horrifying detail, with me all the time, everywhere I go, for I and many other veterans of the war in Vietnam can't see clear of them.

As a survivor of the war in Vietnam, I brought back memories not quite like those who return with souvenirs from a trip. Instead of tangible trinkets adorning a desktop, these gruesome mementos inhabit my spirit like a debilitating parasite, eating away at me, a little at a time.

I have decided to tell the parts of my story that I am at liberty to share; because I do exist. If you, my reader, have no military experience, maybe my story will enlighten you as to the burdens that others carry till death. If you do have military experience or share your life with someone who does, perhaps you will find some relief in knowing you are not alone. Either way, dear reader, you might certainly agree that War Is Hell.

Chapter 1 The Pledge

I thought for sure I was going to die. I was being attacked, stabbed by dozens of sharp knives all over my face and my body. Voices grew louder, strong arms restrained me, and I thrashed out blindly to protect myself. I was screaming and fighting for my life but could not break free from my enemies.

Eventually, I recognized familiar voices, and I made out the faces. Hardly the enemy, Tex and Ed were my two best buddies, like brothers to me. I found myself not in the hostile jungles of Vietnam, but in my own bathtub where they had put me. The frigid shower, pelting down on me with full force, had felt like daggers. Realizing I was safe, I calmed down. Though considerably embarrassed, I tried to get my wits together. Naturally, I suggested we all have a drink, just like old times. Tex said they'd see what they could wrestle up while I changed into dry clothes. My hair still wet, I could smell the coffee brewing from down the hall as I headed to the kitchen, where Tex poured me a cup of strong, black coffee. Ha! Not exactly what I had in mind.

Tex explained that Ed had gone to make a seafood run, something he and I used to do together some fifteen years ago in the Nam. He also promised to fix my back door. I didn't know what he was talking about. "Well, for a few days you wouldn't answer your phone or respond to your doorbell, so Ed and I jimmied the back door. No problem; I can fix it."

With that, Ed returned with bags of take-out and a few large bottles of soda. Soda! What the hell was going on!

After we ate, I thanked them for coming by and splurging on dinner. Feeling in control, I stood up to usher them out. I had my sights set on a small neighborhood bar just down the street.

"Hold on, there, buddy, we're not going anywhere. We're going to stay here all night," Tex declared in his calm, gravelly drawl. "We got an appointment tomorrow morning at 0900 hours, not too far from here. AA meeting. And we're taking you to it."

"An AA meeting! That's horseshit! I'm not a fuckin' alcoholic!"

"You may have forgotten, Sam, but after we left the Nam, back here on American soil, the three of us pledged to watch out for one another, and right now, you seem to need some watching. It appears you're not able to handle your booze anymore. Maybe you don't remember our pledge, but your lovely wife, Vicky, sure does!"

"That's bullshit! What do you know about it?"

"Well, we do know that Vicky is very concerned about you. For a while now, she's been telling us you're not the same man she married; she's worried about you, Sam, and she wants her husband back."

"Now that's even more shit! Vicky wouldn't talk to you guys behind my back. And she doesn't have any problems with me. She's just away visiting her grandparents now, as she does every year at this time. Vicky's got nothing to do with this."

Tex and Ed cast a knowing glance at one another. Then Ed questioned, "Why do you think we're here, now, Sam, while Vicky's gone?"

Instead of letting that sink in, I continued to argue with them. I was obnoxious and difficult to deal with. In the back of my mind, all I really wanted was a drink. I became aware of the sweat pouring down my face while a cold, clammy wave enveloped me from head to toe. Suddenly, my stomach started performing like the agitator in a washing machine. Whatever I had eaten, mixed with lots of strong, black coffee and sugary, carbonated soda, had created a toxic volcano that was ready to erupt. I charged back to the bathroom and threw up violently. Purged, I flushed that foul mess away and considered my situation.

Clutching the sides of the sink to steady myself, I peered into the mirror and confronted the haunted image that looked back at me. A face that hadn't been shaved in days, sickly, pale, and swollen; eyes bloodshot and unable to focus, hands trembling, lacking the power to keep me still. My swaying body betrayed me.

Could Vicky be right? Was I no longer the man she married? Such bullshit! *All I need is a drink, and I'll clean up and be fine. This can all be straightened out. I can make them understand.* I washed my face, brushed my teeth, ran a comb through my hair, and returned to my seat at the table, where Tex and Ed awaited.

"You OK, Sam?"

"Yes! That's what I've been trying to tell you guys. I'm perfectly fine! No way am I an alcoholic!"

In his slow, deliberate manner, Tex removed the toothpick from his mouth and twirled it in his long fingers while collecting his thoughts. "Truth is, Sam, maybe you're not an alcoholic; then again, maybe you are. None of us knows how to figure that out. But we do believe those people at AA can. It seems like the best place to start, anyway. That's what we're fixing to do. We are going to that meeting together. No ifs, ands, or buts. So, get used to it, buddy. When I take a pledge, I live up to it, and I'll be damned if you think you can make me betray my word!"

"Tex is right, Sam. What are we, if not our word?"

"Tomorrow, August 5, 1987, 0900 hours. AA meeting just a few minutes from here."

That was one of the longest, most difficult nights of my life. Eventually, they got to me. I remembered our pledge. I thought of Vicky. I went to the meeting.

Chapter 2 In Country

After spending the better part of two days cooped up in various transports, I was rank, stiff, and more than a bit cranky. Though eager to get to my intended destination, I badly needed to do three things: breathe some fresh air, stretch out my 5′-11″ frame, and dig into a good meal. As the day turned out, I would have to admit that two out of three ain't bad.

It was 0432 hours in Saigon when the 727 came to a full stop on the tarmac at Tan Son Nhut Air Base, which at that time, February 28, 1971, was the busiest military airport in the world. After a fitful sleep, I awoke to confront the fact that my long-anticipated tour of duty in Vietnam was about to begin.

Just then, the passenger door opened, filling the cabin with a suffocating rush of foul-smelling hot air as though an evil dragon had exhaled its penetrating stench on the lot of us. The hair on the back of my neck bristled in response to this primal warning. In less than five minutes, I found this place noxious, threatening, and foreboding. Two formidable combat soldiers drifted into the plane and immediately captured my attention. Their faces were gaunt and expressionless; their hollow cheeks sunken from weight loss. They appeared to be deeply fatigued yet extremely tense. But the most frightening of all was the haunted, far-away look in their eyes – clearly a sign of having endured too much trauma. Both wore flak vests, steel helmets, and forty-five caliber pistols. One, a staff sergeant, shouldered an M-16 assault rifle. The other, a young captain holding a clipboard, spoke.

"OK, listen up, men. This is your wake up. You have just landed in the Republic of Vietnam. You are now officially in a combat zone. Sergeant Wilson and I have each been seriously wounded twice and are therefore on the way home. We are seasoned combat infantry marines. Command picked us to be the first faces you see for a reason. That's right ... take a good, hard look. We are the real deal, not paper pushers. Thought you should be introduced to your future mirrors."

My future mirror? I was facing living portraits painted by the atrocities of war!

"I speak from experience," the captain continued in a strong voice, "so I shit you not. From this moment on, you better get very focused and stay that way for the next 365 days if you want to take one of those seats back home. If not, you will go home in a body bag!"

Whoa! The captain did a great job of scaring the crap out of everyone. Man! The truth is, he really didn't have to say anything at all; their faces alone spoke volumes. He continued, "When I call your name, please acknowledge and depart the plane to your waiting transportation. Babcock, Charles; Rogers, Michael; Walker, Sam ..."

Eager to disembark, I was headed down the steps of the 727 when I heard my name called again from someone in an awaiting jeep. My senses heightened, I noted the distant crow of a rooster, which definitely sounded bizarre against the backdrop of aircraft engines. The air was heavy with offensive odors that wrapped around me like an unpleasant dream. But somewhere in my exhausted brain stirred a hint of intrigue that made this place, so far away from home, seem almost seductive. I felt both attracted and repelled at the same time, by forces which I could not understand; it was unsettling.

My memory drifted back to when I had received my orders for Vietnam. I decided at that very moment that I would not try to imagine what it would be like. I was now glad I hadn't bothered because it would have been a complete waste of my time. Nothing about my life up to that point could have prepared me for this. I was a long way from the farm I grew up on. Then the frightful captain's warning about going home in a body bag rang in my ears: '... get very focused and stay that way.' My survival depended on it.

I climbed into the front passenger seat of the open jeep. Two other pilots were in the back, looking as sleepy as I felt, struggling to become alert to their surroundings, as was I.

"Where you gentlemen from in the world?" inquired the sergeant as he drove us away. "California, little town called Santa Clara," came the first voice out of the dark. "Detroit, Michigan," came the second.

"I'm from Charleston, South Carolina," I added. "What about you, Sarge?"

"Little Rock, Arkansas," he replied with a yellowed toothy grin, spitting a wad of tobacco onto the tarmac. "Any politician ever coming outta' there, would be a crook, for sure!" he predicted before getting back on topic. "I see you young pilots are Warrant Officers. You are the best of the best in my book. We enlisted men have to salute you and call you 'Sir', but you still treat us with respect, not like the commissioned pukes who talk down to us all the time. And your only job is to FLY! If there is such a thing as a good combat job over here, you Warrant Officers got it!

"I'm delivering you flyboys to CIA/NSA headquarters at the Caravelle Hotel in downtown Saigon Square. I'll take care of your duffle bags — you know, put them in your rooms. Major Williamson will meet you when we get there. Good fella as far as officers go. Then you will be handed over to Colonel Morrison. Real prick, the Colonel, but then this is his third tour. Third Tour Guys. They are either good as gold and really want to help or they are over the top hard-asses, like the Colonel. Now that they've showed up for the third time and found things got worse instead of better, maybe it's finally sinking in that we're losing this fuckin' war. Best to keep your mouth shut and just listen when he's talkin'."

The sergeant reached into his top pocket for a fresh piece of chew. He then handed each of us a bamboo stick about three feet long and became much more serious. "OK, Sirs, please listen up. Saigon has more pick-pockets than warts on a troll. They are usually a gang of kids ten to twelve years old; some older. The young ones just want your watch. The older ones will cut off your finger to steal your ring and wouldn't think twice about inflicting injury to get what they want. If this jeep stops in traffic and a bunch of younger ones approach us, poke them away with those sticks I gave you. Crack them over the head if you have to. If an older gang shows up, do nothing. I will handle it. By the way, this would be a good time to take off your rings, watches, or any gold necklaces."

No sooner had the sergeant finished his sentence when the traffic came to a halt. For a brief moment, there was no one around us, and then, all of a sudden and out of nowhere, eight or ten boys in their late teens yelling excitedly in Vietnamese rushed toward us like a pack of rabid dogs.

"Sit back, Sirs. I got this," Sarge said calmly, almost as though he was tired of this routine. In the flash of an eye, he reached under his seat and produced a forty-five-caliber pistol. He grabbed the teenager closest to him by the nape of the neck, shoved the pistol into his mouth, and began yelling something in their language. The other kids vanished as fast as they had appeared. Sarge kept this one kid captive, holding the back of his neck in a vice grip with the pistol stuck in his mouth. The kid began to cry. Sarge didn't buy it. Finally, the traffic began to move. Sarge pushed the kid hard to the ground still yelling at him in Vietnamese while keeping the pistol trained on him. Then he drove on as if nothing had ever happened.

"Man, you gotta' be shittin' me!" exclaimed a voice from the back seat. "Would you have shot that kid, Sarge?" asked Rogers.

"Fuckin-A I would have, and he knew it! You, Sirs, need to get one thing straight right upfront. If you don't have the balls to blow some gook away when you need to, then you will not make it back to the world. You will die. This really is war, gentlemen ... and the ugly truth is, it's all around you ... all the time."

I was sitting there numb, not saying a word. I had been in Vietnam less than one hour; the sun hadn't even come up yet, and this, this THING just happened. My only thought was, what the hell have I gotten myself into?

I felt I should change the subject and somehow sound normal, so I gave it a try. "I understand we are briefed in Saigon for two days and then shipped out to our assigned units."

"That's right, Sir. Get in a little Saigon nightlife tonight if you can, but take someone with you that has been in-country for a while."

The sun I had left at home was now showing its brow over the horizon like a dirty egg yolk, filtered through the smog of Saigon. I wished I could reach out and touch it. It was my only reality. In the jeep, we became immersed in the busyness of the streets. The scene was beyond description to my virgin eyes. The crackle of hundreds of moped engines filled the air to an almost deafening pitch while leaving trails of blue-black smoke that lingered long after they had sped away. Unfamiliar odors of food rose from wood fires that lined the street corners as mamasans cooked breakfast on open pits. Loose black pajamas and woven straw hats were everywhere as these intriguing people hurried off to work, to school … to war.

Even at this early hour, the temperature was already approaching 90 degrees. The heat was like an uninvited and obnoxious guest that overwhelmed everything else. I pulled a military issue black bandana from my flight suit pocket to wipe my face and neck, and for the first time, realized that I was pretty much soaked through and through from the combination of heat and fear.

"You will get used to it, Sir," Sarge reassured me.

"Come on, Sarge, no way you can get used to this heat."

"Ain't talkin' 'bout the heat, Sir. Talkin' 'bout all this other shit. It's different, that's for sure, but there is a certain peace about it too. Hard to explain. You'll have to be in-country for a few months before it sinks in. Guess what I'm sayin' is, when you know deep down inside yourself that in a split second you can kill anybody, anytime, anywhere ... well, the fear just leaves you. You take your balls back. Know what I mean?"

"No! But I will take your word for it." Right then, I didn't have a clue as to what he was talking about and wondered if I ever would.

We pulled up to an impressive establishment in the heart of downtown Saigon — the Caravelle Hotel, a surprisingly opulent oasis in the middle of this city of squalor. Just another thing here that did not make any sense. Wrapped around the hotel was a large open patio that I realized, upon closer inspection, was actually a restaurant. I took it all in as we followed Sarge into the building. Red glazed tiles covered the terrace floor. Rows of orderly tables dressed in white linen were paired with exotic, high-backed bamboo chairs. Ceiling fans resembling palm fronds quietly whirred overhead. Large Asian-styled pots holding eight-foot-tall palm trees decorated the perimeter of the room. Already at this early hour, many tables were filled with members of the press as well as pilots and other military personnel: Americans, South Vietnamese, and several Aussies who were easy to spot by their slouch field hats, folded up on one side. I felt like I had stepped into a scene from a Humphrey Bogart movie. When we entered an elevator on the first floor, Sarge opened a small panel next to the elevator buttons the hotel guests would use, took two keys from around his neck, placed each into a keyhole, turned one key and then the other. After entering a code onto a keypad, he pushed three different buttons in a programmed sequence. Then, we started to move.

"We're going three stories down, Sirs. I will leave you with the good major. Safe tour to you gentlemen, and remember, there are no heroes over here."

The door opened, and we stepped into the hallway while Sarge remained inside and pushed another button. As the elevator door closed behind us, I regretted that I never got Sarge's name.

"Good morning, gentlemen, I am Major Williamson. Welcome to CIA/NSA Headquarters, Saigon. Please follow me for coffee and a quick breakfast. Your briefing will begin in twenty minutes."

Looking back, although I did not know it then, it was the best breakfast I would experience for some time. The poor quality of food that awaited me at base camp was so bad I could never have imagined it given what I was blessed with – and took for granted – while growing up. The wonderful aromas from my boyhood kitchen of crispy bacon crackling while fresh buttermilk pancakes sizzled – with blueberries when they were in season — and strong brewed coffee would be replaced by the greasy odor emanating from the mess hall: a sorry mix of powdered eggs and powdered milk, cheap meat that could not be identified, unappetizing spam, and two-day-old recycled coffee. And they called that slop 'breakfast'. I arrived in the Nam hitting the scale at 170 pounds, and within six months, my weight had plummeted to 130 pounds, barely enough to power a man nearly six feet tall. Ultimately when discharged, I would leave forty pounds of body mass behind, but I had actually gained weight: the burden of innumerable horrific memories that I would lug around for the rest of my God-given days.

After a quick breakfast of ham, eggs, French toast, and robust coffee, we were taken into a large room with illuminated wall maps of Southeast Asia, China, Russia, and the Philippines. A dozen officers and enlisted men were busy scurrying from one place to the other with quiet efficiency, some talking on headsets, and others focused on moving small model planes, ships, artillery, tanks and other things I couldn't make out on the large maps that filled up two entire walls of the briefing room. A number of grids were marked off in different colored grease pencils. Judging by the way everyone was going about his business, the work that was done here looked very complex and important and kept this staff busy. Major Williamson escorted us to a table facing the maps.

"Welcome to the war gentlemen. I am Colonel Bill Morrison. Major Williamson and I will be briefing you today and tomorrow. Please remember that everything you hear, see, or read here is classified top-secret, and you are bound by your agreement with the United States Government to guard top-secret information for as long as twenty or more years. To be quite blunt, you screw up and you spend the next ten years in Leavenworth at hard labor. We clear?"

In unison, "Yes, Sir!"

"Don't interrupt me or ask questions. We have too much information to cover for that. Major Williamson will take your questions after my presentation. Much of what you will learn here is the 'Big Picture,' which is not what you will be privy to once you get to your assigned units. Having a big picture or bird's eye view of the war will help you make sense of things. As you can see, here is a map of Russia and China. These little countries to the south, Vietnam, Laos, Cambodia, are like little piglets sucking on the hind tit of Mother Russia and China. Problem is, they are well stocked with arms, munitions, food, clothing, medicine, supplies, and most of all, training and possibly hands-on personnel. We have not been able to confirm it, but we believe either Russian or Chinese soldiers, perhaps both, are operating many of the enemy's SAM missile sites. The SAMs are high tech, and its unlikely Uncle Ho's boys can handle that. There will be real professionals trying to shoot you out of the sky. Keep in mind, the United States has one main objective in Southeast Asia, and that is this: to stop the spread of communist aggression that has begun in Vietnam before it advances worldwide."

The first morning of my first day and the bullshit had already started. 'Make sense of things! Spread of communist aggression!' I wondered if he really believed this crap or if he had just said it so many times that he finally bought into it.

I would later learn that even though we were exposed to privileged and sensitive information, some of the facts had been glazed over with a political spin. For the first time, America had stuck its big toe in the wrong pond; and the pond had an endless supply of piranhas.

We've all seen those movies, the ones with surreal maps of war toys in movement, played out with virtual figures to depict who is where, doing what to whom, and keeping score. The 'why' of the conflict is hardly addressed because the justification behind the hostile actions of war is usually based on political agendas, which generally are difficult to defend and rarely make sense.

They wanted me to accept the fact that there was an imminent communist threat to American soil because mainland China and Russia were oozing south and from here, would somehow make a hop, skip and jump to main street America. Maybe my opinions had been jaundiced by all the protests, demonstrations, and nightly newscasts that brought this distant war in Vietnam right into our living rooms, but frankly, this was quite a stretch, to say the least.

At this point, however, it really doesn't matter; the die had been cast. When I enlisted, I took an oath to 'support and defend the Constitution of the United States' and to 'well and faithfully' discharge the duties of my office. I am here, in the Nam, my uniform bearing the insignia of a warrant officer. I will fulfill my sworn duties. I have a job to do and I will do it well.

The colonel and Major Williamson went on for hours attempting to ingrain in us the importance of our presence in Southeast Asia and giving specifics on how well we were doing to accomplish our goal here. Mercifully, the two finally changed the subject after what had been a grueling five hours.

"Now, to your assignments. Rogers, you will be going to Da Nang Air Base. Report to Colonel Edwards at the 208th Headquarters Command Squadron. He will give you a similar briefing with more specific details on the base camp you will be assigned to. Babcock, you will be going to Cam Ranh Bay. Same applies to you. Report to Colonel Sigwall, 109th Headquarters Command Squadron. He will take it from there.

"Mr. Walker, since you are under the umbrella of my command, I can get specific on your assignment. You will be going to the 365th squadron about thirty-eight klicks from here in a little place called Long

Thanh North. Rathole really. Just a single strip airbase carved out of a rubber plantation on the edge of one bad-ass jungle full of gooks.

"Here on the map, you will notice these little figures. Each one represents one hundred or more VC (Viet Cong) or NVA (North Vietnamese Army) regulars. As you can see, there are six such figures less than one-half mile from your base camp."

"So why don't we do something about them?" I found myself asking, stupidly.

"You need to stand up, Mr. Walker." The colonel drew himself up to face me head-on, his eyes drilling a hole right through me. I stood ... and in the 'attention' position.

"What part of 'Do not interrupt me with questions' did you not hear?"

"Sorry, Sir."

"SORRY? Sorry, is what you tell your mama. There is no room for miscommunication or failing to listen intently to instructions over here, Mr. Walker. It gets people killed. Do you understand me?"

"Yes, Sir!"

"Good! Now sit down. I will indulge your question since you will no doubt be posing the same question to the major. They leave us alone; we leave them alone. Fact is, the little bastards are cowards. They mingle and live in the village among civilians or in the orphanage a few klicks south of the village. For the most part, they listen to our communications, but every now and then, they'll try to send in a few sappers, you know boys with explosives strapped to them. They're all hopped up on dope, running through your perimeter to blow up a few planes. We killed two sappers at Long Thanh just last night, in fact."

The colonel said this last part with the smugness of accomplishment. I remembered what Sarge had said about the colonel being a prick. At that moment, it wasn't hard to believe. But before I could let my mind wander about that, what he said next got my full attention.

"Anyway, you'll be flying most of your missions into Cambodia where officially we have never been. Rogers, you and Babcock will be going into Laos. Same thing applies. We are not there, either. Remember, you heard this from me, as your Supreme Commander, but the fact that I was shot down in Cambodia on my second tour means I also speak from experience. All three of you need to know upfront that if you are shot down and can't get yourself within ten klicks north of the Vietnam border, known as the 'Fence', our Navy SEAL boys simply can't get to you. We can't risk going in any further. If you punch out of your aircraft and you are on the ground, you will no doubt be scared shitless, and your adrenaline will be in over-drive. I can promise you it is a come to Jesus moment. I have been there. Very important, gentlemen. For the first five minutes, do nothing but check out your condition for broken bones or gaping wounds. If you are too screwed up to move, key your mic and transmit Alpha Foxtrot Uniform three times, five minutes apart. Yes! AFU stands for what you think it does. The dinks haven't figured that one out yet. Won't mean shit to 'um, but an AWAC will hear you. They may also have time to confirm your position with their equipment when you make the second transmission. They will relay the information to a rapid deployment SEAL Team. The team will not be dropped at your location. Usually about five klicks from you. Stay put, gentlemen. We have lost more than one pilot because they started moving. The SEALs have been known to try and find you beyond the ten-klick limit, but that's their call, not ours. Normally, anything beyond ten klicks is out of their reach.

"Oh! Another thing. Very important. Just seconds before you ride the rails out upon ejection from your cozy cockpit, everything will take on an air of slow motion. Be sure to look over at your tracking computer for your grid coordinates. Without that, you are toast unless the AWAC can fix your position. We have to know exactly where you are and your distance from the Fence to attempt your rescue. If your plane does not blow up, we just gave Charlie a lot of top-secret information. But with the grid coordinates, we can send in the F-4s to destroy the aircraft. Clear?"

Again, in unison, "Yes, Sir!"

"If Charlie is after you ... well that's when things can get dicey. Obviously, it's OK to start talking on your radio at that point, 'cause the little bastards have already found you. Of course, you have a pill in your survival vest should you decide to use it. It's painless and will put you to sleep ... forever, or you can die the hard way. I pray you never have to use it. You will get this same information before each mission briefing at your assigned units. Just wanted you to hear the bad news from me first. Now, this last part of what I am about to tell you is very sensitive."

Leaning in, slowing his pace and lowering his voice, he continued, "There are a couple of things that can happen to a pilot that will prevent him from making it back. The first scenario is getting injured when you punch out and then dying from your wounds or exposure. Second, you can be held captive as a POW by the NVA in Hanoi. That much you already know about. This last one is becoming more common, based on our latest intel. Third ... a surviving pilot can be shipped off to Russia."

"Shipped off to Russia! Are you serious?" challenged California Babcock in disbelief.

"Afraid so, son. Hey look, it all sucks, OK, but at least if you end up in Russia, you'll probably be treated half decent. Rumor has it they want to learn all they can about American pilots, since we are the best in the world, so they give you a Russian wife and a job, probably flying and instructing Russian pilots. Bottom line is you will never come home. Apparently, Henry Kissinger knows all this but can do nothing about it. No one said this was going to be easy, gentlemen, and remember … you all volunteered for these top-secret slots. OK! That's enough for now. I will see you at 0600 hours. See Lieutenant Collins on your way out. He has passes for you men to see some of the city tonight. Don't be out too late, and don't drink the Vietnamese beer."

"How come we shouldn't drink the local beer?" I wondered aloud, breaking the no questions rule once again.

"Because it's fermented with formaldehyde, and you can't afford two days to recover from the hangover."

***

It had been a long journey, and the first day in the Nam was a mind-bender. After going to our respective rooms, taking much needed hot showers and putting on clean flight suits, California Babcock, Detroit Rogers, and I met in the hotel patio restaurant for dinner.

I don't know whose mouth hit the floor first when our waitress greeted us. Exquisitely dressed, she wore a black silk body-fitting tunic over white silk pants and sexy red stilettos with fingernail polish and lipstick to match. Her lustrous hair was blacker than midnight but shined like an opal. It was tucked behind her ears, revealing two luminous pearl earrings. She was stunningly beautiful and greeted us with a French-Vietnamese accent. "I see you gentlemen are new to my country. May I offer you complimentary martini?"

"Well yeah, vodka martinis would be good, but how'd you know we are new to your country?" I retorted with a college boy grin.

"Because you not yet have sun tan. All American GI have sun tan even if they only here few weeks." Her seductive black eyes were locked onto mine and holding fast. "I see you are pilots! What you fly?"

Like fingernails on a chalkboard, Miss Saigon just got personal ... too personal.

"Like you said, we just got here, so we don't know yet," blurted California Babcock.

"Sure, you know. All GI well trained before coming to fight here. It OK! You can tell me. I am on your side. GI number one. Maybe you come back after tour of duty and take me home with you. I make number one wife for you!" She ended with a big smile, a sexy giggle, and left us to fetch our drinks, well-assured we'd be following her with our eyes, if not our feet.

"Man! What is going on here?" whispered Detroit Rogers across the table to California Babcock and me.

"Don't look at me, brother," I said. "She is the first Vietnamese I have ever spoken too … and she isn't even all Vietnamese. Did you hear that French accent?"

"Yeah, and what a doll!" whispered Detroit Rogers. "Hey, Major Williamson said they were all prostitutes. I mean, you don't think ...?"

"No way, man! Not this one." I was positive. "She is working in a classy hotel as a waitress. The major said bars, man. This is no bar!"

Her name was Pi. She served us martinis, Vietnamese noodle soup, some type of fresh fish with vegetables, a big basket of freshly baked French bread, and a few bottles of French wine. We topped it off with a round of B&Bs and coffee. After that, fully sated, it was lights out for all three of us. The nightlife of Saigon would have to wait. Well-fed, lightly buzzed, and emotionally exhausted, we were officially 'in-country'.

Chapter 3 Base Camp

After another series of briefings that ate up most of the next morning and part of the afternoon, California Babcock was shipped out by helicopter to Cam Ranh Bay, and Detroit Rogers hopped a C-130 to Da Nang. The paths of our lives had intersected at one point for barely two days. In this brief moment, we got to know each other. In this brief moment, we wished each other well. We would never meet again. Pilots passing as pawns of war. Sometimes, in the present, something brings back a memory of my first day, and I think of Babcock and Rogers. Did they make it? If they did, how did their lives turn out? If not? Well, I can't say I want to know those details. It's more pleasant to think about the alluring Pi and that night so long ago when we three were still so innocent.

Struggling to get into a comfortable position among various boxes and crates that had been already loaded onto the back of a large army truck, I was the only passenger headed for Long Thanh North. The young driver had an array of junk piled on the passenger seat and no room for me upfront, but I was content in the back. It felt good to have some privacy, some time to be alone with my thoughts.

An army deuce-and-a-half truck is powered by a diesel engine the size of a small freight train and sounds about as loud. It bellows smoke from a four-inch vertical exhaust stack located behind the truck cab that emits foul-smelling diesel fumes, which, unfortunately, I was forced to inhale for the duration of the trip. We had been traveling for about two hours when the truck came to a stop at a guard post outside of what appeared to be a small airbase. I noticed that the guard had briefly removed his gas mask to process the driver, and just as I began to wonder why he needed the mask, the back of the truck filled up with a gut-wrenching stench. In very short order, the diesel fumes combined with the putrid stench made me sick to my stomach. I stuck my head outside and threw up violently. Before lifting my head, I called out to the guard, "What in the world is that disgusting smell?"

"Dead sappers, Sir," he shouted above the deuce-and-a-half's roaring engine. Then, looking up, I could see two body bags lying next to the guard house. "Looks like I am stuck with them for a while," he gestured, explaining that they were supposed to have been picked up that morning, but something happened to delay their removal.

I was pretty much horrified by the site of the body bags and the nauseating odor of death.

"They tried to get through the wire last night to blow up a couple of planes. Two of our guys, Navy SEAL types, cut their throats."

Adding to the already macabre scene, and as if right on cue, two tough-looking soldiers the size of professional football players and wearing tiger stripe fatigues, showed up. You got it. Enter stage left. Two Navy SEALs. I learned that they had dropped by the day before to check on a downed pilot they had rescued and just happened to be gazing through a Star Light Scope (infra-red night scope) in one of the bunkers when they spotted these two sappers trying to sneak through the perimeter. It would be the last thing those sappers would ever do.

"These the two gooks we sliced last night?" asked one mean-ass looking lieutenant.

"Yes, Sir, that would be them."

The lieutenant unzipped both body bags just enough to reveal the heads of the dead sappers. He pulled out a wicked-looking curved knife with a deer foot handle and cut an ear off of each corpse. Then he wrapped the two ears in a dirty cloth, which he returned to his pocket.

Leaning out the back of the truck, I couldn't help but ask, "What did you do that for, Captain?"

With a friendly smile, as though we might have been talking about baseball, he approached the truck. The lieutenant unbuttoned his fatigue shirt and pointed to his necklace with pride. "Just adding to my collection. These are gooks whose throat's I cut. I take these babies," patting his pocket, "back to base camp, salt 'um down, put 'um in the sun for about three weeks, and then I string 'um up with the rest."

I wanted to vomit again but somehow managed to hold it in. This guy had at least two dozen black, leathery ears that he personally 'harvested', strung onto a rawhide necklace, and wore close to his heart! With that, he buttoned his fatigue shirt and walked off with his friend. I thought things could not possibly get more bizarre, but they would. This human ear necklace was but a snowball in the middle of a blizzard.

By now, I felt like I was in a really bad dream and couldn't wake up. I just came over here to fly. What was with all this weird shit that was going on around me? My definition of war was changing by the minute. In barely two days, my whole world had been turned upside down and inside out. I struggled to make sense of so many bizarre and horrible things. Are they all the result of war? Most women are prostitutes? And not just for money but to mess with our heads and betray us to our enemies? Young kids schooled in aggression and violence roaming in gangs, eager to assault trained soldiers? What kind of culture would allow – encourage – their women and children to fight in this war in these ways? And what kind of soldier collects human ears to memorialize his kills, sun-curing them so they can be worn as though they were badges, honorably earned? Better not give this too much thought right now. I've been duly advised to keep my focus in order to stay alive. Only 363 more days to go.

***

When we finally left the guard gate, in stark contrast to my inner turmoil, the driver was unfazed. Maybe it was his southern drawl or his uncanny ability to appear nonchalant while living in the midst of war. The thought of him being stoned on local pot never entered my mind, but I would later learn that he was. He dropped me off in the middle of a deeply rutted red clay road beside a hut covered in red dust, which I entered to a friendly greeting. "Good evening, Sir. You must be Mr. Walker. We've been expecting you. I'm Sergeant Reynolds. Everybody calls me Burt, you know like the movie star," said the sandy-haired, freckle-faced young sergeant.

"OK, Burt. Where do we go from here?"

"Just follow me, Sir. I got your duffle bag. I'm taking you to the FLR."

"FLR? What's the FLR?"

"Fuckin' Laundry Room, Sir."

I followed him down a path to a row of little huts made with corrugated tin roofs and plywood walls called hooches that housed two pilots each. I would soon learn I hadn't earned one yet.

"Well, Sir, I'm sorry, but this cot in the laundry room will have to do for now until one of the short guys zeroes out of here."

"Whoa, whoa, there Burt. What do you mean when someone is short and zeroes out of here?"

"You see, Sir, everyone here is doing their tour of duty in the Nam, right?"

"Right!" I said; I got that much.

"Well, when you 'get short', it means you have less than thirty days left on your tour, and when your time has come to go back to the world, it's called 'zeroing' out. I think you have about two days before the next guy zeroes out, and you get a hooch. The showers are down there to the right. You got hot water only at night. Now would be a good time to go. The mess hall is that way on the left; open around the clock. The latrine is just down past the showers on the left. Tomorrow, you have a briefing at 0600 hours with Major Tipper O'Reilly. He's the CO. Just come back to where you met me, and I will show you to his office."

I dropped my duffle bag in the FLR and went over to the mess hall. It was all but deserted at this hour. I helped myself to a glass of milk, two bananas, a box of cornflakes, a hot biscuit, and a piece of greasy sausage and ate alone. I was hungry, famished, in fact, but it was all I could do to keep it down.

The shower was from heaven, and just what I needed. Mounted at least ten feet in the air and painted black, a ten thousand-gallon metal tank held the water where it cooked in the hot Vietnamese sun all day long. Fortunately, I was the only one in the shower stall that had six showerheads, so I took my time. The gravity flow to the showerheads was forceful. I stood there and let the hot water beat down on me for quite some time. I wanted to wash away most of that day.

Returning to the FLR, I lay on the cot without a sheet. I was really exhausted and still suffering from jet lag. It was very hot and stuffy, and I was completely alone among mounds of clothing, sheets, and towels, some of it already cleaned, but most of it yet unwashed. Amazing how the rank odor of dirty laundry pales in comparison with the stench of dead bodies, especially those that have been lying in the sun all day. There was an eerie stillness in the FLR, except for what sounded like mortar rounds off in the distance. Were they ours or theirs? Somewhere around midnight, I finally fell asleep wondering if the explosions would come any closer.

***

The doors to the laundry room burst open at 0500 hours, filling it with the chatter of a dozen mamasans, the local term for our domestic help. The women were speaking Vietnamese faster than I could think in English. It was a chirpy, rapid language, but pleasant to listen to, sounds that would become very familiar to me over the next several months.

"You new GI! You go now! You go now!"

I was in their workspace, and they wanted me out. Standing up in my T-shirt and boxers, I felt very exposed. I hurried to dig up a clean flight suit from my duffle bag. Before lacing up my boots, I reached back into the bag to retrieve my black kiwi boot polish and used a rag to give my boots a quick luster. Throughout the duration of my tour, I found myself doing this every morning, even though my mamasan had already polished them. I never could break this habit that was instilled in me while in fifth grade in military prep school.

I headed for the mess hall, where I would have many unpalatable meals: powdered eggs, powdered milk, greasy bacon, stale coffee, hard biscuits, and lumpy grits. I settled for a biscuit, something that resembled gravy and a cup of black coffee. I later learned that biscuits and gravy actually had a name, SOS, 'Shit on a Shingle', deservedly so. And so I began my tour of duty with the regrettable cuisine of the 365th combat squadron. It was going to be a long year. Only 362 days to go.

Chapter 4 Sully

"Name's Sullivan. Knoxville, Tennessee. People call me Sully." I watched as he pulled the seat out from the breakfast table and swung his long leg over the back before folding his lanky, 6'4" frame into the military issue chair. It was easy to warm up to a man who offers a friendly nickname, with a Tennessee mountain-boy twang to boot, but his low-key approach was incongruous with his physical appearance. His dark brown hair was cropped much shorter than regulation, and that only emphasized his close-set dark eyes and the bony nose that was too big for his thin face. The short mustache that topped his upper lip gave his otherwise unattractive features a dash of interest. I figured at some point he realized he was saddled with the wrong face, so he cultivated an amiable demeanor and put that forward. That plus his God-given intelligence served him well. Little did I know then that Sully and I would go through the night of our lives as combat pilots together.

"You the FNG?"

"FNG?" I questioned.

"Yeah, FNG, you know, fuckin' new guy!"

"By the way, the name is Walker. Charleston, SC. I go by Sam. When do I stop being the FNG?"

"Simple, Sam. When the next one shows up," Sully said with a laugh.

"So how long have you been here, Sully?"

"A little over a year, now. It's my second tour. Three hundred and forty-seven days to go."

"Sully, are you telling me things are so bad here that you know exactly how many days you have left?"

"How many you got left, FNG?"

"Three hundred sixty-two."

"See what I mean, FNG? You don't have to stop and calculate, you just know."

"Second tour? What's that like?"

"You ever break up with a girl from an insane relationship and then go back to her for one more try?"

I laughed. "Yeah, matter of fact, I did once."

"That's what a second tour is like, except a thousand times worse. Like what the fuck was I thinkin'? Things were way too crazy the first time. You're in the FLR, right?"

"Yeah, right."

"Be careful of an old mamasan named Beetle Nut. Can't miss her. I mean she is REALLY old and her teeth, well, the teeth she has left are blacker than coal. Got that way from chewing on some plant over here that gets her high. She must live on that shit. Anyway, just keep your distance."

"Why worry about an old lady?"

" 'Cause she loves White Willy, that's why."

"White Willy?"

"Yeah. She will sneak into the FLR before the other mamasans show up in the morning and try to give you a BJ before you even wake up."

"Awww, that is soooo gross! Are you serious?"

"Oh, I am serious, all right. I mean, who would want that down on his Johnson? Hey man, we will have enough nightmares to take home without that being one of them."

Taking home nightmares! Guess I hadn't thought of that. Gee ... I wondered, what kind? "How come everything around here begins with the F-word?"

"Fuck if I know! Look Walker, we're livin' in a shit hole in the middle of nowhere, and these gooks spend all day, every day, trying to kill us. On a regular basis, we got incoming mortar and rockets along with snipers during the day and sappers at night, coming through the perimeter to blow us away or to blow up our airplanes, or both. There's always the threat of a major enemy ground assault with some five hundred Charlie just sittin' out there watching us. We got snake bites, rat bites, spider bites, bat bites, mosquito bites, lice, fleas, dysentery, heatstroke, foot fungus, jungle rot, dehydration, gonorrhea, malaria, yellow fever, and the wonderful monsoon season, which begins in a few weeks. It rains non-stop day and night for five months! Man, that alone is enough to make you nuts. Then, of course, we got this new thing Uncle Sam has cooked up called Agent Orange – freakin' poison from the sky, if you ask me, man! The word, 'fuckin', just kinda' goes with the circumstances. You come up with a better one, and I will use it ... Oh, yeah, and these fleas! Be really careful of the fleas."

"How come?" I had to ask but was afraid to hear the answer.

"If you notice, there are no cats or dogs over here. The gooks have eaten them all, so these fleas mostly come from rats, you know, not your normal dog and cat flea. Rat fleas carry lots of diseases."

"Wow! OK! But wait a minute, Sully, what is Agent Orange?"

"Technically, who knows? It's this nasty chemical they are spraying all over the place. Acts as some kind of weed or jungle defoliant. Some dumb ass thinks they can kill the jungle back enough to expose Charlie. Tell me that's not crazy! They are spraying it from C-130s, C-47s and choppers. Trust me – you will run into it. If it's killing that thick-ass jungle, along with all those monkeys, what's it doing to us?"

"Killing monkeys?"

"Yeah. A team of marines found dozens of the little fellas just hanging from defoliated tree limbs, and they were deader than shit."

"So, what is it doing to us?"

"That's just it. Nobody knows. They say it's safe. Yeah, right!" Then he waved his hand in frustration and changed subjects. "When did you get in, Sam?"

"Last night, about twenty hundred," I said, choking on a mouthful of SOS, now adding rat fleas and dead monkeys to my list of things to worry about.

"One thing you left off your list, Sully."

"Oh, yeah, what?"

"That God-awful smell. What is it?"

"You mean you haven't been to the shitter yet?"

"No ... no, I haven't. You mean, latrine? Guess I have been backed up since I got here last night. I've peed elsewhere a few times."

"Call it a latrine if you want to, but over here, they are known as shitters. Some smart-ass general in Saigon, who obviously has never been without indoor plumbing or a toilet in his pampered life, came up with the order that no American GI would dig a hole to bury his waste. You know, like we have been doing in the field for boocoo decades. There were concerns of soil and water table contamination, as if that could possibly matter over here, where these people shit, shower, and use drinking water from the same place! Anyway, this brilliant general devised a method whereby a fifty-five-gallon drum is cut in half lengthwise, and handles are welded to each side. These serve as portable septic tanks when half-filled with a mixture of burnt oil and diesel fuel.

"The drums are positioned under sheets of plywood that have round, eight-inch holes cut into them and are framed out one foot above the rims of the drums. These are placed three feet apart, thereby making a six to eight drum shitter, excuse me, latrine, surrounded by a plywood and screen frame and tin roof. Real piece of work!"

"Aw, gross, Sully. So, what happens if you have to go and the drum is full?"

"If the drum is almost full, do your business by squattin' over the hole. Don't sit on it. If you sit, the splash up from shit, pee, diesel fuel and oil will flat ruin your day. Hit the showers as fast as you can. Hard to tell which is worse, the smell or the burn that is flaming over your butt. Unfortunately, this happens more than you might think.

"Second, and this is the part you can't get away from, is the overbearing smell when some sorry-ass enlisted man has 'shit-burn-detail.' That poor guy has to stay in the area until all the drums are completely finished burning. Usually takes about half a day. Oh! And one more thing to add to that list ... we run out of toilet paper a lot around here."

"So, what do you use, Sully?"

He held his index finger up in the air. "Oh, man!" I groaned in horror.

"Yep. Sure, makes you wash your hands a lot."

"So that's the smell that seems to be ever-present, even if just a little?"

"You got it, Sam. Now for the bad news."

"Gee, Sully. Worse than that ... there is more?"

"Yeah, Sam, not trying to freak you out or nothin'. It's how I had to learn all the ins and outs."

Thank God, guys were willing to take the time to help fill me in.

"No, Sully. I didn't mean to offend. Please, go ahead. I really appreciate everything you are telling me."

"As I said, the monsoon season starts in a couple of weeks. That has a dozen quirks all to itself from flying to living conditions – the shitters. As you know from flight school meteorological studies, during this season, the onslaught of cooler wet air will set up a temperature inversion."

"Oh crap, setting up conditions to hold that stinking smoke close to the ground." I found myself shaking my head in disbelief. Then I added shitters and toilet paper to my growing list of things to worry about.

"You got it, brother." Then Sully changed the subject to one more pleasant. "Say, Sam, there may be a quick way out of the FLR. Guy by the name of Laddy is leaving tomorrow. You could get his hooch if you jump on it. I mean right now. He has a new AC and wants $200 for the buy-in, which gives you his hooch. Several guys are holding out to try and low ball him. If I were you, I would jump on it like grits on gravy before someone without a good AC grabs it. Two hundred is a fair price, Sam. Think he paid two hundred twenty-five for it just two months ago. Like I said, the thing is new. I live right next door, and I'm going by there now if you got the money."

"OK! For the first time, I know what initials mean around here. AC! You telling me the hooches are air-conditioned?" I asked with wide-eyed surprise.

"Yep! Takes two weeks to get one through Sears."

"Sears delivers to Nam?" I could not believe my ears!

"Yes, sir. The shipping is free for the GI."

"Sully, I will take it, sight unseen. Here are two one-hundred-dollar bills you could give to Laddy for me. I really got to use the latrine, I mean shitter, and get to a meeting with the CO."

"You got it, Sam. I'll do it right now."

"OK. Tell Laddy I will drop by after my meeting."

"Sure, Sam, and by the way, why don't you come by my hooch tonight for a beer, or maybe I could meet you in the O Club. Sitting around by yourself in the FLR is no place for a new pilot in-country to be. My door is one down from Laddy. Who knows, with any luck, you might be in a room by tonight. By the way, night hooch door rules. If no one has told you, after dark, two knocks, wait a second and three knocks. Otherwise, you could get your ass shot off."

"Thanks. I look forward to it. Make it the O Club. I haven't been there yet."

Things were starting to shape up faster than I expected. As much as I hated to admit it, I was fighting loneliness already. I simply didn't know anyone in this place. It felt good to finally get connected, and after this lengthy conversation, I appreciated Sully's good nature and his valuable insights. Although he was very down to earth, I learned he graduated from an Ivy League college, and the more we interacted, my respect for his intelligence grew.

About that time, nature was calling, and I made my first trip to the latrine before meeting the CO. Some things in life can leave an indelible imprint. The experience of the latrine attacked most of my senses, and the resultant effect has remained with me to this day. I've heard Hell is putrid. That latrine was good enough motivation to live a life determined to not wind up in Hell.

Chapter 5 Tipper

"Morning, Mr. Walker. Get you a cup of coffee or some water while you wait to see the major?" offered Burt.

"Sure Burt, water would be great, thanks." As he handed me the glass, in walked Major Tipper O'Reilly, barrel-chested, thinning red hair, round face, and grayish-green eyes that had a serious, but 'it's-OK-to-like-me' look.

"Come on in, son. Have a seat."

I couldn't help but notice that Tipper had carefully aligned all the papers on his desk, and all of his pencils were sharpened to the same length. Was he really a neat freak, or did he have a lot of time on his hands?

"Thank you, Sir. Don't you want to hear 'Warrant Officer Walker reporting for duty' and all that stuff?"

"You have been watching too many movies, young man. We don't have time for all the formal stuff around here. This is just a quick meet and greet. Sorry for the short meeting, but I just got word that the brass wants me at the Tan Son Nhut Officer's Club in less than one hour. Too bad, you don't have your in-country check-ride out of the way, or I would let you fly me over. The O Club at Tan Son Nhut is something to behold. Probably the real jewel of this mess over here. Guess it wouldn't be fair to take you there without buying you a drink or two, and if you were flying me ... well, that would be a problem. Anyway, another time for sure. By the way, my one standing order about drinking: eighteen hours from bottle to throttle. That means your last drink."

"Got it."

"What do you like to be called, Mr. Walker?"

"Sam, Sir."

"Sam. Good solid name. I go by Tipper, not Major O'Reilly, and you can drop the 'Sir' in private or in the O Club. Probably best to use the 'Sir and major stuff' in front of the enlisted men."

"Sure, I understand."

"Sam, just a few things real quick before I go. Something you might be surprised to hear. When the shit starts flying up there and down here, well, I would just appreciate you coming to talk to me about it ... you know, man to man," he continued with my undivided attention. I was really trying to follow this!

"Oh, it won't be the flying that gets to you. That's part of you as a young man by now, just like any flyer who makes it this far. It's the other shit that wants your mind. Don't have a word for it really, but it always happens ... to every pilot who's flying top-secret missions. What I am about to tell you I know for a fact that no one, and I do mean no one, speaks about, because you just can't. And I am not supposed to either, but damn it, I believe I owe it to you. Understand?"

"You talking about stuff related to the top-secret missions that I will be flying, Sir?"

"Well, sorta, kinda, but no, not really. It's like this. At some point, usually sooner than later, it's going to hit you like a ton of bricks. You realize on a very deep level you know more about what's really going on over here than you ever imagined, and it ain't pretty, and you sure as hell can't write home about it. You will find yourself making shit up when you compose letters. You must, and that feels weird. You start lying to your family. And you begin to recognize that so does every pilot, yet you can't talk about it ... not even to them over a few drinks. Keeping this stuff inside is tough. That's why you have to know I am the one person you can come to and let it all out. Very important, Sam, or you will go nuts. Got it?"

"Yes, I do, Tipper. Truth is, I was wondering just how this part of what I will be doing is handled. Good to know there is an outlet."

"Son, I know it's hard to fathom that what you're doing here doesn't exist. Fact is, over here, you don't exist, except right here in front of me. This top-secret stuff sounds murky to talk about when we try to personalize it ... well, because it is murky. It goes against our nature. Just want you to know that all of us in this business, well, pilots anyway, struggle with it, but together, we will make it."

"Thanks so much, Tipper. You have just clarified the number one thing that has been rattling around in my head since I got here."

"OK, I got to get going. Burt will have your schedule for this afternoon. I just spoke with Colonel Simmons. As you know, we are attached to the Headquarters Company, and his office is in the compound where you will observe a mission briefing. He likes to meet all new pilots, so drop in and meet him before the briefing."

"Yes, Sir ... and thank you."

"Oh, yeah, one more thing before you go – you will be flying your first mission tomorrow. I need you in the air. Two pilots got shot down last night. We got a fix, no word from the SEAL Team yet. I already have one pilot grounded from dysentery. Another bitten by a rat. You know, stomach injections. Got to watch him a few days before he can fly again, and two more on R&R. I need you to fill a slot. OK, get moving and know that my door, this one or my hooch, is always open."

"Thanks, Tipper ... I really appreciate your time."

"You bet."

Burt caught me on the way out. "Mr. Walker, I have your schedule for today, Sir. This is the only time I do this. You will be in the system after today. It's your responsibility to check the duty roster, which is posted by eighteen hundred hours next to the mail slots and on the bulletin board in the O Club.

"As you can see, Sir, you are due for your indoctrination briefing in an hour and a half, where you'll observe a mission briefing. You don't have to do anything, just watch and listen. You have time to drop by Supply and pick up your gear now if you want. That should only take a few minutes. Sergeant Wilson knows you are coming, so he probably has everything laid out. You will need your flight helmet, survival vest, and sidearm to fly with Mr. Higgins for your in-country check-ride after you observe the briefing."

"You're obviously on top of things, Burt. Very efficient. Thank you."

"My job, sir. I take it seriously."

"Where do you mail a letter around here? Just want my folks to know where I am and that I arrived in one piece and to give them a mailing address."

"Our mailing address is on the second page of the package I gave you. The mailboxes are just around the corner to your left. I am also the mail clerk. Mail goes out by chopper every day at eighteen hundred. Usually takes about ten days to get a letter from the states and vice versa. And, Mr. Walker, please take the time to read that information package. There's a lot of stuff in there that you will find helpful."

"Will do."

It was great to be so busy.

Chapter 6 Laddy

I knocked on the door of Laddy's hooch. He opened immediately while sipping a cup of coffee. "Hi, Sir, I'm Sam Walker."

"Yeah, Sam, I'm Laddy. Sully dropped by with your two-hundred and said you'd stop by before your check-ride. Come on in." He continued with nothing but compliments regarding the pilot responsible for my check-ride flight. "Tex! Good man. You will like him. He knows his stuff and then some. Probably the best pilot in the squadron, but then that's why he has the best job. In-country check-rides and an occasional VIP trip. That's all Tex does, that and building model airplanes from balsa wood, which he is also very good at. This is his fourth tour. I can't even imagine what that must be like. I am ending my second and have no plans for a third. This mess should be over soon anyway. Say, Sam, you sound southern."

"From Charleston, South Carolina. You sound northern."

"Yeah! Bronx, New York."

"Is Laddy your real name?"

"Hell no. It's Tony Ladana, but growing up, everyone called me Laddy."

"Not Tony?"

"Nope. Way too many Tony's in the Bronx!"

With that, he gave me a stronger than expected handshake; perhaps that was a Bronx thing. He stood about 5'8" with a stocky, muscular build, developed through years of weight lifting, something he told me was the wise thing to do where he grew up. No question, I'd want him at my side if I ever had to walk down a dark alley. I couldn't help but notice he had the same gaunt look of the marines I met a few days ago when I arrived in Saigon. Fact is, whether you were a combat soldier or a pilot, the constant exposure to war took its toll.

"Guess all that North-South bullshit is put in perspective over here?"

"Makes you realize, the stuff we think means something back home, that somehow makes us different, don't mean shit over here," said Laddy, chuckling knowingly.

"Yeah, you're right. I never thought much about that anyway, to tell you the truth."

"Really? I thought you southern boys hated us 'damn Yankees'?"

"Not all of us. There are still a lot of ignorant rednecks who have never gotten over the Civil War, but not all of us. Sad, really."

"Well, I kinda' thought so. We have quite a few southern pilots here, and I don't see an attitude with any of them, but then, like you, they're educated.

"Say, Sam, I got a few things here you might find will come in handy. A hot plate, coffee percolator, and a popcorn popper. Got three cans of Maxwell House coffee – unopened. Good coffee over here is right up there with good Scotch!"

"Sure, Laddy, thanks! What'll you take for the lot?"

"Nothin', all yours, Sam. Wife back home has got more stuff than we need. Say, Sam, you're in the FLR, right?"

"Right."

"Grab your gear after your check-ride with Tex. My roommate left this morning, and the top bunk is empty."

"Oh, man! You just made my day. A night with AC. Can't wait."

"Not just any AC, but 5000 BTUs of AC. It keeps this hooch at sixty-seven degrees. You are also getting the best mamasan. Her name is Nuwee. I will have her put clean sheets on your bunk."

"You mean we get our own maid?"

"Yeah. Uncle Sam pays them a measly twenty bucks a week, which is a lot in their economy, but even so, I give Nuwee a little extra, but that's up to you. Be good to her, Sam. She is in her fifties, has a daughter. Husband off somewhere up north fighting. She is not a prostitute by any stretch of the imagination, so don't insult her. We have twenty-five mamasans here for the pilots. Two of them are prostitutes. Tipper tends to look the other way. My advice is leave them alone because they will just use sex to try and get into your head and with the stuff we know, that can spell disaster."

"Yes, I will. I grew up with a black mamasan back home. Her name is Otsie. She has been with my family since I was two-years old, and I just love her. She is my other mama. Nuwee and I will get along just fine."

"Then you know how it works. Glad to hear it. That was one of my concerns leaving here. Some of these pilots simply weren't raised right and don't honor or appreciate domestic help. It's foreign to them."

"Believe me, I got it. Respect and dignity. Say, Laddy, if I am not interrupting your packing, I sure would like to hear a little about what living here is like from someone who has completed two tours."

"Glad to, Sam. I can walk and chew gum at the same time. How long do you have?"

"Looks like about an hour. Got to watch a mission briefing then meet with Tex at around ten fifteen."

"Sounds about right. Most mission briefings only last about thirty minutes."

"Here, enjoy a cup of real coffee. Hit the latrine before you fly."

"Oh, wow! This is really good."

"Well, you're going to get two quick years of experience in one lesson. How's that?"

"I'm listening." Laddy had my complete and undivided attention.

"Like I said, this is my second tour, and God as my witness, my last. I will roll it all together for you and hit the important survival stuff. The rest is no biggie. You will learn as you go. You ever read *A Tale of Two Cities* by Charles Dickens?"

"Yes, I have. 'It was the best of times; it was the worst of times.'"

"Well," Laddy responded, "that's a perfect description of life in the Nam. One day you might find yourself swimming in clear, warm tropical waters and that night you're taking incoming while you're trying to sleep in your hooch.

"Your mind is not cluttered with worldly garbage, here. There are no telephones, no TV, no newspapers, no car to hop in and run across town. No wife nagging about the bills, picking up shit from the cleaners, no kids with homework and runny noses, no street lights, no parking tickets, no cops. There is just 'now' to think about … you don't own any keys because you don't need any. On that side, life is real simple. On the other side ... well, let's just say it keeps you on your toes. You learn to live in the moment because that's all you got. Your wits are going to be tested on a daily basis, but they'll be sharper than you have ever known them to be, and they will stay that way. Your sanity will go to the edge more than once until you finally realize that you can handle 'crazy' or you have become 'crazy' and didn't know it. Making sense so far?"

"Some of it. Keep going; you describe it so well."

"You got to embrace all of it, Sam. Even the parts that scare the shit out of you. I didn't, my first tour, and I wish I had. Let yourself live this experience. The stuff you try to hide from will end up getting you anyway, so meet everything head-on."

"Whoa, Laddy! Time out a moment. You totally lost me. What stuff head-on? Give me an example, please."

"Let's see ... OK, try this one. About every two months, every pilot gets grunt duty. Officers have to take berm bunker duty for three nights in a row. You are in charge of four bunkers and two towers. Thirteen men total. Two in each bunker, two in each tower. You share a command bunker with a sergeant. The sarge is helping the guys in the bunkers and towers monitor night movement. Your job is to watch over the operation, which, unfortunately, usually means for most guys, napping, reading a book, or writing letters home. But you could spend time in the bunkers supporting these nineteen-year-old kids who are-half scared out of their gourds. Stay up, Sam! Get in those bunkers with your men! Talk to them. Put them at ease, and if the shit hits the fan, you get to pull down on an M-60 and blow a couple of gooks away yourself. Things here can get upfront and personal very quick. Best part is, those same kids may be working on your airplane during the day. Think they will be looking after you? Bet your ass they will. In their eyes, you are not one of the aloof flyboys anymore. You're one of them. Trust me, it counts. It's what General Patton did!"

"I get it. I get it. I'll do it!" I was inspired.

"It does get rough over here, Sam. Really rough. I won't sugar-coat the reality of your tour. You will be pushed beyond your ability to go one more foot, and when that time comes, you'll discover there is something in you that you didn't know was there that will make you go forward one more time and one more time and one more time until it's all over and you stand where I am standing now. Just remember, if I made it ... you can make it. You will do things in an airplane you never dreamed possible ... and look back and say, 'Damn, I did that ... and lived!' Of course, you may blow a few aircraft rivets or an engine or two and even puke or pee in your flight suit, but you make it. Oh! This is important! Here, take this jar of Vick's Vapor Rub and keep it in your flight suit."

"Vick's Vapor Rub? What's this about?"

"Dysentery!"

"This stuff stops dysentery?"

"No, but when the pilot next to you shits in his pants and you're an hour away from home, put some of this under each nostril. The menthol will keep you from gagging." The things I was learning from

Laddy were priceless. Got a very strong feeling most of it came from his actual experience.

Laddy was staring into his coffee cup saying these words like he was far away. "This place will change you, Sam. Hopefully, it will change you for the better in the long run, once you get over the numbness ... so I hear. Just make it out alive and in one piece, Brother, and everything else for the rest of your life will be a cakewalk."

"Wait a minute, Laddy. You said 'numbness.' I have already been feeling that. Does it get worse?"

"Hate to tell you, my friend. It gets a lot worse, but it is one of the mechanisms that also keeps you alive. Frankly, I don't think the human brain was made to take this kind of life. Part of it starts shutting down to protect itself. Truth is, it was the first thing my wife noticed after my first tour. I was only in the states for four months when my ass was shipped back. Don't know that I ever got in touch with much. Fact is, I know I didn't. When I met my wife in Hawaii for R&R after six months on this tour, she just started crying and couldn't stop. She said I had changed so much that she didn't know me anymore."

"Wow, that sucks."

"I haven't said this to anyone, Sam, but, in a way, I am more afraid of going home than staying here. I just want to feel whole again, man. Don't mean to scare you with all of this shit, but, yeah, this place makes you go home, well ... different, really different, and the hard part is that no one, including yourself, knows how to change it. I heard a guy say that when he got home and saw his parents, he felt older than his own dad."

Laddy snapped back into the present and changed the subject, "The monsoon season starts in a few weeks."

"Yeah, Sully told me."

"Five months of non-stop rain. The flying gets tougher, to say the least. You know, bad weather to contend with on top of enemy fire. Sometimes, the weather can be worse than being shot at. It's good you will have at least a few missions under your belt like I did before the monsoon sets in. Say, Tex will make you shoot an imaginary teardrop approach into Vung Tau today. Be sure you get it down. You will be using it a lot to get in here when the rain and wind have all the instrument landing systems shut down."

"Wait a minute," I gasped, "are you telling me that I will actually be flying by the seat of my pants in bad weather without the equipment to guide me in for an instrument approach?"

"Yep. Best to start practicing it while the weather is still good, so you have it down pat. Once you can visualize the teardrop approach in your mind, set it up with your first procedure turn when your RDF (radio direction finder) needle swings one hundred-eighty degrees. You will be over the tower at that point. Sounds scary, but it really works. You must practice it in good weather first like I said. When the time comes to actually use it in bad weather ... well, you will just have to trust your instincts."

"Wait a minute, Laddy, we don't use the RDF for instrument approaches. It's just there to find the tower. That thing is as old as Methuselah!"

"Be glad you got it. It will save your ass!"

"Did you have to use it for landings?"

"Yep! Twenty times on this tour, and I lived to tell about it," he said before continuing. "Now for the 'on the ground stuff.' The rats, roaches, and snakes come out around here like crazy in monsoon season. The rats and snakes especially get bad. Keep your hooch door closed at all times. With AC, you will want to do that anyway. Don't let some pilot talk to you from an open door at night. Make the guy come in and close the door behind him. Little shit like that can get you in trouble. I had to learn it the hard way my first tour.

"Rats are looking for a warm, dry place, and your bed is ideal. If it happens, don't panic and try to kick it. You could get bitten. Instead, move slowly, pick up your ammo can of grenades, and drop it from about one foot. The weight will kill it. Next, very important. DO NOT handle the little turd. Wrap it up in the sheet and be careful not to get any blood on you, the blanket, or your bed. Stick the sheet outside your door, and Nuwee will burn it the next morning.

"Snakes. We got 'um all. The ones to look out for around here are called Banded Kraits. They have wide orange and black bands, which make them easy to spot. That's the good news. The bad news about the Krait is that it's nocturnal and pretty deadly; it kills 77% of its victims.

"You will be amazed at how long you will learn to hold your bowels and bladder at night, but if you do have to use the latrine, don't go half-asleep or drunk; wear your boots and take a flashlight. Also, very important, shine down in the shitter hole and around the outside edges before you sit down and keep shining your light in that area as long as you're in there. Personally, I don't step out of that door for any reason without my boots on."

"How come no one tells us about all this stuff in briefings?"

"They just don't, because it is all in that briefing package you are holding. You got a lot going on, Sam, but I would make a point to read that stuff before you go to bed tonight.

"Last thing, and I know you gotta' go. Tips on the monsoon season. During monsoon, you're always fighting to stay as dry as possible before you go flying. When you're wet and going on night missions, you'll feel like you're freezing your ass off 'cause you're probably approaching hypothermia. Sitting in that cockpit for four and a half hours with temperatures around fifty degrees in high humidity and no way to change your conditions can really play with your mind. Stuff your flight jacket and two pair of dry socks in your flight helmet bag. Don't forget it, Sam. Not ever! Throw your flight helmet bag in the cockpit as soon as you are dropped off at your aircraft. If you walk around with it during your aircraft pre-flight, the rain will go right through the helmet bag, and your jacket and socks will be soaked. Try to take a thermos of hot coffee or some kind of hot soup. It will keep you sane, man."

Laddy was giving it to me straight, and I knew it. "It never crossed my mind to pack a thermos, Laddy."

"Take mine. I'll leave it on the desk for you. Plenty of thermos bottles back in the Bronx.

"Oh, yeah. Get over to the tailor. Little hut behind us, short trail through the elephant grass. Get zippers sewn into your boots. Costs five bucks a pair. You can't get those suckers off otherwise to change your socks when you're strapped in the cockpit."

I thanked Laddy again for his valuable information. There was so much to digest, and I wanted to think about all of this, but I had a full day ahead of me. It was better to stay focused on the task at hand.

When I opened the door to leave the hooch, I almost collided with a small Vietnamese woman. Dressed in loose-fitting white pajamas, Ho Chi Minh sandals, and a pointed woven-straw hat, there was nothing to distinguish her from many of the other local women I'd seen.

She immediately bowed her head and said, "Oh! Please excuse, sir. I want to tell Mr. Laddy goodbye. Sorry to see him leave."

"You must be Nuwee! Sorry I almost ran into you." Studying her face, I could not guess her age, but her gnarly hands indicated a lifetime of hard work.

"Yes, my name Nuwee. What your name, sir?"

"I'm Sam. I'm moving into Laddy's hooch, and I understand you will be my mamasan. Laddy's told me all about you."

"OK, Mr. Sam. Nuwee take good care of you."

Bowing once again, she scurried around me and into the hooch, closing the door behind her. I was determined to get to know her as a person, and I would do just that.

Chapter 7 Wai Lyn

Sitting behind a large desk covered in papers and magazines with two large fans blowing overhead, sat Sergeant First Class Harry Wilson. His feet propped up on boxes, he was sipping coffee, chewing a cigar and reading a copy of Sports Illustrated. At once, he seemed the stereotypical supply sergeant; as laid back as if he owned the place, fully aware of the power he wielded in this coveted position. I predicted he'd treat me as though he was doing me a favor when issuing anything out of 'his' supply room, without the slightest hint that he would actually be doing his job. He would surprise me.

"Welcome to the Nam, Sir. I got most of your stuff already laid out on the table over there. Just need to know what kind of sidearm you want to carry. Either a thirty-eight caliber or forty-five caliber ... so what's it going to be?"

With that, the sergeant got up from his comfortable perch and walked around the large desk to shake hands. I noticed that his shirt was too big in the shoulders, but at his midsection, the buttons appeared to be straining to keep it together without popping off. For several reasons, most GIs were fit and trim, usually the thinnest they'd be in their adult lives, but Sergeant Wilson's job gave him lots of time to sit and read, and it showed.

I leaned forward to shake the sergeant's hand and to look him in the eye. "Forty-five caliber would be great."

"You sure, Sir?"

"Yes, I'm sure. I've been shooting a forty-five for years. My uncle taught me when I was a kid."

"Your call, Sir. You're the first pilot to ever request one. Just wouldn't want to be lugging one around the jungle myself; you know, if you get shot down and all. You'll be humping a survival pack, a canteen of water, and this here heavy-as-a-brick sidearm. Oh, say 'bout twenty-five pounds total. Lot of weight to carry while trying to outrun Charlie. Know what I mean?"

"Let's hope that day never comes, but all the same, the forty-five, please."

"You got it." The sergeant placed the black Colt on his desk along with its holster, belt, and extra magazines. "One more thing, Sir. You have to wear this sidearm at all times around here. Still sure you want it?"

"I'm sure," I said, strapping it on.

"This, here, is your flight survival vest, flight helmet, and two pairs of flight gloves. We had to take the morphine out of the medical emergency pack; you still got atropine for nerve gas. You have to sign out the morphine pack before each mission. Just be sure to turn it in, or some dumb-ass MP will come looking for you thinking you shot it up. Know what I mean? This duffle bag has your towels, soap, shaving shit, extra underwear, socks, stuff like that. Here you got one ammo can of six hand-grenades, two ammo cans of M-16 rounds, five-hundred rounds per can. A box of fifty tracer rounds in each can. Here's your M-16 assault rifle with twelve magazines and magazine belt. One pillow, one mattress, and one blanket. Your mamasan takes care of the sheets. Please sign here, Sir. Anything not returned at the end of your tour will be deducted from your pay and you actually could be subject to legal charges, depending on what's missing!"

"Got it." I signed the paper. It felt good to have a weapon, and then some.

"I understand you're in the laundry room for now, right Sir?"

"No. Already got a hooch, actually."

"Lucky man. Most don't get one that quick. You will need to lock most of this stuff up," he added, handing me a combination lock.

"Tell you what, Sarge, I'll take my flight helmet, survival vest and forty-five now. Got to fly shortly. I'll pick up the rest of this stuff when I get back."

"Suit yourself. I live here. Got a room, my hooch, in the back. Only NCO with an AC. If I am not up front, just come around and knock on my door."

"Thanks, Sarge."

"Good luck to you, Mr. Walker. Don't know how you flyboys do it."

"Do what, Sarge?"

"Take-off into ... whadayacallit? The wild blue yonder, every damn day. You got to have some brass balls, young man. Just to know when you leave here, you could be checking into the Hanoi Hilton is enough to make me afraid for you boys. Don't know how you do it. I really don't. Just want you to know I say a little prayer every time I hear one of you leave the ground and a little prayer of thanks when I hear you coming home."

"That's really nice to know, Sergeant Wilson, and thank you. That means a lot to me."

Boy! Wasn't expecting such sincerity. Felt a little bad about having figured him wrong. Too many WWII movies.

***

After turning the corner, I came upon the headquarters compound. It looked like a freakin' fort. It was surrounded by a double-walled, twelve-foot high cyclone fence with six strands of barbed wire on top. On each corner of the compound was a concrete bunker with two soldiers manning M-60 machine guns. I approached the smaller bunker, which was also the entrance to the compound where a soldier stood watch.

"Welcome to the three-sixty-third HQ Command, Sir," snapped the young corporal. "Please show some ID, Sir."

I was reaching for my ID when I heard a loud whoosh just behind my head. In a flash, the corporal flew around from behind the bunker, yelling, "Get down, Sir!" while grabbing me by the arm and pulling me to safety.

"WHAT? What's going on? What the hell was that?"

"Sniper, Mr. Walker! Just tried to take your head off."

"What are you talking about, Corporal?"

"Just stay down and back here with me. Got to make a call. Snakehead two, this is Blackshield four three, how copy?"

"Blackshield four three, go ahead."

"Snakehead two, we got sniper fire from jungle tree line at two o'clock my position."

"Roger, Blackshield. We are already on it. We heard the shot."

Within seconds, a Cobra gunship lifted off from Bear Cat base camp, where they served as our air cover, as the base camp was within five-hundred yards of Long Thanh North. The Cobra unleashed hundreds of automatic twenty-millimeter rounds along the edge of the jungle targeting the spot along the tree line they had been directed to.

"Blackshield, Snakehead here. That should quiet things down. Will keep our ears open for the dumb ass."

"Thanks, Snakehead."

"OK, Sir. You're good to go."

"DAMN! Just that quick, huh?"

"Yes, Sir. Charlie has a lot of balls messing with us like that. Must be some gook not familiar with how bad those Cobra jocks are. Probably blew his sorry ass back to Hanoi."

"I'll say. That was quite some show of retaliation."

"Just glad they missed you, Mr. Walker."

"No shit!" NO SHIT! I was rattled. I did not allow myself to fully comprehend what a close call that was. I had to stay focused and start to live with the fact that I was always in danger of being taken out. A freaky way to have to live, yet perversely exciting at the same time. Just like they told me when I first arrived.

I approached the front entrance to the compound where a guard armed with an M-16 unlocked the door by pushing a series of large buttons on a console. The door opened, and l crossed the threshold, not knowing what to expect. Surprisingly, the interior space did not look at all like military issue decor; it could have been anywhere in the states. Framed pictures on the walls, Asian bamboo screens here and there, a scattering of Oriental rugs, nice teak furniture, and there she was again – another very attractive Vietnamese woman, also wearing a fitted black silk tunic with white silk pants.

Her flawless features were framed with gleaming jet-black hair pulled back in a bun and pinned in place with what appeared to be a delicate piece of carved ivory. She was shapely, well dressed, and undoubtedly aware of her good looks. As she approached me with a confident gait, I thought she was really hot. Then she extended her hand and greeted me with a dazzling smile that highlighted her exotic beauty. Within minutes, Wai Lyn could make you forget you were in a combat zone.

"Hello, Mr. Walker, I am Wai Lyn, Colonel Simmons' personal assistant. May I get you a cup of coffee or a glass of ice tea?"

"Yes, ice tea, thank you. That would be great."

"Unsweetened or sugar?"

"Unsweetened. Excuse me, but I thought this was a top-secret area of the base," I blurted out and immediately felt foolish.

"But of course. You assume that I don't have a clearance because I am Vietnamese and I am not wearing a uniform," Wai Lyn answered coyly, smiling all the while.

"Well, yes. Of course, that's what I was thinking."

"It happens all the time. My father is a general in the South Vietnamese Army and has served as an adviser to your government since 1963. My mother is French. I was educated in Paris and then went to the United States where under a diplomatic visa I studied under the diplomatic attaché program. I have only been back in my country serving in this capacity for six months. I hope my appearance and position does not offend you," she added with a slight bow.

"Offend me! Oh my, no … no, not at all. Just caught me a little off guard, that's all."

"One moment while I get your tea. Colonel Simmons will be with you shortly. Please ... have a seat."

I had taken one sip of tea when I heard someone speak to me from around the corner. "'Off guard' aren't words we like to hear around here," came the warm voice with a chuckle. "I'm Colonel Harry Simmons, head of the three-sixty-third. I see you've met Wai Lyn. Nice touch, don't you think?"

"Well, Sir, if I'm allowed a buffoon moment, I think I just had one."

"Know what you mean. When Saigon sent me Wai Lyn, I thought the general at HQ was playing a practical joke. Must say, it makes the tour a little more bearable," replied the colonel with a wry smile. As I followed the colonel into his office and took a seat in front of his desk, I couldn't help but wonder if he was poking her.

"So where is home back in the world for you, Walker?"

"Charleston, South Carolina, Sir. Well actually, Johns Island, which is one of the Sea Islands seventeen miles south of Charleston."

"Sea Island! What's that? Some kind of resort town?" inquired the colonel.

"No, not at all. Just the opposite. It's a very rural farming community. My dad is a tomato and soybean farmer there."

"No kidding! I grew up on a corn and wheat farm in Nebraska. Nothing like a farmer's life – hard, honest work. You get to know The Almighty on a real personal level. You'll get to know him here, too. Trust me on that one. Flying combat on a dark and stormy night with Charlie trying to shoot you out of the sky tends to get your attention."

"Yes, Sir." The colonel had softened a bit, perhaps due to our common backgrounds. I had no way of knowing at that moment that the words he just spoke would prove true for me more than once.

"My door is open to you, Sam. Besides, I don't get too many farm boys through here. Make a point to drop in after hours and have a drink with me. I try not to hang out too much at the O Club. I don't think it looks right."

"Yes, Sir, I understand."

"Besides, I'll have Wai Lyn join us. That should be enough of an incentive," the colonel said, smiling.

"You bet, Sir. I will definitely be dropping by."

"Good, and just remember, the day will come when you do go home, Sam."

***

As part of my orientation, I sat through a thirty-minute mission briefing in a chair a few feet behind the two pilots and two TOs (Technical Operators) who were assigned to carry out this mission.

I found myself looking at a smaller version of the wall map I witnessed in Saigon. Lieutenant Ken Young delivered the briefing. He gave the two pilots sitting in front of him on-target times, off-target times, and the flight vectors for nine ground artillery battery sites, some of which were American, others were South Vietnamese, Australian, and a few Korean. Each artillery battery site also had different radio frequencies, call-up times, and 'fans' or directions of fire from their big guns. The lieutenant took special care to point out eight known SAM missile sites along the Vietnam-Cambodia border, also known as the 'Fence'. The last thing he covered were emergency transponder squawk frequencies and finally, the same grim but important information that Colonel Morrison had covered in the event of being shot down.

Now, this was a lot for any two pilots to remember, so they were allowed to take notes on an erasable board using a grease pencil. Once in the aircraft, we would input all of the briefing information for the mission into multiple on-board computers and then wipe clean the erasable boards.

I understood that the next time I would find myself in this room, it would not be as an observer, but as one of the pilots assigned to a mission. Advanced flight school trained us on mock-up missions, but now that I found myself facing the real thing, it was quite different. Real missions meant dodging real bullets and deadly missiles, dealing with bad weather, beating back fear, and managing the adrenaline. As a pilot, others would be depending on me, as well. On top of that, with each mission, we had to confront the possibility of a plane crash, injury, death or worse – becoming a POW. I realized in the first few moments of watching the pilots taking notes that this was a game I had not yet played. Was I ready? My insides were queasy. I sure hoped it didn't show on the outside.

Missions were generally four and one-half hours long. Pilots returned from every mission completely drained after having been on an adrenaline high from take-off to touch down. To recover, usually a few beers or a couple of shots of hard liquor did the trick, or so I'd been told, along with eight to ten hours of sleep. Then this cycle would repeat itself when the next day brought the next mission. You could see it in the faces of anyone who had been in-country more than three months. No one kept track of Saturdays or Sundays or holidays or birthdays because they just didn't matter anymore. Every day was simply another day with the next mission, and surviving that brought you one day closer to the end of your tour.

Just as the war was fought on a grand scale, each individual soldier fought a constant battle to stay healthy – physically and mentally. Weight loss and strength loss was a common result of poor diet, dehydration, dysentery, and stress. Deplorable sanitary conditions, extreme weather, venomous critters, and disease-bearing insects could wreak havoc; just dealing mentally with these omnipresent threats added considerably to the stress of warfare, taking a heavy toll; insidious, just like Chinese water torture.

Being a pilot just made things tougher. No matter how lousy you might be feeling, you could not avoid taking your assigned mission. In a plane you always had to be at the top of your game, not only to protect your life but also the lives of those flying with you. Throughout your tour of duty, all of these physical assaults and mental stressors piled on and would leave us forever changed, that is, if we were fortunate enough to survive.

Chapter 8 Tex

Just as the briefing was about to cover specific targets, I felt a hand on my shoulder and heard a question carried on a throaty Texas drawl. "You must be Walker?"

I stood up and turned around to meet CW4 Higgins. His thick dark hair was invaded with premature gray. A matching mustache painted on his leathery tanned face deeply etched with life. Eyes that knew too much. He looked to be about the age of Tipper, somewhere in his mid-thirties. After smoothing his mustache with the back of his right index finger, he thrust out his hand for a shake. His vice-like grip was more than necessary to make his point. His steel-gray eyes were locked into mine, perhaps looking for a sign of the pain he inflicted.

Then with a broad grin, he introduced himself, "Name's Higgins, but everybody calls me Tex. Good to meet you, Walker. Where you from in the world?"

"Charleston, South Carolina, Sir."

"Good God, son, can you get a thicker southern accent?"

"It's Charlestonese, Sir."

"Charlestonese? Geechee if I ever heard it, but then I am from Amarillo, Texas, and I been told I sound a little southern myself."

"Yep! I would say so," I heartily agreed.

"Well, from one southern boy to another, whadaya say we go kick the tires and light the fires and see what Charlie is up to?" Tex said, stretching his arms like he had just been napping, but perhaps just to put me at ease.

"That's what I am here for, Tex."

"Yes, you are ... and then some, I can assure you." Didn't know what that meant, and I wasn't going to ask.

"See you got your gear. There's a jeep waiting out front. Let's get movin'."

"Yes, Sir!"

"Drop the 'Sir' crap. I told you it was Tex."

"By the way, I go by Sam."

"Sam! OK, Sam. Huh! I know a fella with a horse named Sam."

The jeep took us out to the flight line. I was eager to finally fly a plane. The aircraft were all parked between twenty-foot high revetments to protect them from incoming rockets and mortar rounds; if one plane caught fire, it would be isolated from the other aircraft on either side. Before entering the cockpit, the long-sleeves of the Nomex flight suit, definitely not tropical wear, had to be rolled down to the wrist, flight gloves had to be donned and attached tightly with Velcro. Flight suits had to be zipped to the top and flight helmets put on. Blocked off from any breeze that just might have been blowing, and dressed in all this necessary, heavy, tight, uncomfortable paraphernalia made climbing into the cockpit an unforgettable experience. The cockpit temperature hung around one hundred-forty degrees Fahrenheit. Trying not to panic or pass out from the heat was a challenge. It took everything I had to concentrate on the task at hand. Once inside the cockpit, I began drinking from my canteen like a man stranded in the desert.

"Whoa, son. Hold on there, Sam," snapped Tex as he took the canteen from me. "You're gonna need most of this later."

"Later? What do you mean later? How do you even get to later in this kind of heat?"

"OK, Sam, I know the heat is unsettling. I need you to get focused, and you will be fine. Go ahead and turn on generator number one and connect your oxygen mask. We can go to intercom through our mask mics and get some fresh air in our lungs at the same time."

The oxygen was hot and tasted rubbery through my new mask.

"There you go. Now, let's remember, the more focused we are, the quicker we get through the pre-flight check and get this bird aloft where the air is a little cooler. Not much, but every degree counts over here."

Tex's drawl crackling through my helmet's headset had a calming effect. He had obviously been doing this a while and accurately anticipated my discomfort. "Oh yeah, don't forget to pack your flight jacket on late afternoon missions that take you into the night."

"You're kidding me, right?"

"No. Not at all. Notice how you're soaking wet sittin' here right now? You get up to altitude at night and you're going to be freezing your butt off 'cause you're wet," Tex explained.

"You see, some dumb dude, who couldn't possibly have been a pilot, took all the heaters out of these planes to make room for more avionics before they shipped them over here from the US. Even if we had 'um we would have no place to put 'um," Tex snickered. "Under ordinary circumstances, most things that turn out to be funny over here, really ain't funny at all. But sometimes, you just got to laugh to keep from going nuts."

Tex was a trip, one heck of a psychologist, and also very pragmatic. Who would ever think to talk about getting cold and the need to take along a flight jacket at a time like this, when we were burning up? I felt like a cake in the oven about to be baked. Tex and I were strapped in shoulder-to-shoulder and ready for take-off.

"So, where we going, Tex?" I managed to choke out despite my dry mouth.

"Oh, first, just going to run you around the patch a couple of times for a few touch-and-go landings. Guess you been on thirty-day leave like most of us before coming over, right?"

"Yep!" I was fighting not to say 'Sir'.

"OK, I got your radios," said Tex. "Long Thanh Tower this is Blackshield three four five ready for take-off runway zero three."

"Roger, Blackshield three four five. Cleared for take-off. Say intent."

"Tower, we want to run a few touch-and-goes and then head southeast for a little tactical work." Tex's voice was steady and calm.

"Got you covered, Tex. Taxi to the apron of runway zero three and hold."

"How you doing over there, Sam?"

"Ready for take-off, Sir … I mean, Tex."

"You're a little afraid, are ya?"

"Good to go, Tex!"

"Yeah, but are ya a little afraid?"

"What difference does it make?"

"Well, if you're not a little afraid, I don't want to be flying with ya … got it?" snapped Tex.

"Yeah, right. OK, I get you. I am a little nervous," I admitted.

"You bet your sorry southern ass you are! You wouldn't be sane if you weren't."

"Blackshield three four five cleared for take-off."

"Roger, tower. We're rollin'."

I lined up on runway zero three and shoved the throttles to the firewall for take-off. Full power. Passing through V-1 to V-2, gear up, flaps up. Truthfully, my heart was racing like crazy, and my breathing was short and rapid, but it was a smooth takeoff.

"OK, young man, left turn, come downwind to runway zero three and level at seven hundred feet. And another thing, take your death grip off the stick. Relax … breathe. Staying as calm as you can is the key to staying alive up here. I know your adrenal glands have kicked in, and you're dealing with a physiological pneumonia that's foreign to you. It happens to all combat pilots over here. It is what will keep you alive and at the same time could wear you out if you don't get a grip on it."

I felt a sense of relief. Tex was good. He was being a big brother, nothing like the hard-ass flight instructors that gave check-rides in flight school. He had a way of telling me what I was feeling and experiencing when I couldn't really put a finger on it – this, my new and separate reality. At that moment, I realized that I finally knew what it was to be a real pilot. Tex kept talking as I was lining up for final approach.

"My job is not to teach you how to fly. You already know how to do that. My job is to make you fully aware of your psyche while under the pressure of combat flying. Flying this plane should be second nature to you. Your constant state of self-awareness is fundamental so that you will 'respond' and not 'react' to the circus that's going on around you. Staying in touch with yourself at every moment will determine whether you make it out of here or not. Understand?"

"Yeah, Tex. Thanks. I understand."

"Long Thanh Tower, this is Blackshield three four five on final approach for a touch and go. Going around one more time."

"Roger Tex, you're clear. No other traffic."

"Blackshield three four five, you will have two Huey Cobra gunships at five hundred feet, one-half mile out at your 10 o'clock position on your climb out."

"Roger, copy Tower. I have a visual on the Cobras. Thanks." To me, he added, "Those boys in the Cobras are why you can sleep relatively safe at night."

As we took off and made our way around the patch one more time, Tex pointed to the Cobra gunship base camp, Bear Cat, that I had already been introduced to. "Yeah, their call sign is Snakehead, right?"

"Now how would you know that?"

I gave him the quick version of the sniper incident, and Tex just shook his head.

"Look, down there, Sam. Cobra helicopter gunships are one bad-ass aircraft. I love 'um, but wouldn't want to fly 'um."

"Yeah, how come?"

"Well look at the damn things. Helicopters make no aerodynamic sense. Should not be able to fly in my opinion. You know what they call the main nut that holds that rotor blade on?"

"No, can't say that I do."

"The 'Jesus nut'. If that comes off, you're just a hunk of metal falling to earth."

"Think they could have come up with a better name?"

"Not really, Sam. Think that word says it all. Without Him ... well, you're just not saved. Anyway, back to work. Pick up a heading of one eight seven and climb to and maintain five thousand. That's your hard deck over here. Out of range of Charlie's small arms fire. Don't forget it.

"Tower, this is Blackshield three four five. Going tactical. Call you back in a few."

"Roger that, Tex. Got an FNG?"

"Yep." Then Tex spoke to me.

"Taking you down to the coast. Little airstrip near a village called Vung Tau right on the beach. If you're lucky, you'll get down there two or three times during your tour. It's where we get our on-board computers serviced. Usually a two-day job so you get a little unofficial R&R. Three French hotels right on the beach. Great seafood, good wine, and wonderful women. The small base is run by our mates the Aussies. Craziest bunch of bastards to ever fly an airplane, but you got to love 'um. They are really tight with the American flyboys here."

"That's good to know."

"Be sure to plan one of your R&Rs to Australia. Now that's a place ya gotta go. Nicest people in the world and they love us GI's. I have been there three times and haven't paid for a drink yet."

"Seriously?"

"Yep! They won't let you. Walk in any bar or restaurant, and the minute you open your mouth, they got you tagged. Heck, had free meals in some restaurants and they were lavish and expensive. The owner will come over and give a complimentary bottle of wine, and when the check comes, the owner comes back, takes the check, and says, 'Our pleasure, Yank!'"

"Yank?"

"Don't let that offend you. Americans are all Yanks to them. Who cares, right?"

"Right. Besides, I am a southerner who always got along with and liked northerners."

"Same here, Sam. Never understood prejudiced people anyway."

It was about a fifteen-minute flight to Vung Tau, and I listened to Tex go on and on about the Aussies. Though talk of Australia kept me entertained, at the same time, I was wondering what Tex was up to. I knew this wasn't a joy ride. He was up here to test me. Laddy had told me to watch him, that he was very good at getting you to relax or think nothing was going on and then hit you with a real zinger.

"There is a lot of Charlie between the Vung Tau airstrip and the village, two miles to the south, where the hotels are located. About one-hundred Aussies live in the three hotels. Mostly pilots and aircraft mechanics. Each hotel has a guarded perimeter around it as well as the airbase. Sounds like quite the vacation spot to be spending your tour ... you know, hotel on the beach and all!"

"Sounds almost too good to be true," I agreed.

"That's just it. It is too good to be true. For some reason, a nest of VC lives between the airbase and the hotels. Word has it they have a listening post set up to monitor our ships a few miles off the coast."

"Why?"

"Why? Because our ships fire their big guns on inland targets all the time. Let me tell you, when you get a target time and direction of fire from a mission briefing and it is coming from one of those bad boys, be damn sure you don't miss the firing times and coordinates. One shell would vaporize your ass. Anyway, these hotels get hit with rockets and mortar from time to time, and the ship munitions are too large to help. Get it?"

"Yeah."

"Unfortunately, so does Charlie."

"So how do these guys defend themselves?"

"They got three of our Cobras. You will see them when we get there. We also assigned a Navy SEAL Team down here. Now that's a crazy bunch."

"Yeah, so I've heard." I kept the souvenir ears to myself. Still made me sick to think about it.

"OK, Sam, enough chitchat. We need to call Vung Tau and get set up for an approach. This is one laid back bunch. They get mostly choppers. Quiet most of the time. Vung Tau Tower, this is Blackshield three four five, over."

"G'day, Mate. How goes it, Tex?"

"Doing well, Robby. Hey, I was down under a few months ago on R&R. Had a great time."

"Did you shag a Sheila, Mate?"

"Whadaya think?"

"You, Tex? It's not if you did, it's more like how many!"

"OK, OK. Enough. I got a young FNG here. You're gonna' burn his virgin ears. We are five miles north. Request a teardrop into runway two eight zero. Full stop."

"Tex, you could have just said, 'doing my usual,' and you would have it."

"Don't you boys ever use proper aviation terminology?"

"We try hard not to, Mate. It's rather a Yank fancy way of getting around in the air, you see! Just tell us what you bloody want without all the 'Roger' 'Dodger' 'Over' 'Tear something', silliness."

"Lighten, up Robby. We will see you in a minute or two."

"OK, now this is where I get to say, 'Roger Tex, cleared for your teardrop'. Should I cry now or later?"

I tried hard not to burst out laughing. I felt like I was about to land in a comedy show. I was surprised at how everyone seemed to know each other on a first-name basis. Voice recognition with no faces, and there never would be. Probably best in this life-or-death environment. I was starting to get the game.

"OK, Sam, I did not give you an instrument approach plate or dial-in outer marker frequencies, because there are none. Only very large airfields over here have precision instrument landing systems. Places like Long Thanh have minimal instrument approaches that can get you in, but down here at Vung Tau, nature has given you the ocean and runway two eight zero. You can get on the deck over water and make it in if the weather is bad. If it's foggy and visibility is poor, don't go below twenty feet. Some of these sampans have sails, and their masts are up to fifteen feet. Actually, the end of the runway is only fifty feet from the sand dunes."

"So how am I supposed to shoot this instrument teardrop approach?"

"Ah-ha! Perfect question. Simple answer. You make one up in your mind."

"WHAT?" They never taught us anything like that in flight-school!"

"You ain't in Kansas anymore, Dorothy. This is reality sandwich time."

"You messin' with me, right, Tex?"

"*Au contraire,* Sam! I couldn't be more serious. The Vung Tau Tower, like ninety-nine percent of all controlled airstrips over here, has an RDF on top of the tower. It's used mostly by the chopper pilots to find the airport. What I want you to do is get out of your altitude level at 500 feet, cross the tower and shoot the approach at 200 feet."

I understood, and I went for it. "OK, level at five hundred feet, on a heading 100° degrees. I have just intercepted the RDF ... I now have a 180° needle swing. Starting a descending left procedure turn, to a heading of 055° degrees for fifteen seconds. Instrument cross-check good. Now making a descending right turn to final approach to a heading of two eight zero. Holding altitude at two hundred feet, one-half mile from final. Have visual of runway. Tex call final."

"Robby, hate to bother you, but we are on short final to full stop."

"Got it, Tex. Oh, yeah, cleared to land."

"Call checklist, Tex."

"Fuel tanks on main."

"Check. Fuel tanks on main."

"Altimeters match, two hundred feet. Koch reading two niner two eight."

"Check. Altimeters match, two hundred feet. Koch, two niner two eight."

"Props full forward."

"Check. Props full forward."

"Manifold pressure steady."

"Check. Manifold steady."

"Flaps down, forty-five degrees."

"Check. Flaps down, forty-five degrees."

"Gear down."

"Check. Gear down. Call three in the green, Tex."

"Three in the green. Gear down and locked."

"OK, Sam, grease this sweetheart on the numbers."

"OK, Tex, I have my imaginary glide slope picture. Coming out of two hundred for touch down to full stop."

Suddenly Tex sat up straight and screamed at me, "SAM, WE ARE TAKING FIRE! WE ARE TAKING FIRE! SAMPAN UNDER MY WING. TWO AK-47'S, SAM. DID YOU HEAR ME? TAKING FIRE!"

"Fuck'um!

"What did you say?"

"Oops! Guess that just slipped out. I'm committed to land, Tex." And I did. Stood on the brakes and came to a full stop.

"My call, Tex. A go-around would have left us hanging out there and just given them more time to hit us. Figured the safest and best thing to do was land. Charlie, at least those two, don't appear to know one end of an AK from the other. Will Cobra's take them out?"

With that, Tex threw his head back and slapped me on the back.

"Perfect call, Sam! Perfect, and without a second's hesitation and you kept your cool. That's what I like to see in pilots! Let's taxi back to the end of the runway. I was just messin' with ya. No ground fire from the sampan." While I let that sink in, Tex turned his attention to the Tower.

"Vung Tau, this is Blackshield three four five." Nothing!

"Vung Tau Tower, this is Blackshield three four five. You copy?"

"Yeah ... yeah, Tex. Sorry, I was napping."

"Kiddin' me, right?"

"No. Out like a drunk!"

"That freaks me out a little, Robby. Say, we want to do a short field power take-off, and we are out of here."

"Sounds bloody dare-devilish to me, but then it's your ass, not mine. Have at it, Tex. Talk with you next time."

"OK, Robby, and try to stay awake will ya? Blackshield out."

I pushed up the sun visor on my flight helmet and disconnected my O2 mask. Tex and I were sitting shoulder to shoulder; he giving me the look of an approving father and offering me his canteen.

"Drink of water?"

"In the worst way! Thanks!" I slugged down three big gulps.

"OK, now comes the hard part," Tex warned.

"Hard part? What was that we just did?"

"That was make-believe. Getting us off this short runway is going to be real." It was the most serious I had seen him all day. "See those eucalyptus trees at the end of the runway?"

"Sure, they're hard to miss; they must be one-hundred feet high."

"Nope! One hundred-thirty feet to be exact," popped Tex.

"So why don't they cut them down or something?" I retorted.

"Can't. They're on the property of the village chief who has leased this airbase to the Aussies. Chief says trees were here one-hundred years before the war, and they will be here one-hundred years after the war. We have to deal with it," grunted Tex, who went on to say, "OK, take one more gulp of water – you've earned it; then O2 mask on, visor down and taxi back to the ocean end of the runway."

I did as instructed, grateful for another gulp of water. The aircraft empennage was hanging out over the sandy beach, and my main landing gear was only a few feet from the end of the concrete runway.

"OK, remember your short-field take-off?"

"Oh, yeah!" I said, now back on intercom, face visor down and sweating like crazy again.

"Good man. Now there is one little twist to getting out of this place. You are going to have to hang this bird at exactly three knots above stall speed to make it out of here, which should put you about ten feet over the tops of those eucalyptus trees. If you aren't hanging this baby just above a stall, we are in trouble. Get it?"

"Oh yeah, I got it loud and clear, Tex."

"OK. You stay glued on your airspeed. I'll watch the trees."

"Got it."

"My hand is on the other stick with you on this one. I will only jump in and help if I see that you're about to kill our asses."

"Roger."

"One more thing, Sam."

"What's that, Tex?"

"If you don't make it, and we crash, the gooks will probably get to us before we're rescued, and we'll wind up wearing a Vietnamese necktie."

"What's that supposed to mean?"

"Oh, they cut your throat and pull your tongue out through the slit. Damn gooks! No imagination!"

"Sounds pretty gross. Don't follow you."

Chuckling before he said it, "They're always the same color!"

"Oh, that's comforting."

"No," countered Tex. "Just one more good reason not to screw it up."

I lowered twenty degrees of flaps to assist in lift, locked my brakes, and went to full power on both engines. The plane sat there shuddering like a chained dog that was being beaten and couldn't get away. I released the brakes and pulled the stick back into my lap. The second we left earth, I retracted the landing gear to reduce drag; within seconds, my stall warning alarm went off, and the cockpit stall warning light was flashing in my face. I was holding her at exactly three knots above a stall. If I breathed heavy, I would lose her. If a plane stalls, it means that it has quit flying and will literally fall out of the sky. The only way to recover is to push the nose over into a dive, add power, and build up enough airspeed to regain flight. Of course, this maneuver causes a loss in altitude, and when you're only fifty feet off the ground and already at full power, the recovery maneuver is impossible. Adrenaline! It had me. My eyes were glued to my airspeed. One wrong move, and we were toast. Vietnamese necktie?

Tex came on the intercom, "That's right, easy does it. Real easy. You got it. Easy does it. Let's keep hearing the alarm and keep that light flashing just a few more feet … that's it … easy does it! Good! You're over and clear!" shouted Tex with his dead calm drawl like it was a walk in the park.

I pushed the nose over a little, flaps up, and maintained a normal rate of climb and headed home at five thousand feet. I had been squeezing the stick with a death grip again. Got to watch that!

"If I had put my hand out the window, I could have picked a eucalyptus leaf!" I said to Tex in short breaths. "That felt a lot closer than ten feet from the tops of the trees."

"Oh, it was, young man. More like two or three feet. Perfect. Didn't want to tell you how really close it was going to be. It's called 'flying by the seat of your pants' and you obviously know how. It's what you were trained for. Good job. OK, Sam, drinks are on me when we get back. You're gonna' love the Officer's Club!"

Yes, I'm gonna' love a drink! I thought to myself. Then it hit me; I don't remember ever saying that about drinking.

***

After landing, Tex took me through a quick performance evaluation, and we walked over to the O Club. Although I had been here once before with Sully, I was so focused on what he had to say that I did not make note of anything else. However, now that I looked around, I realized there was not much to the place. In fact, after having heard so much about it, I was almost disappointed. The room measured about twenty by forty feet, with a concrete floor, plywood walls, and exposed beams beneath a tin roof. Nothing special; it was built just like the hooches. Someone had made a respectable effort to create Asian décor by fashioning the bar out of bamboo and dressing it up with a dozen high-back barstools. Eight make-shift tables surrounded with dining chairs crowded the space. But after several visits, I came to realize that what made this place so special was not what it looked like, but because of what went on here. The O Club was our refuge, a safe place to return to after a mission when you'd be wound up tighter than a clock. A place where you could reset that pulsing adrenaline to 'low', helping you unwind so you could ultimately fall asleep. It was a safe place to share your non-classified experiences with others who were all in the same boat as you. And, of course, it was a place to drink.

Then I spotted her – an uncharacteristically tall Vietnamese girl in her twenties who appeared to be the only bartender here. Instead of silk, she looked right at home dressed in an army green T-shirt and Levis. Her dark, lustrous hair was gathered into two long pigtails that trailed over her shoulders. For a brief moment, I wondered what she did before the war. Then I snapped back to the present when in one efficient movement, she emptied the case of beer that she had been carrying into a large military ice cooler before turning her attention to us.

"Hi, Mr. Tex. Usual? I see you have new pilot."

"You got it, Ling."

"What your name, Sir?"

"Sam."

"My name, Ling. Nice to meet you, Sam. What you drink?"

"Dewar's Scotch and soda, please."

"OK. Scotch, same as Mr. Tex. He always get double. You want double?"

"Thanks, Ling. A double it is."

"Looks like we drink the same thing," I remarked to Tex. "Yeah, been drinking Scotch whiskey since I was in college."

"Same here. They say it is an acquired taste. Not for me. Liked it from the first sip."

"Me too, Sam."

Ling placed Tex's drink in front of him and then mixed mine. Tex picked up his drink and turned toward the room, hoisting his glass in the air. Clinking it with a pen from his flight suit pocket, he drew the attention of the two at the end of the bar and others who were sitting at a table in a corner.

"Here! Here! Gentlemen!" Then Tex clinked my glass and raised his again, "To Sam here. A broke-in FNG. He just finished his in-country check-ride and actually passed the first time out!"

The others lifted their drinks without saying much of anything other than a few low-key 'congrats'. One guy said, "Welcome to the Nam, Sam."

After acknowledging with a nod and a quiet 'Thanks', I turned to Tex. "You said, first time. You telling me some pilots don't pass the first time?"

"Buddy, I gave that same check-ride to a fella three times just a few months ago. Think his last name was Walters. Guys around here call him the 'goat roper' for some reason. Tipper put him in maintenance inventory and lets him fly one mission a month so he can collect flight pay. Ask me, he has no business in an aircraft. His daddy must be a damn U.S. Senator or something. Anyway, the first-time pass rate for that check ride is under twenty-five percent; but most pass it the second time."

"It's unbelievable that a pilot took three times to pass."

"No, Sam. Not unbelievable; it's downright dangerous is what it is. You ever see that boy beside your name on the schedule roster, you come get me. By the way, now would be a good time to walk over to the wall there and check your mission time tomorrow. Always check it when you walk in the door."

"How come when I walk in the door?"

"Well, if you're not flying until say the next night at two a.m., you're free to get drunk!" he explained, referencing the eighteen-hour rule.

We both laughed. Tex signaled Ling for another round, and I got up to check my mission time. On the way to the schedule, I noticed that for some reason, Ling went to a little cabinet to get Tex's Scotch but took mine off the shelf behind her. Oh, well, none of my business. I checked the schedule and returned to my seat at the bamboo bar.

"This round is to you for not panicking when I screamed in your ear that we were taking ground fire. That's what usually flunks pilots the first time. So, tell me again, what were you thinking?" questioned Tex as our glasses met. Before responding, we each took a big gulp of our drinks, not just a little sip. "Well, I was on short final. You know, everything hanging out … low and slow. The way I figured it, best to stay on course and land. If we were taking rounds, at least we would be on the ground in a few seconds. To start a 'go around' or 'get out dodge' procedure would just have exposed us to being airborne that much longer and remaining a target," I replied with retrospective confidence.

"Right answer! But no thought of being hit or killed?"

"No! Why?"

"Because a lot of pilots do, that's why. Hold on to that one, Sam. Truth is, if you let your head get wrapped around that kind of thinking, you'll forget what you're doing, and that can spell disaster. You're going to do OK over here, Sam. Just know your limits, keep your cool, watch this stuff," nodding to our glasses, "and you'll do just fine."

"Thanks, Tex."

We continued with a bit of small talk until I finished my second and final drink; I had to stick to the rule – eighteen hours from bottle to throttle. Truth be known, most pilots fudged by at least six to eight hours. The day to day pressure on a combat pilot can and does get very intense.

"Tex, I am going to call it an early evening. I got to get my gear unpacked, read the information manual I have been carrying around all day, and get a good night's sleep. I've got my first mission tomorrow."

"Good man, Sam. Keep up the good habits. Got to tell you, REST is the number one thing you need before any mission. Sleep well, my new friend, and good luck to you tomorrow. I see where you are flying with Carl Wiggins. Good man! An Aircraft Commander."

"How do you become an Aircraft Commander?"

"The squadron nominates and votes on two new ACs every six months. Rank and the CO have nothing to do with it. The boys in the squadron know who they want, trust me. They know the Aircraft Commanders are breaking in the new pilots, and they better do it right, because they will soon be flying with them. Now, get out of here and get some rest. And Sam ..."

"Yeah, Tex?"

"Drop by my hooch after your mission tomorrow. I want to hear all about it."

"Sure thing. Good night."

Chapter 9 First Mission

That night, my fourth in the Nam, I slept like a baby in my air-conditioned hooch. I was up, showered and eating what passed for breakfast when a pilot sat down next to me and introduced himself.

"Sam?"

"Yeah."

"I'm Carl Wiggins. Good to meet you. Looks like we are flying together today."

"Yeah, nice to meet you, too, Carl."

When he followed up with, "Something wrong, Sam?" I figured he had read my quizzical expression.

"No! I guess I was expecting an Aircraft Commander, to be, you know, a little bit older."

"Not necessarily. I am twenty-five and a Chief Warrant Officer. Been here nine months. First tour... and hopefully, my last."

Carl, with his light hair, clear skin, and blue eyes, had a very boyish look, but his hands, like mine, were older than the rest of him. We exchanged small talk, hometowns, family, and school, and discovered we had something in common. Like me, he grew up on a farm where manual labor just came with the territory. Carl exuded self-confidence, which could be a bad thing, but I would soon see him perform as First Pilot under extreme pressure, and there he earned my respect.

When we entered the briefing room, two Technical Operators were already there, and Carl took care of the introductions. "Scotty, Jimmy, I would like you to meet Sam Walker. Be good to him today. This is his first mission."

Scotty spoke up. "Yes, Sir. Good to meet you, Mr. Walker. We will be looking after you, Sir."

"Good to meet you, Scotty ... and thanks."

Jimmy shook my hand, smiled, and nodded before we all sat down, waiting for the briefing officer who walked in as I was sipping my coffee.

"Good morning, gentlemen, and welcome to your first mission, Sam. May I call you 'Sam'? We met yesterday when you sat in on most of a briefing."

"Of course."

"Good. Please call me Ken. Let's get started. We have a lot to cover, and you have wheels-up in less than forty-five minutes. Sam, I will be giving this briefing in a little more detail for your benefit. The other men know, for example, what radios one through seven represent. It is on your in-flight checklist, but it is something that is critical to your mission and worthy of a little extra attention. Especially, since this is something you will be handling as co-pilot."

Carl leaned over and whispered reassuringly, "Don't worry, I'll be giving you a hand."

I was excited; not nervous or afraid. Knowing that I was in good company with a crew who showed a personal interest helped.

"Sam, I am assigning you a call sign of Blackshield 876. With Carl's assistance, you will be handling all comms. Please use your erasable board and grease pencil to take down the following frequencies: First Radio, VHF, handles three contacts: Long Thanh Tower, 231.09; Departure Control on 248.68; and Tactical Control on 288.30.

"OK, this is the artillery situation. Unusual this morning. Something pretty major is going on. I have been doing this for four months now, and I have never seen these many guns focused on one target area. At least for now. Doesn't mean it will stay that way. Just so you know, Sam, this is a tricky part of your mission. Can't get all the intel on the current situation, except that we got four players: us, the South Vietnamese, the Aussies, and the Koreans.

"Second Radio handles American artillery on FM 45.90. American Artillery to the 'Fence' this morning has three different firebase batteries operating and one U.S. Navy battleship, the USS New Jersey – call sign, 'Black Dragon'. She sits three miles off the coast of Vung Tau, firing sixteen-inch guns. Firing time, 1010 - 1050. Firing fan from 080 -120 degrees.

"American Artillery Firebase One: grid coordinate XY10065773, call sign 'Deep Purple'. Firing time, 0915 - 1015. Firing fan from 095 -120 degrees.

"American Artillery Firebase Two: grid coordinate XY10065768, call sign 'Blue Wave'. Firing time, 1000 -1030. Firing fan from 095 -110 degrees.

"American Artillery Firebase Three: grid coordinate XY10065763, call sign 'Rolling Thunder'. Firing times, 1015 - 1045. Firing fan from 100 - 115 degrees.

"Sam, these three batteries have been in place for about six months now. The New Jersey has been on station for three days. Except for the ship, notice the firebases are all on this east-west line of 1006. This is a ridgeline that is four hundred-eighty feet high. When these boys give you the altitude arc of their trajectory, they do not include their ground elevation. Be sure you add four hundred and eighty feet to their numbers. By the way, these are very big guns, Howitzer M110s. Four guns per battery."

"M110s? Those shells are eight inches in diameter!"

"You got it, Sam."

"Now, notice their times and fans of fire overlap. They are walking their rounds to the southeast. Directly in your path to the Fence.

"Third Radio: Aussie artillery on FM 39.60. Grid coordinate XY1006774, call sign 'Matilda'. Same ridgeline. Little over ten klicks east of Rolling Thunder. They only have one battery up this morning. Using our M110s. Firing time, 1025 - 1040. Fire fan from 090 - 110 degrees.

"Fourth Radio: South Vietnamese artillery on FM 28.90. Grid coordinate XY11089369, call sign 'White Duck'. They are not part of this operation. Nothing going on at the moment, but you never know with these guys. They often start shelling without notifying anybody. Be sure to call them, Sam. Sometimes, it is difficult to understand them. Scotty, here, seems to have no problem with that. You get in a jam and need help, hand it off to Scotty." Scotty looked over at me with an affirmative nod and a smile.

"Fifth Radio: Korean artillery on FM 23.46. Grid coordinate XY12009015, call sign 'Sunset'. They are on top of a knoll. Elevation four hundred thirty feet. Firing time, 1115 - 1130. Fire fan from 080 - 130 degrees. Good luck with that bunch."

"Whadaya mean, Ken?"

"Just like the Vietnamese artillery. Very unpredictable. Firing times and fans seem to jump all over the place. Also, very hard to understand. Their English really sucks."

With that, Carl spoke up. "Don't worry, Sam. Leave the Korean boys to me."

Ken continued. "Sixth Radio: Standard VHF in the event you lose Radio One. Have the volume up. It monitors the Guard Frequency 243.0. Sam, 'Guard' is an emergency frequency for pilots and fighter jocks needing vectors to targets, and if any of you get in serious trouble, it's the frequency for a 'mayday' call. These fighter jocks are usually listening to us, and helping them is important. They know we are out there somewhere and may need their help. Let me tell you, if you ever need them, they are with you in seconds."

"Ken, you telling me fighter pilots are depending on us for flight vectors?"

"Yep. Every now and then. You got to figure, Sam, these boys fly a mission, land, grab a beer, play a game of pool, take a nap, and fly again before you get home the first time. Shit, they take-off on afterburners and reach Mach 1 within seconds. You think they have time to call up artillery?"

Everybody laughed, but it was the truth. Our missions were generally four and a half hours long, from take-off to landing.

"Radio Seven is top-secret comm. It is sitting in front of Scotty. He has the M-16, which makes him the legal 'armed guard' that is required in order to transport the radio to your aircraft. Sam, you and Carl signed for it and were given two keys. Please show them." We were wearing the keys on chains around our neck and held them up for Ken to see. "Thanks. Know that sounds sophomoric, Sam. Just covering everybody's ass."

"Understood."

"OK, here we go, targets and times. Sam, now we do not speak, only write. For your eyes only, gentlemen."

"Whatever you say, Ken, but how come?"

"I am sure you have been told there is a lot of Charlie around us. We have to assume they are always listening. We just don't know how well. The NVA certainly doesn't have the technology, but the Russians and Chinese do. Just can't take the chance."

With that, Ken flipped a switch on his podium, and the wall map changed dramatically. I did not see this the day before when I observed a briefing. But now, behind the plexiglass map, there suddenly appeared what looked like a hologram of green neon targets, each marked with a skull and crossbones symbol. Under each target, there was a Roman numeral, grid coordinates, and the 'Target Up Time'. This was a very advanced technology that I had not previously been exposed to. Obviously computer-generated, I wondered where this program came from and how it worked, but now was not the time to ask. There were fourteen targets in all. No wonder the missions were so long. We were all busy writing. It took a good ten minutes. The need to write it all down kept me from actually thinking about it. My first mission. Fourteen targets. Skulls and crossbones. Death – for whom and how many? I did manage to ask, "How come I didn't see this yesterday?"

"Like I just said, Sam, for your eyes only. That means men in front of me going on a mission. Yesterday, you weren't going on that mission. You remember the definition of top-secret information, 'information which is given only on a need-to-know basis.' Tex had been told when to come get you yesterday."

Man, I was impressed. These guys operated with surgical precision. The briefing ended, and we were driven out to the airfield. The four of us climbed into the rebuilt military version Beechcraft King Air, strapped in, and got settled. Sitting in the co-pilot seat of the cockpit with Carl in the left seat was worse than the day before with Tex. It was just as hot, but this time, programming the computers and executing the pre-flight checks took longer, much longer. Behind the pilot sat the TOs, Jimmy and Scotty. Their seats were at right angles to the pilot's, and they sat shoulder to shoulder with their equipment in front of them. Both Scotty and Jimmy had worked hard to sit in those seats. After passing qualifying tests, they attended several months of technical training and learned code in Vietnamese, Chinese, and Russian. Scotty had a real knack for languages and could understand quite a bit of Vietnamese. In my opinion, with these skills and vast knowledge, Technical Operators were smarter than us pilots. And they were willing to carry out their tours of duty in a plane, over which they had no control. They put their complete trust in our judgment and flying skills. Although our missions would take us directly into danger, our plane did not carry any weaponry other than the pistols each of us selected upon arrival at base camp, and TOs carried M-16s. Our best defense was avoidance; we were not equipped for engagement. Although we each had top-secret clearance, the dissemination of mission-related information was controlled on a need-to-know basis. We pilots did not have access to the TOs' information, nor they to ours. Only by working together efficiently and according to protocol could our mission be executed.

"OK, Sam. Real quick. We need to get moving. Do a quick comm check. They will not ask where we are going or our intent. Believe me, they know who we are. They don't dare ask what we are up to! Call sign is all you need. Got it?"

I did an intercom check first with Scotty and Jimmy, followed by the tower, Departure Control, and finally, Tactical Control. Contact with the AWAC, known as Ramrod, was through Radio Seven – cryptic, top secret. Carl and I inserted our keys and unlocked the heavy, gray lead box that encased Radio Seven. A small red light came on, letting us know the TSR (Top-secret Radio) was working.

"OK, Sam. Give the tower a call again and get us out of here."

"Long Thanh Tower this is Blackshield 876."

"Blackshield 876, go ahead."

"876 is ready for take-off."

"Roger 876. Taxi to apron for runway zero three and hold."

"Roger that."

We had to wait for one of our birds on a long final approach returning from its mission. Sure would be good to know what things were like out there today, but then I reasoned we were about to find out firsthand. The bird landed, we were cleared for takeoff, and then I went to Departure Control.

"Departure Control, this is Blackshield 876, how copy?"

"Read ya, Blackshield 876. Squawk transponder 70705 and identify yourself."

"Roger 70705." I entered the numbers 70705 and pushed the I.D. button.

"Blackshield 876, I have you. Turn to heading three five five, climb and report fifteen thousand."

"Roger, Departure, turning to three five five, will report fifteen thousand."

"OK, Sam. How ya doin' over there?" Carl checked in with me, perhaps to remind me he was there if I needed him.

"I feel like adrenaline is spurting out of the top of my head, but other than that ... good."

"I want you sipping water every five minutes. Adrenaline dries your mouth out, and you got lots of talking to do for the next thirty minutes. I know you already know the procedure, and I don't mean to be coming across as telling you your job. It's just what an AC does the first couple of months, OK?"

"Yeah, sure, Carl. No problem here."

"OK, be sure to call each artillery firebase at least ten miles out. Confirm fire time and fan."

"That's not set from the briefing we just got?"

"No freakin' way, Sam. They change that shit within minutes sometimes."

"OK, we are level at fifteen thousand."

"Departure, this is Blackshield 876, level one five thousand, switching over to Tactical."

"Roger, 876."

"Tactical, this is Blackshield 876, how read?"

"Blackshield 876. We were listening. If that's you squawking 70705. Gotchya."

"Blackshield 876, that's us. Climbing to level two zero on a heading of three five five. Will call back before we go silent."

"Roger that, Blackshield 876. You have four F-4s at ten o'clock, one mile, your altitude moving north."

"Roger that, Tactical. Got 'um."

"Blackshield 876, you also have eight helicopters at eleven o'clock, low."

"Roger, Tactical. Got 'um."

The first and second artillery sites were as advertised. We flew well behind their fans of fire without incident, and then, when flying behind the fire fan of Rolling Thunder, we got a call, and everything changed. All of our plans went out the window, and the situation got very dicey. I realized we could actually get blown out of the sky!

"Blackshield 876, be advised, changing our fire fan forty degrees to the south."

"Whoa, Rolling Thunder! This is Blackshield 876, we are four klicks away at flight level two zero, crossing your new fire fan. Can you hold?"

"Negative, Blackshield. Critical."

Suddenly, the urgent voice of the battery commander came through. "Blackshield 876, this is Major McGee. Just got a call. We got about one hundred of our guys pinned down with a regiment of VC and NVA within one-click of their position. Looks like they are also being flanked from the south. Got to fire now to stop them."

Carl jumped in, speaking quickly, but clear and calm. "I got this, Sam. Major, this is Blackshield 883, same bird. What is your trajectory arc?"

"Blackshield 883. Standby. Give me five seconds."

"Roger, Rolling Thunder."

"Blackshield 883. We top out at nineteen thousand five hundred, max. You should be OK. I got seasoned boys on my guns. We are commencing fire."

"Shit, Carl, that's only five hundred feet below us!"

"Not really! Remember, we got to add almost five hundred feet to that number. That is actually right on top of us. OK, boys, strap in tight."

Carl went to full power and pushed the nose over eighty degrees until we red-lined at 470 knots and then pulled straight back on the stick. We were in a vertical climb. Within less than twenty seconds, we had gained two thousand feet.

"Shit, Mr. Wiggins," Jimmy declared, "if I had wanted this kind of flying, I would have signed up for the Blue Angels."

I hit my intercom. "He just saved your ass, Jimmy."

"I was fuckin' with ya, man! I dig it, actually."

Below us, all hell had broken loose. It was like watching a silent fireworks display because you can't hear anything while suited up in the cockpit, only what comes in from your headgear. Looking down, we could actually see four M-110, eight-inch Howitzer guns firing. The bright flashes from the business end of the Howitzers, even at this altitude, were startling. To think eight-inch diameter shells were passing right under us was unnerving, to put it mildly.

"OK, guys, we are at flight level two two and will be out of their fan in thirty seconds. Sam, it's past time to contact Matilda."

"Matilda, this is Blackshield 876, how copy?"

"Yeah, Blackshield 876. G'day mate. You're late and may be in trouble with us. We had to change our fan to help Rolling Thunder. Say position and altitude."

"This is Blackshield 876, five klicks west of you at level two two."

"OK, Blackshield 876. Our arch is two four thousand. Say again, our arch is two four thousand. Very close to you. Not good! WE ARE CHECKING FIRE! WE ARE CHECKING FIRE! You need to turn ninety degrees and fly over us immediately! Call back when you pass us, mate."

We safely passed over the artillery within seconds. The big guns resumed fire. "Matilda, this is Blackshield 876, how copy?"

"Gotchya, mate. Almost put you Yanks on the barbie."

"Roger, Matilda. Too damn hot for a barbecue."

"Bloody good show, old boy. Don't know what you Yanks are up to, but good hunting."

"Thanks, Matilda. Do you have grids on the target that everyone is hammering?"

"Roger, grid XY10004363."

"Thanks, we may need it." Sure enough, we did.

"This is F-4, call sign Fox 21. Anybody read?"

Carl jumped in. "Yeah, I got you, Fox 21. This is Blackshield 883."

"Blackshield 883, Fox 21, can you give me vectors to XY10004363? Heard you on this comm. There seems to be a lot of heavy shit going to that grid. Also, our target."

"Roger that, Fox 21. You airborne?"

"Will be. Four birds rolling off Tan Son Nhut. Target time 80 seconds. How copy?"

"Copy, Fox 21. Take outbound radial three one eight. When you see target area, should be lots of smoke, recommend you turn west at least ten miles out, and come back in for strike on heading of one six zero. You got three batteries and one ship. All hot. That will keep you out of harm's way."

"Roger copy, Blackshield. Thanks a bunch."

"You got it, Fox 21."

"Blackshield 876, you are cleared back on course. G'day to ya, mates."

"Roger. Thanks, Matilda."

"OK, Sam, hand off White Duck to Scotty, and you call Sunset."

"Sunset this is Blackshield 876, how copy?"

"Rawer brawksweel. No chain. No chain."

"Carl, what is he saying?"

"I got it, Sam."

"Thank you, Sunset. Blackshield 883, out. He was saying, 'Roger, Blackshield. No change' meaning their fan had not changed."

"OK, if you say so."

Suddenly we heard from Scotty. "Sirs, we got a problem with White Duck! Something happened; I don't know what. Only one guy there, and he speaks very broken English."

Carl jumped in, "What's he saying, Scotty?"

"Something about 'fire sunset.' Keeps saying it over and over. I don't get it!"

"NO! He means they are firing to the west," Carl corrected. 'Fire sunset.' He doesn't know how to say the direction, 'west'."

"I didn't think they were supposed to be firing," I commented, rather confused by all this.

"Tell him, 'Thank you. We got it.'" Carl broke right in a ninety-degree bank as he was talking. He leveled out for a few minutes and then broke left and got back on course.

"Whoa, what was that?"

"I had to be sure we were out of their way, Sam. Asking him his arc and fan would have been a waste of time. Why they let guys who can't speak English get behind big guns is beyond me. Talk about poor customer service!"

Scotty, from the back, "Yeah, and they call it 'Friendly Fire.' There is a word for that, right?"

Chuckling, Sam responded, "It's called an oxymoron. And you're right, nothing friendly about running into gunfire."

"OK, guys, everybody take a breath and get a drink of water. Will be twenty miles out from the Fence in zero five. Now we really go to work, Sam."

"Is artillery always like that?"

"No, sometimes it gets a lot worse. Go ahead and sign off on Tactical Control. Put all radios in standby mode."

"Tactical, this is Blackshield 876."

"Go ahead, 876."

"Gone dark, Tactical."

"Roger that, but you know we will be listening."

Carl again. "OK, fellas. Silence from here. Sam is the only one talking. Sam, get off of Tactical and come up on Seven (the top-secret radio), and call Ramrod (the AWAC)."

"Ramrod, this is Blackshield 876, how copy?"

"Blackshield 876, this is Ramrod. You squawking 70705?"

"Roger, Ramrod. That's us."

"Thought so, we have been watching. You boys have been busy. Afraid it was just a warm-up. We got boocoo shit on the Fence. Blackshield 876, don't know your call sign. You an FNG?"

"'Fraid so."

"Who you got in the left seat?"

"883, how goes it, Tommy?"

"Not good. Keep sharp, Carl. Back to you 876."

"876. Go ahead, Ramrod."

"Turn to heading zero two zero. We got two SAMs fixed. They haven't moved in days. Will squeeze you between them. Be advised you got a thirty-knot headwind, twenty degrees west of your nose. Make a five-degree crab to 015 degrees. You only have one half-klick distance on either side of SAM tracking. No room for error, fellas."

"Roger, Ramrod. Heading 015."

"OK, now the real problem. We got a damn rogue down there who keeps moving on us. Last known position was thirty minutes ago. He was just to the east of you. The son-of-a-bitch lit up and took out an F-4 two hours ago. By the time we fixed his position, it was all over, and he went into hiding again. The F-4 pilots punched out and are on the ground in one piece. Got their fix. Hope they can get to the Fence. Went down about twelve miles to the north. SEAL boys on the way."

I swallowed hard. "Roger, Ramrod. Thanks." I kept it short, certain my fear was showing.

"OK, Blackshield, here we go. You are sixty seconds from CCO (Critical Cross Over)."

Carl spoke up. "We trust you, Tommy. Guess we got to."

"No, you could turn around and go home!"

"Bullshit! Holding steady on zero one five. Let us know when we are clear."

"You bet."

"Carl, how close are the SAMs that we are flying through?"

"At least three miles. Anything beyond that range, they won't fire."

"OK, Blackshield. You are clear. Come back up on transponder squawk 71722, when you are twenty miles north of us on your return."

"Roger copy, Ramrod, and thanks for the help."

"That's what we're here for."

I put the new squawk frequency into the transponder before I cut it off. Now, no one in the entire world, except for Ramrod, knew we were in Cambodia, and even if someone did know where we were, they would have no way to track us.

Radio Seven was top secret. The keys we used gave us access to one encoded frequency only, which had been programmed for this particular mission just before we took off. Our transmission was encrypted. Other than communicating with Ramrod, it would be used for what we were about to do. This frequency would only be used for this one mission, and then it would disappear forever. It would be zeroed out before we landed. As per top-secret protocol, no official record of anything we said or did would remain anywhere, other than in our memories or nightmares, as the case would be. Officially, we were never here, but tell that to the hundreds of thousands of Vietnamese and Cambodians whose sons never came home.

Scotty's urgent voice came through the intercom. "Sir, we have a hot potato. I mean a really big hot potato!"

"What do you mean, Scotty?"

"Well, for the last three or four days, me and about six other TOs have been tracking two advancing enemy regiments. When we first picked them up on radio, they were several miles apart and on two different trails, but they were both heading south to Vietnam. Apparently, in just the past few hours, they met up, and there's a lot of chatter going on back and forth between the two regiments."

"Can you get anything useful out of that chatter?"

"Best I can tell, one regiment radio guy is up in front, and the second regiment radio guy is in the rear. Both regiments are now together and stretched out in single file. Their radio transmissions are about two klicks apart from each other, so given that distance, I estimate there must be about three thousand or more NVA, and they are definitely on the move for an offensive strike."

"Heading directly to our guys!"

"Yeah, for sure. We have a lot of troops along the Nam side of the Fence, along with the Aussies and South Vietnamese. I suggest we get the fixes on the positions of those two regiments and then go to TSR (Top-Secret Radio) to confirm computer accuracy."

Within the next ten minutes, Carl and I fixed both radio positions. Scotty was right; they were two klicks from one another. Then Carl confirmed computer accuracy through the Navy. Best not to mention how that was done. Next, we placed a call to Saigon Headquarters on TSR. While we waited on standby, they communicated with Langley. In less than fifteen minutes, we got the green light. I called the lead pilot of the B-52 bomb squadron waiting on the tarmac at Tan Son Nhut Air Base. Within five minutes, six B-52Ds, 'Big Bellies', took off, carrying a total of 219,000 pounds of bombs. I realized that if it weren't for us spooks, those bombers might not have left Tan Son Nhut that afternoon.

The lead pilot and Carl talked non-stop, verifying information and confirming our computers were in sync before Carl gave him the vectors to the target. I went on Guard Radio, and said, 'Arc Light' three times and repeated the target site coordinates. Nothing else. Everyone listening to Guard Radio would now be aware of the imminent attack and be able to get clear of the area and to stay away for at least thirty minutes. Naturally, we got the hell out of the way and then, from our cockpit, witnessed the firestorm that was unleashed some miles north of our position.

The Boeing B-52 first took flight in April, 1952. Years later, modifications yielded the D model, whose sole purpose was to drop bombs. Aptly nicknamed Big Belly, the B-52D featured an enlarged cargo area, significantly increasing its ordnance capacity both inside and external to the plane. From our vantage point, less than ten miles from ground zero, we saw the Big Bellies approach and unleash their deadly loads; six planes, each dropping bombs in succession as they moved across the doomed enemy regiments. We could see, but not hear, the parade of bombs released from these planes, appreciating those precious moments before the bombs would hit, and change everything. As I wondered how many seconds those on the ground had to confront their fate, the first bomb struck, followed by many others in rapid succession. Each strike sent up a giant red fireball that gradually turned black as smoke and destruction painted a picture across the afternoon's blue sky. Eventually, the Big Bellies, having completed their mission, flew away from their target, now buried under a massive cloud of black haze and debris, which would take several hours to finally settle. In barely ten minutes, about three thousand enemy had been blown away.

Before returning to base, we were directed to coordinate additional bombings, though not as great in scale as that first one. I orchestrated the deaths of approximately 750 additional enemy, bringing my day's total to 3750. Totaling my kills seemed like a natural thing to do. I hadn't really thought about it; I just did it. I shuddered to think about what that number could be by the end of my tour. A queasy feeling grew inside.

***

Three and a half hours had passed since we first climbed on board, and we were now headed home, having completed our top-secret mission, my first.

"OK, Sam. We are twenty miles north of the Fence. Cut the transponder back on and squawk. Wait a few minutes and call Ramrod."

"Got it. Ramrod, this is Blackshield 876, how copy?"

"We have you 876. Be advised; you need to either slow down or go into a holding pattern. Looks like we may have more than one rogue playing hide-and-seek down there. He came up for a radar check and went right back down. He is on your side of the Fence. Just don't know how far in or where he is. Sorry fellas. Not good news. At this point, I will bring you out a different way. Stand by."

"Roger, Ramrod. Is this normal, Carl?"

"No, not at all. Never had it happen before." Carl pulled power back to sixty percent and went into an elliptical holding pattern. After a few minutes, Ramrod called.

"Blackshield 876, I can't keep you out there forever. We got to take a run at this. I have two birds coming in that need to cross over and another one behind you. Copy?"

"Roger, Ramrod. What we got? Any luck?"

"No, Blackshield. The prick has not come back up. 876, pick up a heading of one five two degrees. CCO in five minutes. Got to tell you, this one is dicey, fellas."

Carl answered, "Know you're doing your best, Tommy."

No sooner had Carl made the transmission when Scotty's voice screamed over the intercom, "WE ARE BEING TRACKED ... WE ARE BEING TRACKED ... SAY AGAIN. MISSLE IS TRYING TO LOCK ON!"

Without saying a word, Carl immediately went to full power and shoved the nose over in a vertical dive straight for the ground.

"Carl, we are red-lining! No! We are past red-line by twenty knots!"

"I know, Sam, we may pop a few rivets, but we're OK. Pushing outside the envelop a little. Got to shake this asshole before he locks on. If he does, it's all over."

The aircraft was vibrating violently as it screamed from our flight level of 22,000 feet down to five thousand feet and then dropped below that. This was a condition I had never experienced before, and it was not a pleasant one. Carl had me get on the controls with him, instructing me with his quiet calm, "OK, buddy, start pulling back with everything you got." There was no question in my mind that Carl knew exactly what he was doing. I thanked God for that.

From the vantage point of a pilot's seat, it's extremely unsettling, to say the least, to see the ground below coming up at you so fast. The triple canopy jungle that covered this part of the earth was beginning to fill the view from our window with dense green foliage, much too close for comfort. Carl had pulled most of the power off, but we were still red-lining. At one thousand feet, we finally leveled off and then, to my great surprise, Carl pushed the nose over once again.

Having just started to exhale, I jumped. "Hey, man! What are you doing?"

"Puttin' this bird at tree-top level, Sam, and making zigzag turns to the South China Sea."

"What about artillery?"

"Say a prayer and hold your breath. We would have to be right on top of a gun to take a hit at fifty feet above the trees. Probably safer from artillery down here than up there. It's Charlie with his small arms we got to worry about now."

At only fifty feet above the jungle treetops, Carl continued making ninety-degree bank turns first one way and then the other, jitterbugging as fast as the aircraft could take it. As a result of all those non-stop abrupt maneuvers, both Scotty and Jimmy had thrown up. Puke covered a lot of their equipment. I was to find this was not an unusual occurrence. TOs had not been trained to withstand this type of flying as pilots had been.

"TAKING HITS! TAKING HITS!" Jimmy screamed into his mic. Enemy ground troops had found us, and an AK-47 had just stitched half a dozen rounds through the fuselage only inches above Jimmy's head. I had heard the term, 'staying cool under fire', but only had a textbook definition in my mind until now, when the enemy was trying to take us out of the sky. Then, as suddenly as it had begun, it was over. All was quiet, including us. We just kept flying. After thirty-five minutes, we could see the South China Sea from fifty feet.

I could not process all that transpired on this, my first mission. So much of my mental energy had been focused on the mission itself that I had not anticipated the many dangers we would encounter on the way to and from our mission. On some level, I knew it would be dangerous, but I hadn't really let that sink in. We had flown above a raging Howitzer gunfight; almost wound up on 'the barbie' as victims of friendly fire; avoided a hostile SAM lock-on; had taken hits from ground-fire that could have easily taken us out, and pushed our aircraft well beyond what I understood to be its limits. To say nothing of the actual mission. Any of these situations gone bad could have blown this plane and the four of us in it clear out of the sky.

Now we were flying home, missing a few rivets, decorated with a row of neatly placed bullet holes, and splashed with putrid vomit. This mission had taken its toll on us. In addition to puking their guts out, Scotty and Jimmy had both peed in their flight suits. My mouth was so dry I could hardly talk; I was soaking wet from sweat, and my hands were shaking uncontrollably. Only Carl seemed to be none the worse for wear. I admired his calm under pressure, which left me inspired to perform like that, too. After we hit the coast, he brought us back up to five thousand feet, heading back to Long Thanh.

"You have the controls, Sam."

"I have the controls, Carl."

"Take us home, Brother."

Chapter 10 Tex's Story

Tex knew exactly what I would face as a pilot with top-secret clearance and what it would do to me. That's why he had invited me to his hooch after my first mission. In the eyes of most, he was not only the best pilot in the squadron, having logged more total combat flying hours than any six of us combined, but he also had an extraordinary capacity to relate to us pilots. I knocked on his hooch door.

"Yo!"

"Tex, it's me ... Sam."

He opened his door, which I noted he always kept double locked.

"Come on in, Sam. Real mother fucker up there, ain't it? Have a seat," he motioned while closing the door behind me. I walked in quietly and then, like a rag doll, abruptly crumbled to the floor, where I remained, wailing and writhing, primal sounds emanating from deep within me.

"NO! This can't be true. Please tell me it isn't so, Tex. This is not what we are doing. Please, Tex. Tell me this is not what we do every day. This is totally insane!" Looking up at him from my place on his floor, I saw the tears in his eyes and a look on his face that I would never see again. It was a look of deep compassion for me. For he had known that it was only on one's first mission that we would find out what it was that we actually do. No one had whispered a word about it. No one could have. Not only because it was top secret, but because the reality was too hideous to face. Verbalizing made it real, and that was just too much.

"Yes, Sam, it is insane. There are no words for it. There is nothing I can say that will change it. It will cripple your soul, Sam. A part of you will die over here, my friend, and you will never get it back. What we do up there will humble us for the rest of our days. I didn't leave the Nam after my first tour because I get that, and I want to help young men like you get through it. That is why I stay. I am here to guide you through this insanity. What we do is beyond us. It is beyond beyond."

Tex squatted down beside me. Placing his hand on my shoulder, he spoke softly. "I know it sounds impossible right now, Sam, but you've got to get a grip, or you won't make it. Understand?"

"But I killed so many people! Almost four thousand men are dead because of me! In one afternoon! My first mission! It may sound stupid, I mean, I'm here in the Nam, but I guess I just focused on the flying, blocking out the real reason I'd be up in that plane. My God, what have I gotten myself into? I don't know if I can do this job, Tex."

"Tell you what, Sam. You just gotta make an adjustment, you know, change your point of view. For sure, that is a big number, four thousand. But there's another number I want you to consider. Do you have any idea how many of our guys, the Aussies and South Vietnamese would have found themselves between the enemy's crosshairs? Guys like you and me? All those good soldiers would have been massacred. Damn! Think of all their mamas and papas, wives, sisters, and brothers back home, getting that God-awful news. What you did today saved their lives. Remember that! That's what your job is all about, Sam, saving lives – for our side."

I wiped my tears on my sleeve and blew my red nose. I pushed myself up into a sitting position and drew my knees into my chest. "I hadn't thought about it that way. I guess I see your point, but I don't know that I can do it. Right now, I am numb all over."

"You have to learn to live with this, Sam. Accepting this job makes you insane. Doing this job means you can handle insane. If you can master this way of thinking, you will make it."

"How do you do it, Tex?"

"I just know that today, in this moment, living this insanity, I will make it until tomorrow, and then I will do it one more day and one more day and one more day ... until that blessed day when it will all be over. Of course, by then, I may be over, too, but I don't know what that looks like, either. I do know that I will fight until that day. I will fly. I will fight. I will stay alive, and when that day comes, I will deal with it. And, so will you."

Tex extended his hand, and grasping it, I pulled myself upright where we stood quietly, face to face. "Upset, scared, confused, and pissed off, all at the same time, right?" He summed that up well.

"Yeah, that's about right."

"That's why I wanted you to come by. Now you know. You know what we really do and why it is so important to not breathe a word of it."

"Who knows besides us ... you know, who knows in Washington outside of the spook circles?"

"The President, Kissinger, McNamara, and the Joint Chiefs. That's it."

"You mean Congress doesn't know?"

"Nope. And supposedly, not even the Vice President."

"This is a lot to handle, Tex."

"I know it is Sam. Say, how about a few good snorts of some twenty-five-year-old Scotch and stay for supper?"

"They make Scotch that old?" The Scotch was older than I was!

"Oh, yeah. Some even older. Stuff costs a damn fortune. I brought a case with me from the States. And picked up another case when I was in Australia. In round numbers, about three hundred a bottle."

"What? Three hundred a bottle? You sure you want to share it?"

"Now I wouldn't be offering it if I didn't want to, would I?"

"Mighty nice of you, Tex. I never needed a good stiff drink more in my life than I do now!"

From a small cabinet in the kitchen, Tex took out two expensive looking cut-crystal whiskey glasses and rested them on the desk next to his bottle of Chivas Regal. I could read a snippet of the gilded label, ... aged for 25 years ... oak barrels. After pouring about three inches for each of us and raising his elegant glass, Tex gave it a light tap to signal his simple but appropriate toast, "To the finer things in life."

"Oh, man! This is so smooth. It tastes better than anything I've ever had. How do you drink Dewar's after drinking this stuff?"

"Who said anything about drinking Dewar's?"

"When we were at the O Club, Ling made us both Dewar's and soda."

"No, no, my friend. Ling poured you a Dewar's and soda. You didn't see her take my Chivas from under the counter. If you got something special you would rather drink, just let her know. She is very obliging and won't give it to anyone else. Just slip her a little extra tip."

"Wow! Sure missed that one!"

I was admiring Tex's place, taking it all in. It appeared that Tex, or somebody, had constructed a hooch that would withstand incoming mortar and rocket attacks ... well, to a point. He had a double-width bunk bed only one foot off the floor. The four corner posts, if you could call them that, were actually six by six, eight-foot-high beams, framed on.. the top with four by fours, supporting the roof against a cave-in. On the. other side of his hooch, the same sturdy construction protected an impressive stereo set, a small refrigerator, and living area. Two over-stuffed chairs shared an ottoman, and two sets of headphones rested on the end tables on either side of the chairs.

"Gee, your hooch is twice the size of mine. Got to say, Tex. This is impressive."

"Yep! And I got it all to myself. Home, actually."

"What do you mean home? I thought Amarillo was home?"
"Not really. I grew up an orphan, Sam."

"Damn!"

"No. Don't damn it. It wasn't bad. You can't miss what you never had. You know, like parents."

"How old were you?"

"Just an infant. Dropped off at the front steps. They said I was no more than two weeks old."

"So, you were never adopted?"

"Nope. The Depression was in full swing when I was growing up. Young married couples were not focused on starting families at a time like that. By the time the nation was climbing out of the Depression, and people started resuming a normal lifestyle, World War II broke out, and I had missed the window of opportunity to be adopted. Anyway, when I was eighteen, they had to cut me loose. Only problem was, I had no place to go, so I joined the service. I boot-strapped through night school and got my college degree in aeronautical engineering."

"What's boot-strapping mean?"

"Uncle Sam lets you go to college while you're still in the service, but there is a catch. You got to give him the years back in service that you spent in school. I was staying in anyway, so it didn't make any difference to me."

"So, then what?"

"I started taking private flying lessons and got my license. Loved airplanes since I was a kid!"

"Yeah, me too!"

"True for most pilots. The real ones, anyway. Take the 'goat roper.' He probably can't even spell airplane. Anyway, after college, I got commissioned as a second lieutenant. I was in intelligence, and all I wanted to do was fly but could not get into flight school. About the time I made Captain, I resigned my commission and became a Warrant Officer, which guaranteed me flight school. The rest is history."

"And this is your fourth tour."

"Well, yes and no. I have never really left."

"You telling me you have been here ... how long?"

"Never bothered to add it up. Let's see; after my first tour, they wanted me to extend for six months, which came with a bonus."

"What kind of bonus?"

"Ten thousand dollars, tax-free, and thirty days leave anywhere in the world. You bet, I took the money! Went to California and put eight thousand down on a piece of land I had read about, near Santa Barbara. Two hundred and fifty acres with a dirt airstrip and an old hangar. Best part, is that four hundred feet of it are right on the beach."

"Get out of town!"

"Yep!" Smiling, Tex poured us another round. I was so wrung out from the mission that I was already feeling the first one. "Anyway, I did the same deal a few times, and each time put eight thousand more toward the property. I was thinking about buying a Piper Pawnee and becoming a crop duster after I get out. Now, I am not so sure."

"What? About getting out?'"

"No, I'm getting out of the military, for sure. That's already planned. That part is sweet. I been in so damn long, eighteen years, that I have made a lot of friends in high places. A three-star general buddy of mine is promoting me to full bird colonel after this tour if I promise to become his personal pilot. After eighteen months of time in grade, I can retire on a colonel's pension. Not a bad deal ... not a bad deal at all."

"I've never asked you how much is left to this tour?"

"My current tour ends shortly after yours. Then I have those eighteen months before I get out."

"Good for you, man. I'm happy for you. You earned it, for sure. So, the Pawnee ... you going into crop dusting?"

"Well, Sam, I was thinking about it, but after seeing what a mess this Agent Orange shit is causing over here, I'm having second thoughts about spraying chemicals."

"Yeah, Sully mentioned it was killing monkeys!"

"I been around this stuff for four years now. Let me tell you, we're killing a lot more than monkeys, my friend. I did a little research. This stuff they gave the sweet little name 'Agent Orange' ain't no damn Florida tangerine. It's called Paraquat. Toxic as they come. Kills plants, animals, fish, and yeah, people. Part of the Geneva Protocol under the Geneva Convention and registered under the League of Nations in 1929 prohibits the use of certain toxic chemicals. Of course, back then, we didn't have these things called 'herbicides', the name implying that it only kills or controls plants. Bullshit! If you ask me, we are in direct contravention to the Geneva Accord. I can't help but wonder what that stuff might be doing to us. Anyway, you been through enough today. More on that topic later. Let me show you around, and then I'll cook us a little something to eat."

Tex said this like he was giving me a tour of his home, and in a way, I guess he was. I was conflicted. On the one hand, I felt sorry for him, but on the other, really happy for him. I would learn, as I got to know this man, he was as solid a human being as I would ever meet. He was content with himself and with the life he had made, never blaming anyone or anything for his circumstances.

"Tex, this place is built like a brick shit house. You do this?"

"Yep, sure did. Stole it from supply. Well, I say stole. We GIs are government issue, and this stuff is government issue. Can't hardly steal from yourself, now can you?"

"Nobody tried to stop you?"

"Nope! 'Cause nobody saw Tipper and me do it."

"You mean Tipper helped you?"

"Well, we helped each other. This is heavy shit to handle by yourself. Besides, his hooch, same size as mine, is designed the same way."

"I get it. Being CO, he just had it delivered."

"No, no, Sam. Even he can't do that. We had to wait for the changing of the guard. When the Supply Officer in charge of the stockpile of lumber zeroed out, there was a three-day lag before his replacement came in. Let's just say it was there for the taking, and there was a shit load of it. The opportunity presented itself – midnight raid. No one saw us. Chinook choppers bring all kinds of crap in here on a regular basis. Typical Uncle Sam screw ups. We got enough lumber over there to build a small hotel. Problem is, there is no proper paperwork to allocate the use of it for anything. Truth is, the lumber probably belongs to someone else. Chopper pilot dropped it off at the wrong location. I mean literally dropped it off. Released a hook and cable from a hover and hauled ass outa' here."

"That's really kinda' cool. I guess there is an upside to this place after all."

Tex poured us a third Scotch and started cooking some rice and beans. In his well-appointed kitchen, I spotted three hot plates and several pots and pans.

"Don't know why, Sam. Guess it don't really matter, but I've taken a liking to you, son. Southern boy and all. Besides, you're the best FNG I've ever flown with. Tell you what. I am gonna let you in on somethin', but it has to stay right here between us, OK?"

Couldn't wait. This was going to be good. I took another sip of my 25-year-old Scotch and leaned in.

"The Supply Officer, fella by the name of Captain Crane, is leaving in two weeks. Over there in that chest, I got skill saws, drills, hammers, nails, you know, all the stuff you need. Whadayasay we make a midnight raid on the lumber yard in a few weeks and get your hooch safe? I need to build something besides model airplanes, anyway. Going a little stir crazy for somethin' to do in my spare time."

"Man, that would be absolutely awesome, but what will the other pilots think?"

"Who gives a shit what they think. By the time they figure it out, a new Supply Officer will be settled in for a year, and they'll be out of luck."

We sat down to two heaping bowls of brown rice and red beans and a can of pickled beets, while Tex pointed out his many model airplanes. He had designed, hand-crafted the parts, and built each one out of balsa wood. Each was more a work of art than a model airplane.

"I like your P-51," I mumbled with a mouthful of food.

"Yeah, me too. Cadillac of the sky."

"How long did it take you to make it?"

"Gee, I don't really know, Sam. Sometimes, I get into those planes and just lose track of time. I guess the P-51 has about two hundred hours in it. Still need to paint it."

"WOW! That's really putting your aeronautical engineering skills to work." Although I had been admiring the models in all their glorious detail, I was stunned to find that Tex invested that many hours to create just one.

"That large book over there in the corner has blueprints of most military aircraft. I use a scale of 1:60. I bought hundreds of sheets of balsa wood and balsa framing pieces from Sears. Had to write them a letter and special order it. Took me two months to get it, but it was well-worth it."

Tex and I talked for hours before I called it a night. Returning to my hooch, I hit the shower, then crashed onto my bed. It had been an exhausting day – mentally and physically – but it ended well, in fact, a lot better than I could have imagined. I slept like a dog until late morning, glad that I wasn't scheduled to fly again until that afternoon.

Over the coming months, I found myself hanging out in Tex's hooch a lot. He was the only friend I had that seemed to keep his wits about him in dealing with the day-in and day-out craziness. He seemed to enjoy my company, and I certainly enjoyed his. He invited me into his world of hand-crafted model airplanes. His skill was amazing. I watched him by the hour as we talked of many things. He wanted to know what it was like to grow up with a mom and a dad; what it was like to have a sister. These were things, he admitted, that he never had the courage to find out about, and he wasn't completely sure he wanted to know. Guess he picked the right fella to finally ask. As I told him about my family-life, he smiled a lot. He would look at me with a best-friend nod and thank me. Tex had taught me many things, yet I taught him about a part of life that he had never experienced, something that I had simply taken for granted. Guess I had to come all the way to Vietnam to realize how fortunate I was.

Chapter 11 Black Void

Time passes slowly when your life is about nothing other than going to war every day; when all you do is simply exist, just hoping to survive only to wake up the next morning and repeat this endless and numbing cycle. It crowds your mind like ten people in a VW bug. There seemed little room for anything else. Add to this formula unrelenting torrential rain, 100% humidity, armies of black flies, hordes of mosquitos, and the misery factor is off the charts. I never realized how unfriendly Mother Nature could be. In the Nam, I learned first-hand she has a nasty sense of humor.

The monsoon season was in full swing and had been so for over three months. If I had not experienced it, I would never have believed it could be this bad. In the Nam, it rained buckets, day after day after day; back home, the heaviest rain I ever knew looked like a drizzle in comparison. It was not only relentless but also unforgiving; the force was so strong, it stung like needles, and left you feeling wounded. Efforts to bundle up against it were futile; you'd always wind up soaked to the bone. As if that wasn't bad enough, the rainfall seemed to defy gravity and came at you from all sides. Going anywhere meant sloshing through thick mud so deep that at times it was strong enough to suck the boots right off your sorry feet. Paths turned into knee-deep rivers and important roads were washed out. Military vehicles, even large tanks, were unable to maneuver and often wound up stuck in the mud, stranded and inoperable.

All of this water wreaked havoc on our well-being and took a sizeable toll on our forces. Breeding grounds for mosquitos proliferated, and malaria spread throughout our troops. Not everyone took their weekly malaria pill; I always did. In addition to the enemy, we battled disabling diseases such as amoebic or bacillary dysentery, typhoid, cholera, and blackwater fever. Countless of our military suffered from trench foot and ringworm, and leech bites were as common as mosquito bites. We were threatened by poisonous snakes that were driven from their hiding places and were now more apparent than before. Many best-laid plans would come to a grinding halt as work became impossible to complete. I could only imagine the significant costs of this awful and indefatigable enemy, courtesy of Mother Nature.

By this time, I had seventy-eight missions under my belt as first pilot, and I felt confident that I could hold my own when I flew with co-pilots who had more time in-country. Monsoon season, with its ceaseless rain, seemed to underscore the futility I felt. It was during monsoon season that I experienced one of my most challenging missions. It happened to take place during a pitch-black night.

Night missions were a very different experience from those I flew in daylight. As a pilot, in order to maintain situational awareness, you are constantly surveying the scene from the cockpit – the ground below and the sky around you. On a night mission, there is nothing to survey – just complete and utter darkness. Because the black of night has neither features nor details, it provides no information or reassurances and can hide imminent threats. Night missions are more draining, too, because of the increased difficulty to maintain vigilance. On this particular night, I embarked on a mission very deep into Cambodia. I was flying completely on instruments from the time of takeoff. The monsoon rain was pelting down in sheets, and visibility was less than a quarter-mile. At 2330 hours, artillery was quiet. We had been given firing times and fire fans for three firebases that would be active on our return trip. Fortunately, they would all be firing to the northwest, which was always easier for us. The ride to the Fence was very bumpy until we climbed above the turbulent weather to eighteen thousand feet.

Sully was my co-pilot. "Ramrod, this is Blackshield 743, how copy?"

"Roger, 743. You squawking 86890?"

"Roger that, Ramrod."

"I got you, Sully. Turn to a heading of three six zero. Taking you between two SAMs several klicks apart. Hold your heading. No winds aloft of consequence. Just to let you guys know, on your way home, I will bring you back across the Fence at the same spot."

"Yeah, how come, Ramrod? We always go back a different route."

"Weird, really! For the last ten or twelve hours, we have been picking up a few new SAM sites. Looks like they are putting more and more of them along the Fence on mobile half-tracks. The bastards keep moving. Not good! We got two new ones six miles inside Cambodia. Never seen that before. OK, Blackshield, you are over CCO, good hunting."

"Roger that. Thanks, Ramrod."

Flying north into Cambodia, we were above a cloud layer, which made no difference for ground references because this area had no distinguishing features anyway. In daylight, solid triple canopy jungle is a field of green as far as the eye can see, but at night, there's not a hint of light, as the area is completely devoid of modern civilization. We were flying between cloud layers, one above us, and one below. That meant no stars, no moon, just infinite blackness. In these conditions, the flight experience was far from normal and more than a bit unnerving because it went on for hours. With none of the typical visual cues that I counted on while flying, I actually felt motionless, as though the plane was suspended in mid-air from some giant-sized puppet strings. Only by looking at the airspeed indicator and computer grid clicks would a pilot know that he was actually moving his plane through space. We had an ominous name for this kind of thing, 'flying in the black void'.

A few hours in the black void could play with your mind if you let it. The only element that showed itself in the pitch blackness was the red glow from the array of instruments in the cockpit. Noting them in the dark, I was reminded of what had been drummed into every pilot's head a thousand times during the instrument flight phase of training, 'Always trust your instruments'.

At 0200, the totally unexpected happened, and there had been no way to see it coming. Upon reflection, it was remarkable that after training for all the possible scenarios imagined, this, the one that no one had ever thought about ... actually happened ... it happened very fast ... it happened without warning ... and it was happening to me and my crew.

After so many hours in flight, Sully decided to stretch his long legs. He straddled the rudder pedals and pressed his feet against the metal plate that covered the aircraft fuse box. Apparently, the crew chief who had worked on the fuses before our mission had forgotten to completely tighten the toggle bolts that held the fuse plate in place. Not necessarily a problem ... unless you accidentally kick it. When Sully stretched, his left boot pushed in the corner of the fuse panel, which struck the fuses, shorting them out. Within seconds, an electric arc could be seen flashing under Sully's boot, followed by thick acrid smoke that filled the cockpit. I could no longer see my instruments. I dared not make a maneuver change.

Before Sully could utter a word, in less than a split second, I acted instinctively, reaching up to switch off both bus bars, which shut down the generators, preventing the electrical short from spreading through the wires, and stopping the smoke. The air in the cockpit cleared through the ventilation system. We were carrying over a thousand pounds of fuel in four tanks, two inboard tanks, close to us, and two in the wings. Each tank's gauge sensor was connected by a wire that ran through the fuse box. Had I not stopped the travel of the wire burn by shutting down the generators, we would have known about it by now, or perhaps not, as death would have come within a millisecond of the fuel igniting, and we would have been obliterated.

Although oxygen was supplied under pressure, the face mask intercom was now non-functional. There was no way to communicate with the crew while wearing the mask. I immediately came out of eighteen thousand feet and continued to drop to ten thousand, because below ten thousand feet, we did not need supplied oxygen and could remove our masks. I spoke up in a firm but calm voice, as our masks dangled from a strap in front of our helmets. "OK, men. Listen up. We have had a cockpit fire. We have lost all electrical."

"Yeah, no shit! Think so?" came a scared voice from the darkness behind me. It was Jimmy. I had him and Scotty assigned to my missions as often as I could get them. Not only were they the best at what they did, but also, the three of us had become friends. The squadron had voted on new Aircraft Commanders, and I was now one of the two. It gave me a little clout in determining which TOs would fly with me.

"Let's keep our cool, and hopefully, we will get out of this. I cut off both generators and had to leave them off, which means we have no comms, no lights, and no flight instruments other than one altimeter, the RDF, one attitude indicator, one turn-and-bank indicator, and that old compass up there floating in alcohol." This was mounted between the two pilots and close to the top of the cockpit, away from anything electrical that could influence it with a magnetic pull. The flight instruments now working ran off of an air venturi system and therefore did not need electrical power. I continued, "Scotty, put your red lens on your flashlight and keep it fixed on that compass for me."

"Yes, Sir. You got it."

"Sully, same for you, but keep your flashlight on my flight instruments."

Another voice from out of the dark. Jimmy again. He was usually pretty quiet. "Excuse me, Sir. But how we gettin' home without comms or navs? We sure seem to be in some deep shit, Sir."

"You pray, Jimmy?"

"Yeah, Mr. Walker. Sometimes."

"Well, this needs to be one of those times."

Scotty spoke up, "Seriously, Sir. You think we can get over the Fence without Ramrod and miss those freakin' SAMs and then somehow miss three different artillery firebases that are supposed to be firing by now?" For the first time since I had been flying with Scotty, I could tell he was very worried. So was I, but I had to be the last person to let it show.

"OK, fellas. First thing we got to do is stay calm and get a grip. We got a few things on our side. I got our location grid off the computer before we shut down. I have taken up a heading that should take us back across the Fence the way we came, just like Ramrod planned. Second, all artillery firebases are firing to the northwest. Once over the Fence, I will pick up a heading to the south-southeast. Based on my last known position, in the next twenty minutes, we will either be shot down or get over the Fence."

Scotty, holding his flashlight steady on the compass, commented, "You sure tell it like it is, don't you, Sir?"

"Yep, 'fraid so, Scotty. I am giving you the worst-case scenario so you will be prepared. Be sure you are strapped in, and your survival pack is secure to your ejection seat. If we are going down and can get out, I will say, 'EJECT! EJECT, EJECT!' Since you two eject from the bottom of the aircraft and Sully and I would go out the top, there is no way we can run into each other. Remember your emergency radio procedures.

"Jimmy, since you are sitting behind Scotty, you go first. Scotty, follow immediately, and you don't have to wait for me to say 'Eject' three times. Get your asses out of here on the first one if you can. I will be coming off the rails by the time I say it three times. If you say, 'Huh?' you will be talking to a smokin' hole."

The next twenty minutes seemed like two hours. Then another two minutes passed. After twenty-three minutes, I spoke up. "OK, guys, we made it through, but we still got some important shit to figure out."

"How are you going to find home and land with no radio and no instruments in this weather?"

"I'm working on it, Scotty. I'm working on it." I pulled the PRC-25 radio out of my survival vest. "Tactical should be monitoring the PRC-25 distress frequency. Tactical this is Blackshield 876 on FM 777, how copy?"

"Got you 876. Did you go down? Did not hear the mayday."

"That's a negative, Tactical. We're still up here, but we got electrical problems. All comms inoperative. All navs down. Declaring an emergency and need your help."

"Yeah, 876. What you got in mind?"

"Tactical, I know this is a long shot, I mean a really long shot, but can't come up with anything else. Need a few things from you."

"Go ahead, 876. What is it?"

"I am on a heading of one five five, leaving ten thousand for five thousand. Just crossed the Fence. Can you check all artillery batteries from Fence to Long Thanh along this radial?"

"Roger, Blackshield. Standby."

Tactical came back within seconds, "OK, Blackshield, one of my guys is on it. Go ahead."

"What are the winds aloft at five thousand down to the surface?"

"Blackshield 876 winds calm. Less than three knots. Say intent."

"Tactical, I need you to contact Long Thanh Tower. Tell them of my situation. They do not keep a PRC-25 in the tower. They will need to get a pilot to bring them one immediately."

"I'm on it, 876. Stay on your heading of one five five, and you will be clear of all artillery."

"Roger, Tactical. Thanks."

It seemed like forever flying in complete darkness, except for the two small red beams in the cockpit. It was a challenge flying in the soup with only a turn-and-bank indicator, attitude indicator, the RDF, altimeter, a World War II compass floating in alcohol, and of course, my watch, but then I realized, these were the only instruments the great pilots Charles Lindbergh, Amelia Earhart, and Beryl Markham had in front of them when they were in the cockpit. I had never thought of that until this moment. Now they inspired me. If they could do it then, dammit, I could do it now!

Tactical got word to the tower, and the tower sent a jeep to pick up a pilot who just happened to be Tex. Fortunately for us, he had been up at this hour working on a model airplane. His was the only light that shone from the pilot hooches when the tower boys went looking for help.

"Sam, this is Tex. Sounds like you got both feet in a Texas cow paddy, son!"

"That's putting it mildly. Man, sure good to hear you on the other end. Shit, I was afraid it would be the goat roper since his hooch is closest to the tower."

"No, I don't think they'd leave him alone with a PRC-25." Even at a tense time like this, we both managed to laugh. "So, what's your plan, Sam?"

"Well, you know I got no nav aids, no comms, no lights. I have an estimated time to you of twenty-two minutes. I am on a heading of one five five degrees at five thousand. Tactical has checked artillery on that heading. Winds are calm, and I am at seventy percent power."

"OK, what's next?"

"Got to get out of this altitude at some point."

"All good, except for one thing."

"What's that, Tex?"

"You don't know what's in front of you or coming your way. So, hold on a minute."

"Roger copy."

"Departure Control, this is Tex. How copy?"

"Go ahead, Tex."

"I got Blackshield 876 on PRC, FoxMic 777 declaring an emergency. He is about fifty miles north at five thousand on a heading of one five five degrees. His comms and navs are down. Repeat his comms and navs are down. Get on your horn and get traffic out of his way. Notify Departure Control at Tan Son Nhut to do the same and get back to me. This is an emergency. Got it?"

"Roger, Tex. Stand by."

Tex was on the catwalk around the tower when Departure Control called back. "Tex, this is Departure Control, how copy?"

"Go ahead, Departure Control."

"All clear, Tex. Also got a call from Tan Son Nhut. All clear with them as well."

"Roger, Departure Control. Thanks."

"Good luck, Tex. Departure out."

"Sam, Tex here. You are clear. I am standing on the tower catwalk. When I hear you coming, I will let you know."

"Thanks, Tex. What then?"

"I will correct your heading if needed but get your ass out of altitude. Pull power, drop gear and flaps and try to pass over the tower at around two to three hundred feet. You should be able to see us. Ceiling is around four hundred fifty. Shoot a visual approach."

Knowing Tex was down there talking us through this calmed all of us down, especially me. Laddy's words came to mind, 'You will do things in an airplane you never thought possible'.

"OK, Sam. I can hear your engines. Start your decent."

I broke out of the soup one-half mile from the tower. Seconds passed. I felt my tension release. We had made it through the worst of it. Thanks to all my practice, the approach should be a piece of cake, and it was.

"Departure, Sam's on the ground. Our boy is safe."

"Good to know. This is one for the books, for sure."

Maintenance let me know the following day, without any doubt, that if I had not cut off the bus bars to the generators when I did, we would have been vaporized.

Chapter 12 Telegram

Checking mail was something most guys did every day. They had wives or girlfriends who wrote constantly. I was lucky if I got a letter every ten days or so from either my mom or my sister. Letters from 'The World' were like gold, but I felt funny asking my sister to write more often. She had two children and a husband to care for. I did get one letter from her that seemed a little odd. Something about my brother-in-law, who would be in charge of a congressional delegation coming to Vietnam and that I should be on the look-out for a telegram from a U.S. Senator requesting that I be his personal bodyguard. My sister was eight years older and had been teasing me my whole life, so naturally, I thought she must be pulling my leg. Just messin' with me. Telegrams in Vietnam? I don't think so; especially not to my base camp. U.S. Senator? I didn't know any senators. Anyway, I pretty much forgot about it.

My mom would write short sweet notes, which I really appreciated, but a letter from your mom was not the same as a letter from your girl. I never kept up with any of the girls I dated in college. Nothing serious had ever developed with any of them. You had to be nuts to get serious with a girl at the University of Georgia. There were four girls for every guy, and I attended the School of Journalism where the ratio was double that. After eighteen months of flight school, I had forgotten most of their last names and could barely conjure up any of their faces. Writing to 'Ashley' addressed to 'somewhere' in Georgia, probably wouldn't work.

***

I was walking back to my hooch from the mail slots one day when Burt busted out of the CO's office and stopped me.

"Glad I caught you, Mr. Walker. The CO wants to see you."

"Sure, Burt, when?"

"Like, thirty minutes ago. Never seen him like this. Got to tell you, a special courier delivered a telegram by helicopter to him about an hour ago. He has been beside himself ever since. Suggest you come right in."

"Sir, I found Mr. Walker. Would you like me to send him in?"

"Have a seat, Sam. Perhaps you can explain this telegram. I will skip the salutation and well wishes to me as CO and get right to the meat of the matter as it pertains to you." He read,

I will be arriving with a Congressional Delegation at the Caravelle Hotel in Saigon by 1400 hours on 2 June 1971. STOP. I request that Chief Warrant Officer Sam Walker meet me at the hotel to accompany me and offer me protection as my personal bodyguard during my stay in Saigon until the afternoon of 4 June 1971. STOP. A car and driver will meet Sam on the tarmac at revetment J-343 at the Tan Son Nhut Air Base at 1100 hours on 2 June 1971. STOP. Best Wishes. I am respectfully yours, Albert H. Finley, United States Senator.

"You want to tell me what's going on here, Sam? I have been in the military for twenty-two years, and I have never seen or heard of anything like this."

The major appeared to be more perplexed than angry. We got along great. Shared a few laughs and drinks at the O Club and had flown one mission together that went well.

"To be honest, Tipper, I am not sure myself. All I can tell you is that my brother-in-law is a brigadier general and works as a liaison officer between Congress and the U. S. military. He has served two tours over here as a helicopter pilot. My sister sent me a letter weeks ago telling me to look out for a telegram from a member of Congress. I thought she was playing a joke. Who gets telegrams in the middle of the freakin' jungle?"

"Apparently, you do young man! Delivered by helicopter via special courier. Scared the shit out of me, if you want to know the truth. Thanks for being honest, Sam. Sounds like your brother-in-law just wants to see you and get you out of here for a few days."

"You think that's all there is to it, Tipper?"

"Nah, don't think so! The telegram came to me as your commanding officer from a freakin' U.S. Senator. And not just any Senator, I might add. He is Chairman of the Armed Services Committee. On top of that, there is a special permit attached for you to carry both a sidearm and an M-16 in the streets of Saigon. That part scares me a little."

"Way over my head, Tipper."

"Way over your head? How the crap do you think I feel, Sam? Anyway, be sure you look your best. You know, clean flight suit, shine your boots. Be ready for wheels up at 0930 in the morning. The XO and I will be flying you."

"What? You two never fly together! And why are you flying me?"

"Because that's what the telegram says!"

The next morning found Tipper and the company Executive Officer, Major Wayne Robinson, looking their best. I had never seen Tipper with his boots shined, and the Major – his hair was always longer than regulation, and he wore a mustache – but today, his hair was super short hair and his mustache was gone! They were ready to meet THE senator. Only problem was when we taxied to Revetment J-343 there was no senator. Instead, there was a highly polished, black Ford LTD

Town Car. Standing beside it was a young Vietnamese man wearing a chauffeur's uniform. When he saw our plane approach, he held up a sign that read, 'MR WALKER.'

Major Robinson had removed his flight helmet and turned around to address me, "There aren't six cars like that in all of Saigon. Who the hell are you, Walker ... I mean, REALLY?!"

"Just a John's Island farm boy over here doing my job, Sir."

"Oh, yeah! I'm beginning to wonder just what that job might be!"

"Lighten up, Wayne," Tipper spoke up as he shut down engine number one for me to step off the plane. He shook my hand, told me to enjoy myself, and warned me not to let my weapons out of my sight. I just got a glaring stare from Robinson. I barely knew the guy and now realized I wanted to keep it that way.

"Sam, drop by my office when you get back. I want to hear all about this little adventure. And I certainly hope you don't have to use your weapons!"

"Sure thing, Tipper."

While Tipper and Robinson sat in the cockpit, watching, the chauffeur opened the back door for me, and after I settled into the posh leather seat, he poured me a vodka on the rocks from the little bar in the back seat before closing the door. I tried to suppress my smile while tipping my glass toward them. Tipper was shaking his head in amusement. Robinson was red-faced by now. Maybe he didn't approve of early morning drinks.

At any rate, I found myself in the backseat of a freakin' air-conditioned American-made luxury car at Tan Son Nhut Air Base, in the Republic of Vietnam, with a Vietnamese chauffeur, sipping expensive vodka from a crystal bar glass. I thought I must be dreaming. *This kind of stuff just doesn't happen to me.*

The Vietnamese chauffeur settled into the driver's seat and said politely, "Good morning Sir. I am to take you to the Caravelle Hotel in Saigon Square."

Although the Caravelle was only five miles away, in bumper to bumper traffic, this would take thirty to forty minutes. Rationalizing that it was highly unlikely I would ever find myself in a chauffeur-driven limo in Saigon again, I decided to celebrate with the fine Russian vodka and crystal glass at my disposal.

"That would be nice, thank you," I replied and helped myself to another drink. The label read Stolichnaya Russian Vodka. Huh! Never heard of it. Here I am, enjoying fine Russian vodka, and they're trying to kill me. By the time I reached the hotel, I was buzzed.

Chapter 13 Vicky

"Mr. Walker, we've been expecting you. The congressional delegation has not yet arrived, but we can show you to your suite."

The front desk manager, a Vietnamese man in his fifties, wore an ill-fitting black suit, and his white shirt collar had a brown stain around the neck. In an unsuccessful attempt to cover his shining dome, he had combed his thinning hair across his balding head. His gold-framed eyeglasses appeared almost new, but when he turned his head, I noticed a yellowing strip of scotch tape holding one side of the broken frame in place. Despit

e his good job, the poor fella could not afford to dress the part and, even worse, had no mamasan to take care of him. While his faded appearance would be out of place in a five-star hotel almost anywhere else in the world, it was just another anomaly I found typical in Vietnam.

"Suite? Did you say suite? There must be some mistake."

"No, no mistake, Sir. All members of US congressional delegation get nice suite. Balcony view of our beautiful city. But we have small problem. Maybe you could help us?'

What's with this guy? Here I am, a guest at his hotel, and he's asking me to help him with his problem? But tempered by the vodka, my curiosity peaked, and I asked politely, "Yeah, what's that?"

"It crowded here behind desk. Four cases of alcohol for your delegation. Can we deliver them now to get them out of way?"

Though stunned, I recovered quickly, "By all means. I would be only too happy to help!" And with the biggest grin I've had since arriving in-country, I headed to my suite where cases of alcohol were being delivered right behind me. The bellman began unpacking the booze and lined up the bottles in the spacious suite's bar. He put the Dom champagne in the refrigerator. After I was left alone, I sized up the stash and realized I was looking at several thousand dollars' worth of top-shelf liquor. Eight bottles of McCallan Scotch caught my eye. I remember Tex having mentioned it as much more expensive than the 25-year-old Chivas Regal Scotch he had served.

After taking a luxurious hot shower in an oversized stall of Italian marble, I dried off with a huge fluffy towel and dressed in the thick terrycloth bathrobe and the silk slippers provided by the hotel. I poured a three-finger shot of the top of line Scotch, sat on the balcony and sipped it as I awaited room service. I enjoyed an awesome breakfast of ham 'n eggs, roasted potatoes, toast and pastries, and a large pot of freshly brewed coffee. Now this was the way to fight a war!

After relaxing a good hour, I dressed in a clean flight suit, strapped on the Colt 45, and slung the M-16 over my shoulder; no way I would leave them in my room. I checked with the front desk and learned the delegation was due in about two hours. I had time to kill, so I left the hotel and turned left on Tu Do Street, where I spotted two attractive western women entering a store that sold Asian furniture. No sooner had I entered it than I heard the fetching voice of one of them call out to me, "So what's with that get up, GI?"

I turned to face two American women, clad in T-shirts, jeans, and sneakers. Each was very attractive, but in a wholesome, all-American girl sort of way, especially the one who spoke to me.

"Oh, this! Well, I am actually working. I am serving as a bodyguard for the next few days."

"Yeah, right! A guy in a flight suit, wearing a pistol and carrying a rifle just doesn't make sense, that's all," said the prettier one. "Hi, I'm Vicky Pullman," she continued, extending her hand, "and this is my friend Lisa Durham. We are Pan Am stews on layover. This is my fourth trip to Saigon, and I just haven't seen anyone but the Military Police carrying weapons in the streets; so, I am a little curious ..."

"Oh, well, I can explain that. Actually, I'm a pilot; that's my job. But I'm here following orders. I'm one of the bodyguards assigned to a US Senator, who is part of a congressional delegation arriving today."

"By any chance, is it Senator Finley – the Republican Senator from Illinois? He's my Senator; I'm from Chicago," gushed Lisa.

I responded with a conspiratorial wink, "I really shouldn't say. Well, hold on, let's see here," I said as I pulled the itinerary from my top pocket. "There is a cocktail party for the delegation at the rooftop bar of the Caravelle Hotel tonight at 2000 hours, ah, that would be 8 p.m.," I stammered.

"We know military time; we use it. The cocktail party sounds great," Lisa responded, and then Vicky spoke.

"So, you're staying at the Caravelle. So are we! Cocktail party, huh? We don't have anything to wear to a cocktail party," Vicky said in an almost teasing tone. This girl wasn't just nice to look at; she was vivacious. Her confidence and grooming indicated she came from a good family.

"Well, neither do I. You're looking at it." I laughed. "Besides, it's not like a 'cocktail' cocktail party. These guys and the military types with them will have been traveling all the way from the states and will arrive here totally jet-lagged and drained. So, I should have said 'a very casual cocktail party'."

"Does that include the guns, cowboy?" giggled Vicky.

"Afraid so. I can't leave these weapons in my hotel room, and not only that, part of this 'get up' as you call it, really does come with the job of protecting the delegation if necessary."

Vicky gave me a curious, but inquisitive smile. "Well, for a flyboy, you don't sound stuck on yourself."

"Well, when I'm not flying, I try not to take myself too seriously. Anyway, I better be getting back to the hotel. I hope to see you both tonight, and I am sure you would be welcomed by all." I turned and left the furniture store, wondering if I had made as good an impression on them as they had made on me. I had certainly hoped so. Then, I thought, *What are the chances of running into two gorgeous American flight attendants in downtown Saigon, in a furniture store, no less?* Limo, expensive vodka, luxurious hotel suite. Kinda hard to get a grip on my changing realities. Whoa! I sure hoped they would show up at the 'very casual cocktail party'.

***

That evening I was seated at a large table with my brother-in-law, two U.S. Senators, and four U.S. Congressmen along with a half dozen aids and as many MPs. They sure didn't need me for protection. Everyone was dressed in crisp tropical jungle fatigues and looked very much out of place, like orphan boys at a Sunday school picnic for which someone had given them all new clothes. The fatigues were brand new, and never having been worn before, they did not look like the ones seen on real soldiers. No one had an insignia or name tag, except for my brother- in-law and the MPs. It was obvious that everyone, except for my brother-in-law and the MPs, had been enjoying far too much booze. They all seemed extremely worn out from the long trip, and the alcohol hit them pretty hard.

Then, Vicky and Lisa glided into the room like two angels floating on a cloud. In stark contrast to our drab attire, they wore colorful silk T-shirts and white silk skirts that stopped just above the knee. They wore Vietnamese high heels, not stilettos. Both wore their hair up in a French twist, held in place by ivory chopsticks. The girls had obviously been shopping since the last time I had seen them, and they had dressed appropriately for this very casual cocktail party.

Like a cadre of lost soldiers, everyone almost came to attention when these beautiful women joined the party. I got up and hugged them like they were old friends and introduced them around the table. I ushered Lisa into my seat next to Senator Finley, and I pulled up two chairs to sit with Vicky. We ordered more drinks, and the laughter and small talk continued for a couple of hours until my brother-in-law stood and announced they had an early morning chopper ride and should all be getting some shuteye. Then he pulled me aside.

"Where in the world did you meet these two?" he whispered.

"This afternoon, around the corner at a furniture store."

"You could get lucky. Tell you what, if you end up with one of them in your room, just tie a sock around your doorknob, and I will leave you alone tomorrow. We have enough security for the congressman. Take a couple of bottles of champagne if you want, and I know you also like Scotch. There should be a case or more of Macallan Scotch for Senator Finley. Take three or four bottles with you for your friends back at your unit. He'll never miss it. I will send someone to pick up the rest of the booze before we leave. We go from here to a few places up north, and these guys like their liquor."

"WOW! This is really nice of you, Charlie. Vicky did say she would come by for a nightcap! You sure about the Scotch? A buddy of mine at the squadron mentioned this Macallan brand to me a few weeks ago. He said the aged stuff was like five hundred a bottle."

"Sounds about right. Thank Uncle Sam!"

After the party broke up and I was back in my room, there came a knock at the door. I opened it to find Vicky, who had let down her thick mane of chestnut hair.

"May I come in for a nightcap?"

"Of course, I put a few bottles of champagne in the fridge this afternoon."

"Wow, you flyboys drink the really good stuff, huh?" she commented as I poured the Dom.

I explained that the fine booze came ahead of the delegation, probably from some U.S. diplomatic source. We brought our champagne to the balcony, where we sat and talked for hours. She was not only beautiful but also cheerful, smart, and had a great outlook on life. Man, did I just meet the girl of my dreams ... when I wasn't even looking ... here in a war zone? Insane!

Eventually, we stumbled upon something we had in common, loneliness, a side effect of spending so much time in the air. Though I was a pilot and she was a stewardess, we both agreed it's easy to lose your connection to the world below; you reach a point where the plane becomes your normal and your earthly home is nothing but a place to stash your things. While we bonded over that connection, the champagne kept flowing.

"Sam, I would love to write you … that is if you would want me to," offered Vicky through a coy smile.

"Are you kidding? I would love it! That would be great. Let's exchange addresses now, while we're thinking of it. There must be something to write with on the bedside table."

Vicky entered the bedroom to look for a pad and pen while I opened a new bottle and filled our glasses. I entered the bedroom to find that she had already slipped under the covers. Parking our glasses, I noticed she had, in fact, written out her address, and I hastened to join her between the silk sheets. The overhead palm frond fan was humming quietly, and the scent of handmade lime soap drifted in from the bathroom.

"Hope you are not offended, but I am really attracted to you, and I don't know if this chance will come again," she whispered.

"Ohhhh! I'm not offended!" We made love all night and polished off the bottle of Dom. I put the sock on the doorknob around five a.m., and while I was awake, I wrote out my address for her. We slept until noon, ordered room service, and dined on the balcony where we continued to talk about our childhoods, our families, our hopes, dreams, and expectations. We discovered we were very much alike.

"I have to say that meeting you was the last thing on earth I would have expected. It's good to know that everything over here doesn't have to be crazy-making."

"Is it? I mean is everything really as bad as all that?" Vicky asked with concern.

"It can get pretty crazy. It's not just the flying. I live in a base camp about thirty-eight miles from here. It's in the middle of nowhere. The food is so bad ... the ... well, there is no sense in getting into all of it now. I'll be OK!"

She walked over to me, curled up in my lap, and rested her head on my shoulder. "You have to stay tough, and you have to stay brave all the time, don't you?"

I felt I had been transported to a different place and time. I felt very disconnected from my life as a pilot in Vietnam. Around three or four in the afternoon, we opened another bottle of Dom and started the lovemaking all over again. At a certain point, we admitted to being both exhausted and hungry, and I ordered room service once again. We threw on some clothes and ate on the balcony.

"Please write me, and I'll write you. I have an R&R coming up in a few months. Maybe we could meet in Hawaii!" I blurted out.

"Are you serious? That would be incredible!" Vicky seemed very excited about the idea. "I have some time off coming to me with the airline. I could probably swing it, and it wouldn't cost me anything to fly there."

"Tell you what, as soon as I get back to my squadron, I'll put in the paperwork, and we can make plans from there. This will be great!"

Suddenly, I had something to look forward to, and I needed that more than I had realized. We embraced and kissed for a long time. I had never even imagined such a thing as this. Vicky and I were quite compatible. Vicky fell asleep, but I wanted to stay awake all night, just to savor every minute of her presence. Eventually, I crashed hard and woke up hours later. A smile spread over my face as I recalled the events of the previous evening, and I rolled over to face Vicky. But there on the pillow, where I expected to see her lovely face, I found a note:

Dear Sam,

I'm so glad we met – in a Saigon furniture store, no less! I enjoyed the casual cocktail party and the party after that. We had so much to talk about and you're really a great guy. I hated to leave without saying goodbye but you were sleeping so soundly, I did not have the heart to wake you. Fact is, I am terrible at goodbyes.

Oh, my head is throbbing; and it will only feel worse in the pressurized cabin. Poor me. I've never had that much champagne in my life!

I'm not sure about Hawaii. Maybe we can meet, if you're still interested.

Now I really must run; I have a flight to catch.

Please stay safe!

Vicky

I was stunned! I went to sleep believing I had met my soul mate, and I woke up feeling like I'd been given the brush off; I had been used. *If I'm still interested!!!* A sharp knock on the door interrupted my pity party. As I got up, I crumbled the note and threw it on the floor. Pulling on my robe while approaching the door, I noticed my sock on the floor. Apparently, Vicky had done me the favor of removing it from the doorknob on her way out. Does she do this kind of thing a lot?

It was my brother-in-law. "Hey, Sam. I see the sock is gone. Where's the stew, what's her name, Vicky?"

"She left. Had to catch her flight," I managed to explain through a champagne hangover.

"Well, get showered and come on down to eat. We leave for Tan Son Nhut Air Base in one hour. I've arranged for a chopper to take you back to your squadron. So how was it with Vicky?"

"She was wonderful. I'm too much of a gentleman to say any more."

"Yeah, I get it. I must admit she's really something."

"We exchanged addresses. Maybe we'll get together again sometime."

"Good for you, Sam. Something to look forward to. See you downstairs."

After I showered and dressed, I quickly packed my gear. I noticed that Vicky had taken my address and left hers. I took it and somewhat reluctantly retrieved the crumbled note and stuffed them both into my pocket. At that moment, I had no real expectation of seeing her again but rationalized that without that note and address, it would be all too easy to think the whole thing never really happened. I would need tangible proof to remind me otherwise. Either way, at least I had something new to think about. Time would tell ... always does.

***

After reaching the airbase, the congressional delegation went one way, and I went the other. I met Chopper number 376 on the helipad tarmac.

"I'm Warrant Officer Sam Walker, here to catch a lift to Long Thanh North," I said to Warrant Officer Smyth, who was sitting in the door of the Huey gunship.

"Sure, Sam. No problem. I am waiting for my co-pilot and door gunners. They should be here in a minute. Got to tell you this is not a direct flight to Long Thanh North. First, we're dropping off mail to a firebase camp twenty miles east of Long Thanh, and then we're dropping ammo at a firebase between there and Long Thanh. I see you're a pilot. Choppers or fixed-wing?" Smyth asked.

"Fixed-wing."

"Ever been on a chopper?"

"No, this will be my first time."

Just then, Warrant Officer Stone and one door gunner, Corporal Lanston, arrived. "Hey Stone, where is my other door gunner?" questioned Smyth.

"Don't know. He was a no-show at Flight Ops," replied Stone.

"Sam, you qualified on the M-60?" asked Smyth.

"Well, yeah," I was shocked by his question, "but ..."

"No buts in the Nam. The job is yours. You will find a flight helmet and mic in the back. There's a flak jacket on the seat over there. Put it on. Now let's get out of town," said Smyth, motioning me to get onboard.

The Nam was like Disneyland, someone had suggested, because you never knew what a new day was going to bring. I was having a real hard time trying to get my head around what had just happened to me. Only two days ago, in another reality, I was escorted from this same airbase in a gleaming, air-conditioned, chauffeur- driven Ford LTD to Saigon, where I would soon spend two unforgettable evenings in the arms of a beautiful woman, who was somewhere on this same tarmac this very moment about to depart for LAX. And now I was departing the Tan Son Nhut Air Base on a chopper, as a door gunner strapped in behind an M-60. Go figure.

The constant vibration of the entire fuselage seemed to heighten the eggbeater noise of the rotating helicopter blades. This was definitely not an airplane!

"OK, mic check! How does everybody read me?" squawked Smyth.

"Loud and clear," we all responded like obedient school kids.

"How you doing on that M-60, Sam?" asked Smyth.

"Oh, I'm here. Hanging in the breeze." Trying to sound nonchalant as I contemplated the powerful weapon in front of me.

"OK, Sam. You only fire if I give the word. Keep your blast down to a twelve-shot burst if possible. And, for God's sake, hit what you're aiming at," ordered Smyth with a comment that made me want to vomit.

"Are we expecting hostile fire?" I ventured.

Lanston interrupted, "Sir, where we are going, you can count on it. Let me give you a few pointers. Don't lean out the door too far in your harness. It makes you a bigger target. Leave the sun visor up on your helmet. Easier to fire with it up. If we start taking rounds, forget the twelve-shot burst rule. You just hold your trigger down and let Charlie have everything you got. Another thing, just because I have a target and I am engaging on my side of the chopper does not mean you have one on your side, and vice versa."

"Got it," I said, grateful for the advice, which now filled my head, replacing the champagne hangover with something much more troubling.

We were two minutes from landing in Firebase Zulu 87 when all hell broke loose on my side of the chopper along a tree line about fifty yards away. Over the mic Smyth started screaming, "RETURN FIRE! RETURN FIRE!"

I was firing on full-automatic. It was hard to miss given our low altitude, such a big gun and the target only fifty yards away.

Smyth on intercom. "Way to go, Sam. You missed your calling, buddy! Think you blew away at least four gooks. You quieted four muzzle flashes pretty damn quick."

"You saying I killed four people, Smyth?"

"Gooks, Sam. You killed four gooks."

I screamed, "GOOKS, VC, CALL'UM WHAT YOU WILL. THEY WERE PEOPLE!" I was shaking uncontrollably.

"Hey, genius. You gotta' remember, they were trying to kill you, kill us. They fired first. Lanston, get with Sam."

"On it. Here, Mr. Walker. Let me give you a hand." He unhooked my harness and sat me down. I was still shaking from head to toe.

"Take a couple big gulps of this."

"What is it?"

"Whiskey and one crushed up valium. It will calm you down." I took several big gulps ... then a few more.

"There ya go. Give it a second. It calms the nerves ... ya know. First time?"

"First time? First time, what?"

"You know, blowing away Charlie?"

"Yeah."

"I get it. It's upsetting, but you'll get used to it"

"I am a pilot, Lanston, not a damn door gunner, OK?"

"Whatever you say, Sir, but today you are a door gunner, and we may have more coming up ahead. Gotta get you strapped in again."

We flew for twenty minutes without incident. The chopper then hovered five feet over an artillery firebase. Red dust stirred up from the rotor blades covered us like tainted talcum powder, while Lanston pushed a duffle bag of mail out the chopper door. Then we continued to fly.

Ten minutes later, we were taking fire again. This time it was on Lanston's side. Screaming obscenities, he opened up with a wild look in his eyes. When it was over, he turned to me with a big grin and gloated, "Now that's how you deal with these little bastards!"

Once again, I was witnessing a different facet of how this war was being fought and what it was doing to young men who, at nineteen or twenty, should have been in school or learning a trade, not killing people. I couldn't help but wonder how do we go from living in this day-to-day craziness to being normal again? Just how exactly is that supposed to happen?

At the next base camp, which was a Marine Special Forces outpost, we landed, but as the rotor blades maintained their wop-wop-wop deafening roar, we were covered in even more red dust. I helped Lanston push six large boxes of ammo over to the edge of the door. Bending over to avoid the rotors, a few Marines ran toward us to unload the cargo that would support the very thing I had just experienced up close and personal; the goods that would tear more men to shreds. I had never seen anyone actually shot before ... and this time, I had pulled the trigger! I was numb and pushed the thought from my mind. I would not speak of that incident again. Not ever.

When I could see that we were approaching Long Thanh several miles ahead, the strangest feeling came over me. I was coming home. No, that can't be right, I thought. This is Vietnam, and that's the rat hole where I live. Then it hit me. I didn't have it as bad as most of the guys over here. For instance, the two firebase camps I had just gotten brief glimpses of were barren and devoid of everything. The guys living in those bunkers were always covered with red dust and dirt; most likely got shot at every day and probably had to kill every day. I wasn't flying helicopters like the guys I was riding with at the moment. For the first time since my arrival, I found myself saying a quiet prayer of thanks. My thoughts turned to Vicky. She should be in the air headed home by now. All of a sudden, I wondered if a commercial jetliner could be in danger flying in and out of Vietnam.

Smyth went to intercom, "OK, Sam coming up on your base camp. Thanks for your help today. Good job."

"Yeah, you bet. Thanks for the lift." I unhooked my harness, removed my helmet and flak vest, thanked Lanston, and left the chopper. I walked away and did not look back. I struggled to make sense of the past forty-eight hours, during which my emotions had gone from the highest of highs to the deepest depths of despair; from loving to killing. Is a human being designed to endure these extremes? As I increased my distance from the chopper, I could not help but recall, 'It was the best of times; it was the worst of times.' Years later, I would learn this distress would leave its imprint: PTSD.

***

The return address told me the letter was from Vicky. Since we last met, I had tried hard to convince myself that what we had was just a fling, for which I should be grateful, but when I saw the envelope, I flinched. I took a deep breath with a 'please God' and opened it.

Dear Sam,

I left Saigon filled with emotion and very confused about what had happened. During the time we spent together, I consumed far more alcohol than I could handle. Previously, I had only enjoyed champagne as a toast, not by the bottle!

I sure got carried away – with the champagne, with you, with the excitement of it all. I was really drawn to you. The circumstances were so romantic, every girl's dream, but when I woke up that last morning, I felt embarrassed for having thrown myself at you. Then, on my way out, when I found the sock on the doorknob, it really crushed me. I know what that means! Maybe a good-looking guy like you does this all the time, but I felt cheapened, used. That's not who I am. I honestly hope you're not that type either. I don't think so, but I do need reassurance if I am going to be your pen pal.

My flight was very difficult; I looked awful, my head was pounding, my stomach was churning, and on top of that, I was just so sad. It was the first time I had to paste on a smile and force myself to do my job. It took a few days before my head cleared and I started to feel better again. Since then, I've been giving this a lot of thought.

When I recall our long talks, how we shared, how hard we laughed, how much we had in common, I felt I should write to explain myself. Maybe we should give ourselves another chance. If you'd still like to meet in Hawaii, let's do it. If you've changed your mind, or if that was never really your intent, I will accept this as a lesson learned. No matter what, please stay safe.

Vicky

***

Dear Vicky,

I appreciated your letter. Explaining things from your point of view was helpful because I have been struggling to make sense of things. I had no idea how you felt when you left. I, too, had the worst flight of my life that day, but that's a story for another time.

For the record, I never thought you threw yourself at me; quite the contrary. I thought we were mutually attracted to each other, so why fight it.

It's funny. I thought our time together was absolutely magical; the best time in the midst of some pretty awful times for me. But the way things ended, I felt dumped, and you felt used. Too much champagne? That stupid sock? We can do better. I agree we should give it another try.

Neither of us lives normal lives. Not many young women volunteer to visit combat zones. Not many young men do the crazy job I have. The odds of us meeting were almost impossible. But we defied those odds.

I am getting this letter out to you ASAP, before my next scheduled mission, and I will file the papers for my leave soon as I return. I'll send you the itinerary when I have the dates. I am so glad you wrote and shared your thoughts and feelings. We need to be open about such things. Let's trust our instincts and give this a shot!

Affectionately,
Sam

Chapter 14 Security Blanket

The days turned into weeks and the weeks, well, they ever so slowly drifted into the next month, but time did pass. The monsoon season, though nearing its end, gave no sign of relenting. There was no point in trying to stay dry unless you were preparing for a mission. It had reached the point where we walked around thoroughly drenched by the unyielding rain as though it didn't exist. 'Not existing' was our silent mantra, anyway.

In the last two months, we had suffered the loss of four pilots and eight TOs. The squadron across the runway, flying a different type of mission than the ones we were flying, had lost two pilots only a few nights earlier. Out of fuel, they landed intact one-quarter mile from the end of the runway in eight-foot high elephant grass. By the time a rescue team had reached them, they were still strapped in their seats, but their heads had been cut off and were nowhere to be found. Their torsos showed no sign of fatal injury. They had both been very much alive when they were decapitated. I shivered to think about our enemy's depravity.

After a pilot accumulated one-hundred-forty hours of back-to-back flying, it was standard practice to be taken off flight status, getting time to rest and recoup before going back out again. I had reached that number, as I always did, well before the end of the month, because there were many times when I flew two missions a day. Pilots and TOs, with good reason, seemed to stay on edge more than others, even during these earned breaks that kept us grounded. We had our ways of dealing with the stress, none of them good, and one of which was drinking. Truth is, my drinking was starting to scare me, but I brushed it off, perhaps, in retrospect, too easily, rationalizing that 'everyone else was doing it'. On this particular night, for some reason, I only had two drinks before retiring, and I was counting on the hissing drizzle outside and the constant hum of my AC to lull me to sleep. As I was about to drift off, there was a coded knock at my hooch door. I got up and opened it to find Tex standing there with a huge wagon in tow.

"Where did you get that?"

"Outside the maintenance hangar. Let's get movin' before they miss it. I told you we would turn your hooch from a sow's ear into a silk purse. Get dressed. Now is the time."

The wagon was eight feet long and three and a half feet wide; basically, a steel frame mounted on two jeep axles outfitted with jeep tires. Normally, it was used to move aircraft engines. Tonight, it would be put to good use doing something else.

"Except for your mattresses and desk chairs, we gotta load up everything and dump it at supply."

"Supply open at this hour?"

"Don't worry. The sarge knows we're coming."

"So, Sergeant Wilson is in on this caper?"

"In on it? It was his idea to begin with. Wilson is a little like me. No family back home. Saw the advantage of sticking around a few years and cashed in like I did."

"How long has he been here?"

"'Bout the same as me. You caused me to add it up. I've been here four years and three months. Wilson got here a week ahead of me. Man, you should see his hooch!"

"Think he'll let me?"

"Tell you what. When I drop the key off later, I'll bring along a bottle of Chivas. We can all have a little drink before you and I get to work."

"You mean we are starting construction tonight?"

"Not unless you got other plans."

"Of course not, I ain't flying. I'll keep my mouth shut and just follow your lead, Tex."

"Now you're getting the idea."

Sergeant Wilson helped us unload the wagon and then gave Tex a key to the lumber yard gate. We rolled the empty wagon to the lumber yard in the rain. After stacking two wagon loads of lumber in my hooch, we went down to Tex's hooch and loaded the wagon with his skill saws, hammers, nails, and other carpentry tools.

"OK, Sam. Time for a Scotch break."

Sergeant Wilson's hooch almost defied belief. While we shared the Chivas, I learned that his father, now deceased, had been a cabinet maker and taught Sarge the trade. Sarge had built floor to ceiling cabinets from teak and mahogany, a mahogany bed frame, and a large table made with teak planks and matching teak chairs.

"This place is freakin' unbelievable, Sarge! I mean really beautiful. Where'd you get all this mahogany and teak?"

"Ouch, that came at a stiff price. You won't find any of that in the lumber yard. Actually, I bought it at a lumber mill just outside of Saigon. Dirt cheap really. The problem was getting it here."

"Yeah, so how?"

"Chopper, but that wasn't the problem. It was finding a chopper pilot who could and would take the time to do it. This stuff sat for over a month before I could get it delivered, and it cost me a whole case of Irish Whiskey that had to be special-ordered. That took another month to get here. And you better believe it wasn't at GI prices. Twelve bottles, plus shipping from the states, cost almost three hundred bucks. Tex and Tipper said, 'Screw that', and settled for standard GI-issue pine in their hooches."

We had two rounds of Scotch, and then Tex and I got to work. Sergeant Wilson came along and gave us a hand. We toiled into the night, and around 0200 hours, we called it quits, but we were back at it early the next morning. For the first time since I had been in-country, I felt genuinely cared about by the guys I was serving with. It felt like I had brothers, and in a sense, indeed, I did. Their actions were without any pretense or ulterior motive. Just two fellas wanting to help me out. After another exhausting day, we completed the task.

***

When I awoke the next morning, I had to blink a few times before realizing that I was still in the same place. My hooch looked absolutely amazing! It had been completely transformed; what had been dreary metal was now golden wood. Not even a hint of green and gray remained. Sergeant Wilson insisted that the military-issue desk chairs had to go because they spoiled the look. Remarkably, he made me two new wooden chairs to take their place. However, what I appreciated more than anything about my remodeled hooch, was that I now had significantly more protection from mortar rounds, due to the strategic design and sturdy construction of my new furnishings. Generally speaking, indiscriminate mortar rounds came our way three or four nights every week. Charlie was focused on taking out aircraft, not people. People, well pilots, could be replaced within hours. Planes could not. Mortar fire always came from a different location but rarely lasted more than ten minutes, making them all but impossible to counter. Once the assault started, it was unnerving; although you had no idea where the destructive mortar would be landing, you had no doubt that you were under siege. We had been trained to quickly don our flak vests and steel pot helmets, then roll under our bunks where all we could do was hope for the best. Now that my hooch could likely withstand a direct hit, I found myself able to drift off to a twilight sleep in my reinforced bunk. I figured my reinforced hooch improved my odds of surviving a hit; however, I was careful not to become too cocky, because if I had learned one thing about living in a combat zone, it was never to assume anything.

Climbing out of my newly fortified bunk, I discovered I was sore all over. In handling all of that lumber, I had abused a number of muscles I forgot I even had. I was glad I wasn't scheduled for a mission. It gave me a chance to get rid of the soreness and to dive into the Sears catalog to choose some carpeting and peel-and-stick wallpaper. As I was sitting at my desk, enjoying my morning coffee and flipping through the catalog, there was a knock at the door. There stood my childhood friend, Dicky Hatfield, now an army captain assigned to a nearby artillery battery. To say the least, I was totally surprised to see him and threw out my arms in a welcoming gesture. "Hey Dicky, what the hell brings you to this part of the war?"

"Stand up straight and salute me, you warrant puke!"

"Fuck you, Dicky. Warrant officers don't salute. Don't you know that by now, you dumb-ass captain?"

"Seriously Walker, as your superior officer, I am owed that respect."

Turning my back on him, I limped back to my desk, where I ignored him by posing a question. Holding up the Sears catalog, I asked, "Which of these carpets do you think looks best: the black and orange or the black and tan?"

But Dicky was not looking at the catalog; he hadn't heard a word I said. Now that he had stepped inside, his eyes darted around with wonderment as he took in my newly remodeled hooch in all its wooden splendor.

"You have got to be shittin' me, Sam! Who the fuck lives like this over here? And with AC, no less!"

Just then, Nuwee slipped in. "Good morning, Sam. Some fresh fruit for you. I put in fridge. What boots you want shine today?"

"Those, please, Nuwee," I pointed, "and thanks for the fruit."

"Sure thing, Sam. Excuse Nuwee, please." She left with my boots in hand, as quietly as she had entered.

I opened the fridge, grabbed two beers, and tossed one to Dicky. I retrieved the fresh fruit and brought it back to the desk. "Enjoy that cold one, CAPTAIN Hatfield, and help yourself to some fresh fruit. I'm glad you came by. I'm not flying today, and I assume you're not shooting any guns, so here is a toast to us ... brother. To the good old days in the Low Country!"

Dicky pulled up a chair and helped himself to some mango. He acknowledged my toast by clinking beer cans. We went back so far that he knew me well enough to know that I was not going to buy into his superior soldier bull shit.

"You know I was just raggin' you with the superior rank shit ... right?"

I took a long pull on my beer.

"I'm not pissed off at you, Sam," he admitted quietly, "I'm pissed off at myself."

"About what, Dicky?"

"Well, we were classmates, hunting buddies, played on the high school football team, double dated, both went to UGA. I mean, we did everything together ... right?"

"Yeah, pretty much. What are you getting at?"

"How did we end up in the same ungodly place but, well, under such different circumstances? Looks like I really blew it!"

"Rank, alone, really doesn't mean shit over here, Dicky. A lot more depends on what it is you actually do."

"Exactly! That's what I'm getting at. You fly a really cool airplane. You got a hooch that looks like a damn mountain cabin with AC and a fridge, and a mamasan takes care of you."

"What are your living conditions like?"

"That's my freakin point! There are ten of us at my artillery battery, and there's no such thing as a hooch. We live out in the open, on a fuckin' dome of orange dirt with three fuckin' Howitzers that never seem to stop. Choppers bring in ordinance every four or five hours churning up a constant dust bowl. Sam, it's bad, OK? Day in, day out, I'm fuckin' covered in fuckin' red dust. I can't hear myself think. My bed is a rope hammock under a lean to, and I'm lucky if I get four hours sleep a night. There is only one shitter, and it's barely twenty feet from my hammock. You can't escape that stench!

"Cold beer!! Fresh fruit!! I eat fuckin' K-rations three times a day! We got one fifty-five-gallon drum perched on poles for a shower. I'm lucky if I get a shower every three days, but even when I do, I am covered in red dirt before my balls dry. Then there's the monsoon. Last season, I wound up with jungle rot on both feet and my crotch. Not a night went by I didn't wake up with at least four or five leeches on me. Shit, man! I'm twenty-four years old and almost deaf from those freakin' guns. And, oh, I'm a CAPTAIN in the US Army!!"

"Damn, Bro! You do have it bad. I feel for ya. There's one thing about the Nam you have to understand: everything is a trade-off. Take what we do, for example. Different types of trade-offs."

"Sam, I have no idea what you're talkin 'bout."

"It's like this, Dicky. No doubt, you definitely live in shitty conditions. That red dust and that constant gunfire would drive anybody nuts. However, you do have one of the safer jobs over here. Right?"

"Well, yeah. Guess I do."

"On the other hand, in terms of living conditions, I got it pretty good. However, my job is very different than yours. Every time I fly a mission, which is nearly every day and often twice a day, I stand a seventy percent chance of not coming back to this comfortable little hooch, with my AC and mamasan. I face the real possibility of being shot down and killed or becoming a POW, almost every day. Trust me when I tell you, I have already had several 'come to Jesus' moments doing what I do. So, you tell me, CAPTAIN without wings, want to swap jobs?"

"No, mother fucker, I want to keep my job and have your hooch!" He stood up, grabbed me by the shoulders, looked me in the eye, and said, "I get it, Sam. Trade-offs. Think that makes me sound like a chicken shit?"

"Of course, it does. But I promise not to remind you of it when we're back home."

After a hardy laugh, a few more beers, and some reminiscing, Dicky rose to leave. Facing each other squarely, we snapped to attention. We saluted each other. When he arrived, Dicky demanded a salute because of his rank. When he left, he gave me a salute because of my job.

Chapter 15 Miss America

Serenity is hardly the state of mind of a pilot on a combat mission. The luxury of that peace was not mine when I spotted the hamlet below me. I fixed its position in my computer to use as a navigation checkpoint at grid coordinates Z3008-Y2006. The on-board computer operates on a global grid, and this checkpoint was almost at the end of the world in computer jargon. Amid miles and miles of endless jungle treetops, this hamlet was a distinct place that allowed me to update my position just before receiving my instructions for flying in between SAM sites. Sometimes we skirted the outside peripheral edge of a SAM tracking system by no more than a quarter-mile. I couldn't afford not having an accurate update before this risky phase of any mission.

The hamlet was not a place that stood out. In fact, in the course of many missions, I had flown over it several times before I ever noticed it. I had either been too busy in the cockpit or my eyes had not focused on that particular spot along the Mekong River while crossing over the border into Cambodia. If the hamlet had a name, only those who lived there would know it. My best estimate placed it about seventy-five miles southeast of Phnom Penh, the capital of Cambodia, and ninety-seven miles northwest of Saigon. There was not another hamlet or village as far as the eye could see from 15,000 feet. This place defined 'the middle of nowhere'.

My first sighting of Hamlet Z3Y2, as I came to call it, touched a part of my soul. I can no more explain the feeling than the one I experience upon seeing an original work by a favorite artist or encountering an intriguing woman who steps into an elevator and fills my senses. And so ... my love affair began with Z3Y2.

The hamlet had been carved out of a dense mahogany and teak jungle that rose to form a towering perimeter around a few dozen or so bamboo and grass-thatched huts, called hooches, that encircled a main lodge which stood at its center. The hamlet was surrounded by a few acres of rice fields. The rice fields were in proportion to the hamlet population. This was always a good sign, indicating that these people were not supporting the North Vietnamese or a Viet Cong contingency. Their rice harvest fed the village, and no one else.

I noticed a small group of children at play on the bank of the Mekong River as their mamasans washed clothes on nearby rocks. The river seemed to serve as the western border of the hamlet where several sampans allowed a means for these peaceful, gentle, people to expand their world outside of this remote existence. I wondered how far away they ventured and if they knew of the huge city, Phnom Penh, to the northwest. Something told me they didn't, but if they did, they probably didn't care. If ever a storybook scene could come alive, this hamlet stepped right off the pages of Jungle Book and into my consciousness where it would long remain.

There were many missions when thick cloud cover below separated me from visual contact with the hamlet, and on those days when my computer clicked off the grid Z3008-Y2006, I went into a lazy 360-degree turn just above the cloud tops. This circling flight ritual had become familiar to the villagers at Z3Y2. I sensed somehow that we knew that we were waving to each other. It felt good to wave on those cloud-covered days. Even though they couldn't see me, I knew they heard me. I wondered in those moments what, if anything, the villagers down below thought of me, high overhead. You see, in a mystical sort of way, we knew each other.

During my one-year tour of duty, I got to know them and their habits, in an odd, yet personal way. Coming from a countrified farming family, I could identify with much of their lifestyle. I observed their rice paddies and how they rotated their crops from one plot to the other. When new plantings sprung up, I cheered them through their small harvest. At times, I saw the cleaning of large game. This told me these people were hunters as well as farmers and obviously self-sufficient. Some members of the group were fishermen; their boats were always out at certain times during the day. They used cast nets and fishing lines, just like I did back home. Others would clean laundry, wash dishes, or bathe in the river. Either they practiced personal hygiene or simply loved to feel the refreshing, cool river currents washing over their bodies. They were either Cambodian or Vietnamese; being that close to the border, there was no way to know for sure. I had met members of both nationalities on many occasions and found them to be open and generous people, who just wanted to be left alone to live their lives. Come to think of it, isn't that what most people want?

***

Upon leaving the mission debriefing, a lieutenant I had not yet met stuck his head out into the hall.

"Excuse me, Mr. Walker. You got a minute?"

"Yeah, sure. What's up?"

Lieutenant Ed Bearman introduced himself. He had something he wanted to talk to me about and suggested we meet at the O Club.

"Sure. See you there."

There were more officers than usual at the O Club, that afternoon. Noting that we were flying more and more missions, someone commented, 'Business was picking up'. Several new pilots had come on board, and others had been transferred in to help keep up the pace. Ed Bearman was one of them.

"What're you drinkin', Ed? First one is on me. Big spender, right?" Drinks only cost twenty-five cents here. Uncle Sam sure made it cheap and easy for us to stay lubricated.

"It's the thought that counts, Sam. Vodka tonic. Thanks. I'm the new scheduling officer, and I have a favor to ask of you." Ed paused to sip his drink.

"Sure, Ed, if I can help."

"Oh, you can help, but it might take a little coercing with Tipper. I understand you guys are pretty tight." He chuckled. "I would like to become your Assistant Seafood Procurement Officer. I'm from the Eastern Shore of Maryland and pretty much grew up around seafood. You're going to need a co-pilot to fly with you anyway, so I figure it might as well be me."

"Sure, Ed. Sounds good to me, and you're right, this is something I need to bring up with Tipper. Shouldn't be a problem, though. You just want to enjoy Vung Tau, the French girls, and the beach! Can't blame you for that."

"That may be, but you should know my request comes with a bonus right up front."

"Yeah, what would that be?"

"The Miss America USO tour is putting on their last performance in Can Tho in two days. Figured you and I could work that in with a seafood run."

"You serious, Ed? How long they been here?"

"Almost a month. They were scheduled to be in Cam Ranh Bay just two days after I left to come here."

"Boy! Bet that pissed you off!"

"It made me nuts is what it did. Anyway, I got one of the flyers with the show schedule on it, and they will be in Can Tho in two days. Like I said, their last show. Who knows when we'll have an opportunity like this again?"

"Let's make it happen, my new friend. Tell you what, I'm in the habit of grilling one of Pole's steaks out at the Pit at least every other week. Lots of us do. Tipper and I ran into each other at Pole's hooch yesterday buying steaks and made plans to cook them tonight. I'll get right on this. Miss America Show! No shit!"

Although the Pit was nothing more than a picnic area under a tin roof, dinner there had become a good habit for all of us. It gave us time to hang out together in a comfortable setting, as it was a viable alternative to both the O Club, where it was far easy to drink too much, and the mess hall where you had to choke down the awful slop that posed as dinner. Named for the large fire pit that had been dug in the center, it included several grills and half-a-dozen picnic tables. Usually, Tipper had a few enlisted men build a fire every evening, and we simply helped ourselves to coals from the burning wood fire and placed them under a grill to cook our own steaks or whatever else we managed to get our hands on. All too often, it was barbecued Spam, which might sound disgusting, but I was to learn that Spam was better barbecued than cooked up by the mess hall. Barbecued, you could pretend it was something else. Later that evening, I met up with Tipper as planned.

"Hey, Sam. How goes it, buddy?"

"Good, Tipper. Going to freshen my drink. How 'bout a little Scotch?"

"Sure. On the rocks would be great."

Back in my hooch I prepared our drinks – a generous pour of Macallan Scotch on the rocks for each of us.

"Tell me what you think of this," I asked Tipper as I handed him his drink back at the pit.

"Damn, son! This is like the expensive stuff Tex occasionally pours, which I understand we are of the lucky few to enjoy."

"Well, I sure don't have a case of this. Just a few bottles."

"Where'd you get them?"

"Compliments of the senator."

He winked as he took another sip, and then changed the subject, "Sam, I see where you put in your paperwork for R&R to Hawaii."

"Yes, Sir, that's right. I requested ten days."

"You meeting your Pan Am girl? Wasn't it Vicky?"

"Yes, Sir. That's the plan if I get approved. The date is flexible for her. She said she thought she could make it work."

Tipper put his hand on my shoulder. "I just approved it for you a couple of hours ago. Let the young lady know you will be there."

"Thanks, Tipper. That's awesome!"

A few minutes later, Tipper was spreading coals under a grill when a pilot approached us.

"Sam, I want you to meet Major Rodney Mitchell. Mitch just transferred down from the 521st up near the DMZ. This is Mitch's third tour. We were roommates at Da Nang on our first tour. He is going to be our new Executive Officer."

I reached out and shook Mitch's hand. "Good to meet you, Sir."

"It's nice to meet you as well, Sam." However, his perfunctory reply told me otherwise; meeting me was anything but nice for him. Then he continued by asking a question for which there was no good answer.

"Wow! Man, which part of the south are you from?" Mitch teased, but he wasn't smiling.

"South Carolina."

"So, tell me how a southern white boy is going to like sharing the cockpit with a black man like me?" Mitch snarled. There was no mistaking his disdain, and I was angered to have been judged so unfairly. I thought I'd diffuse the situation and get it on track with some humor.

"Excuse me, Sir. You're black? I hadn't noticed. Oh, yeah, now I can see it. Gee, yeah ... you're a black man!"

Mitch took a hard look at me not knowing how to react at first and then a large smile spread across his face, and he started to laugh. Tipper and I joined in. I would later learn that Mitch didn't smile too often, and his laughter was even rarer, but when he did let go, it was infectious.

"Come on, Sam. You're telling me you're not one of those prejudiced Southerners?"

"Not a prejudiced bone in my body, Sir. I grew up with black people. I've been close to them my whole life. Hunted with them, fished with them, picked tomatoes with them. Sure, there are prejudiced people in the South. In fact, lots of 'um, but then I think there are prejudiced people all over, and it's not just prejudice against blacks; there is prejudice against whites, too."

"Sorry, Sam. Shouldn't have jumped on you like that. I just get a lot of it, and I assumed you were, you know, being from the South and all. By the way, please drop the 'Sir' stuff. It's Mitch."

"You staying for steaks, Mitch?"

"No, Tipper. Got to get going. See you gentlemen around."

I sensed that Mitch felt bad about jumping to conclusions about me. "You sure Mitch? You can have half of mine," I offered.

Mitch stopped dead in his tracks.

"You serious, Sam? You would share your steak?"

Tipper jumped in. "Tell you what. Let's cut these two bad boys three ways. Plenty for everybody. How do you like your steak, Mitch?"

"Medium rare would be good, Sir."

"Yep, same as Sam and me."

"Say, getting ready to fix another round of drinks if you like Scotch."

"Yeah, Sam. Thanks."

After taking a healthy swig of his drink, Mitch closed his eyes, tilted his head back, and smiled. "Man, now this is what I call a really fine drink. Haven't had much expensive Scotch, but I know it when I taste it. Where did you get this stuff?"

Tipper, shaking his head and smiling, said, "It's a long, very long, story, Mitch, and you wouldn't believe it anyway."

"Tipper's right. I'll tell you about it sometime when we got absolutely nothing else to do," I promised, never imagining how soon that opportunity would present itself.

Tipper and I enjoyed dinner with Mitch, and the three of us talked mostly about flying. The ice had been broken. After devouring the steaks, Mitch, tired from the long flight from the DMZ and our drinks, decided to turn in for the night, and Tipper suggested that he and I drop by the O Club for a nightcap. This would be the opportune time for me to broach the subject of making Ed my Assistant Seafood Procurement Officer. Only a short while ago, Tipper had asked at one of our monthly squadron meetings if any of us knew anything about seafood. I raised my hand and explained how growing up on a tidal river pretty much kept me in a johnboat during the summer months. My dog, Sandy, and I would sometimes spend the entire day on the river, as I fished, crabbed, and threw out the cast net for shrimp. So, needless to say, I got the job. About once a month, I would fly down to Vung Tau to order fresh shrimp and lobster, which would be packed on ice and loaded the next day for my trip back. This job got me a night at a hotel and a few hours on the beach. Not bad extra duty, and it kind of balanced out my other job.

It was not unusual for a Warrant Officer to get any type of extra duty, as long as it was related to flying. In addition to Seafood Procurement Officer, I also worked as a test pilot. Now, this might sound glamorous, but believe me, it wasn't Chuck Yeager stuff. Whenever we lost an engine, from mechanical malfunction or bullets, it was rebuilt and had to be tested before being returned to use. Being a test pilot was not without its risks, but somebody had to do it, and I just loved to fly. I also had high confidence in our mechanics.

"Guess we'll be grilling fresh seafood in a few nights," I said, after ordering our drinks.

"Yeah, I'm really looking forward to it, especially since we missed it last month," said Tipper. "Who are you taking with you, Sam?"

This was my opening. "Lieutenant Ed Bearman, Sir."

"Isn't he the new scheduling officer?" asked Tipper.

"Yes, Sir, he is."

"Well, how convenient of him to schedule himself for a seafood run and a night in Vung Tau. You flown with him yet?"

"No, Sir. I was having a drink with Ed earlier when I learned he grew up on the Eastern Shore of Maryland; he knows a thing or two about seafood. Probably would be good to have him along,"

"Well, Sam, you have to have a co-pilot. We may as well have two good noses picking out seafood. The last thing we need around here is a bad batch of shrimp and lobster. By the way, be sure to get the Tiger Prawns, not plain shrimp. They cost a little more, but they're worth every penny."

"Yes, Sir. Tiger Prawns and lobster, it is. What do you think about me taking him along for most trips, since like you said, he has a nose for it?"

"OK, with me, Sam. He is the scheduling officer, not me. As long as it doesn't interfere with his other duties, that's fine."

I dropped by Ed's hooch on the way to mine to let him know we were all set, and now we needed to make an important phone call.

"I say we give Tom Harris a call now, Ed. We got a tight window of opportunity here, and I got no idea what this guy's schedule is like. When we arrive in Vung Tau, we'll need Tom to helicopter us to and from the fish market."

"You're right, Sam, but do you know where he is staying? I mean, can we reach him by phone? That's pretty unusual for over here."

"He's at the Vue Sur L'Ocean Hotel. You got any way to find that number? It's only ten-thirty. Someone should be at the front desk."

Ed put on his boots. "Let's go to my office."

Once there, after a few minutes shuffling through drawers, he finally found a three-ring binder that had all the hotel phone number listings. Scanning down the page, he spotted the number, dialed it, and handed me the phone.

"Good evening, this is the Vue Sur L'Ocean Hotel. How may I help you?" announced a sweet female French-Vietnamese voice.

"Yes, good evening. This is Sam Walker. Could you tell me if Lieutenant Tom Harris is in, please? Yes, sure. I will hold."

She rang his room. "Hello."

"Yeah, Tom, this is Sam Walker. How goes it, mate?"

"Bloody well ol' chap, and to what do I owe the honor of a call from a Yank pilot at this hour ... or at any hour for that matter, ol' boy?"

"How would you like to go to Can Tho tomorrow to see the last Miss America USO show?"

***

The next morning, Ed and I arrived in Vung Tau to a waiting chopper with Tom at the controls. After a short flight, we set down on a helipad next to a Land Rover. From there, we were at the docks in less than fifteen minutes, where I met with Mr. Kim's daughter in a small office. I gave her my order, paid her in advance, and told her I would see her father at first light. We were back in the air in a little under an hour.

"You think you got enough cologne on, Tom?"

"I jolly do hope so, mate. You never know, we might get a walkabout with these American Sheilas."

"Walkabout my ass! These girls will have MPs all around them. Bet a GI can't get within twenty feet of them."

When we arrived at the hangar where the show was being held, there were well over five-hundred folding chairs set up, and the first six rows were already filled with eager GIs. We managed to settle into good seats in the seventh row.

A USO show was probably the highlight of anyone's tour of duty, second only to R&R. The entertainers were, without a doubt, talented, gorgeous, and genuinely determined to deliver an unforgettable experience to us fun-starved, love-starved GIs. The lift we got was nothing we could have done for ourselves or each other. It might have been the only time we felt special; that these people, the entertainers and their crew, who were all living comfortably in the USA, came to see us, sing to us, tell us jokes and make us feel good, just because they really cared. And most impressive of all was that they were willing to take such risk in order to do so.

The USO Miss America Review staged in August 1971, featured Phyllis George, who had been crowned Miss America eleven months earlier, and six other pretty and talented state title winners: Miss New Jersey, Miss Nevada, Miss Arizona, Miss Arkansas, Miss Iowa, and Miss Texas. They wore white, sleeveless, body-hugging mini dresses and skin-tight white knee-high boots. Between the bottom of the hemline and the top of the boot, it was all leg – tanned, toned, and very sexy. In contrast, their long hair had been styled into two juvenile pig-tails, each tied with an over-sized white bow. This made them appear younger than they actually were, and tended to remind you of the girl next door or your kid sister. So, there they were, provocative, yet innocent. Probably done on purpose to tone down their sexuality, as if anything could, considering there were only seven beautiful women frolicking on stage in front of at least 500 horny young men!

These girls were mesmerizing. They were playing to a captive audience, and did they ever know it. Having seen their schedule, I couldn't help but think that they were a brave bunch. They had already performed at some high-risk bases, although Can Tho was not one of them. I was glad they had made it through their tour without incident, and that this final stop should not expose them to danger.

Toward the end of an unbelievable, non-stop two-hour show, Miss America announced that the final act would be 'ladies' choice'. The audience grew quiet as she explained. All seven of them would leave the stage and venture into the audience to select a guy to dance with. She asked us to imagine we were back home at a dance when ladies' choice had been announced. She suggested we think about how we would feel, hoping to be selected. With that, the six state beauties descended the stage and fanned out across the audience, wading deeper into the rows. As each beauty chose her dance partner, the audience hooted and howled as the perky girl held hands with her guy, guiding him to the stage. Finally, Miss America descended the stairs, and all eyes were upon her as she entered the audience. Of course, from the seventh row, I was watching her intently, which was pretty easy as she was generally heading in my direction. I figured I would have a great view of her as she selected her lucky guy. As it would turn out, I had an excellent view; in fact, it could not have been better, for suddenly, Miss America stopped right at my row, extended her arm, and pointed at me!

I froze. The luckiest guy in the audience could not move a muscle, and his brain failed to function.

Smiling broadly, she rotated her hand, palm up and crooked her index finger, giving me the 'come hither' signal. I'm thinking, *Yeah, right.* Am I dreaming? I could not believe what was happening. Tom, sitting next to me, gave me a sharp elbow in the ribs and said something in Aussie to get me moving. Not nice to keep Miss America waiting. All I remember were the excited sounds of whoops and cat calls; I have no memory of actually getting up and following Miss America to the stage. Dancing was a disaster; my legs moved as if they were filled with lead, and my feet felt like concrete blocks, but somehow, I tried to move around the stage, following her lead.

Phyllis George, so gracious, was as friendly as she was beautiful, and she tried to engage me in conversation as we rocked back and forth. I'm not sure I was able to speak in complete sentences or was even coherent, but I am fairly certain I did not step on either of her dainty feet. Thank God for that! When the dance ended – and I have no idea what song was played – each of the girls gave her blown-out-of-the-water dance partner a warm hug and an innocent kiss on the cheek. The seven of us lucky dogs returned to our seats while the audience cheered and made happy sounding noises as though it was New Year's Eve.

There was a melancholy aspect to these shows, however, buried beneath the hoots, howls, cheers, and applause. Every one of us had just been keenly reminded of what we were missing. Young, lovely American girls just swooped in, strutted their stuff, twirled around, and were whisked away, never to be seen again. All the anticipation and excitement had been building for days, if not weeks, and poof! It was all over in a few hours. The letdown manifested itself in a variety of ways. Some guys would go on and on for days about how great the show was, while others would insist it wasn't what it was cracked up to be. Depression set in if you let yourself think about it. It was like yanking a favorite toy from a baby's hands.

After the show, back at our plane, Ed and I were completing an aircraft pre-flight walk-around check when the girls, surrounded by MPs, walked within thirty feet of us to their waiting helicopter. All of them waved to us; one called out, 'Be careful', and Miss America blew us a kiss.

"That little 'kiss to the wind' was meant for you, ol' chap. Looks like you made a bloody topper impression."

"Yeah, Tom, 'kiss to the wind' is about right. It's gone with the wind, too. Got to tell you guys, I don't get it ... I mean I really don't get it."

"Get what, you lucky bloke?"

"I mean, it was great and all that, but over here, this kind of stuff really screws with my head. First Vicky, the Pan Am flight attendant, and now Miss America. Man, I am in Vietnam! This kinda' shit doesn't happen to me when I'm home. I think I am going crazy."

"What's this about a Sheila being an American Stew?" Tom's curiosity had been peaked.

"Never mind!" Ed and I said in unison.

Ed was on the intercom by now. "I get it, brother. I can see where the things, the unbelievably good things that have been happening to you, could make you nuts. It would make me nuts. It is just so far off the scale, man. Like you said, this type of thing doesn't usually happen back in the world, but over HERE? I get it, OK. I get it."

We flew in silence back to Vung Tau. I thoroughly enjoyed piloting this flight. Since I wasn't on a mission, my adrenaline wasn't pumping, and I was free to fly a course that did not put our lives in danger. I hugged the coast, flying at a low altitude so we could take in the beauty of the beaches and shoreline below. It really was a beautiful country. I know I could have been gloating about the experience I just had, but the truth is, I just found it all so confusing. In many ways, Vicky seemed more like a dream to me than a reality. And now this. Who the fuck dances with Miss America? Anywhere? Who has that kind of luck?

After landing at Vung Tau, Tom flew us back to our hotel in the helicopter. I flew upfront in the co-pilot seat, and Ed was in the back. Something ominous on the ground below caught my eye.

"Say, Tom, over there at two o'clock about a quarter-mile from the hotel outside your perimeter. Is that what I think it is? I didn't notice it yesterday."

"'Fraid so, mate. Compliments of your bloody American SEAL Team. Craziest bunch I ever met, but I got to tell you, that thing you are looking at, the remnants of that little caper they pulled off, has kept us safe. We are no longer harassed by Charlie."

"How long has that been there?"

"Oh, going on about two months now. Just a few nights after you were here last. The putrid stench is almost gone, thank God. Heat, rain, buzzards, ravens, ants ... you know. All the flesh has either rotted away or been eaten. Guess there is no appetite for hair."

Twelve skulls, each mounted on a tall bamboo pole, rendered a grizzly warning, compliments of the SEALs. Every skull had been completely picked clean, devoid of all skin, eyes, tissue, but matted clumps of black hair still remained, moving stiffly in the breeze. It was a ghastly sight. If it was unnerving for me to look at, I can't imagine how the VC felt. I found it interesting that the VC did not remove them. Perhaps they thought if they did, the missing skulls would be replaced with their heads, and that is exactly what the SEALs would have done.

***

Ed and I had separate rooms at the hotel, both overlooking the South China Sea. Even though there was no sun in the sky and a slow drizzle was falling, I asked Ed if he wanted to go for a dip in the ocean.

"Yeah, sure, Sam."

We met in the lobby and walked out to the beach, heading toward a slow-rolling surf.

"Sam, since you're an AC, I got to ask, is it OK to have a few drinks if we're flying tomorrow? It's not a mission or anything. You know, the eighteen-hour rule?"

"Sure. I plan on having a few beers, but that's it. Just don't overdo it, Ed. These Aussies are a rowdy bunch and will try to get you to drink all night. Plus, there is a Navy SEAL Team that stays in the hotel. Talk about over the top. Great fellas, but they have a high tolerance for everything, including how much they can drink."

I swam out about forty yards offshore and floated on my back. I was by myself. Peacefully suspended in the sea, with drizzling rain sprinkling over my face and body, I felt cleansed and refreshed. Once again, I had just gone through diametrically opposed experiences within hours of each other. How does one mentally process the beauty and vitality of seven gorgeous American girls along with the beastly arrangement of twelve hideous rotting skulls – all in the same evening?

***

The next morning, I had to meet with Mr. Kim, as promised, to maintain our trusting relationship on a personal basis. I had ordered a lot of seafood, four hundred pounds of it, to be exact, half Tiger Prawns and half lobster, and paid in advance so that he could pay the fisherman when our catch came in. The Tiger Prawns were already packed on ice, having been caught the day before. I returned to the hotel, where I found Ed on the terrace overlooking the ocean.

"The seafood will be delivered to the airstrip by thirteen thirty. With any luck, we should be wheels up by fourteen hundred, just you, me, and four hundred pounds of shellfish."

When it was time for us to leave, the Aussie airstrip crew knew what we were doing here and were a lot of help. "G'day, Mr. Walker.

Your two coolers are stowed and tied down there, mate. She should be good to go. I drained any excess water before I weighed 'um in. You're looking at a little over 238 kilos. That would be five-hundred and twenty pounds in your language. I put a dipstick in your fuel tanks. You got about a quarter of a tank in each. You know, mate, plenty light enough to clear those eucalyptus."

"Thanks for your help. The eucalyptus and I have already met." Handing him a case of beer, I added, "A little something for you and your crew."

"Thanks, mate. American Budweiser! Good show! Is this the one made from horse piss?"

"WHAT? What are you talking about?"

"We Aussies always see this beer advertised with a string of Clydesdale horses pulling a beer wagon."

"No way, brother. It's one of America's favorites."

"Just jerking your chain, mate. Love the stuff."

***

You would have thought we were delivering gold bricks when we landed at Long Thanh. A mess hall truck was waiting with four guys to haul the seafood to the refrigerators, and another dozen or so guys just wanted to take a look at these tasty creatures from the sea. Guess they just wanted to make sure the rumors were true.

Around five that afternoon, things were well underway at the Pit for the seafood bash. Two huge pots of water were boiling over propane burners. The cooks were simmering a seafood spice mixture that I was assured was not military issue. The Spec-4 cook who happened to be Cajun said he had it sent to him from New Orleans, or did he say 'Nawlins'?.

The barbecue fires were already burning. The Tiger Prawns were either boiled or grilled. The lobsters were all grilled. Several quarts of cocktail sauce had been prepared. Ten pounds of butter was starting to melt just sitting on the picnic table in the heat. To wash it all down, there were three large military coolers brimming with beer on ice. It started raining again, but no one seemed to care. It actually cooled things down a few degrees, and the patter of rain falling on the tin roof of the Pit sounded nice. The turn-out was large, and a party atmosphere filled the space under the roof. Most of the hungry crowd took a portion of everything.

Tipper stood on one of the picnic table benches to make a quick announcement. "Listen up, people. A toast to Sam and Ed for bringing back such a bounty from Vung Tau. These boys obviously know their seafood. Grab a beer and dig in!" He was still holding his can of beer in the air as all heads turned to admire Wai Lyn walk in with Colonel Simmons.

"Good evening, Harry … Wai Lyn," said Tipper as he stepped down off the bench before taking a long draw of his beer.

"Evening to you, Tipper. Gentlemen. Couldn't resist the offer to dig into some of this fresh seafood," replied Colonel Simmons.

Wai Lyn caught the eye of several pilots she knew. She gave a little bow of acknowledgment without saying anything. She looked absolutely stunning tonight. Anyone would have taken her to his mom's for Sunday dinner ... and then, gratefully, to his bed afterward. I approached the colonel first.

"Good evening, Colonel Simmons. Glad you could make it, Sir."

"I hear you're the man who brought all this in from Vung Tau."

"Yes, Sir. Ed Bearman and I. Quite a trip," I remarked.

"Yeah, I haven't been to Vung Tau. One of the disadvantages of too much rank and not getting to fly much with my job." He chuckled. "I believe you have met my assistant Wai Lyn?"

"Yes, we met outside your office when I first arrived, and we've spoken several times since. Good to see you again, Wai Lyn. I am glad you could join us." That's what I said, but what I was really thinking was that the old colonel was probably rolling in the hay with this beautiful China doll a couple of times a week.

"Oh, thank you very much, Sam, but I do feel a little awkward and out of place. I am the only female to attend," she smiled coyly, slightly bowing her head.

"I am sure you won't find anyone complaining. Say, may I get you a cold beer or something from the O Club? Afraid beer is all we have at the Pit," I apologized.

"A Budweiser would be fine. I like your American beer, especially if it is good and cold."

When I returned with a very cold Bud from the bottom of one of the coolers, she was standing alone. Colonel Simmons had gone over to sit with Tipper. I wiped off the can and opened it for her. "Here you go, Wai Lyn. I'd be happy to get you a glass from the O Club if you prefer," I offered, ever the gentleman.

"No, the can is fine. It keeps the beer cold. So how are you, Sam? I see you come and go on your way to mission briefings, but we have not really had the chance to get acquainted."

"Yeah, I know. I have gotten glimpses of you as well. I didn't think it would look good to just drop in on you since you work for my boss's boss." *But I do undress you in my mind every time I see you,* I thought.

"It would be OK. Colonel Simmons is a very nice boss. He encourages me to get to know American GIs. He says there is a good chance that my family and I will be able to move to your country when the war is over because of my father's service to the United States and his high rank. Colonel Simmons says I probably got only a quick look at American life when I was in school in Virginia, and he is right. I want to learn more about your country. It would be sad to leave Vietnam, but I know my family and I would have a better life there."

"Say, would you like some seafood?" I posed this question out of my own desire to get started on those prawns and lobsters that I had been thinking about since yesterday.

"Yes, of course. Tell me what you want, and I will fix us a couple of plates while you get us a few more cold Buds. I'll meet you at that table over there."

A few minutes later, Wai Lyn approached our table carefully balancing two plates heaped with lobster and prawns, a cup of cocktail sauce, and a cup of melted butter. She was so graceful with her arms loaded, it amazed me. The seafood was so fresh and delicious, we both ate until we just couldn't take another bite.

Wai Lyn was a good person. I found out that she was my age and did not have a boyfriend – Vietnamese or American. That may have been why she was so friendly. I know I pulled back several times when I was given an opening to say more. I couldn't help it. I had no idea where things were going with Vicky, but now that I had an R&R approved to meet her in Hawaii in less than a month, I could think of little else. Another woman, at the moment, just wasn't in the cards for me. Besides, I had always been a one-woman man.

The seafood party ended around 2200 hours. I walked Wai Lyn back to the compound where she had her own room. I was shocked to find that she actually lived on base. She was the only female to my knowledge that did. She said it was too dangerous for her to live in the village of Long Thanh. The VC knew of her father and probably would kidnap her if she were not under US government protection. I learned later that she never left the base except to visit her father in Saigon once a month, and that was via the base chopper where she would be escorted with care. Her restricted living conditions could have been tough for her to deal with, but they sure beat the alternative. Daddy, however, was not the main reason she couldn't live in the village. The real reason was that Wai Lyn knew all our secrets.

Chapter 16 Red Mullet Island

Mitch and I were assigned a Black Ops mission. My first. We were to deliver a satchel of classified documents to Da Nang Airbase and return. It sounded simple, especially because we were approaching the dry season, and except for an occasional thunderstorm, the weather for flying couldn't have been better.

Our flight path would take us from Tan Son Nhut Air Base, direct to Dalat and over to the coast at Nha Trang. From there, we would go 'feet wet' along the coast up to Da Nang just south of the ancient city of Hue, a few miles south of the DMZ. The trip was approximately five-hundred miles. Flying along the coast added about one-hundred miles extra, but it was safer, and we wouldn't have to contend with dozens of artillery batteries.

Lieutenant Young began the briefing.

"Good morning Mitch … Sam. You are to pick up a satchel at Tan Son Nhut Flight Ops. The satchel will weigh approximately seven pounds. It contains top-secret documents that are to be personally delivered to General Howard Matthews at Da Nang. He will meet you there, at Flight Ops. Spend the night, turn around, and come home. You got an easy mission this time ... except for one thing."

Mitch couldn't resist, "Why is it always ONE THING?"

We all laughed. Lieutenant Young sobered quickly.

"Da Nang has been under rocket and mortar attack just about every night for the last three weeks. Conditions tonight could be dangerous. Stay on your toes. Don't let your guard down. If you are lucky, it could be just another sleepless night in a bunker. If that is the case, you need to be careful flying home with little to no sleep. Have a good trip."

Mitch and I picked up the satchel and were back in the air in less than thirty minutes. Pretty good for getting in and out of one of the world's busiest military airports. Not only were thousands of Americans stationed here in the early 70s, but also Bob Hope played here to a crowd of 10,000.

We leveled at twelve thousand feet headed for Dalat. All was going well. No surprises. We flew over Nha Trang and continued flying north. Mitch was flying first pilot.

"OK, Sam, what I am about to do is unauthorized, but you got to see this."

With that, Mitch started coming out of altitude and leveled at five-hundred feet above the water and one mile offshore.

"Wow! This is one beautiful country, Mitch. I have been to Vung Tau and south to Can Tho but never flown north of Vung Tau. The beaches go on forever, and the water is crystal clear. There are so many islands off the coast. Are they inhabited?"

"Maybe one or two, if they are close to shore. Other than that, no. I have always been amazed at how many are not. We've been flying at less than five-hundred feet over a half dozen tropical islands for many miles. Thought you should see some of this up close. Its unforgettable beauty. Now I'll take us up to at least 5000 feet. No sense in pressing our luck any further since we're both going on R&R soon. No time to risk things."

Mitch and I had gotten to know each other a bit. He was from Detroit. When I told him about the incident with the pick-pockets on my first day in the Nam, Mitch was unfazed. He had grown up in a tough neighborhood and learned early on how to defend himself once he was outside the security of his home. When he was still a kid, his father left his mom with four mouths to feed. As the oldest, Mitch had to grow up fast; he started working after school when he was only ten. In high school he proved to be a good athlete and was awarded a football scholarship to a little-known college. By then, he had assumed the persona of someone not to be messed with, and kept his feelings to himself. After graduation, he worked to help take care of his mom, brother, and two sisters. Ultimately, he was drafted, entered OCS, and then went on to complete Special Forces training. He told me that looking back on his early life, everything he went through prepared him for that difficult and grueling experience. A few years later, he made it into flight school. The rest was history.

"Da Nang Tower this is Blackshield 876, how do you read?"

"Blackshield 876, loud and clear. Say intentions. Over."

"Da Nang, this is Blackshield 876, we are approximately five miles to the south, feet wet. Request landing to a full stop."

"Roger Blackshield 876. You are cleared to land runway twenty-seven behind the C-130 that is on long final. You should have him at about your two o'clock position, three miles out."

"Roger, Da Nang. We have him."

"Blackshield 876, call turning from left base to final behind C-130."

"Roger, Da Nang. Will do."

After landing, we taxied to a revetment where a jeep was waiting to take us to Flight Ops. General Matthews was waiting for us with two of his aids. We introduced ourselves and handed him the locked satchel. He passed it to one of his aids like it was a loaf of stale bread. Somehow, it appeared to have lost its importance. It may as well have been sent via elephant.

"Welcome to Da Nang. This place is a real shit hole. We take rockets and mortar every night, so keep your pants on ... literally! Captain Miller here will show you to your quarters for the night. Meet you at the O Club for a drink in thirty minutes. You fellas might want to freshen up after such a long trip. We have Navy mess here. Some of the best food in Nam. See you in thirty."

As Captain Miller walked us over to the hooches, I was getting a distinctly bad vibe just from the look on his face and the way he carried himself. His bland features were pinched into a scowl as though he had just smelled something putrid. Extremely skinny, he relied on his rank, not his nature, to dictate the arc of his relationships. He had an attitude, and it wasn't good. You could just tell even though he hadn't even opened his mouth. Captain Miller was born with a corncob up his ass, and it wasn't sweet corn. Not sure a hog would even eat it. Once he started talking, it only confirmed my suspicion. He really was an asshole. Speaking directly to me and only to me, he explained, "We only got one hooch available that has two bunks. One pilot on R&R. The other was shot down and killed last week. That is if you want to room with the major here?"

I erupted, so angry at his flagrant display of prejudice, "Excuse me, Captain Miller, but in case you haven't noticed, THE MAJOR outranks you. Based on what I have learned in the military, THE MAJOR is due the respect of being addressed first, not me. I am a Chief Warrant Officer. THE MAJOR outranks both of us, you prick, not to mention this is his third tour of duty in the Nam."

"Well, you know, I just figured ..." Miller trailed off, lamely.

"Figured what, Captain Miller?"

Mitch put his hand on my shoulder. "It's OK, Sam."

"NO ... NO! It's not OK at all! What's the problem here, Captain Miller? Are you one of those prejudiced white assholes from Alabama or just a prick in general?"

Mitch stopped me. He turned to address Captain Miller for the first time, with complete calm and dignity, qualities Captain Miller would neither appreciate nor acquire if he lived to be one hundred.

"Captain Miller, you are a general's aid. What you do and how you present yourself is a reflection on him. I know this because I was a general's aid at one point in my career, too. One thing about the job is certain: one screw up, and it goes in your record as having screwed up in the presence of a general officer. It tends to ruin one's military ambitions. Get my drift?"

"Yes. I mean, yes, Sir."

"Good. Now please leave us."

"The general will expect you in the O Club shortly." Captain Miller turned and left.

"Thanks, Sam. You didn't have to do that, you know?"

"Well, I think I did. When I see that kind of blatant prejudice, it makes my blood boil."

"Yeah, I kinda' noticed it got you upset, but I guarantee Miller got the message."

We joined General Matthews for drinks. Captain Miller didn't make it. Imagine that! We were directed to the Navy mess hall, where the food, as promised, was exceptionally good. We wondered aloud why our base camp couldn't do the same, but that's one of those questions that has no answer. Perhaps having a general as the CO made all the difference.

Satiated and relaxed, we headed back to our hooch for the night. Stars were shining, and a slight breeze cooled the air. Suddenly, all hell broke loose! We were under heavy mortar and rocket attack. We realized we didn't have flak vests or helmets, having left them on our plane. We were exposed, crawling on hands and knees. Thankfully, a young, quick-thinking sergeant saw our dilemma and grabbed us both.

"Follow me … and stay low."

We ran in a crouched position for about fifty yards before falling to the ground inside a bunker where two men operating an M-60 machine gun were firing on the perimeter. Two others were firing M-16s. Mitch and I stayed curled up on the dirt floor. The deafening barrage went on for almost an hour before it stopped as abruptly as it had started. The sergeant who had guided us to the bunker had probably saved our lives. Outside, there were several fires burning out of control. Mitch tapped me on my shoulder and pointed without saying a word. One of these fires was our aircraft burning. No words were necessary. Now we understood Da Nang's infamous nickname, 'Rocket City'. We wondered how we would ever get out of this hellhole. It proved to be a long night. Although it remained quiet, we both slept fitfully until we were awakened early by a staff sergeant from Flight Ops.

"Good morning, gentlemen. Sorry 'bout your plane. I've been sent over to take you to the hangar to check out a Beaver the CO says you can have to fly back."

On the way to the hangar, we talked about the Beaver. Fortunately, both Mitch and I were qualified in the De Havilland Beaver DHC-2, a great, beefy Canadian-built single-engine airplane. At four hundred fifty horsepower, it was no puddle jumper, but at the same time, was built for tough terrain. Next to maple syrup, it was the best Canada had to offer. The sergeant took us to the corner of a large hangar where the Beaver had been parked some time ago.

"Whadaya think, Mitch?"

"These old birds are solid, but this gal has been sittin' here a damn long time, Sam."

After thirty minutes of going over the plane, the mechanic spoke up. "OK, gentlemen, I think I should change the engine oil. Then I can start the engine with an auxiliary power unit (APU) and check her out further. I should be done in about an hour if I don't run into any problems."

We took off to grab some breakfast and returned. Later we would regret not having eaten more. The mechanic started talking as we approached. "OK, a few things. Good news first. The battery is taking a charge. Oil pressure is good. I drained what little fuel was in her tanks and topped them off with new fuel. Now for the not-so-good news. The engine is running a little on the rough side. Both magnetos need replacing, but we don't have spare parts here. Keep the rpms under twenty-five hundred, and you should be OK. But no guarantees. The tires have dry rotted to some extent, but they are holding pressure.

I suggest you land at Cam Ranh Bay. They have a Beaver unit there and can take care of you."

Mitch spoke up. "Thanks for your help. How 'bout standing by with that APU until Mr. Walker and I can do a walk around pre-flight."

"Yes, Sir. Glad to."

"Thanks."

Mitch took one side of the Beaver, while I checked out the other. Over breakfast, we acknowledged that we had a long flight ahead of us, and the day was not waiting. Now we realized that in the Beaver, we would have to fly a lot slower than planned.

I checked the Beaver's logbook. "This plane hasn't been flown in five-and-a-half years, Mitch. Says here it was flown for the Army Corp of Engineers doing survey work as part of building this airbase. It was used for hauling supplies to a few outposts after that. Then, for some reason, it was just parked here and abandoned. Nothing in the logbook that indicates any trouble."

"Typical military," Mitch commented. "Probably just a few pilots using it until they finished their assigned job. Somebody pushed this baby back in the corner of this large hangar, and she was forgotten. I am sure as Da Nang Airbase expanded, choppers took over the hauling function. One thing about the Beaver, she is a sturdy airplane and good for dirt strip landings. Once everything got paved and built up around here, she probably wasn't needed. Let's just hope that we don't have problems in the air because she has been sitting up for so long."

"Yeah, I was thinking the same thing, Mitch. It's covered in red dust inside and out."

We found some rags in the hangar and wiped the cockpit down as best we could. We were given two old flight helmets. It was all they could spare. I was first pilot. Mitch was riding co-pilot. The Beaver had one radio, which was cutting in and out as we taxied for take-off. I hoped it just needed to warm up. I turned on my pilot-to-pilot mic. "Whadaya think, Mitch?"

"I don't like it Sam, but then I don't like the alternative of waiting around Da Nang for days to get a ride back to Long Thanh either. I say we go feet wet and fairly low all the way to Vung Tau then hang a right and get home. If she is running rough by the time we get to Cam Ranh, we can make a judgment call."

"I agree. Let's see if we can get this old gal off the ground."

We climbed to 2500 feet and stayed over the water, away from possible ground fire. In the bombing, we had lost our survival vests and the PRC-25 rescue radios, as well as several other useful items. Barely twenty minutes after take-off, the Beaver's radio stopped working. Not a good thing.

Just as we were contemplating the implications of flying without a radio, things got worse, much worse. With a loud bang, the manifold gasket blew, causing the engine to send out a flame approximately two feet in length along the cowling. Through the windshield, we could see the fire coming toward us, and we could feel the inside of the cockpit getting hot, very fast.

I hit the mic button to Mitch. "WE GOT A PROBLEM!"

"Yeah, I can see that! What about that island off the coast straight ahead? Think you can make it?" Mitch said with a sense of urgency.

"Yeah, we have plenty of altitude. We can make the island and attempt a beach landing. I am cutting off the engine and fuel. Best if we dead-stick in and avoid the chance of blowing up or being spotted."

With the engine off, Mitch and I could talk without the mic.

"What do you think, Sam? How will you access the best approach?"

"It looks like the island has its longest beach on the east side. That's also the side away from the coast of Vietnam. If Charlie doesn't see us land, he won't know we're there, but then the same is true for the friendlies. If they don't see us, they wouldn't know to come to our rescue. What do you think: east-side beach or west-side beach?"

"Go with your first choice. East side. We don't want any company. Let's land on the larger beach and away from the Vietnamese coast. We can figure out rescue later. Crap! Sam, we don't have PRC-25s either. Without radios, this could be a long stay."

"Yeah, tell me about it. How does that saying go? It wasn't the first thing or the second thing or the third thing that caused me to get here. It took all three of them! I think that applies to us about now."

We touched down on a deserted tropical Island. The beach sand was soft, but not soft enough to flip the Beaver, just soft enough to bring us to a fairly quick stop. We both sat still and quiet in our seats for a minute or two without saying a word. Then Mitch spoke up.

"Sam we are screwed! No radio of any kind, no survival vest, one canteen of water, and no food."

"Let's check the storage compartment of this old bird. You never know!" I said, ever the optimist. I jumped out and opened the cargo bay door.

"Oh, my God in heaven! Look at this, Mitch!"

I had found a duffle bag loaded with goodies. It contained two machetes, a survival knife with whetstone, a first aid kit, a canteen, mosquito repellent and netting, two net hammocks, two ponchos with poncho liners, a small bag of phosphorous tablets, a box of matches, an entrenching tool, large field binoculars, a steel pot helmet, a topography map of Da Nang including the area south and a full quart of tequila. Back in the corner of the compartment were two M-16s and two boxes of ammo.

"Gotta love these flyboys. Someone just walked off and left all this stuff! Doesn't seem right," I said. "But thank God for that!"

"Who knows. Mechanic in the hangar said this plane had been sitting there for years. We don't know what was going on at the time. Probably a crew that had to leave in a hurry to catch a chopper ride. If they were zeroing out, they sure as hell didn't care about what they left behind."

I could not help but smile over my discovery. "Looks like we're going camping for a while, Mitch."

"I'm from downtown Detroit. Do I look like I have ever been camping? I went through Special Forces survival training, but we had radios and food."

I turned around to look at Mitch. "No, man, you don't look like the camper type, but you're in good hands. I grew up more outdoors than indoors. We need to set up a shelter, gather firewood, see what kind of food might be on this island, but first of all, I see supper right in front of us. Come on, Mitch. Let's get movin'. We have a lot to do before dark."

"Damn! I'm stranded out here with some kind of Jungle Jim?" Mitch followed me, shaking his head.

"Nope, just a farm boy who spent a lot of time in rivers, creeks, and on the beach. I grew up camping a lot, and I mostly lived off the land when I camped. See those fish in that shallow gully about thirty yards ahead of us?"

"Yeah, those red-looking things? What about 'um? You don't have anything to catch them with."

"Follow me. All we need is a few bamboo poles."

"Bamboo poles? If you haven't noticed, we don't have any fishing line, hooks or bait." Mitch was shaking his head, again.

"Don't need 'um. Notice that the gully is flowing out to sea. It will get even shallower as the tide goes out, and eventually, the mullet will leave the gully and follow the tide. So, we need to catch a few of those suckers before they get away. We simply run alongside the red mullet, forcing it to hug the bank, and whack the water next to the fish as hard as you can. It will cause them to jump on the bank and voila, supper! Of course, you have to catch them before they wiggle their way back in the water."

Mitch looked incredulous.

We cut a few bamboo poles, which were in abundance on the island. Then we stripped down to our boxers and went fish whacking. Mitch was the first to whack the water hard enough to cause a red mullet to jump up on the bank.

"Great job, Mitch! Now jump on him! Grab him behind the head and hold him down!" I yelled.

"Say what? Man, this thing is slippery as hell, and he sure doesn't want to be caught."

Mitch started laughing while he rolled in the coarse beach sand, trying to land a three-pound fish that was in the fight of its life. Ultimately, the fish won. It wiggled back into the water and got away. Now that he knew what to expect, Mitch ran back for his bamboo pole and went right back at it. Another mullet was on the bank within minutes.

"Help me here, will ya', Sam?"

I dropped my pole and ran over. I fell to both knees straddling the fish and held its head down with both hands. Amazing how strong a determined three-pound fish could be.

"Go get the survival knife, Mitch."

Mitch was back in a flash. I took the knife, cut the fish's throat, and eviscerated it on the spot. I took a bamboo stick and stuck it through its tail, pinning it down in shallow water. Mitch watched all of this in awe.

"Wow! Sam, you know your stuff. How come you put him back in the water after you cleaned him?"

"We don't have any ice, Mitch. That will keep the fish from spoiling in the sun while we catch a few more. Come on, let's get back at it before they all catch a ride on the outgoing tide."

We caught two additional red mullet. When we went back to retrieve the first one that had been cleaned and pinned down under the water, we found a very large blue crab feasting on its head. I took out the survival knife and speared the hungry crustacean. "Looks like I'll be serving a crab appetizer before the main course, Mitch," I deadpanned.

Mitch grabbed our duffle bag, and we headed toward the tree line and the base of the hills just fifty yards off the beach. I followed, carrying our dinner: three cleaned fish, and a large blue crab. Despite all our misfortune, this would be a good night. Mitch continued looking over his shoulder at me, shaking his head in disbelief. The spot we chose was shaded by coconut palms. There was an overhang from the tall hills that came right down to the beach, which offered us good shelter.

"Mitch, do you think Charlie saw us land?"

"Doubt it. You dead-sticked at least two miles before touching down on the island, and we had at least a 15-knot headwind from the south. He may have seen us if he were looking in our direction, but there is no way he could have heard us. There was nothing to hear. As you were landing, I was looking at the coastline of Vietnam. I didn't see any hamlets, roads, or movement of any kind. Still doesn't mean Charlie wasn't watching. Time will tell; always does! I guess the question is, if Charlie does come, how many, from which direction, and when?"

"Yeah, I was thinking the same thing. We better wait until dark to cook these fish. That way, Charlie won't see our smoke during this moonless night. Whadaya say, we try to climb this hill and take a look at the coast through these field binoculars?"

Under a palm tree, I dug a deep hole in the soft beach sand, lined it with leaves, put our fresh catch in the hole, covered it with more leaves, and then put a layer of sand on top.

"There! The fish and crab should be good for a few hours until we can get back down here to cook them," I said with satisfaction.

We put our flight suits and boots back on and started the trek up the hill, which turned out to be more like a small mountain. Probably built up over thousands of years from coral. The hill was hard going. Mitch and I took turns in the tough spots with our machetes. After about an hour we had reached the top. We laid down on a small grassy knoll overlooking the western side of the island. Barely one mile of sea separated us from the Vietnamese coast.

Like cavalrymen on their bellies scouting for buffalo, we took turns scanning the coast with our new-found binoculars. Nothing. No sign of life. Not even sampans. We moved a few feet off of the knoll, out of sight on the eastern side of the ridge, and sat up. Mitch pulled out the topography map that we had found in the duffle bag.

"Sam, best I can figure, we are here … on this island. If this is where we are … well, we are in the middle of nowhere, which is a good thing. See where the coast of Vietnam juts out a little right here?" Mitch put his finger on the map and then pointed north to that spot on the coast.

"Yeah, got it."

"Well, if I'm right, this has got to be where we are. There is nothing on the map that shows any inhabitants along the coast of Vietnam for at least ten miles in each direction. This island, according to the map, doesn't even have a name. Although this map's at least five years old, I bet we're safe here, at least for a while."

"I hope you're right, Mitch. Let's head back down while we have enough daylight. The going should be easier since we already cut a trail through the spots that had dense foliage. By the way, on our climb to this vantage point, I spotted a mango tree, an avocado tree, and a lemon tree. Let's gather some fresh fruit to go with our seafood," I suggested, growing more acutely aware of my hunger and assuming Mitch felt the same.

We were back at camp in no time. We cut large pieces of bamboo and used the entrenching tool to dig holes in the beach sand under the overhang. We buried the poles a few feet into the sand. Then we strung up our hammocks. We laid our ponchos in the hammock and then covered them with the poncho liners. We had a bit of a mattress that we hoped would keep insects from biting through the hammock netting. We dug a small pit at the entrance to the overhang and gathered firewood, which was in abundant supply.

"I think we should wait until it's completely dark before we light a fire, Mitch."

"I agree. No sense in pushing our luck. Looks like the wind is offshore blowing out to sea. Whatever smoke we make should be moving away from the mainland. Whadaya say we have a little tequila with fresh lemon while we wait for supper?" Mitch grinned as he groped in the duffle bag for the bottle.

"Sounds good to me!" I cut a few wedges from a fresh lemon. I smiled again over the prospect of our having a before-dinner drink on this deserted island. Darkness fell, and the night sounds of the island came alive. Unfortunately, the bugs came out, too, so we put on insect repellant and covered our hammocks with the mosquito netting for later. When it was dark enough, we built a good fire. I put the fish and crab on a spit and turned them every fifteen minutes when I doused them with fresh-squeezed lemon juice. Mitch had walked out on the beach to observe our position and came back with great news.

"We're in good shape, Sam. I could not see the fire from the beach, and the smoke is not visible against the woods of the hill."

We dined on fire-roasted mullet, crab, mango, and avocado. It was surprisingly tasty and boosted our spirits. The smoke helped drive back the mosquitoes, and the repellent was doing its job.

"Mitch, the way I figure it, when we don't land and report in at Long Thanh North tonight, someone will make a call to Da Nang by tomorrow morning. Da Nang will let them know we took off today. When Long Thanh doesn't hear from us by tomorrow night, Tipper will be all over it. He knows us well enough. He will know we are in trouble."

"Yeah, you're right, Sam. We need to figure out a rescue plan."

"Well, they will be looking for us in daylight. They will probably be using Jolly Greens or Hueys to find us. We run the risk of someone other than our rescuers finding us if we light a signal fire and make smoke during the day. We should spend our time up on the grassy knoll or down by the Beaver. Whadaya think?"

"Sam, a chopper might be too low to see the downed Beaver if they are flying along the coast on the other side of this island. That's a small knoll up there, and we don't have any bright cloth to attract someone looking for us. I think we'll need a fire, but building a fire up on the knoll would probably be the worst idea."

"Not if we built the fire at the last minute, Mitch."

"Say what?"

"We build the fire at the last minute. If we see a chopper headed our way, we light a stack of palm fronds soaked in fuel and oil. It would immediately send up a column of smoke." My plan caused me to grin.

"You mean fuel and oil from the Beaver?" questioned Mitch.

"Yep! That's the plan."

"How are we supposed to get fuel and oil to the top of the hill? We don't have any containers."

"Oh, yes, we do, brother." I held up the bottle of tequila, which, at that time, was two-thirds full.

"What? And pour out that good stuff?" Mitch was serious.

"Who said anything about pouring it out. Like we said, we probably have a few days. Here, drink up, buddy. Want another slice of lemon?"

"You're a trip, Sam. Got to say, I never thought being marooned on a tropical island could be so much fun. You going back to South Carolina when you go home?"

"Haven't really thought about it. Why?"

"Cause the camping bug has bit me. I actually like it a lot." "Yeah, as long as Charlie stays away, this will be a good time!"

Mitch passed the tequila back to me. We threw a few more logs on the fire.

"What're you gonna do when this is over, Mitch? You know, when you go home?" I asked, gazing into the flames.

"You gotta remember, Sam. I am a lifer. I go wherever Uncle Sam tells me to go. Just hope it ain't a trip back to the Nam. Man! Three tours are enough. Know what I mean?"

"No, this is my first tour, and I plan on it being my last. I couldn't imagine making two more trips to this place. Three is crazy. I don't know how you do it, Mitch."

"Yeah, it hasn't been easy. I got a girl back home, Sarah ... Sarah Heyward. If it weren't for sweet Sarah, I don't know that I would have made it, to tell you the truth."

"Sarah? You have never mentioned her ... how come?" I asked.

"No reason, Sam. You know me by now. I'm a private kinda guy."

"OK, I will give you that much. So, tell me about Sarah."

"I met Sarah at Walter Reed after my first tour. She's an army nurse. I went home with parasites from being in the bush over here too much. You know, Special Forces crap. Anyway, we started seeing each other, and she got transferred to the same airbase as me, so we figured it must be fate. Yeah, sweet Sarah Heyward. I asked her to marry me on my first R&R, and she said, yes. Gonna marry that girl when I get home!"

"WOW! Congratulations, Mitch. I am happy for you, brother. So, when is the wedding?"

"Soon as we can after I get home. You should come to the wedding. It will be just outside of LA."

"Sure, I would love to, and I definitely want to meet Sarah."

"What about you? Anyone special?"

"Well, I'd have to tell you that long story that Tipper said you wouldn't believe."

"Looks like we got the time and the tequila. I'm all ears."

I started at the beginning and included every detail; well, almost every detail!

"Man, talk about fate. Don't let this girl get away, Sam."

"Don't plan on it, Mitch. In about three weeks, Vicky and I are meeting in Hawaii for my R&R. OH SHIT! What if you and I are still stuck on this freakin' island?"

"Don't think we got to worry about that, Sam. Yeah, maybe on my first tour that could have happened, but not now. Just way too many choppers and planes flying around. Somebody will see us if Tipper doesn't get to us first."

"Or Charlie!"

"Hey, Sam, we aren't sittin' here with just sidearms, Brother. We got two M-16s and at least a thousand rounds. Besides, I think the only way Charlie will know if we are here is if we tip him off ... and that ain't gonna' happen."

"Oh well! Just a thought. Let's get some sleep. Tomorrow will be another challenge."

***

The next morning, we found some ripe coconuts on the beach, almost as though they had been delivered by room service. A few good chops with the machete, and we had fresh coconut and what was left of the mango for breakfast. We were running low on water. Dry mouth from the tequila didn't help.

"Whadaya say we check out this island, Sam?"

"Sounds good to me."

We walked the beach to the south end of the island. Carrying our canteens, two M-16s, and the machetes, we hugged the tree line to avoid being seen from the Vietnamese coast just in case the enemy was watching. The island was about three miles long and not quite a mile wide. We arrived at the southern tip in twenty minutes.

"Look, Mitch, over there." I pointed to a spot on the side of the island closest to the mainland. "It's a small cove. See the poles and ropes on its shoreline? You can tell some boats have come and gone. Looks like a small dock from here."

"Yeah, I see what you're talking about, but who would use it? Vietnamese fishermen or the enemy?" wondered Mitch.

"Don't know, but now we do know that people use this island. We just don't know who, why, or when."

Suddenly, we realized we weren't as safe as we once thought. On our return, we hugged the tree-line and kept an eye out for anything edible and any sign of water. Luck was with us on both counts. Having discovered a row of banana trees, we managed to cut down a ripe stake of the thick-skinned fruit. We also found a small freshwater spring just minutes from our campsite where we drank our fill after topping off the canteens. Several small animal tracks decorated the edge of the spring, but no human footprints. While all of this good fortune was somewhat calming, we understood we had to remain vigilant.

Once back at camp, we decided to catch a few additional red mullet while the tide was right and effortlessly caught two large ones. After cleaning them, we layered slices of lemon and mango in the fish cavity, wrapped them in banana leaves and buried them in the smoldering coals from the night before. This would cook the fish slowly so they would not spoil in the tropical heat.

Energized with cool spring water and several bananas, we made our way back up to the crest of the ridge and the grassy knoll we had found the day before. From our secluded perch, we spent most of the afternoon taking turns with the binoculars, scanning the area for any movement on the not too distant Vietnamese coastline, or the secluded inland coves that could easily conceal enemy boats. Nothing. At least nothing we could see. We decided to wait until dusk before going back down to our campsite. We wanted to see if any campfires appeared on the mainland.

"Sam, what do you say that tomorrow morning we start putting a stack of dried palm fronds and light wood over there a few feet from the top of the crest. When we finish our tequila, which may have to be tonight, we can add oil and gas to the bottle to soak the palm fronds. One match should do it. There is plenty of room on this knoll for a chopper to pick us up."

"Sounds like a plan, Mitch." Then I lowered the binoculars and got serious. "OK, this may be bad news. Take these and look about one mile down the coast to the south. See it?"

Mitch was frowning while he looked through the binoculars. "Yeah, I see it. Looks like a pretty good size campfire. Problem is, we don't know who they are or how many. But we do know that only humans build fires."

We made our way back to the campsite and made a somewhat smaller fire. The fish were already cooked and delicious with the added flavor of lemon and mango. We drank more tequila, ate several bananas, and what was left of the mangoes and avocados.

"Let's get an early start in the morning, Mitch. We can fill this tequila bottle first with oil and gas and start getting the materials for the signal fire up to the knoll. Now that we know someone is fairly close by, I think we should keep our eyes open and keep watch from the knoll. If Charlie is coming, at least we will be able to see him. Also, it's the best place for a rescue helicopter to pick us up."

"I agree, Sam. Let's get some shuteye."

Fully aware that we were not alone on this island, neither of us slept as soundly, and we were up at the crack of dawn. Within an hour after daylight, we had eaten, filled the tequila bottle with oil and gas from the Beaver, and taken our first armload of palm fronds to the grassy knoll close to the crest. Mitch and I took turns. One kept watch for movement on the coast and looked out for a rescue chopper while the other gathered palm fronds and wood.

We waited and watched all day. Nothing!

About two hours before dark, Mitch said, "Sam, why don't you go down and catch us a few fish and get a fire going? I'll stay here and watch for a fire on the coastline again and then come on down."

"You got it!" I gathered several lemons, mangos, and avocados on my way downhill. As I was leaning down to pick up a few ripe mangoes under a tree, I startled a nearby covey of quail. The sound of their wings taking flight and their noisy, urgent chirping scared the crap out of me. It could have easily been an NVA ambush lying in wait. My senses heightened; I was reminded that we were not alone. I allowed myself to wonder how this adventure would end, but only for a moment.

I gathered wood for the fire and got back down to the gully, but much of the water had flowed out with the tide, and most of the fish were gone. Thirty more minutes and I would have missed the tide completely, but I managed to get one medium-sized red mullet. It would have to do. I cleaned it and had a fire going when Mitch arrived back at camp.

"Something is going on, Sam. The fire we saw last night has moved about a mile down the coast, closer to us. I also spotted a second fire about two miles north of here. If we light that signal fire tomorrow in broad daylight, which is what we will have to do to signal a helicopter, the enemy should be too far away to get to us, unless they happen to be an anti-aircraft site, which I doubt."

"I hope you're right, my friend. I pretty much missed the tide. All we have is one mullet between us, but there is plenty of fruit."

"Hey, Sam, thank God for that. If it weren't for your skills, I would be living off candy bars and water." As the fish cooked, Mitch reached into the leg pouch of his flight suit and produced a shiny silver flask. "Thought I would save this until we really needed it. I know you're a Scotch man, but this will just have to do," he declared as he handed me the flask. "It's Old Grand-Dad Bourbon."

I took a healthy gulp and returned the flask. "Thanks, Mitch. I can handle it. Sure beats nothing at all. In fact, it hits the spot!"

Mitch took a belt of the bourbon. We split the mullet and ate fruit. We sat around the campfire polishing off the flask while talking about home, our girlfriends, flying, and the hope that tomorrow would be another easy day on the island. We could not have been more wrong!

"Surely, Tipper will have someone out looking for us by tomorrow. I say we get up to the crest early. Let's take most of our supplies and stay put all day. If we see a chopper coming down that coast and we light a fire, once he sees our smoke, we should be out of here in under thirty minutes."

***

It was about eighteen-hundred hours, nearly dusk, when we saw the chopper coming up the coast from the south. It was a Huey C-model. When it was about five miles away, we torched the signal fire, as planned, unleashing a bellow of black smoke up into the sky. Our hopes soared, but a few minutes later, the chopper went flying by as though they had not seen us. Mitch peered through the binoculars as the Huey passed by and then dropped them by his side in despair.

"Sam, those pilots had to see us. My bet is, because we don't have a radio, they thought nothing of the smoke. DAMN!"

They probably didn't see the downed Beaver, either. As we watched them disappear along the coast to the north, we understood clearly that they would not be coming back to rescue us. The feeling of helplessness and danger was almost overwhelming.

"Sam, I'm afraid we have screwed up big time!"

Mitch grabbed all of our gear and tore down the hill, yelling over his shoulder. "I say we head out for the south point and dig in with the entrenching tool. I noticed several palm trees that were down on the beach. We might be able to roll a few in front of a foxhole for protection. I say we dig in about thirty feet from the cove, where no doubt Charlie will be coming ashore. We just sent him an open invitation."

Since Mitch had been in Special Forces before becoming a pilot, I was now following him and trusting his lead. Soldiering, especially at his level of training, was not my forte. Before we rounded the end of the beach coming up on the south point, Mitch had us crawl on our hands and knees so we wouldn't be seen, sticking close to the tree line. Concealed by small shrubs, we edged our way toward the south point and the cove.

"We're in luck, Sam. If we stay on our hands and knees, we'll be protected from discovery by those small sand dunes and shrubs that lead out to the point. It looks like a palm tree log has washed up on the beach just about forty feet from the boat landing near the cove. We can dig in behind it."

Mitch and I remained low, which made digging with the entrenching tool a little more difficult, but working feverishly, within forty minutes, we had dug a foxhole three feet wide, five feet long, and four feet deep. We crawled back for our ponchos, poncho liners, machetes, mosquito netting, canteens, and two cans of M-16 ammo. We dragged several dead palm fronds behind us to cover our tracks and to camouflage the foxhole.

We used more palm fronds and the ponchos to line the foxhole to protect us from the damp sand and placed the poncho liners over the tops of the ponchos. We placed the palm fronds over the foxhole in a manner that looked natural and yet completely concealed us from sight. We had smudged our faces and hands with smut from the campfire and wrapped our heads in two black bandannas. The foxhole was actually pretty comfortable as we sat on dry poncho liners, peeping through the palm fronds and listening, loaded M-16s at our sides. Our camping trip was over, trumped by the twist of war.

"How long do you think it will take them to get here, and how many will they send?" I asked Mitch.

"Well, Sam you can bet they saw the smoke. They may think we are still on top of the hill, and therefore, we would be able to see them cross over to the island in daylight. My bet is they will wait until dark and pull up right here, forty feet in front of us. Once they are all standing, we let them have it. The element of surprise should give us a huge advantage, especially if we are outnumbered. My guess is that they won't send more than two boats, three to four soldiers per boat."

It got dark, and we waited. Mitch and I said very little to each other, and what little needed to be said was spoken in a whisper. Wrapped in mosquito netting and leaning against the inside wall of the foxhole, we listened. We prepared mentally and physically for a very long and tense night. Around 0300 hours, we could hear what sounded like two small boats headed in our direction. Our heart rates accelerated as though the boogie man had turned the corner ... and indeed, he had!

"OK, Sam, this has got to be Charlie. We'll be able to see their outlines without a problem. Be sure they are all out of the boats before you fire. Let me go first. I will take the first guy on the right and work in. You take the first guy on the left and work in. Hit each one at least twice," Mitch instructed in a low, calm voice, which seemed to help, even if just a little!

As the boats got closer, we could hear the motors slowing down and then we could hear them chatter. They were definitely speaking Vietnamese. Mitch was right; they had sent two boats. Once they pulled into the cove and stopped at the small docking area, they were so close I felt as though I could reach out and touch them. Surprisingly, they were very easy to see in the dark. The first boat docked, and a VC jumped out to tie it off, and the second boat did the same. Then the soldiers from each boat stood up and stepped out on the boat dock plank. Six of them in all.

It was like shooting fish in a barrel.

They had not planned for the element of surprise. Within less than ten seconds, Mitch and I had taken out all six of them. There was no movement. They were all dead. Shooting a person twice in the chest with an M-16 from less than thirty yards away doesn't leave much room for error ... or for life.

We waited a bit before exiting the foxhole and approaching them, our M-16s at the ready just in case. A voice chattered from the radio of one dead soldier. Neither Mitch nor I understood Vietnamese, but we could bet that whoever was on the other end of that radio would be looking for these six soldiers and two boats by morning.

"Sam, we should take the high ground and stay there. Let's get back to the knoll."

I did as I was told. Breathing heavily, I asked, "We should just leave the bodies and the boats?"

"Yes, when the other VC come looking for these guys, we'll have a clear shot at them from the knoll. Sam, I don't know what's coming, but this could get bad, really bad. But before we leave, take their AK-47s and grab their ammo belts. We might have to fight off a lot more of these guys before it's over. We may need the extra weapons and ammo."

It was a heavy load. Going through the two boats, Mitch found a mortar tube, which he slung over his shoulder as well as a satchel with a half dozen mortar rounds.

"OK, Sam. Let's bury all but two of the AK's. That's all we need. Otherwise, it's too much for us to carry."

In little under an hour, we made it to the top of the knoll, and immediately, Mitch started to dig a foxhole.

"Mitch, it's still about an hour before the crack of dawn, I am going down to the campfire to bring back the rest of our supplies and what little fruit we have left."

"Great idea. How about filling up the canteens while you're at it?"

"I'll do that first. See you in about two hours. Say, Mitch?"

"Yeah, buddy?

"Thanks for being such a great grunt."

Mitch laughed, "Ain't over till the fat lady sings, my man. Unfortunately, I think the worst is yet to come." Turns out, he was right.

It took me longer than I expected to find the spring of water in the dark. The island had gotten spooky. I had gotten jumpy. My short-lived experience as a door gunner was bad enough. This could be worse. I kept stopping and listening for any sounds of boats coming to shore or voices that might already be onshore. Nothing! Good! I found the spring and took a long drink, double-tasking as I simultaneously held the canteen underwater to fill it.

I raced back to the campsite and grabbed the duffle bag. I filled it with all the bananas, mangos, and coconuts I could carry and headed back up the hill. Dawn was just breaking. That's when I heard the first mortar round go off. Then the second followed by an explosion offshore.

I dragged the duffle bag of fruit behind me and crawled up to the foxhole Mitch had just dug. "Get in and get down!" Mitch ordered.

"What's going on, Mitch? Was that you firing mortar?"

"Yeah, that was me. They aren't waiting on darkness again. Got one boat. The one closest to the island. There are four more boats out there coming this way. Looks like six to eight men per boat. Sam, grab the two AK-47s and the ammo belts and come with me. I'll take the mortar tube and mortar rounds. We need to move down this ridgeline and stay out of sight. We can fire again a couple of hundred meters down the ridge."

Fortunately, the going was easy. We were moving through something that reminded me of broom straw back home.

"Why are we making this move?" I wanted to know.

"We don't want to give away our foxhole position. If we fire a few mortar rounds further down the ridge, they might think there are more than just the two of us up here and spread their men out to come after us. That way, we wouldn't be fighting them all at once. After I fire a mortar round, move down another fifty yards and start firing away with the AK-47, they will know we got their guys when they hear their own weapons being fired at them. I know you already know this, but there are rules of war. The VC and NVA use green tracer rounds every fourth bullet. The Americans and our allies use red tracer rounds every fourth bullet. What we don't want to do is have a rescue helicopter show up for us and see us firing green tracer rounds off this ridge because we don't have a radio to tell them who we are. Best to use Charlie's ammo on Charlie until the cavalry shows up for us."

Mitch's thinking under fire was calm, focused, and tactical. He was a good man to be in a battle with. His first mortar round fell only a few feet short of the bow of the lead boat; however, it was close enough to throw the occupants off balance and pitched them overboard. Now these eight were forced to swim ashore, and it was likely that at least some of them would have lost their weapons. I fired two full magazines of AK-47 rounds. None found a mark. The boats were too far away, but at least they knew we were firing their weapons. That sent a psychological message, if nothing else. They had to be wondering why we were on the island, and how many of us were here. I went back to Mitch's location.

"Sam, look through these binoculars. Notice to the right of the lens you should see an elevation scale."

Grabbing the binoculars, I focused on the lead boat. "Hey, these guys are wearing pith helmets and brown uniforms."

"Yeah, I couldn't help but notice. They're all NVA. They are usually better trained and better equipped than the VC we dealt with before daylight. Do you have a range reading, Sam?"

"Yeah. Looks like twenty degrees down from here."

I watched Mitch make the adjustment on the mortar tube. He fired. He missed the boat by ten feet. "OK ... OK … Here goes another shot. Just one small correction." He fired again. This time, the mortar round hit five feet or so in front of the boat. "OK ... OK ... one left, Sam." Mitch fired. It was a direct hit!

"Good shot, Mitch. That's eight more we don't have to worry about."

"Yeah, but there are still a lot we do have to worry about. They will probably concentrate on this position, so let's get back to our foxhole. When they get to the top of the knoll, we'll be in a pretty good firing position to defend ourselves and take them out."

Mitch was breathing heavily, and so was I. The adrenaline factor had taken over. One thing about adrenaline: You can't will it to kick in, and you can't wish it to go away, but it always shows up when you need it most.

"Sam, I will keep my eyes open. I have a panoramic view from here, so we will know where they land. How about you gather some palm fronds. I think there is enough gas and oil in the bottom of our tequila bottle to get a small fire going if help shows up."

I raced downhill. I had to go several hundred feet to find dead, dry fronds. Returning to the knoll on my way back up, Mitch and I both saw it at the same time – the Chinook was about five miles to our south at approximately fifteen-hundred feet. What a sight for sore eyes!

Mitch tossed me the tequila bottle and a box of matches. There were only a few ounces of fuel left. I just hoped it was enough to get the job done. I lit the fire, and a small column of black smoke went skyward. Within seconds, the Chinook acknowledged our position by flashing its landing lights and coming out of altitude directly for us. We were elated!

The Chinook landed a few hundred feet north of us on the top of the ridge. No sooner had the helicopter touched down than an RPG (rocket-propelled grenade) took out the cockpit and both pilots. I could not believe my eyes! With the arrival of our rescuers, my face had just been morphing into a smile, not yet fully formed, and now it was contorting with horror and despair. Those guys in the cockpit just gave their lives, or more accurately, had their lives snuffed out, in order to rescue me and Mitch. It was almost too much for me to bear. I could only hope our lives would be worth it.

Six Navy SEAL guys came piling out of the back of the Chinook with M-16s and M-60 machine guns blazing. They laid down a line of fire in the tree line below them where the RPG had been fired. All went silent after a few minutes of intense firing. Then a strong voice yelled out, "Get away from the chopper! Drop down behind the ridge! Take cover!"

The SEALs were all but rolling down the hill when the Chinook went up in a burst of flames. The fire had reached the fuel tanks. The same voice called out again, but not as loud this time.

"OK, men, regroup over by the signal fire. Let's move it out."

In less than five minutes, I was looking out of the foxhole and directly into the face of one mean-ass Navy SEAL lieutenant, the rest of the SEAL Team in place in tactical positions. The lieutenant spoke to us, "You men OK?"

"Yes, Sir, we're OK. We were actually enjoying a little tropical island vacation until the NVA dropped in."

"Well, we still got trouble. Look yonder! Five more boats coming this way, and they ain't the Chow Mein family delivering noodles and egg rolls."

The lieutenant was busy barking orders. "Rodrigo, take two men and move. I want you to space out at least three hundred meters along this ridgeline. Give me a foxhole every fifty meters. Put your M-60 in the middle one. I will take the rest of the men and put in foxholes from here to within fifty meters of your first foxhole. Got it?"

Rodrigo, already on the move, responded over his shoulder, "I will give you a call once we are in place."

With lighting speed and incredible efficiency, the SEAL Team set-up a fearsome line of defense along the entire ridge. They were equipped with a deadly arsenal and were ready to unleash its fury. Each SEAL was armed with a forty-five-caliber handgun and also carried an M-16, mortar tubes, at least a dozen mortar rounds, two claymores, and a half-dozen hand-grenades.

This was the American soldier, not just any soldier, but the elite of the elite, the United States Navy SEAL. They were armed to the teeth and would fight to win. With more and more NVA arriving on the island, I thought I would be watching a ferocious firefight, the kind I had only heard about and, frankly, dreaded participating in. In minutes it would unfold before me ... and I would be right in the thick of things. But as fortune had it, the assault would not originate from our knoll, but rather from above, and what I would witness would curdle my blood.

The lieutenant got on his PRC-25, "Guard frequency, this is ST-6 Green Hornet, anybody read?"

Nothing!

"Say again to anyone on this frequency, this is ST-6 Green Hornet, how copy?"

"Yeah, Green Hornet, this is Falcon 909, how copy?"

"Falcon 909, Green Hornet needs support for an extraction. How copy?"

"Green Hornet, you're coming in a little broken, but I can read you. Say location."

"Falcon, we are at grid coordinate Y7887Z4434. It's a small island about fifty miles south of Da Nang, one mile offshore. How copy?"

"Green Hornet, be advised you are talking to three F-4s with spent ordinance. I will pass this along to the boys on the USS Oriskany. They are probably your closest bet. I will stay with you on this frequency until they start talking to you."

Rodrigo advised the captain on his PRC-25, "Everyone dug in and in place. Looks like Charlie is about a quarter-mile from putting in a little further up the beach than his last position. The two foxholes on this end can reach them with mortar."

"Fire at will, Rodrigo. Help may be a little while in getting here." I interrupted the lieutenant and Rodrigo.

"Sir, we got more company on the way."

They turned to see what I was talking about.

"Look there to the north about three miles up the coast. Looks like six boats, bigger ones, headed this way."

"This is going to be a real battle. That's a whole platoon coming."

For the first time, I recognized the Navy SEAL lieutenant. "Probably not a good time, but we have met before. Long Thanh about six months ago. You're the guy with the ear collection, right?"

"That would be me. Thought I'd heard that accent before. What-the-fuck you doin' this far north?"

"Just camping out until these assholes showed up."

"What?"

"Had a delivery to make at Da Nang. Engine trouble on the way back," I explained, pointing to the downed Beaver.

"Green Hornet, this is Silver Fish 332, how do you read?"

"Silver Fish, this is Green Hornet, go ahead."

"Green Hornet, we are a pair of A-1 Skyraiders from the USS Oriskany. We should be on target within the next 10 minutes. Approaching from the north. Please confirm your grid Y7887Z4434."

"Silver Fish, this is Green Hornet. Be advised that the grid coordinate is correct, but that is our exact location on top of the island. You got six boats headed for the island about two miles to the north of this location, and another six boat loads of Charlie landing within the next ten minutes on the northern end of the island. Suggest taking out the six Charlies on your way to us. You got any fire from the sky you can drop on the little bastards trying to fuck up a camping trip?"

"Roger copy, Green Hornet. We see the boats. They're toast. I will get back to you in a minute. Silver Fish out."

In two passes, the Skyhawks took out all six boats. Caught them completely by surprise. Six boats and everyone in them, gone for good, just like that.

"Green Hornet, we have neutralized the target. Be advised we were headed home when we got your distress call and diverted course to come help out. What little ordinance we had left was spent on those boats. All we have remaining is one napalm each. See what we can do for you. Stand by."

"Roger, Silver Fish. These boys just hit the island. Suggest dropping about fifty yards inside the jungle directly where they put in with their boats. That should do it."

I felt relieved as I watched the two A-1 Skyraiders roll in on their target for the kill. One moment, I was admiring the skill of the pilots, the grace of the aircraft – one of my favorites – and the next moment I was horrified to see the dense, green jungle below us become a raging inferno! There was not even a single scream; there wasn't time. I had never before seen napalm dropped while I was on the ground, only when in the air, from my vantage point as a pilot. This strike gave me a whole new and hideous perspective. Napalm isn't a bomb; it's a pyrotechnic gel that carries burning fuel along a speedy route directly to its earthly target. Depending on the formula, it can burn at temperatures up to twenty-two hundred degrees Fahrenheit. Together, the gel and the fuel make a deadly couple, far worse than Bonnie and Clyde. Moving with incredible velocity and covering a wide path, the gel sticks to everything in its way, holding the intense flames in place while they severely burn everything and anything having the misfortune to be there. In mere seconds, thousands of people, structures, and natural environments have been destroyed by napalm. Remarkably, a few severely disfigured survivors have lived to tell their ghastly tale and of their endless suffering.

As the A-1s made a low pass over us before heading home, the offshore wind brought up the overpowering stench of burning flesh. "Green Hornet, that should quiet things down. We will stay on this frequency with you. I heard over Guard that a Chinook is on the way to pick you up. Should be there in under thirty. You copy?"

"Roger copy, Silver Fish. Good job. Thanks for the help. I heard the Chinook also. There is no more activity below or on the shoreline. We will be out of here before Charlie can regroup. You guys can sign off. Thanks again. Green Hornet out."

Death! So much death! All because of one old Beaver with a malfunctioning manifold. How many were killed? I did not know; could not estimate. I would not estimate. Some time ago, I realized that counting kills seemed as inhumane as collecting ears.

***

We all boarded the Chinook that arrived to pick us up, as promised. I sat next to the Navy SEAL lieutenant. The inert body bags holding the two American chopper pilots who lost their lives less than two hours ago lay next to us. I started talking to the lieutenant and asked him his name.

"Marcus Philips. Everybody calls me 'Cus.'"

"So how did you find us, Cus?"

"I heard your CO down at Long Thanh was coming off the rails when he couldn't get answers. We got a call from top brass to find you guys, or else. My team was ready to move within ten minutes, but we had trouble getting a Chinook out of Tan Son Nhut Air Base. That delayed us by almost four hours. Then we had to stop in Nha Trang for gas on the way up to you fellas. That delayed us another two hours. They were busier than Aunt Bee in a chili cook-off. Helicopters were lined up at the gas pump, and we had to wait for fuel. Just glad we got you two out in time. Two bad about these Chinook pilots. Don't think they even knew what hit them. Both young warrant officers. Damn shame."

We both looked over at the black plastic bags, which contained the remains of two American pilots. It was the first time I had actually flown in an aircraft with bodies, and they happened to be pilots who were also warrant officers, just like me. It was eerie and hit way too close to home. I was just glad it wasn't Mitch and me in those bags, and then I thought … how selfish! Each of these two young men was someone's son, and perhaps a brother, a father, a husband, a best friend. They had families who loved them, too, families who were about to receive devastating news. I shifted my gaze and thoughts away from the dead pilots.

Mitch seemed to sense where my head had taken me and spoke up, with a bit more cheer in his voice. "I was with Jungle Jim down there, on that island. Sam, here, can catch fish with only a pole. Apparently, he never learned about fishing line, hooks, or bait!"

"You're pulling my leg now, Sir. I am a Frog-Man, and we went through thirty days of survival school, and I ain't never heard of no such thing. How're you gonna catch a fish just using a pole?"

In Mitch's tale-telling fashion, he applied a bit of polish to this adventure that would become known as 'When the Red Mullet Met the Bamboo Pole'.

***

As soon as we got back to base, Mitch and I reported to Tipper for debriefing. He was clearly relieved to see us and listened with keen interest as we gave him a play by play of all the events that took place on what will forever be called 'Red Mullet Island'.

"Knocking red mullet out of the water with a bamboo pole! You're bullshitting me at this point, right?" Tipper laughed.

Mitch was talking excitedly. "Never would have believed it if I hadn't seen it with my own eyes. Thing of it is … and I haven't told this to Sam yet … that's the most fun I have had since I was a kid! In the middle of that first fish whacking lesson … even if just for a second … the war went away. We were like two young boys, without a care in the world, running through the sprinkler system in our boxers on a hot summer's day."

"Wow! You two keep up these adventures, and you will have enough to write a book." Changing the subject, Tipper added, "I know it's become old hat around here, and I feel foolish sometimes for even suggesting it, but Pole got in some great steaks, and a couple of them have your names on 'um. I bought them for you two while you were missing."

"Now that's faith, Tipper. The kind my sweet mama in Detroit raised me with."

"We both know from our first tour, Mitch, it really is the only good lesson we take home."

***

When I returned to base camp, a letter was waiting for me. A quick look at the envelope, and I knew it was from home. Holding the letter in my hand, a wave of emotions swept over me, taking me completely by surprise. Receiving a letter from home was always a pleasure, but this one stirred up a spiraling storm of sentiments. Perhaps, with letter in hand, I was suddenly struck by how close I had come to being killed, not once, but twice; the Beaver could have crashed and/or enemy fire could have taken me. And what kind of letter would my family get? As these many feelings swirled around in my head, once again, I was reminded of 'the best of times and the worst of times'. Meeting Miss America and camping in the natural beauty of the island were so out of place for a war zone, while arming-up to kill or be killed was not. Experiencing both, especially in such a short time-span, was really messing with my sanity. I needed time to sort all this stuff out. I put the letter down, unopened.

***

The next day, after a sound sleep – I hadn't realized how exhausted I was – a hot shower, and another tasteless breakfast, I opened the letter. Written in Mom's familiar cursive, I heard all the words spoken in her voice, as though she was talking to me from one of the chairs in my hooch:

Dear Son,

I hope my quick note finds you well. We see so much of the war on the nightly news that frightens us. We never know how close you are to the atrocities we watch.

Everything is fine at home. Your father is busy overseeing the soybean harvest. He and Henry planted a little over one thousand acres this year. The market is good. He went dove hunting last weekend at George Hill's farm and brought home 23 birds. Otsie is cooking them like only she can. She is always asking about you and mentioned how much she knew you would like to be sitting down to these doves smothered in bacon, onions, and gravy.

I am so sorry to hear the food there is bad. I think you used the word, 'repugnant'. I guess my mother's insistence on testing you on the vocabulary section of her Reader's Digest every month has paid off. I often have to look up some of the words you use.

I know you have this love of flying, and somehow, I try to make all of this OK, because I know you're doing what you love. I try, but I can't imagine what it must be like for a pilot over there. I will never forget the day you buzzed our house in that little Piper Cub. You were only seventeen then. Now look at you!

I have mailed you a case of canned She Crab Soup. I know it's not homemade the way you like it, but I got it at Harold's Cabin. It is supposed to be very good. Be sure to share some of it with your friends. We miss you and love you and count the days until you're home safe.

Love, Mom

Many parts of that letter rekindled wonderful memories that I had buried deep, soon after arriving here. Now they made me feel good, but not for long. Despite all of the pleasant updates that Mom shared, I was left feeling deeply saddened, for I realized that the people I loved most in the world were suffering on my account.

Yes, they were miles away from the war zone, completely safe and able to carry on with their lives, but each morning they would wake up and remember that I was here, fighting a nasty war and at risk every single day. They functioned under a constant level of stress that gnawed away around the edges of their lives. Worry, fear, and hopelessness had become their constant companions. Now go and multiply this madness by the hundreds of thousands of families who are all suffering from the same malady. War is hell for everyone involved, whether on the front lines or the home front.

What could I do? Only one thing. Just stay alive – for my family as well as myself. What the hell should I do now? I could simply write back, believing they'd find a moment of happiness when lost in my letter. But what would I say? Then I remembered the Major, Tipper, warning me that *you will find yourself lying to your family because you sure as hell can't write home about any of what really happens here*. Did that have to become my truth, too?

I picked up my pen, and I wrote:

Dear Mom,

I really appreciated your letter. My life is very different now- fighting a war I hardly understand, in a foreign country with a culture that I will never understand, so, it was good to be reminded of my life at home. I've met a lot of soldiers who did not have it as good as I did growing up, and I realize just how lucky I am to have such a fine family. Of course, that includes Otsie. Please tell her that I often brag about her cooking, and I could smell those doves, smothered in gravy, from here! In fact, you can place my order for the first home-cooked meal when I come back: dove smothered in bacon, onions, and gravy!

Please tell Dad I am happy to hear the soybean harvest went so well. Man, I would love to get my hands in that dirt again and make something grow. I look forward to helping out when I return.

Please don't worry about me too much. Things are not so bad for me here. You know how much I love to fly; well, I caught a break recently, and it was pretty interesting. Another pilot and I had the opportunity to test-fly an old bird, and for our troubles, we got to land it on a beautiful island where we camped out a few days. There are many small islands here off the coast, and from up in the air, they sure look amazing. The sand is pure white, and the sea is a stunning shade of blue-green, clear and sparkling like jewels, nothing like our beaches at home.

Most of these islands are uninhabited; so was this one. The island was an exotic oasis. Surrounded by the beach, its center was a tangle of thick, lush tropical plants and trees. They were all in full bloom with fruits and flowers. Just imagine; coconuts, mangos, avocados, bananas, and lemons were growing all over the place and free for the taking. I taught my co-pilot, a real city boy, fish whacking, and he got real good at it. We had roasted red mullet for dinner every night. He said that with all the things I taught him about camping, he felt like a kid again, but not a city kid. And he taught me a few things, too.

Oh, I almost forgot! Right before the camping trip, I met Miss America; actually, I danced with Miss America. I know you're thinking that I am not much of a dancer, and I agree, but I had to. You see, she asked me, and right in front of a whole bunch of people, so I just had to. It was the right thing to do. That's how you and Dad raised me.

Well, that's all for now. I'm counting the days, too. Be back before you know it.

Your loving son,
Sam

***

Ha! How about that! And all of it true ... just left out a few details. I mailed the letter.

Chapter 17 Hawaii

After fastening my seatbelt, I felt strangely uncomfortable. Instead of occupying my usual place in the left seat of the cockpit, I was just one of Pan Am's many passengers flying from Saigon to Honolulu. As I settled in to experience the flight from this unfamiliar vantage point, I planned to enjoy the relative comfort and ordered a drink when offered. Of course, the stewardess reminded me of Vicky, who else would I have on my mind at this point, finally heading to the Hawaiian R&R that almost never happened? I replayed in my mind the time Vicky and I met in the furniture store and how events conspired to this day when we would reunite in Hawaii. We managed to right our relationship through numerous letters that crisscrossed the globe after that fateful meeting in a Saigon furniture store. Perhaps my journalism degree was put to good use; my writing skills enabled me to share my thoughts honestly and to solicit hers with sincerity.

As our trip to Hawaii grew closer, I addressed some things that I felt were important. I let her know that Uncle Sam required all military personnel and their families to attend a half-hour briefing on the do's and don'ts of R&R. Also, from what I've been told, every soldier goes through at least a day of culture shock in their new location. Apparently, after having adapted to life in a combat zone, you just don't snap out of it the moment you find yourself back in the civilized world. I had to prepare myself to expect everything to be different – people, activities, sights, sounds, aromas. All of this could be a shock. Not necessarily bad, just different. One guy told me he just kept flushing the toilet in his hotel room over and over. Something he grew up taking for granted now seemed so strange to him since we don't have indoor plumbing in the Nam.

On R&R, lots of guys are jumpy for days. They can't believe they are out of danger and are unable to relax and enjoy things. Not having to psych yourself up for a combat mission every day just doesn't feel right, in fact, it's actually uncomfortable! You'd think we'd be relieved, but unfortunately, that's not how it works. It's not something you can turn off with the flip of a switch.

The toughest thing, I told Vicky, and frankly this was difficult to put in writing, is the numbness that sets in over here. Like a deadening of your natural emotions. Many of us suffer from it, and we tend to bring it with us wherever we go. In the Nam, we lose touch with who we are. That essence gets lost, buried under the weight of what we do and what we've seen. In other words, I warned, I may be a little off-balance at first, but I was confident we'd be able to deal with it.

Vicky always wrote back promptly, and that inspired me to respond in kind, and so a steady rhythm of reading and writing developed between the two of us, and without a spoken word, our relationship deepened. Many times, it was a challenge for me to decide what to write about. There was not too much I could share with her about my life in the Nam, obviously, nothing about the nature of my top-secret assignments, nor did I want to tell her anything that would cause her to worry about me. Or of anything gross, like the week I spent mostly on the shitter, battling parasites. Boy, when those microscopic bastards take hold of your intestines, you have a serious fight on your hands. I was grounded until the meds worked their magic. So, I usually glossed over things and wrote about my family, my childhood growing up in the low country close to nature, learning how to farm, camp, fish and hunt, learning the names of plants and trees and stars. I told her how I transformed from Huckleberry Fin to GI Joe when I was about to start the fifth grade, and my father decided that I would continue my education at a private military academy.

Vicky told me about her parents, who ran a family business in southern California where they all lived. She was also close to her paternal grandparents, who lived nearby and her maternal grandparents in New England, with whom she'd spent summers in Cape Cod while growing up. She admitted, since she was an only child, that she may have been spoiled in terms of getting a lot of attention from these six special people, but also that they instilled in her the value of a good education, a strong work ethic, and the willingness to help those less fortunate than herself. They encouraged her to see the world before settling down, and that's why she decided to become a stewardess after graduating from UCLA. At some point, I drifted off to sleep and awoke to the announcement that the pilot was preparing to land, which I had sensed because my ears were popping.

My eyes were blinded by the brilliant Hawaiian sunshine. I had never anticipated that my feelings would be so intense as I scanned the area looking for Vicky. Taking in my surroundings as I climbed down the stairs to the tarmac, I knew I was not in the Nam anymore. It seemed like I had stepped out of a black and white movie and into a technicolor one. Once inside the terminal, I heard Vicky's voice before I saw her running toward me. She threw her arms around my neck, looked me in the eyes, and planted a romantic kiss on my lips. We were off to a good start.

After the R&R briefing, we took a cab to the hotel, and since Vicky had already checked in, we went directly to our room. I had barely closed the door when we were tearing each other's clothes off. Having spent the afternoon getting reacquainted, we fell asleep, entwined, a tangle of arms and legs. Emotionally spent and suffering from jet lag, we slept until almost noon the next day.

I awakened to the smell of Hawaiian coffee, pancakes, and ham with fresh pineapple and papaya. Vicky had ordered room service. As she was placing the breakfast tray on the bed, she said sweetly, "Once again, I didn't want to wake you, Sam. You were sleeping so soundly."

"Gee, I didn't fly six thousand miles to sleep, but thanks, I guess I needed it more than I realized. Did you sleep OK?"

I propped myself up, and Vicky sat next to me sipping her coffee while I picked up some fruit from the breakfast tray. "Yes ... yes, I did. It was wonderful sleeping in your arms. I don't know when I've slept better. I usually don't rest well in hotel rooms, but this is entirely different – and far better! When I am traveling for work, there is no chance of sight-seeing. Typically, we check-in to our hotel late in the evening and check-out very early in the morning, in order to be at the airport at least three hours before the flight. Our schedules don't leave time for much else."

"Do you like your work?"

"Yes. Despite what some people think, we are far more than glorified waitresses in the sky. I take my job seriously because I've been trained to know that it's a serious job. If something goes wrong, seconds matter, and I have to be on top of my game. You know, lifejackets under the seat, oxygen masks dropping in front of you, kicking off your shoes before sliding down the escape shoot. I'm sure you can relate. Thank God I have not had those emergencies, but I feel prepared to act if need be.

"Then, there are those times when you know you have made a positive difference, and that makes being a flight attendant rewarding – at least for me."

"Such as?"

"OK. Well, there was this time a few weeks ago. I had a cross-country trip from LA to New York, my most traveled route. This particular passenger was probably in her late seventies, and she had never flown before. She pushed the flight attendant button as soon as she sat down. She was going to her grandson's wedding on Long Island. She was so sweet; excited about the wedding but so nervous about flying. I reassured her as best I could before takeoff, but I could tell she was still very nervous, so I brought her a glass of sherry, and that seemed to help. I had work to do, but I made a point of checking on her throughout the entire flight. Once dinner had been served and cleared, I found myself actually squatting in the aisle next to her seat, and I talked with her until she fell asleep. I've never done that in my two years of flying, Sam. I know I helped her, and that made me feel really good about my work.

"So, tell me, what about you? How are you making it in Vietnam? You know, the flying?" she asked as she poured me another cup of hearty Kona coffee.

"I'm glad the monsoon season is nearly over. Constantly flying in bad weather just brings another level of stress to the job and gets to be old very fast. I never would've thought it would be so demanding, but I never experienced the monsoon before. I've never been completely soaked through to my skin. I've never lost my shoe walking through the mud before. At least the last part of my tour will be in the dry season.

"I'm flying with a bunch of awesome guys! My buddies keep me going. Maybe there's a pilot just a month ahead of me who has flown ten or twenty more missions than I have, and I see that he somehow keeps it together, and that inspires me to keep going. That's how I make it. I've learned to take one day at a time, and somehow the days pass by."

"What are your plans when your tour of duty is over?"

"I am a 'Government Issue' GI. I have a six-year commitment, so it really depends on what Uncle Sam wants to do with me. There are signs of the war cutting back, thank God. I am close to Tipper, my CO, who told me he thinks the military has a lot more pilots than they need, and because the war is winding down, they may give a lot of us an early-out."

"Would you take an early-out if they offer it?"

"In a heartbeat!"

"When will you know?"

"Tipper indicated things were in the works, but in military speak, 'in the works' could mean next week, next month, or next year. Certainly you, my love, will be the first to know."

Vicky had been rummaging through her suitcase and found what she was looking for. Handing me a new pair of swim trunks, she urged me to try them on. They fit perfectly. She stood facing me wearing a flowered bikini, which, on her, was very flattering.

"You know what, Vicky?"

"No, what?"

"I just love your navel. So small and cute. And your tummy is ... well ... so pretty. Just got to kiss it." I did, and then went on from there. Something we had never done before. It was nice. Very nice. It was late afternoon when we managed to get out to the beach.

Before dinner, we had drinks on our balcony and enjoyed the picture-perfect ocean view and the faint strains of Hawaiian music. Discussing our plans for the rest of our stay, scuba diving and snorkeling were on the list, and we decided to make arrangements for these adventures the next morning.

"I did some research – actually I asked a number of other stews – about what they recommended, and everyone suggested visiting the Pearl Harbor and USS Arizona Memorials. I'd love to do that. My father was a pilot during WWII. He spent most of his wartime in Europe, but I'd like to see what's here out of respect and be able to talk to my dad about it. I would imagine you'd like to do that, too, Sam."

"Sure," I said, topping my glass. "As a GI, that certainly interests me. And since I studied World War II during my military school days, I think I'll find it very compelling."

After a lovely dinner facing the beach, we sat at the outdoor bar, enjoying the Hawaiian musicians on the ukulele and drums, and watching lovely Hawaiian women doing the hula, which looked pretty impossible to me. Everything was so different here. The palm trees swayed in the cool breeze, and it was so comfortable, we stayed for quite a while. Our waiter kept refreshing our drinks. I thought of the culture shock warning and figured I had made a quick adjustment. First full day, and I'm absolutely fine here. Looking back, I had a little help from the Scotch ... and Vicky.

***

The next day, we didn't open our eyes until nearly noon. Vicky sat up and moaned, then stumbled out of bed, making her way to the bathroom. Through the closed door I could hear her retching. Not good. After a shower, she returned, her wet hair wrapped in a towel, her beautiful face a bit peaked. She flopped into a comfortable armchair.

"I don't know how you manage, Sam, but just like Saigon, I had way too much to drink last night. I might enjoy it while I'm drinking it, but the next day, there's hell to pay. My head ... my stomach ... I feel shaky."

"All you need is a little food in your stomach. I ordered room service while you were showering."

"Food? I don't know. Not now. Maybe later. I just want to feel normal again," she groaned.

"You will, you will. Don't make such a big deal out of this."

"Big deal! Well I usually don't have to run to the toilet the second I get up! And I usually don't start my day barfing my brains out! Here we are in this beautiful paradise. I thought we'd wake up and make love each morning. Instead, I'm a wreck. This isn't what I imagined. Maybe you did."

With that, as if she needed to emphasize her point, she flew back into the bathroom and retched again. She cleaned up and hobbled back to the chair.

"Don't you think we drank too much?" she asked weakly.

"Well, I see that you're having a bad time, and I'm really sorry, but you know, I'm OK, perfectly fine. Maybe because I carry more weight than you; you're so slender. You and I have different limits."

Although her body was lifeless, her head thrown back and eyes closed, she was listening. "Well, maybe you're right. I shouldn't try to keep up with you. Just the same, today it's nothing but black coffee and 7 Up for me. I have to lie down now," she moaned and crawled back into bed.

We spent the rest of that day at the hotel. After a few hours rest, we migrated to the lounge chairs on the beach and later dined at the hotel terrace restaurant. A woman of her word, Vicky stuck to 7 Up but didn't seem put off by my choice of beverage.

***

Over the next few days, we set out in a leased car with a picnic lunch in tow, and rented scuba and snorkeling gear to explore various beaches and the underwater life of Oahu. The neon-bright colors of various fish species, interesting coral gardens, and the exotic undersea plants moving with the tides were enrapturing and not to be forgotten. It was like being in a life-sized aquarium. As soon as we pulled our mouthpieces out, with the wonderment of children, we raved about the thrill of swimming up close with these incredible life-forms in their natural habitat. These were wonderful days.

Then it was time to spend a day shopping. Not a guy's favorite thing, but just being with Vicky and watching her get so excited in the shops of Honolulu was enough for me. She bought a few souvenirs for herself and some things for a few special friends. After I bought Vicky a puka shell necklace and a fragrant perfume, I was done shopping. It was odd, but I couldn't find it in me to buy anything for myself or anyone else that I would want to take back to Nam. It just didn't seem right. I was glad one shopping day was enough for Vicky. It seemed like a waste of vacation time to me; probably would to a lot of guys. But it made her so happy; I did not complain. However, before leaving the island, I did buy Nuwee some macadamia nuts. I wanted to show her my appreciation, but a more personal gift seemed inappropriate.

Besides, we had been made aware of the fact that the friendly South Vietnamese who helped us out might suffer the price after the war ended, so it was best not to give tangible gifts to these fine people. Yes, nuts are tangible, but they would soon disappear without leaving a trace!

***

The following day, we drove to the USS Arizona Memorial at Pearl Harbor to pay our respects and experience these historic sites firsthand. Since I was already familiar with the history of the surprise attack by the Japanese bombers that devastated Pearl Harbor, destroying the Arizona and resulting in the deaths of more than one thousand sailors and marines, I never imagined that visiting the site would have such a powerful effect on me.

From Pearl Harbor, we joined others taking a tourist boat to the USS Arizona. Through the clear, dark water of the Pacific, you could see the ravaged hulk of the Arizona lying in the silt about 40 feet below the surface. The brilliant white concrete and steel memorial stood over the warship, perpendicular to it without touching it, almost as though it was guarding the sacred remains from further assault. Its 184-feet span was high at each end and dipped down in the middle, forming an inverted arch. Windows dotted the sides. Our guide explained the memorial's form resembled a bridge. Architect Alfred Preis, an Austrian-born American, drew his inspiration from our country's history: the height of the first peak symbolized the strength of America before the attack; the dip in the middle captured the nation's shock and depression after the attack, and the second peak represented America's recovery and rise to power after the war.

The memorial was intended to honor the fallen. Of the 1177 men on board that fateful day, 1102 of them remain in the wreckage of the ship. The Arizona had become their tomb, a sacred place standing in testament to their service, never to be forgotten.

We learned that President Eisenhower approved the creation of this national memorial in 1958, with a budget of $500,000 to be publicly financed. After an initial flourish of interest, fundraising understandably took a back seat during the Korean War, and by 1960, donations had stalled. When several Hawaiian newspapers in support of the memorial publicized the dire situation, they caught the attention of Elvis Presley.

Elvis, at that time the King of Rock and Roll, was all too happy to headline a fund-raising concert, and his illustrious manager, Colonel Tom Parker, saw an opportunity for good publicity. Having been discharged from active duty on March 5, 1960, Elvis was an unwavering patriot and staunch supporter of the U.S. Armed Forces. On Saturday, March 25, 1961, little more than a year later, Elvis went all out to entertain those fortunate enough to attend in a sell-out performance at the 4000-seat Block Arena in Pearl Harbor.

Tickets cost between $3.00 - $100.00, and there were to be no free giveaways. The event poster advertised it as "Guaranteed 100% Benefit Performance. Absolutely all receipts from ticket sales must go to the USS Arizona Memorial Fund." Elvis not only paid all the other performers, but he also bought a $100 ticket for himself and several more $100 tickets to treat staff and patients at a local hospital, proudly donating $67,000 to the memorial effort. The concert is rightly credited with spurring on additional fundraising until the budget was in place.

Dressed in a gold lamé jacket with sparkling silver sequined lapels, a fit and handsome Elvis performed fifteen songs beginning with Heartbreak Hotel. The 45-minute concert was the longest of his career, and he would not stage a concert for the next eight years. Elvis would visit the USS Arizona Memorial several times after its completion. Upon Elvis' death in 1977, in a show of gratitude, the US Navy placed a wreath for him at the memorial.

On a sadder note, we learned of another concert at the Block Arena, on December 6, 1941, the evening before the infamous attack on Pearl Harbor. The Battle of Music featured several ship bands from the

Pacific Fleet competing for the championship. While the Arizona band had not qualified for the finals, it was invited to entertain the crowd with their music. That would be their last performance, ever, for each band member lost his life the next morning in the dreadful surprise attack.

We entered the memorial and walked from one end to the other, viewing the exhibits along its length and learning along the way. At a point in the center, the floor of the memorial was open to the water, directly above the ravaged hull of the ship. Here, it was customary to toss the *leis* we had each been given into the water out of respect for those entombed below. The brilliant tropical flowers stood in stark contrast to the murky remains of the once glorious battleship. I wondered about the after-life and whether the spirits of any of the fallen were comforted with these heartfelt gestures. I was struggling to imagine the horror experienced in the last minutes or hours of the 1102 men who were consigned to this watery grave. I had not really thought about my own death; I mean specifically. I know that I could lose my life in this war, but I never let myself think about the details. I had always imagined I'd live to a ripe old age and be buried in the family plot, under a moss-covered shade tree, not far from other Walkers. Now it occurred to me I could be entombed for eternity in some remote enemy land, in the burning wreckage of my plane. And would it have been worth it? World War II had a noble and righteous goal, and although the price was terrible, the Americans seemed to rally around the flag in support of our efforts. The Allies victory changed the course of history. Not so with the war in Vietnam.

I realized that the only person speaking was the guide; we visitors had been so deeply touched as we continued our experience we learned more about the infamous attack. On December 7, 1941, the brazen Japanese assault not only caught its target unaware but also in the worst possible condition. For our audacious attackers could not possibly have known that on December 6, the Arizona topped its tanks with 1.5 million gallons of fuel in anticipation of its return to the US mainland scheduled for December 8. The filled tanks fueled raging fires and violent explosions that added to the calamity, hastening the death and destruction, and shocked our nation to its core. President Franklin Roosevelt in addressing our stunned citizenry called this "a date which will live in infamy".

Meanwhile, Isoroku Yamamoto, Japan's Commander of the Combined Fleet of the Imperial Japanese Navy, prophetically penned in his diary, "I fear all we have done is to awaken a sleeping giant and fill him with a terrible resolve." He was right about that, for we never forgot. Sixteen months later, on April 18, 1943, the US killed Yamamoto on Bougainville Island in the South Pacific. Thanks to military intelligence, we shot down the aircraft in which he was being transported. We blew his ass out of the sky. The successful execution of Operation Vengeance was just one example of our 'terrible resolve'. It demoralized the Japanese and rallied the Americans.

We all know that ultimately the Allies would bring the enemy Axis to its knees. Although Germany officially surrendered May 7, 1945, bringing an end to the European conflict, the Japanese did not surrender until August 15, 1945, but not before we detonated atomic bombs in two of Japan's most populous cities – Hiroshima on August 6, 1945, and Nagasaki three days later. Convinced the U.S. would continue to inflict unimaginable damage, Japan's Emperor, Hirohito, announced his willingness to surrender on August 15, 1945. On September 2, 1945, in Tokyo Bay, on the deck of the USS Missouri, Japanese Foreign Affairs Minister Mamoru Shigemitsu signed the Japanese Instrument of Surrender while U.S. General Richard K. Sutherland and hundreds of American sailors watched history being made.

At the end of the long walk through the memorial, I beheld the interior wall known as the shrine, which seemed to be over two stories high. Neatly chiseled into white marble were 1102 names, each belonging to a man who met his maker that infamous day. While contemplating all those names, the enormity of the loss struck me. And these were only the men who were killed in this particular attack, on this particular vessel. Good men, duty-bound, husbands, fathers, brothers, and sons.

The price the world paid for World War II in terms of death and destruction was staggering. Estimates range from between 70 million to 85 million deaths throughout several countries around the globe. This includes not only military deaths but also civilian casualties and many who succumbed to starvation and disease. Almost 3% of the world's population at that time. Staggering. Mind-boggling. Incomprehensible. And here I am, front row and center, playing a key role in another war. Have we on the planet not learned anything about war? Or just not enough to avoid it at all costs. Will I end up another statistic? Will my name be engraved on a wall? Will my death have been for a just cause? This was really messing with my head. Maybe the R&R Don't List should prohibit visiting war memorials.

Vicky and I boarded the boat for the short trip back to land. On this ride, the visitors were a lot quieter and more solemn than on the first trip. We had planned to visit the Pearl Harbor Memorial next, but I was not at all in the mood. I felt badly about that, but I needed to get out of this place. If Vicky was disappointed, she did not show it. We got in our car and drove on. Vicky broke the silence.

"This memorial is certainly worth experiencing. My father shared very little about his time in World War II. I hadn't thought much about it until today. As a pilot, he was probably in some pretty dicey situations – oh, Sam, I'm sorry! I realize you are too! I didn't mean to be so insensitive."

"It's OK, Vicky. I understand."

"It's just that I got so involved in all the World War II information, and naturally, I thought of my dad. When we heard all those fatality numbers, I was so grateful that he was spared. And then I thought about all those families. So many good people receiving such tragic news. Oh, this is so upsetting. Good thing the sun is shining because I am feeling so depressed. How about you, Sam. Your wheels must be spinning, too."

"Yeah, they are. But right now, I'm going to turn these wheels right into that parking lot over there. Looks like a nice open-air place where we can relax and get something to eat."

It was so nice to be able to sit down in a comfortable spot, the cool breezes rustling the palms and soft Hawaiian music playing in the background. We were uncharacteristically quiet, our spirits having been crushed by the weight of history, up close and personal. Even Vicky wanted a drink. We discussed how fitting the memorial was; everything about it, its significant design, the inclusion of a fitting place to gently drop our *leis,* the historical story told, and the names of the fallen honored. It made us proud of our government. We wondered in vain why the Japanese didn't surrender when Germany did. Imagine if the atomic bombs had never been dropped. We had more to drink than to eat that day; the alcohol seemed a much-needed salve on our wounded spirits.

***

I guess I should have seen it coming. The next morning, we slept late again, and Vicky was hungover. This time, she was not only miserable but also angry.

"Sam, this is horrible! I feel so wasted, useless. Tired of spending another beautiful morning unconscious and then with my head in the bowl, retching. I don't know how you do it. Doesn't seem to make you sick at all."

"Oh, I don't know, Vicky, I've never seen anyone as sensitive to booze as you are. Maybe you ate something that made you sick. You know, we're not used to this Hawaiian food, and we really don't know what kind of seafood we've been eating."

"Oh, for Pete's sake, Sam. IT'S NOT THE FOOD!" And with that, she charged to the bathroom.

She wobbled her way back, sat down, drew herself up, and declared, "I think you have a problem with alcohol."

"Really? I have a problem? You're the one hugging the commode, not me!"

"Yes, I may be puking my guts out, again, but what good is all that booze doing in your body? Don't you think that's worth considering?"

"Maybe, but what's the point? I really feel fine!"

"Wait a minute! It's coming back to me now. You had to help me get to the car. When we drove away from that restaurant, you drove right over the curb. And driving back here, you drifted a few times. I was too screwed up to say anything; I was practically passed out. But now I remember it. That's not good. You could have caused an accident!"

"You're exaggerating. I was in complete control. I bet if we went downstairs, the car would be perfectly parked."

"OK. You're on. As much as I'd prefer to remain unseen at this point, I'm throwing some clothes on, and we'll go down together to take a look."

Once outside, it became clear I did not remember where I parked the car. I found myself scanning the parking lot but trying not to betray my clouded memory. In a minute, my cover was blown.

"Look over there!" Vicky exclaimed, pointing to our rental car, where it sat at a funny angle, more on the grass than on the pavement. "It was beached, not parked!"

I retrieved the keys from my pocket, and we moved the car to a proper spot. We returned to our room in silence.

"Sam, do you see it now? We both have a problem with alcohol. I have a different type of problem than yours. You might be putting yourself and others in danger, drinking and driving. My God, what about flying? Do you get into the cockpit this way?"

Looking back, I had been caught red-handed, but I put up what I thought was a reasonable defense. I told Vicky that I had fallen victim to one of the warnings of R&R. I failed to appreciate I was in a new and strange environment. I wanted to acclimate quickly so we would have a full vacation. I drank so much here only because I was in a celebratory mood and because the alcohol was so available. I didn't dare tell her that Uncle Sam really makes it much easier to indulge. Back in the Nam, a drink in the O Club only costs 25 cents!

That evening, our last in Hawaii, I suggested at dinner that we limit ourselves to only two drinks each. I told Vicky I wanted to prove to her that I could control my intake. I also wanted her to see that two drinks would not make her sick. It was difficult for me to stop at two, but I did, though I really wasn't sure whether I was doing it for Vicky or for me. Truth is, I had grown very fond of her and did not want to lose her. Our lovemaking was very tender that night. I told her I had fallen in love with her this week, and with tears streaming down her lovely face, she said she had fallen for me. We talked into the night about our hopes for the future and her concern for my safety. I never felt closer to her. She asked quietly, "When will I see you again?"

"I know this is a long shot, but we get two R&R's each year. I've been planning a trip to Australia with a buddy of mine, Ed Bearman. Any chance you'd meet me there?"

"Australia! I'd love that! I'll see what I can do about getting the time off when you tell me the dates. In the meantime, I do have another shot at Saigon in a few months. Let's try and make that work, too."

The next morning, we had to pack and get to the airport, so we did not have much time, but as we moved through the motions, we talked about the wonderful time we had here and the prospect of meeting again in the coming months. Since Vicky did not mention anything about alcohol, I figured we resolved the issue and put it out of my mind.

Chapter 18 Monsters

I had been back from Hawaii long enough to turn the entire R&R into a distant memory. In fact, if it weren't for Vicky's letters, I think I would have convinced myself that the magical time on that heavenly island was only a very vivid dream. Maybe I should have brought back a souvenir; something I could see, feel and touch, that would sit in my hooch and serve as testimony. Our next R&R was still four months away, and Vicky meeting me in Australia meant everything. Now that I was back in the Nam, I realized how important it was to have something to look forward to.

I felt bad for the guys who went on R&R without someone special to spend it with. Two of the most popular places to visit were Bangkok and Australia. From stories I heard, those who went to Bangkok mostly hung out in bars and hooked up with prostitutes. The ones who went to Australia seemed to do less of both, because not only were the Aussies so good to us, but also many of the girls there loved Americans and were willing to show it. I don't think I ever talked to a soldier who had been to Australia without getting laid, because guys returning from Australia regaled us with tales of epic sex with the most beautiful women, and none of these goddesses were prostitutes. But looking back, I realize that any guy who didn't get lucky there would never want to admit it! Guys will be guys.

***

Flying mission after mission in bad weather was wearing thin on all of us. Regardless of one's level of experience, the unrelenting torrential rain demanded intense concentration, sapped your energy, and tested every pilot's flying skills. According to the calendar, the monsoon season should have been coming to a close, but inexplicably, it lingered on. Rumor had it that the Air Force had developed and planted some type of seed in the upper atmosphere to cause it to rain more. We all laughed that off; it seemed so preposterous. I mean who could manufacture rainstorms other than Mother Nature? It wasn't until years later when I found out that what had been rumored was actually true, and it was buried under an innocuous and comical name: Operation Pop Eye.

Our tactics were relentless. We dropped more bombs, clandestinely, on the small countries of Laos and Cambodia than we dropped on Europe and Asia during WWII. Under the friendly moniker Operation Ranch Hand, we sprayed eleven million gallons of Agent Orange to defoliate dense forests, damage native farmland, and contaminate freshwater sources. Devastating napalm was used aggressively and in massive quantities that would dwarf those of WWII and the Korean War. And as if all of that was not enough, we changed the natural weather pattern. I began to wonder what else had we done that no one knew about. At this point, nothing would surprise me, but all of it made me ill. With my top-secret clearance, I was already privy to more than I wanted to know. I still loved my country and believed in the Red, White, and Blue, but I felt as though our flag had cast a dark shadow; our great nation had lost all pretense of human decency, honor, and the American way. At times it was hard to follow orders, to do what I had to do and to not feel like a monster. Well, I was about to look that monster right in its hideous eye.

***

As I suited up for a night mission, I hoped it would be my last in the soup. Sully and I were piloting together again, with Scotty and Ted as TOs. Along with Tex and Tipper, Sully had become a trusted friend whom I could count on, especially when it came to flying. This particular mission would be new for me, one that I had not previously flown. It would take us just across the Fence to a mountainous region where Laos, Cambodia, and Vietnam came together, a hotbed of war. There would be way too many SAMs to contend with and far too much artillery to avoid. On top of that, the night was black as coal. After we were on our way, but before going to pilot-to-pilot mic, I spoke up, "Scotty, you and Ted can relax back there. Nothing wrong up here, just a personal chat with Sully."

"Yeah, OK. Thank you, Sir."

"You've flown this mission before, haven't you?" I quietly asked Sully.

"Yeah, twice, and I gotta tell you, Sam, this one's gonna be a real bitch. Worse than the other two. You tellin' me you haven't?"

"Haven't had the pleasure. Guess I've been spared while breaking in FNGs."

"No way an FNG could handle this!"

"How'd it go on those other two missions, Sully?"

"Between artillery dodging and SAM sites, we were unable to get across the Fence on time and missed two of our target times. Hate to say it, but we've already missed two target times and may miss even more on this one."

"Yeah, I know. Trust me; I've been listening to you over there."

"Blackshield 743, this is Ramrod, how copy."

"743, go ahead Ramrod."

"I need you to go into a holding pattern in about ten minutes. I should be able to get you to your CCO point in about twenty minutes, copy?"

"Roger that, Ramrod."

"743, be advised, while holding you will be over a firefight. Pretty big one. You're at five thousand and clear of small arms, but you will be getting a lot of cloud-bounce light from the parachute flares below."

"Roger copy, Ramrod. Thanks for the heads up."

"OK, Sully, Scotty, Ted ... get your helmet sun visors down now or you will lose your night vision when those flares start going off. Also, go to O2 oxygen mask as a precaution. We could be dealing with a lot of smoke, even at this altitude."

We had settled into a holding pattern. Scotty had turned the volume up on the Saigon FM radio station to help pass the next ten minutes. The Doors song, *Riders On The Storm,* had just started to fill our plane.

'Riders on the storm.
Riders on the storm.
Into this house we're born.
Into this world we're thrown.
Like a dog without a bone.
An actor out on loan.
Riders on the storm.'

With the close of that refrain, the entire sky lit up as if by a gigantic technicolor flashbulb. Suspended between two cloud layers, the four of us in our modest aircraft were the meat in a cloud sandwich. About five hundred feet above our plane, the top layer sprinkled us with steady, drizzling rain. Below us at four thousand-five hundred feet hung a carpet of translucent fog. Flying in a cloud sandwich could have been fun, but in an active war zone on this stormy night, it was rather unnerving.

I had seen my share of nighttime firefights, but this was by far the biggest. The U.S. Marines on the ground below lit up Charlie's position by launching a barrage of one million candle-power flare parachutes. Interspersed among the bright white flashes of gun battle were sparks of color, as our ammo was punctuated with red tracers and the enemies with green. Those of us in the plane could not hear a sound due to our head gear and communication equipment, but given the enormity of the visual display, the sound of this firefight must have been ear-splitting for those below.

I had switched to total instrument flying. After getting a glimpse of the amazing light show, I had to stay focused on my instruments, so my head was in the cockpit while Sully watched below. We were anxiously waiting for vectors from Ramrod when Sully hit the pilot-to-pilot mic, cutting off The Doors just as they warned, ... *if you give this man a ride, sweet family will die. Killer on the road ...*

"Hey, Sam. Take a look, man."

"Take a look? Whadaya mean? Take a look at what?"

"At the monsters in the windshield."

"Monsters? What the fuck are you talkin' about?"

Then I saw them. Ghoulish doesn't begin to describe the menacing images in the windshield that were glaring back at Sully and me. While the gruesome face on a Halloween mask or a horror movie monster may initially shock or scare you, it is not truly unsettling because we view them within the context of a safe environment. This was different. Very different. The face I was looking at was returning my stare. It was real; it was breathing, and it was alive. Sinister was the word that came to mind. The cloud layers that enveloped our plane had created a light bounce from the flares below, turning our windshield into a mirror and breathing life into these monsters. Wearing helmets with sun-visors that covered our eyes and oxygen masks that concealed the rest of our faces, our reflections bore the countenance of something other worldly. When we moved ... they moved. The monster within had been exposed. Night creatures prowling the sky to kill. *Killers on the road.*

The constellation of explosions on the battleground swirled through the translucent cloud layer below our plane. These bright blasts of firepower projected a pyrotechnic light show onto the windshield, backlighting the monsters' ghastly reflection while pulsating through them, infusing these already sinister masks with an eerie glow and the movement of life. It rattled me. Not a good thing for a first pilot to get rattled. Then, suddenly, the radio came alive and snapped me back to reality.

"Blackshield 743, this is Ramrod. How copy?"

"This is 743, go ahead, Ramrod."

"Turn to a heading of three five zero degrees. Report CCO."

Five minutes later, "Ramrod, this is 743. We are CCO. Climbing to fifteen thousand headed to the chicken coop."

"Roger, 743. Suggest you listen on Guard. Looks like weather will be getting worse moving in between you and home in a few hours. Sure pilots out there will be talking about it."

"Thanks, Ramrod. Will keep ears on."

"Mr. Walker, we need a minute, Sir."

"Yeah, go ahead, Scotty. What's up?"

"Well, Sir, this delay in gettin' over the Fence has really screwed up our target times. I was just talkin' to a Blackshield out of Na Dang who is also working close by. They said they could work our next target. No way we can get there in time. I recommend we work the ones we got back toward the south. Also, heard an F-4 say weather really sucks between us and home."

"Yeah, I heard him, too. Sounds like a plan. Give me a heading to a target, Scotty."

"Turn to a heading of two zero three."

"Roger. Got it. Two zero three."

Time passed. Really shitty flying. I was being tested. To avoid the worst of the weather indicated on the cockpit radar screen, I had been constantly changing altitudes, which demanded additional power, and additional power burnt more fuel. The more we burned up fuel in this way, the less fuel remained for the mission and our return. It's complicated to keep up with constantly changing variables – at least when piloting an airplane. It's not like you can pull over at a rest stop, stretch your legs, lay your map out on the hood, light a cigarette, and sip on a Coke while figuring out what needs to be done.

"Sully, how about checking with Ramrod south of us to see if we can get home across the Fence down there."

"You got it."

"Ramrod 262, this is Blackshield 743. How copy?"

"Go ahead, 743."

"Say, Ramrod, we are about sixty miles to your northeast. Our freeway is backed up. Any chance of crossing your bridge?"

"743, we got a mess down here, but come on. We will work you in. Report twenty miles from Fence, and I will give you vectors to CCO."

"Roger, Ramrod. Thanks."

"Got to warn you, 743, slow down and reserve fuel. You might have a wait."

"Roger that."

Twenty minutes passed. Ramrod had us hold ten miles north of the Fence. Each time we called in, the wait time increased. I got on the horn.

"Ramrod, this is Blackshield 876, we are ten minutes from Bingo (critically low fuel level). We need to move now!"

"Roger, we got several Bingos. If you don't mind going wing to wing with a Bronco, I can bring you two over together."

"Let's do it, Ramrod."

Formation flying takes a great deal of concentration, and there is no room for error. The bad weather made this type of flying all the more dangerous. It was very quiet in our plane as we contacted the OV-10 Bronco. Fortunately, our planes were compatible for formation flying. With a lot of flight experience under one's belt, a pilot can maneuver his plane as though it were an extension of his body. The Bronco approached us from our left rear and tucked his right wing in about ten yards behind our left wing. That pilot was good. Together, we crossed the Fence without incident. The Bronco peeled off to the south and was soon out of sight. Visibility was low. The weather was getting even worse.

"Tactical Control, this is Blackshield 743. How copy?"

"Blackshield 743. This is Tactical. Go ahead."

"Roger, Tactical, we are seventy miles north on a heading of one five five for Long Thanh, over."

"Roger 743. Go ahead and contact Departure Control. You got a mess out there."

"Roger copy, Tactical. Departure Control, this is Blackshield 743, how copy?"

"Gotchya, 743. We were listening. Be advised, all instrument landing systems are down at Long Thanh, and Tan Son Nhut is stacked up."

"Roger, Departure. We now have a Bingo." We were dangerously low on fuel.

"Sorry, 743. Suggest you declare an emergency for Long Thanh."

"This really sucks, Sully."

I had no sooner said those words than we hit a wall of weather like nothing I had ever flown through in almost eight years of flying. I was not prepared for anything like this. It was the only time in my flying career that I would experience what is euphemistically called 'an unusual attitude beyond one's control'. This situation would test all of my training, my abilities, and my instincts. Options were limited. I sure as hell wanted to get through this, and I was keenly aware that three others were completely dependent on me for their survival. I had only one chance to do the right thing and do it well.

Emergency protocol called for keeping the wings level and switching to the main tanks, which were closest to the engines. Unusual aircraft attitudes on wing tanks could starve fuel to the engines. I switched the fuel tanks from tip tanks back to mains.

"Sully, get on the stick with me and just help me hold wings level."

"Will do, Sam. This is bad ... really bad."

"Roger that!" Dear God, make me everything I need to be.

Remarkably, our plane was now completely inverted, flying with its nose facing down, despite the fact that the vertical climb indicator and altimeter showed us to be in a three thousand feet per minute vertical climb. Our plane was upside down with its tail pointing to the sky, yet, incredibly, our gauges indicated we were climbing! Our plane was as powerless as a rag doll in a clothes dryer because a vertical storm column had us in the clutches of its updraft. Completely impotent, all we could do was ride it out and pray we remained in the vertical column. If we were thrown into a downward column, the divergent crossover would rip the wings from the plane, dooming us for sure.

"How much of this do you think we can take, Sir?" Scotty asked, trying to be brave, though I could hear the fear in his voice. I was scared shitless, too, but could not dare show it.

"Hang in there, Scotty. We should be OK shortly. Be sure you and Ted are strapped in tight."

"We are. Just never been through anything like this before. You?"

"No, Scotty. Can't say that I have, but we'll be OK."

Truth was, I knew that our wings could be ripped off at any moment, and I didn't know when the storm would spit us out. Then, suddenly it did! At twenty-nine thousand feet, the storm had thrown us out of her top, and I was ready to respond. I throttled back to forty percent power. Sully and I fought with everything we could muster to keep the wings as level as possible. The plane was still inverted, and we were badly shaken. Once again, I had to hide it. I was able to right the aircraft and began a slow descent toward the Fence.

"OK! Comm check. Everybody OK?"

Both Scotty and Ted had thrown up. I could hear the fear and fatigue in their voices when they confirmed they were OK.

"Well, the good news is, we came through in one piece. The other good news is it gave us some free altitude, which we needed. The bad news is we are dangerously low on fuel, gentlemen. I am making an emergency approach to Long Thanh.

"Long Thanh tower, this is Blackshield 876, how do you read?"

"Got you, Sam."

"Say, Eddie, we are declaring an emergency. Low on gas."

"Got that, Blackshield. All instrument landing systems are down. You got a two-hundred-foot ceiling, heavy rain, visibility less than a quarter-mile and wind, fifteen knots at one six three degrees. Don't know how you're going to get in, Sam."

"I don't either. It's gonna be interesting, but I gotta get this bird on the ground. Any traffic out there?"

"You kidding? We have been shut down for over two hours. Nobody, in or out."

Our on-board computers were not designed for shooting any type of aircraft instrument approach. They supported an entirely different purpose. Both Tex and Laddy made it clear that I had to be prepared to fly and land in extremely bad weather or without instruments, or both. As an FNG I was shocked to hear that, but I made it my business to prepare. During the course of many missions over these past several months, I had been taking note of the digital grids as they clicked off in relation to my position, particularly when I lined up on final approach to land, as well as at the one quarter mile mark from touchdown. I had also noted my time, down to the second, from when I crossed the Fence to when I got safely home.

I don't know if anyone else had ever attempted using this information to coordinate a precision approach for landing an airplane in bad weather, but I was about to try. It was my only option. My bag of flying tricks was empty, and the boys on the ground had no way of getting me down.

In my mind, I was formulating options based on several variables that had to be considered. This was not make-believe. No less than our lives were at stake. The weather sucked, we were almost out of fuel, and all nav aids were down, except for that old, World War II RDF. God bless the man who put that antique in a modern aircraft.

"OK, Sully, I just started my stopwatch. I am coming out of altitude for three hundred feet and going to sixty percent power. My best estimate to the tower's RDF is fourteen minutes thirty-seven seconds. My best guess is that we have twenty minutes of fuel at sixty percent ... tops."

"Sam, at three hundred feet we are going to be an easy target for Charlie."

"Yeah, I know. That's the weakest link in this chain. We got poor visibility, and it's pouring rain. Let's just hope Charlie has kicked back a little. Given our fuel situation and the distance to Long Thanh, this is our only option, as I see it, Sully."

"I know, brother ...I agree, and I'm with you. If anybody can do this, you can. It's just that Charlie has a little duck in 'um."

"What?"

"You know ... ducks and water. Ducks like bad weather for some reason. Charlie? Same shit! Nothing about the weather seems to phase the little bastards."

I had one shot at what I was about to attempt. At three hundred feet and at one hundred sixty knots, my RDF needle swung one hundred eighty degrees. The tower acknowledged my fly over. I dropped to just below two-hundred feet. We could barely see the ground, and I got a quick glimpse of the tower when I passed above it. In my mind's eye, I set up a teardrop approach. When I came around to a heading for our final approach, the visibility was down to several hundred feet. Rain was pelting down in sheets. I lined up the grid coordinate on the computer to match the runway. I knew what perpendicular coordinate line should click off at one-quarter mile from the end of the runway. Sure hoped they would match up.

"OK, Sully, give me gear down, three in the green, and flaps, thirty degrees."

"Sam, your call, but you got nothing in front of you that says there is a runway out there. Remember what happened to those two pilots that landed short a few months ago?"

"Call three in the green, Sully ... and flaps. NOW! And stop the small talk!"

"Three in the green. Gear down and locked. Flaps down, thirty degrees."

"My eyes are out of the cockpit, Sully. I want you to let me know when the computer clicks off X7888Z3484."

"Roger."

Twenty seconds passed. "Sam, reading X7888Z3484."

I said a quiet prayer, not my first on this perilous night.

"Roger. Props forward. Power back to indent. We are committed to whatever shows up in that windshield."

A more welcoming sight was not possible. The runway-lights were literally within a stone's throw. Scotty and Ted howled with relief. Sully exhaled deeply. I thanked God for granting my prayers. We touched down on the runway numbers and taxied to the revetment. We would live to tell our unbelievable tale and to fly another day. We did not know it then but would find out the next morning that we had less than five minutes of fuel remaining.

As a pilot, if you fly long enough, the one thing you can always expect is the unexpected. Not necessarily life-threatening shit, but mind-blowing shit. What I experienced that unforgettable night would put me in touch with a part of myself that I had not yet met.

Chapter 19 Shot down

I love flying; I wasn't tired of it. I wasn't afraid of the high risk, and I had learned to live in relative comfort within a shit hole. What I was tired of, was counting the days until my next R&R to Australia and having the remainder of my tour of duty hanging over my head. After returning from Australia, I would have to serve four months before zeroing out. That I could handle. The home-stretch. I had made it this far and damn it, I would get through the entire year. In five days, Vicky was scheduled for a three-day layover in Saigon, and I was able to arrange the time off to spend with her. Then, only two months after that, we would be in Australia together. Thanks to those times I'd be spending with Vicky, things were looking up. However, I continued to feel I was living in a violent black and white movie that I had seen way too many times yet still didn't know the ending.

Among the guys, there was a lot of talk about the war being over soon, but this had been going on for so long, I dismissed it as wishful thinking, as if we said it long enough, often enough, and loud enough, it would come true. I thought it very unlikely that someone would knock on the door to my hooch and say, "Pack your bags, we are out of here!" so I put those thoughts to bed.

Of all the people I had met, it was Sully who had made the most sense. I had only known him for a few days when he advised. 'When you don't think you can go one more day ... you go one more day, then you go one more day ...' and that is how I hung onto my sanity, by surviving one day at a time, not by grasping at fantasy.

The weight of a tour of duty in the Nam can crush you toward the end. Whatever people like Tex and Sergeant Wilson were made of, those who could just sign up for another tour was a trait I neither possessed nor understood.

Alone with my thoughts, when I contemplated the dismal reality of my day-to-day existence, I wondered what decisions I had made at such a young age that got me here. Maybe it had nothing to do with any specific actions I took, but rather it was just a twist of fate based on when and where I was born. And now I was hit with the reality that I was nothing but an expendable pawn, just one of thousands of hapless pawns being played in a losing game.

Now that I had a relationship with Vicky, I no longer considered myself a carefree flyboy. In a loving relationship with someone special, my life took on new value. New meaning. I had never considered my lack of telephone access here a problem, but once Vicky pointed out how difficult it was for two people in love to be deprived of something as commonplace as a phone call, I got it. I realized that in this dark and dreary lifestyle, I didn't have the luxury of hearing her voice if only to hear her say, 'I love you. Good night!' Thinking of what I was missing only made me more depressed. I knew I had to shake off negative feelings. If I wanted to survive, I would need to think positive and stay focused.

***

On a night mission in Cambodia, once again, I found myself flying into a black void. High cirrus clouds blocked any moonlight that might have otherwise lit the dark sky, but at least, it wasn't raining! My co-pilot was an FNG by the name of Jim Watson, who seemed like a nice enough fella. After about three months of experience with another AC, he was just about broken in. Skip, an experienced TO, was also partnered with an FNG, Tommy. The four of us were three hours into our mission on this starless night.

As an experienced pilot, I had learned to trust my instincts, but this time I couldn't get in touch with what was bothering me; I couldn't shake the nagging feeling that had invaded my gut. Then I remembered the night I arrived in-country when the hair on the back of my neck bristled. That, I thought, was primal fear. But this, fear about what? Flying combat? Maybe! Whatever it was had kicked my adrenaline into an afterburner state. I was experiencing the same primal feeling that invaded my psyche during my first five minutes in-country, but now, it gnawed at me even stronger, much stronger.

Ah, youth! At the tender age of twenty-four, you live with the unchallenged promise of tomorrow, even if you're a combat pilot. Although the prospect of getting shot down lingers deeply in any pilot's mind, you don't think the worst can ever happen to you. That belongs to the other guy. Pilots know to snuff out these thoughts whenever they show up; we've been trained to deal with that.

For some reason, the new TO could not get his headphones to work, and Skip had taken his off so that they could communicate face to face. In those few fateful seconds, a SAM locked in on us, and no one heard the ominous warning of the tracking tic.

BOOM! The SAM came out of nowhere and hit us hard. I've heard guys say that you can see a SAM coming at you. In this case, based on my actual experience, that is just plain bullshit! The shock of the impact was horrifying; I will never forget that feeling. The missile had sliced off four feet of the right wing. The right engine was on fire. I knew what had to be done, and we only had seconds to act.

We were about twelve miles northwest of the Fence and still over Cambodia. I made the urgent call, "Ramrod, this is Blackshield 876, MAYDAY! MAYDAY! MAYDAY!" Then to my crew, "EJECT! EJECT! EJECT!" words I had hoped and prayed I would never utter.

I looked to my right, where I could see flames advancing along the wing toward the cockpit, a fire that, in short order, would ignite the fuel tanks destroying the plane and everything in it. I noticed my copilot's side window had blown out, taking half of his head with it. The poor soul never even knew what hit him. Maybe that was for the better. Watson's vandalized body was slumped over in his seat, held in place by his harness. Nonetheless, I felt his neck for a pulse. Nothing! He would go down with the plane. The two TOs had already punched out. It was my turn to go. I sat up straight, helmet pressed against the headrest of the ejection seat, legs squeezed together and against the ejection seat, arms and elbows tucked in. I had been warned in training that while traveling at great speed on the way out of the plane, any body part or piece of clothing that happens to get caught against the airplane would result in grave injury or death. Time to go. I pulled the ejection seat face shield. NOTHING! DAMN! I could feel the heat of the fire advancing toward me. I knew the plane was only seconds away from blowing up.

This was my last chance. I reached down between my legs and pulled the secondary ejection handle. Violently, I was launched into the air. I was literally riding a rocket by the seat of my pants, shooting out of the plane on the ejection seat rails into the black void of the night sky. It felt like my intestines were exiting out of my ass! Propelled by rocket seat from the comfort of my cockpit into the fresh air, I was suddenly blasted by a two hundred-seventy knot wind. It was as though my body had slammed into a brick wall. I was about to pass out from the G-force when a fireball erupted below me and off to the side, catching my attention. The aircraft I had been sitting in just moments ago, had exploded.

The blood rushed from my head. Strangely enough, though I knew my body was hurtling at great speed from the moment I pulled the ejection handle, everything seemed to be happening in slow motion. I had an eerie but acute recollection of many last-minute details, as though I had snapped a picture of the cockpit on my way out to take with me on this impromptu trip. In the photo, my instrument panel had frozen in place, and I could see every dial quite clearly. The computer grid coordinates of my location stuck in my mind. I saw a bulge under Watson's left flight glove. Must have been a college ring. I found myself wondering where he went to school, when my ejection acceleration stopped, my seat separated from me, and I heard the swish of my chute opening overhead. I was forcibly jerked upward by my harness before gravity regained its rule, and I started drifting toward the black jungle below, my survival package dangling on a lanyard, in tow.

At this altitude, the night was as soundless as it was dark. Like a puppet suspended from controlling strings, I floated through pitch-blackness over enemy territory, anticipating my landing in a threatening triple canopy jungle. Everything had happened so fast; barely eight seconds from the missile hit to the punch out. If your response did not kick in immediately, you and your crew would be toast. Fortunately, I survived. I hope that Skip and Tommy would, too, and I prayed for Watson's soul. Now I had to start thinking clearly and strategically if I wanted to live to tell. I had to focus on the immediate present.

I was grateful that Charlie wouldn't be able to see my descent, but anxious that I couldn't judge when I was going to hit the giant-sized trees of the jungle below, the tallest of which could be as much as two-hundred feet high. I imagined a thick blanket of heavy foliage supported by buoyant limbs waiting to catch me, like the safety net ever-ready for the acrobat performing a high wire act.

The triple canopy jungle might sound lovely and exotic, but it is actually a very dangerous place. The plant-life density can be so thick that you can barely advance one step without using a machete to hack your way. Under these conditions, traveling is a very slow and exhausting process. Since you can barely see much farther than the nose in front of your face, you might very suddenly encounter the enemy, prepared and lying in wait for you, having heard you approach. And more than one enemy lurks in the jungle; those that employ a different type of weaponry. These bad boys include a deadly gang of animals, like poisonous snakes – Kraits, vipers, and cobras; predatory cats –

jaguars, tigers, leopards, and annoying critters – leeches, fire ants, and mosquitos.

As I continued to drift towards the hazardous jungle, an alien visitor in the black ink of night, I said a silent prayer. I would soon become not only an uninvited but also an unwelcome guest in hostile Cambodia. I had scrunched my body into a tight ball and was conscious of keeping my knees slightly bent, as I had learned to do in survival training, to minimize impact. It seemed like an eternity before I finally hit the triple canopy, and when I did, I hit hard. I had unhooked my facemask, which dangled from my helmet, and now the piney, minty smell of eucalyptus filled my nostrils as I plunged through a dense sea of leaves and branches that snapped at me as I passed by. When I finally came to a complete stop, I found myself hung up in a gigantic tree, dangling in my harness, completely surrounded by gnarly branches and huge leaves, in total darkness. From this vantage point, as I caught my breath, I figured I was suffering from the violent shock of ejection, not to mention being scared out of my mind. If I had gotten hurt, I couldn't feel it. My adrenaline was pumping like crazy.

I checked my wristwatch, but I could barely read the luminous dial, which I realized had been stained by torn eucalyptus leaves. I wiped the greenish goop away. It was ten minutes after two in the morning. I took inventory of my physical condition, starting with my face and then feeling my body from top to bottom. No breaks, thank God. I was very lucky to discover only a few minor cuts and bruises because broken bones and open wounds in a rescue situation like this drastically reduce your odds of survival. I impulsively turned on my PRC-25 emergency radio and then, just as quickly, cut it off. What was I thinking? I had no idea of how close I was to the ground. For all I knew, Charlie could be sitting quietly right below me, just waiting for me to descend. Don't be a dumb-ass, Walker!

I took off my flight helmet and strapped it to my side. Without the helmet, my hearing tuned into the night sounds of the jungle, and I could feel a breeze on my face. It was unnerving. Like all good flyboys,

I had a little unauthorized contraband in the leg pocket of my flight suit. Two half-pint flasks of Scotch. Macallan. The good stuff. I took a healthy gulp. Truth was, I needed it.

Through a break in the cirrus clouds, a half-moon illuminated the dense top canopy of the jungle as though a huge bucket of silver paint had been kicked over, spilling its contents on top of these exotic plants. Everything for as far as I could see dripped with the radiance of heaven's glow. It was an awe-inspiring scene that flooded me with feelings I will never forget. For me, the moon would never look the same. It seemed so close to me from my tree-top perch that I had an urge to reach out and touch it. There was a mystical presence here; a sense of peace, and as strange as it may seem, I felt a part of it. Even though I had never been more removed from civilization, I did not feel alone. In that magical moment, I didn't want daylight to come.

My breathing started to return to normal, and my vision was adjusting to the moonlight. I took out my compass. I knew I needed to head south in the morning. Taking stock, I was secure in my harness, and from what I could see, my parachute was so ensnared in the eucalyptus branches that I was not in danger of falling to the ground. I was totally exhausted and effortlessly fell asleep. After a few hours, I was awakened by a radiant tropical sun rising over the jungle, which had become alive with the music of thousands of birds. But instantly, my fear returned. I reached into my leg-pocket to retrieve a candy bar and took several gulps of water from my canteen.

I fought the urge to make a radio transmission, but I reasoned that suspended from the top of a giant tree I had a chance of good reception. What the heck! Take the chance! I turned on the PRC-25 and buried my face and the radio inside my flight helmet to muffle my voice.

"Guard, this is Blackshield 867, mayday, mayday, mayday!"

"Blackshield, this is Ramrod on Guard Frequency. You OK?"

"Yeah, so far. I am approximately thirteen miles northwest of the Fence. I know my approximate last grid coordinate. It is Z0087Y0343. A

SAM took us out. Don't know if the TOs made it. My co-pilot did not; he went down with the plane."

"Roger, Blackshield. Copy your transmission. The AWAC you were in touch with on your mission saw you go down. You need to stay off of this frequency as much as possible. Charlie is listening. Key your PRC-25 for thirty seconds at 1800 hours every day. Be brief. Thirty seconds will give us enough time to fix your position and keep track of you. Charlie won't have time to find you in thirty seconds. Key your radio over thirty seconds and you run the risk of Charlie finding you before we do. The objective of this game we play until we rescue you is that WE keep track of you but Charlie does NOT. With any luck, you should make the border in three days. We will have a Jolly Green pick you up."

"Roger Ramrod. If I can get out of this tree, I will start heading south. Will key my radio at 1800 hours for thirty seconds. Keep chatter low and quick."

"Roger that, Blackshield. God speed. Ramrod out."

SILENCE! I never felt so alone, so small, so insignificant, and so vulnerable. I felt pangs of despair and hopelessness. Then I jettisoned those negative feelings right quick. Fuck that! I got a Fence to cross and a girl to love! I put my helmet back on and pulled the clear face visor down for added protection while making my way to the jungle floor. I was a lot higher than I first imagined. I had 150 feet of one-half inch nylon rope as part of my survival gear. I couldn't see the ground, only the tops of the secondary canopy at least forty feet below. I tied off one end of the rope on a large limb. I clipped a climber's ring on my harness and then made a sliding loop on the rope. The crap you learn in survival school that you never think you will use! I disconnected myself from the parachute. I was now committed. What was I lowering myself into?

Inching my way down, I didn't want to make any noise. I tried not to emit a grunt or groan. I still didn't know what was waiting for me below, but if anyone or anything was there, it would not bode well for me. This was hard going. My feet finally found a place to rest on a large, sturdy mahogany tree limb. I had made it to the secondary canopy and recalled the textbook description – moderately tall trees as compared to the ones I just slept in and unusual plants that don't even root in the ground, rather they grow in these trees. Together they create a very dense layer of foliage that blocks much of the sunlight from ever reaching the ground below.

Pulling out my survival knife, I cut the rope, leaving me with about 100 feet remaining. Here it was quite dark as the higher growth did not allow much sunlight to pass through it. I tied off the rope again and started lowering myself when I heard movement below. I froze. I was looking into blackness. I couldn't make out anything. Whatever it was moved very slowly and then emitted the trumpet call of an elephant. Elephant? Man! No way … elephant? I'm above a freakin' elephant? Was this a wild elephant or one that the VC or NVA were using to haul supplies? There was no way to know. I had to stop, collect my thoughts. This was crazy! This situation seemed surreal, and my adrenaline was racing. I needed to calm down. I was in the Cambodian jungle, dangling dangerously from a piece of rope with an elephant trumpeting below me. I waited until I didn't hear him any longer. Then I waited another ten minutes just to be sure. The truth is, I was frozen in place. I was afraid to move a muscle.

The difficulty of my present reality kept sinking in by degrees. I had to get a grip if I was going to make it out of here. I kept at my descent systematically and with intense focus. Having come this far, I sure didn't want to fall to the ground now. Eventually, my rope ran out. I couldn't see the ground too well. I sat on a sturdy limb until my eyes adjusted to the dim light. Finally, the ground below, or I should say, what I thought was the ground, came into focus. It was a good thirty feet below me. I started feeling my way down. Limb by limb. Kind of like when I used to climb trees as a kid. Kind of, but not exactly. I slipped twice and badly bruised the inside of my left leg before finally setting foot on terra firma.

I stood motionless, catching my breath and listening for movement. Nothing! Other than a lot of bird chatter, the jungle was silent. I figured the elephant had moved on. I reached for my flashlight and screwed on the low-light red lens, again, using my helmet as a shield against being spotted. I took a compass reading and then started walking very slowly heading south. I had to check my azimuth every fifteen minutes since I could not see too far in front of me. I would pick out a tree perhaps fifty to seventy feet ahead in a southerly direction. Walk to it. Stop and repeat. It was the only way to stay on course. Another technique I had learned in survival school. Otherwise, you could be wondering in a big circle.

Although I wondered what happened to my two TOs, I couldn't take the chance of raising them on my PRC-25. Even if they were OK and safely on the ground, it would be difficult to find them. After having pushed forward most of the day, I was exhausted. The vegetation was getting thicker, and the going was tough. I had not covered much distance at all. I really needed a machete and a break of some kind. I found a hollow in a large mahogany tree and crawled in, pulling some dead branches around the opening to hide myself. After a fitful sleep, I awoke to find hundreds of mosquitoes lunching on me. I reached into my survival vest for the repellent. It helped. The tree's hollow offered safety and dryness from the heavy jungle dew. I decided to stay the night and get a good rest. I took off my boots and put on a pair of dry socks that I had tucked away in one of my flight suit pockets. Finally, it was time to call in, and I really, really needed to hear a human voice! I keyed my PRC-25 at 1800 hours and whispered.

"Ramrod, this is Blackshield 876, how copy?"

"We have you Blackshield. You OK?"

"Yeah, I'm OK. Anything from the TOs on my flight?"

"Roger Blackshield. We heard from them after your call. One of them is injured, but both are capable of moving. Leave them to us. We have you fixed. Gotta disconnect now. We are coming up on thirty seconds."

The radio went dead. I hated that the call had to end so abruptly, but I knew they were looking after my best interest. I lay there in the dark with a thousand things running through my mind. Skip and Tommy were alive. I wondered which one was hurt and how bad? My thoughts turned to the young co-pilot who had gotten killed. I mean, who was this guy? I hardly knew a thing about him, and now he was dead. His family would soon be getting the news they've been dreading ever since he signed up. Would my family ever be at the receiving end of such news? With a shiver, I put that thought out of my mind to focus on the here and now. Emergency flight rules before punching out called for the co-pilot to dial in a transponder code of 7777 so that F-4s, or 'double uglies' as they were known to Navy flyers, could find and destroy the downed aircraft and all top-secret material aboard. My co-pilot had been killed, and I had failed to do that, but the aircraft was already on fire, and I had seen it explode after I ejected. So, there was little reason to concern myself with that.

My brain bounced to Vicky. I remembered that we were supposed to meet in Saigon in five days. Fat chance of that happening, but then again, Vicky gave me a real good incentive to get out of this jungle. What would she think if I didn't show up? There was no way for her to contact my unit because I had never given her that information. Even if she started inquiring, as a civilian flight attendant seeking information from a top-secret military unit, she would run into a dead-end street. It would be awful for her. Unbearable. I must get out of here!

Now I had to stay focused on surviving. What about the presence of the VC or NVA? They had to be thick as flies in this part of Southeast Asia. Most likely, they would be NVA. I was in Cambodia and close to the Ho Chi Minh Trail. The NVA were seasoned, well-trained soldiers, whereas the VC were guerilla fighters who had rebelled against the South Vietnamese. But whether well trained or guerilla, the simple fact was, they all carried AK-47 assault rifles.

With this thought came the sound of distant voices, and they sure weren't speaking English. My heart started pounding. I felt like a helpless rabbit being hunted by a pack of angry dogs. As the voices got closer, I could hear their footfalls and the cracking of twigs. Now they were very close, passing just behind the tree where I had taken refuge for the night. As they walked by, I listened to their voices and tried to count them. I estimated a dozen. I could tell they were headed north. I was headed south. I was shaking all over. I did not risk moving until I felt confident that they were far enough away. I took a sip of water, ate another candy bar, and took another slug of Scotch. I was hungry, lonely, exhausted, and scared. I tried to sleep, but imaginary enemy voices kept waking me up. They were just the unfamiliar night sounds of the jungle. It was a very long, torturous night.

***

The next morning, after my eyes had adjusted to what little light there was, I took off my dry socks and put the originals back on. They were now dry. Another survival training tip: I had slept on top of the damp socks, and my body heat dried them out. I was very concerned about getting foot fungus. How many times as a GI had I heard that your feet are more important than your gun! I had heard about the trick of rubbing your feet down with eucalyptus leaves. The oil from the leaf was supposed to relieve the fungus, but I just didn't have any leaves handy now. It had never occurred to me up there, while I was drowning in eucalyptus leaves, to take some with me. Now I wish I had. Survival is in the details, and I had to get my act together. Fortunately, I had a small canister of antifungal powder in my survival vest and sprinkled that on my troubled feet.

I stepped onto the footpath the NVA had used. It made the going much easier and faster, but I was definitely taking a chance using their trail; it could have been booby-trapped, so I proceeded cautiously. I simply couldn't go another day pushing myself through impossibly thick jungle growth without a machete. I found myself stepping lightly and stopping every few hundred yards to listen.

I had traveled what I estimated to be two miles when I heard voices up ahead. I looked for cover, but there was nothing close by that would hide me completely, so I pushed my way deeper into the jungle. I finally came upon a large bush and crouched down behind it. My heart was pounding rapidly and my breathing very heavy. I hoped that I would not inadvertently move the bush and betray my presence. It was imperative that I remain calm ... stay perfectly still ... and wait ... and wait.

Again, I remembered something I was taught in survival school. The Vietnamese could smell Americans. Because our diet was so different than theirs, our body odor was dramatically different. And, boy, was I ripe! I could smell myself through my sweat, blood-stained, and dirt-soaked flight suit. Was I far enough away to not be detected? I was further away from them now than I had been last night, but then I was protected in the hollow of a tree. This group was walking fast and talking fast. Last night's group had passed me without notice. Maybe I would be lucky again.

All of a sudden, they were so close, I could see their outlines. I could tell by their pith helmets they were definitely NVA. By the rhythm of their back and forth chatter, I figured they were talking about general things, not the war. Once again, obscured in a forest hiding place, I went unnoticed. I waited for twenty minutes before getting back on the path. My alertness went up a few notches. I moved faster now. I considered how out-numbered I was. It would be me and my forty-five-caliber pistol against a band of twelve NVA with AK-47s. Not a fight I wanted to engage in.

I pushed on for what had to be another three miles. It was getting late, and I was spent. I looked at my watch. The day had flown by. It was almost 1700 hours, and I needed to get well off the trail to make my call and to find a safe place to spend the night. I had a few phosphorous capsules and a box of matches. One capsule would boil a cup or more of water. I had half a canteen of water left, the canteen cup, two teabags, and some instant soup. Just add hot water. I knew I needed hot food in my body if I was going to make it.

About two hundred yards off the trail, I came upon a small ridge. The bluff of the ridge dropped off and away from the trail to the west. I let myself down the face of the bluff where a six-foot wall of dirt protected me from view from the trail. I felt relatively safe. I found a flat, curved piece of palm wood that served as a shovel to dig out an area in the side of the bluff like a small cave. It took a good hour to hollow out an area large enough for me to fit in comfortably. To further protect myself, I placed branches and palm fronds in front of the small cave. I was concealed from sight but wondered if my stench was strong enough to lure a distant enemy. Hours later, I would find out.

I took out a phosphorus capsule and lit it. I heated up a cup of water and made instant soup. I drank it in three or four gulps. There was enough phosphorus still burning to heat another cup of water. With that, I brewed hot tea, and sitting with my back against the wall of the cave, I cradled the warm cup in my hands. I poured what Scotch I had left into the hot tea. It's what my mom would have called a hot toddy, and it was very soothing. I allowed myself a pleasant memory of my mom. She was the most giving person I had ever known. All of my friends loved her. I prayed that she would never be on the receiving end of the tragic news that Watson's mother would receive. Then I banished that thought from my mind.

I sipped the toddy until it was 1800 hours. I was determined to keep my voice down and to limit my call to less than thirty seconds. Ramrod confirmed that tomorrow I should be in range to rendezvous with a SEAL Team for a Jolly Green Giant helicopter rescue, that is, if I didn't get into any trouble. I snickered at the thought. *'Trouble? Man, you're already in trouble!' Who knows, maybe I would make it to Saigon in time to see Vicky. That'll keep me going.*

I took off my boots and put on my dry socks again. My feet were very dirty and smelled foul. I wiped my exposed neck, face, and hands down heavily with repellent. I took the small mosquito net from my survival kit and secured it over the front of my little cave as best as I could. It helped tremendously. I actually slept.

***

At 0300 hours, I awoke with a start to the sounds of NVA chatter, and they were much too close for comfort. I remained completely still, not daring to move a muscle, while I figured out what, if anything, I could do. If they were going to find me, they'd either kill me immediately or force me along with them, to the place where I would either be executed or become a POW, but not before suffering some really unspeakable torture. I made up my mind that if I had to go down, I'd take as many of them with me as I could. Without making a sound, I sat up and got hold of my pistol. My heart was pounding, and sweat soaked my body as I tried to steady myself. BOOM! A shot rang out! But that shot did not hit me. I heard a lot more chatter; they were definitely excited or agitated about something. I remained still, but ready. Not long after, their voices began to fade, and it became apparent they were continuing on their course, away from me and my hiding place. On some level, I felt relieved, but not understanding what had actually happened was unnerving. After that, I remained awake for quite a while; my mind was racing. I thought of my friend, Dicky, the artillery captain, and the conditions on the ground that he and so many other soldiers had to endure in this war. I realized how much better I had it as a pilot – sleeping in comfort and the relative security of my hooch, my air-conditioned hooch. Waking up to a hot meal, returning from my mission to a hot shower, cleaned quarters, fresh laundry, another hot meal, and drinks at the O Club. I realized that despite the commonality of the American GI, each of us, or groups of us, would experience very different realities during our tours of duty.

***

After a while, I managed to get some sleep. When I awoke, I became acutely aware of every ache and pain in my body. That's when I realized I definitely had foot fungus. My feet were swollen, and the blisters on my heels and the balls of both feet were the size of quarters. They had broken, exposing painful, raw, red skin. I used what little antifungal powder I had left, sprinkling the contents on my feet before putting on dry socks. I waited until dawn to put my boots back on. I dreaded it. They were soggy and smelled awful, and I knew that pulling these stinking boots over my wounded feet would set them on fire.

Once out of the shelter of my tree, I scanned my surroundings. There was no sign of the NVA, and I got back on the trail. I had not gone far when I saw it; something that looked like a shredded piece of clothing. Then I realized – no one over here would be wearing black and yellow stripes. I was looking at part of a Banded Krait, what was left of it after having been blown away by a shot from an AK-47. These highly venomous snakes are nocturnal creatures, averaging six feet in length. I guessed that the NVA marched right into its path, startling it when it would be most active. If the snake managed to bite one of them, he likely died within the hour. So, the snake was either shot just for interrupting their march or to avenge one of their own. Much later on, in hindsight, I came to believe the snake might have actually saved me that night by distracting the NVA. Or was it the enemy who saved me that night, from the slithering Krait?

Nothing was going to stop me now. I was emboldened by my survival thus far. Though I could have easily been distracted by my painful feet, I put mind over matter. I was more determined than ever to get out of this alive. I decided to stay off the path for a while, spooked by both the NVA and the snake. After my detour, when I returned to the path, I heard Vietnamese voices. They sounded close, and I quickly took cover behind a large tree. There were only two NVA this time, and they stopped abruptly. I didn't know if they had smelled me. Then one of them did something that really amazed me. He tilted his head back and shot his nose up in the air like a determined hound dog trying to pick up a scent. That's exactly what he was doing; trying to pick up my scent. CRAP! They had found me!

They crouched low and brought their AK-47s to the ready-to-fire position. The soldier that picked up my scent said something to the other, and then they started toward me. When they were less than fifteen feet away, why wait? flashed across my mind. I don't remember pulling out my Colt .45, but I do remember taking dead aim at the young soldier closest to me. The first round rang true. It took off the top of his head from his eyebrows up. I wielded and put two rounds in the second soldier, just as he was about to fire his rifle. Both rounds found their home in his chest. Two NVA now deader than doornails. Can't smell me now, mother fuckers!

I was shaking out of control. I knew I needed to get them off the trail. Grabbing their ankles, I pulled both bodies for at least fifty yards before stopping. I couldn't bring myself to look at them, but I dragged them another fifty yards before giving up. These bodies probably weighed no more than 125 pounds each, but this effort had sapped almost all of my strength, and I just couldn't go any further. I covered them with leaves and branches and continued to head south deciding to stay off the path. Other NVA would surely be looking for me now. A .45 pistol does not sound at all like an AK-47, but it makes a lot of noise!

Though the vegetation was not as thick as the day before, it was rough going for the next several hours. When I came across a stream, I was absolutely ecstatic! After removing my boots and socks, I waded into the cool watery path and slumped down in an exhausted heap. In the last few hours, I had to live by my wits and kill two enemy up. That encounter could have resulted in my untimely end. My adrenaline had kicked in big time, several times. After facing the severity of these threats and having to drag those two heavy, lifeless bodies to their shallow graves, I was mentally and physically spent.

I took a long drink that I desperately needed and sought refuge lying in the stream, letting the fresh, clear water bubble around me, isolating me from this dangerous world.

I had now killed seven people up close and personal. It sickened me. As I studied the blood of other men on my hands and my flight suit, I reached into the depth of my soul. What had I become? Frantically, I scrubbed my hands long and hard to rid them of any trace of my victims. *Out, damned spot!* I thought, scrubbing even harder. Then I walked further upstream to clean waters before I would take another long, refreshing drink. I sat down on a rock to rest my weary body and to eat my last candy bar when I noticed a mango tree just on the other side of the stream and several large mangos that had fallen to the ground. I gobbled up one of the luscious fruits and put another in my flight suit. Refreshed and somewhat rested, I started to breathe normally again. The sugar from the mango had given me a huge burst of energy. I had to keep moving. I had to block this most recent incident out of my mind. I recalled having read somewhere that people in extreme survival situations can die from 'shame' more than anything else. When I thought of killing the two NVA soldiers, I remembered what I had been taught about soldiering, 'Hesitate and you die. It's either you or the other guy.' I concluded I had no other option than to shoot to kill. When I would die, I decided, it wasn't going to be because of shame. Fuck that!

The stream flowed south. It was cool and shallow, barely a foot deep. Walking in the middle of it I was able to make good time. Then, up ahead, I saw smoke. I immediately went deep into the bush, where I crouched and listened. I could hear the clanking of metal against metal, probably cooking utensils, and the soft voices of several people talking. I waited for what had to be an hour. They were still there. I decided to take my chances and go back to the trail, soon realizing that was a mistake. The trail led me right back to the stream and the NVA campfire.

I picked up an azimuth ninety degrees from the trail and headed due west for about a quarter of a mile before heading south again. As before, moving through this thick underbrush was slow and draining. I found myself so tangled in twisted vegetation that I had to back out and try another approach, and I lost valuable time. I had come too far and endured too much to be captured now. I had absolutely no intention of becoming a POW. I decided then and there that I would fight to the death rather than be taken alive. I had spent so many hours in this torturous route that I had lost all sense of time. I was back at the stream, which though not the plan, was comforting. Checking my watch, I found it close to 1800 hours, and I was literally joyful at the prospect of making another radio call and hearing a friendly American voice. Ramrod assured me they had a fix on my position and that I was well-situated for tomorrow's planned rescue near the clearing.

"That's music to my ears, Ramrod. Thanks!"

"Let's get off this frequency, Blackshield. No time to blow your cover now. Ramrod out."

And with that, he was gone. As quickly as the call had begun, it was terminated. I replayed his warning in my weary mind, *No time to blow your cover now!* I would spend one more night in the jungle, my third. Actually, my fourth if I counted the time I spent in the tall tree. I could make it. I would make it. Now I just had to find a safe place to conceal myself for one final night, absent my enemies: the NVA, tortuous mosquitoes, and deadly snakes. I wondered how Ramrod knew I was standing in a stream. Either he could hear it or because he knew exactly where I was. I figured they would have put a topography map over my known position and read the terrain. How else would they have known about the clearing where tomorrow, I would rendezvous with my rescuers? It was comforting to think of the dedicated men working hard to find me and bring me home, and for that, I would be eternally grateful.

As luck would have it, I found another huge mahogany tree that had a hollow in it. I had become an old hand at finding secure campsites in the jungle and making do with so little during my unfortunate stay. In some ways, my days as a country boy growing up in the woods was paying off. In others, I had survival training to thank as well as my experience with Mitch on Red Mullet Island. And the source of my motivation was certainly Vicky, my loving mom, my sister, and my father. I gathered several arms-full of leaves to create a natural mattress, which made a definite difference comfort-wise. I set up my mosquito netting to shield the hollow and placed branches over it for cover. Once tucked inside of my lair, I realized my body was hurting in places I didn't even know I had. But now, I could rest. My rescue was scheduled for 0500, only a few hours from now. Dear Lord, please don't let me sleep past my appointment!

I warmed up another cup of water. Drank my last instant soup and last cup of tea. For dessert I had the second mango. I couldn't remember when anything tasted so good! Fortunately, my feet were dry. I was glad I had washed them and chosen to go bootless when possible. The ground had been dry, and except for my socks being a little soiled from the jungle floor, I knew I had made the right decision in leaving my boots off for a while. Tomorrow, if I weren't rescued, I would have to find eucalyptus leaves and squeeze out their medicinal oil. I would soak my feet all day if necessary. I could no longer ignore the problem; I realized that without my feet, I was a dead man. Utterly exhausted, I fell asleep.

***

I awakened around 0400 hours. Soundlessly, I pulled my damp boots over my dry socks. This was the day that I would be rescued, God willing. I felt rested, restored, and excited despite the pain radiating from my aching feet. As much as I hated to get moving again, I knew it was time for me to go. I decided to get back in the stream and start my trek to the clearing. As long as I stayed in the stream, I could feel my way south. It would be light enough to see in an hour.

The rising sun illuminated the most beautiful thing I had seen in a long time – a clearing about half the size of a football field. The site of my rescue. The morning dew on the green grass sparkled like diamonds in the early sun. It was as if I had stumbled into the Emerald City. And then I saw it! Only one problem, but it was a big one! The little clearing had visitors and not the kind that would welcome me. About a dozen NVA were cooking breakfast next to the stream at the other end of the wide meadow. I took cover before they could see me. I had to turn on my PRC-25, but I needed cover to do that, and I had lost my flight helmet somewhere during this ordeal. I stepped behind a large tree and faced away from the breakfast party. They were at least seventy-five yards away, and I prayed they would not be able to hear me. I made the transmission.

"Jolly Green, this is Blackshield 876, how read?" I whispered into the PRC-25 mic.

"Hold your mic button down, Blackshield ... OK, we got your exact location on a map. Can you see the clearing to your south?"

"Yeah, and right now, Charlie is at the south end, making breakfast. About twelve of them."

"Yeah, roger, Blackshield. Give us a minute. I got two Cobras with me. We need to take out that campsite."

"Roger."

What happened next was an amazing display of military might. In less than two minutes, two single-engine attack helicopters approached from the north. They had flown low, downwind, and away from the clearing so as not to be detected by the NVA, and I knew they were well aware of my location and would keep me safe.

The Cobra gunships fired two flechette rockets, which are made up of several dart-like projectiles clustered in an explosive warhead. Two of these could easily destroy an area the size of a football field. In one pass, they annihilated the unsuspecting enemy camp along with everything and everybody in it.

"Blackshield 876, this is Jolly Green 19. How read?"

"Got you Jolly Green, but I am afraid I am about to lose my radio. Battery low."

"Not to worry, Blackshield. You should have a visual on us about now."

"Yeah, I do."

"Just step out of the jungle. We are coming to you. Will sit down about twenty yards from the edge of the clearing."

A few minutes later, and oblivious to my burning feet, I ran like a track star toward the open door of the huge chopper. A set of strong hands pulled me in, and we were off in a matter of seconds. "Sit back, Sir! Try to relax. I'm medic Hogan Trusdale. I need to take your vitals and get you hooked up to fluids. Here, take this quinine tablet. You have probably been exposed to malaria."

The medic carefully examined my entire body. He said most of my cuts were getting infected and that my feet were in very bad shape. I was also suffering from dehydration and exposure. Under my clothing he found and removed more than a dozen leeches which, to my horror, had attached themselves to various parts of my body. They had been sucking my blood while using me to hitch a ride through the jungle. It's amazing where these slimy suckers made their homes! Within an hour and a half, we landed at Tan Son Nhut Air Base, where an ambulance was waiting to take me to the base hospital. The chopper pilot spoke up as they were removing me from the Jolly Green.

"Sam, at the base hospital, they'll get more fluids in you and give you a good physical. They usually let you get back to your unit within forty-eight hours if you're not in too bad a shape."

"How many pilots have you rescued? And by the way, what's your name? I want to know who to thank."

"Name is Chief Warrant Officer Al Smith, and I'm from South Carolina. You are the twenty-eighth pilot I've picked up, and you are in better shape than most."

"You're kidding, South Carolina? Where in South Carolina?"

"Beaufort."

I shook Al's hand.

"I am from Charleston. Small world."

"Well, sure glad I could save a soldier from my home state. Just up the road, at that!"

"Say, Al, any word on the two TOs that were with me?"

"Yeah, they were picked up late yesterday by another Jolly Green. One of them has a broken arm, but other than that they will make it. Look, I've been doing this a while. This is the eleventh month of my second tour as a Jolly Green jock. Most, and I do mean most pilots and crew that get shot down in Cambodia or Laos just aren't heard from ever again. Most get busted up on impact, get captured or panic or make mistakes. You three guys were lucky. Count your blessings, Sam. You're one of the lucky ones. Get well, now, you hear? The ambulance is waiting for you."

"Yeah, Al. Three of us were lucky, but I lost my co-pilot. Give my thanks to your crew and the guys in the Cobras. You've rescued so many men ... God bless you."

"So sorry to hear about your co-pilot. That's tough. I will pass your good words along. Take care, Sam."

"Hey! When we're both back home, let's get together for a few cold ones and some shrimp 'n grits. It's on me!"

Chapter 20 Convalescence

I was loaded into the back of the ambulance like some kind of sick person. I wanted to sit up, but she would not let me. "You need to lie down and just relax now, Mr. Walker. I am Nurse Specialist Lieutenant Valerie Kern, and I will be taking care of you."

"Whatever you say Nurse Kern," I agreed, acknowledging that she was indeed the boss. She was not only in charge, but also quite tall, extremely professional, and 100% American. I started to feel better already.

In the hospital, I was given the once over more than once. They X-rayed me from head to toe. They pumped fluids into me. My cuts and bruises were attended to. I was put on antibiotics. My feet were soaked in an antifungal solution every four hours. The burst blisters, still painful and raw, were cleaned with something that burned like hell, then dressed with gooey salve and covered with thick white bandages; I looked like I was wearing Eskimo mukluks. The medication they administered to rid me of parasites had me on the toilet for the early part of that night, expelling from me all kinds of gross stuff. After the great purge, weak and exhausted, I slept like a log until ten the next morning when I was awakened by the caring and efficient Nurse Kern.

"How was your night, Mr. Walker?"

"Sam! Please call me Sam."

"OK, Sam, how did you sleep?"

"You kidding? After three nights in the jungle, four if you count sleeping in the tree, and after the parasite medicine ripped through me like a tornado, I slept like a baby. So, when do I get out of here?"

"Probably not for a few more days. Because of your high clearance and the fact that you're a pilot, well … let's just say they will require you to meet with the hospital psychiatrist before you can be cleared to return to your unit."

"Yeah, whatever. Say, my girlfriend, Vicky Pullman is due in tomorrow. Could someone get word to her that I am here? She'll be staying at the Caravelle Hotel."

"I will take care of it myself on my way to the hospital. It's just a ten-minute cab ride from where I live on base. You owe me a drink, soldier," she said with a wink.

"Glad to!"

"So, is your girl from the states?"

"Yes. Vicky's American, but we actually met here in Saigon several months ago." Then I proceeded to tell Nurse Kern how we met and about our time together in Honolulu.

"Wow! I have heard some tall tales over here, but nothing that comes close to that one! Sounds like you have a real keeper, Sam. I look forward to meeting her. Tell you what. I will bring Vicky back here with me; otherwise, she might have trouble getting on base since she is a civilian."

"That would be great, Nurse Kern. Thanks! I really appreciate it, and so will Vicky."

"Make it Valerie, OK?"

"Sure. Yeah, thanks, Valerie."

"Now, let's take a look at those feet." Valerie removed the bandages, soaked my pathetic feet in a salt solution, slathered some antibacterial cream on the blisters, and bandaged them up again. She was good!

"Sam, I must tell you, you are not out of the woods with your feet. You need to stay off them for a few days and stay out of those sweaty boots of yours until these blisters have a chance to heal."

"How much time are we talking about?"

"Three or four days, at least, maybe more."

"Well, I am supposed to be getting a 72-hour pass about now to see Vicky, so that gives me some time to heal."

The next morning, I got out of bed and limped to the bathroom to clean up for Vicky. I took a long shower and removed my bandages so I could wash my wounds and blisters. Boy, did that hurt! In the process, I found more than a dozen leech marks on my legs, crotch, and butt. Gross! It was the first time since my rescue that I had taken a look at myself in the mirror, and I was shocked at the toll those four days had taken. My eyes were bloodshot, my face was red and swollen from insect bites and covered with a dozen or so cuts, scratches, and purplish bruises. Having lost weight, I looked pretty scrawny. I figured that Vicky would get upset with just one look at me but hoped that she would realize that my ordeal was over, and that I was safe and sound and in one piece. I would just have to convince her. By 0800, I was showered, shaved, bandaged up, dressed in military pajamas, and sitting upright in my bed, eagerly awaiting her arrival.

All of a sudden, Vicky burst into my room and rushed to my bedside, exclaiming, "OH, MY POOR SAM!" She threw her arms around me and held on tight. Then she drew back, her eyes scouring every mark on my ravaged face.

"Oh, Sam, you're here," she quivered. "You're safe, and not badly hurt. I am just so, so grateful that you made it!" Then she sat down on the bed beside me, seeming somewhat relieved now that we were together and she could see my condition with her own watery eyes.

"You sure look wonderful, Vicky!" I smiled from ear to ear.

"You look great for a guy who has been through a meat grinder!" For a moment, I sensed she would burst out in tears from the stress of worrying about me, but she quickly changed topics.

"Valerie explained everything to me on the way over here, and she's trying to push your evaluation through this morning so you can get out of here. She said you should use the hospital phone to call your CO, since it's time for your 72-hour pass. I mean, he would let you take this leave as planned, right?"

"I can't imagine him saying no. Come on, let's call him right now. I understand he's gotten word that I made it, but I haven't spoken to him yet." I was reaching for my robe and slippers when there was a knock on the door.

"Come in," I called out and was astonished to see Tipper, Mitch, Tex, and Ed stride through the doorway.

"Oh, my God! All four of you! This is too much! Thanks, guys."

Tipper spoke first, "Well, we knew you just got back and figured you could use a couple of things, especially since Vicky was coming in for a visit."

With that, Tipper dropped an overnight bag of clothes and toiletries on the bed. He and the others introduced themselves to Vicky. They were real officers and gentlemen. At that moment, I felt part of a brotherhood with these fine men that I hadn't experienced before. Though outwardly modeling manners and charm, behind that façade stood a combat warrior, always prepared to take any action necessary, without any fanfare, but with quiet resolve, and calculated moves. Action that would be effective and suited to the situation; lethal if necessary. For the first time, I recognized this as the demeanor of officers and pilots, not often found in non-combatants and civilians.

"Don't let it go to your head, Sam. We really came to check out Vicky, here, since we've heard so much about her." Tex chuckled, then continued, "Well, young lady, you sure got your hands full with this lad. Don't let those boyish good looks fool you. The son-of-a-bitch is up to mischief all the time, and he gets away with it. Damnedest thing!"

"Gee, thanks, Tex, but I think I got his number. Hey look, if a fella can get four men like you to come by, there must be something to him other than his flyboy abilities. Frankly, I judge a man by the company he keeps, and you four just put a few more feathers in his war bonnet."

"When I heard that Sam had punched out into the Cambodian jungle, I was very worried, but at least I knew he'd know how to feed himself," offered Mitch with a smile.

"Damn! You were right about this young lady. Beautiful AND charming!" said Tipper chuckling.

"You said that about me, Sam?"

"Well, yeah! It's true."

"Hey, Mitch, how are my TOs, Skip and Tommy doing?"

"Well, luck was on their side. A Special Forces unit on patrol heard them hit the trees and camped out underneath them until the next morning when they completed the rescue. Tommy has a broken arm, but Skip is in one piece. They were worried about you and were real happy to get the good news about your rescue. I'm sure the three of you will have lots to talk about when you can get together again."

"I've been thinking of writing a letter to Watson's family. Not sure what I'll say, but I'd like to comfort them. At least, I can assure them he didn't suffer."

After each of my buddies told a little about themselves to Vicky, Tipper stood up and changed the subject, "OK, we have to pick up Tommy and Skip and get back to the unit, but I got something for you to consider. Let me run it by you. Sam, you are scheduled to go to Australia on R&R in less than thirty days with Ed here. I've talked it over with a few of the pilots, and we all agree you should move that date up and get your ass out of here ASAP so you can recuperate. Two pilots have volunteered to swap slots with you and Ed. You could leave here in four days, right after your stay in Saigon. Now, that having been said, Vicky, I went through channels to Pan Am and got approval for you to change your vacation dates so you can leave for Australia directly from Saigon, too. You'll be flying a Pan Am commercial flight; Sam and Ed will be on a charter, but you'll all wind up at the same airport."

"Really, Tipper? You did that for me?"

"Well, for you and Sam, here. Once I explained the situation, they were happy to make it work. They don't call Pan Am the Freedom Bird for nothing."

"Sam, no sense in coming back to the unit. Let Ed here pack your bag and meet you at your hotel in Saigon on Friday. We'll let Tommy and Skip know you are OK."

Vicky would arrange for her roommate to pack her bag and send it via Pan Am to Australia so that it would be waiting for her. The guys each gave Vicky a big hug, shook my hand, and left. Of course, Tex stole a kiss square on the mouth, and made sure that I saw it!

"Thanks again for coming, guys. Tell Tommy and Skip I will see them when I get back, and we can compare notes about spending the night atop a giant jungle tree. Please let them know how happy I am that they made it."

As they were leaving, someone I had not yet met, entered. Extending his hand, he introduced himself, "Hello, Sam, I'm Dr. Jerome Cusack, head of psychiatry. I just need to ask a few questions before we can let you go."

"Should I leave the room, Doctor?" Vicky offered.

"No … no, not at all. This should only take a few minutes. That is if it's OK with Sam?"

"Sure, OK with me. Fire away, Doc."

"Sam, I've read the report you wrote. Allow me to go over it. I'd like to read it aloud, and then we can talk."

Vicky had not heard any of the details that Dr. Cusack was about to read, and by her posture, I could tell she would not miss a word.

"After you ejected, you landed in the top of a tree in the black of night. Having spent the night in that tree, you then managed to come down from a height of about 200 feet without serious injury and then survived three additional nights in the hostile Cambodian jungle.

"You lost your co-pilot. He was killed when the SAM hit your aircraft. You came face to face with two NVA, and you killed both of them at essentially point-blank range. Then you dragged them a hundred yards through the jungle to hide their bodies. In spite of sore feet, little if any real food, dehydration, and exhaustion, you kept moving until you were rescued. That sound about right, Sam?" Dr. Cusack looked up at me, anticipating my response.

"Yeah, that's about it, except for almost falling on top of an elephant when I was coming down from that tree, dodging Charlie a bunch of other times, being half-eaten alive by mosquitoes, covered with leeches, and who knows what other kinds of nasty bugs.

"Oh, and a few other things. Just minutes before the chopper was to pick me up, I was in danger of losing contact because the battery in my PRC-25 was almost dead. You know, the little orange light was blinking to tell me I had only about three minutes left. I had finally made it to the rendezvous location, but it was filled with NVA! After all I had gone through, there was no way I was going to miss this rescue. I was determined to get out of that fuckin' jungle!

"Right then and there, Doc, I thought of the funniest thing. I mean this has to be something you'd tell a shrink. While I was watching a dozen NVA eating breakfast in this clearing where I am supposed to be picked up, I thought to myself I should just walk out into the open and explain why I needed them to clear out, ASAP!

"Hey you guys, there, eating that stinking *nuoc cham* shit for breakfast! I can smell you from here. You mind stepping aside? I've got a Jolly Green that needs to drop in here and pick me up. NOW! Oh, and by the way, if you're missing two for breakfast, you'll find 'um upstream with Colt forty-five holes in 'um. Well, only one actually has holes. The other one – I blew half his head off. No holes. So how about you *didi* before the same thing happens to your sorry asses!"

Vicky's face registered a look of horror. Dr. Cusack reached over and rested his hand on my shoulder.

"Most guys wouldn't have been able to talk about any of that, especially so soon after all the trauma you have been through. Here is my contact information if you need to talk, but I have a strong feeling I won't be hearing from you. Now, get your clothes on and get out of here."

***

Vicky and I took a cab to the Caravelle, which held very special memories for us. The same slightly shabby Vietnamese man was at the front desk and recognized me, despite my swollen face and bandaged feet. "Good to see you again, Sir."

Vicky had booked a comfortable suite, and the dining table looked like Christmas morning – at least, my idea of Christmas. Santa had dropped off three bottles of Scotch, a few packages of gourmet foods, water and fruit juice, a stack of paperbacks, shampoo, soap, and lots of toilet paper. I had told her of the perennial shortage!

"Oh, Vicky, you have done too much, Baby. This is unreal. It must have set you back a fortune!"

"My father sent you the Scotch. You being a pilot and all ... well, he already likes you. I haven't had a chance to tell you much about him, but you might recall he was a P-51 pilot during World War II."

"I remember. I look forward to meeting him someday."

We retreated to the balcony where we enjoyed smoked oysters, Gouda cheese, and stone-ground wheat crackers with that wonderful Scotch. Made a great breakfast!

"Sam, I have to be honest with you. You have been through the wringer, my dear man, and you do look the worse for wear. I want you to allow me to do something for you."

"Yeah, OK; what do you have in mind?"

"I want to take care of you. Valerie gave me this first aid kit and told me exactly what to do. First, you need to be sure to take all of this antibiotic. Second, we have to take care of your feet; they need to be kept clean, medicated, and dry. The raw blisters were her biggest concern. I have bath salts, antifungal powder, antibacterial cream, and bandages. She said you had three cuts that were infected rather badly and have to be cleaned daily. We'll keep an eye on them; one on your left leg, one under your right arm, and one on the back of your right hand. I know you have to be suffering more trauma than you're letting on. I mean, come on, Sam, you have been to hell and back and lived to tell about it, thank God. I just want you to let me take care of you these next few days. We don't even have to leave this hotel room until Friday."

"Well yeah, I guess you're right. My body is pretty beat up. My cuts are uncomfortable. The one on my leg hurts, actually. My feet are on fire. To tell you the truth, now that I'm taking notice of it all, I feel like shit. So, I'm all yours! Pamper my brains out! No argument here! Just keep the Scotch coming!"

"OK, then. While you enjoy your modest feast, I'm going to run your bath, then give you a massage with some great lotion I have. Then we'll take care of those cuts and blisters. Later we can have dinner sent up and dine on the balcony with the door open to get the AC."

"Gee, and to think I could be spending the night in the hollow of a tree in the Cambodian jungle. I was becoming arboreal."

"A what?"

"Arboreal. You know, animals that live in trees."

The Scotch had gone right to my head; I needed the relief.

I had never let a woman take care of me like this. The truth is, I never felt this lousy in my life. I was worn out. My body ached all over, and I was still more than a little in shock over the whole ordeal. The God that had known I would be shot out of my plane and land in that Cambodian jungle, who helped me down the tree and guided me through those long and challenging days and nights, was the same God that had seen to it that Vicky and I were destined to make this date in Saigon that we had set up weeks ago. The timing could not have been more perfect. Once again, my fortune would swing from the worst of times in a hostile jungle to the best of times, with tender, loving care from Vicky.

Sometime after dinner, I fell asleep in her arms. A few hours later, I was awakened by what sounded like distant screams. The screams were mine. I was shaking uncontrollably and in the grips of a cold sweat. Vicky held me, rocking me and stroking my forehead tenderly.

"It's OK, Sam. You're safe now. You're with me." She went to the bathroom, returned with a cool, damp washcloth, and tenderly wiped down my face, neck, and chest.

"Here, take off your T-shirt and put on this dry one. And take these aspirin. You're running a fever."

"Yeah, OK! Thanks, Baby. Thanks."

I collapsed into my feather pillow and slept and slept and slept. It was late morning the next day before I opened my eyes again.

"Welcome back, flyboy." Vicky leaned over and kissed my cheek.

"How long have you been sitting there?"

"Oh, I don't know, a couple of hours. I enjoyed watching you sleep. Been drinking coffee and reading *War and Peace*. Want some breakfast?"

"Sure, I'm famished."

When room service arrived, I hobbled to the balcony to enjoy fresh papaya juice, bacon, eggs, biscuits and washed it all down with a pot of French roast coffee. After breakfast, I drifted off again and slept a few more hours. When I awoke, Vicky smiled at me. She was curled up in a comfortable chair with that heavy copy of *War and Peace* in her lap.

"I feel alive again. You know, so rested, and actually hungry. Let's get out of this hotel and do something fun tonight," I suggested.

"No can do, soldier! I got strict orders from Valerie and your doctor to keep you off your feet until we leave for Australia. I am very content just being here, hanging out, and taking care of you. You don't have to feel pressured to do anything, OK?"

"Yeah, I know. I just think it will be good for us to get out a little, that's all. I need to be sure I can get around anyway. How about dinner out tonight? I know of a great restaurant with beautiful views. It actually floats on the Saigon River."

"Tell you what; I'll give Valerie a call and get her opinion. Let's see what she has to say about us going out."

Valerie made it quite clear that it was too soon for me to venture out, insisting we wait two more days. Turns out, she was right. After three days, I could actually walk on my feet without pain, but they were wrapped in yards of gauze so thick that I was fortunate Vicky found socks large enough to cover them. Over these white bundles, I wore sandals a few sizes bigger than my normal size. I felt like a real dork, especially with this gorgeous woman on my arm, but have to admit I was comfortable. Anyway, I figured more people would be looking at Vicky's beautiful face than my Paul Bunyon-sized feet.

In the cab on our way to dinner, I told Vicky the tragic story of My Canh Café. Although now considered safe, one fateful summer evening in June, 1965, it was the target of a terrorist bombing. The explosion destroyed the dining area, killing about thirty-two people, including thirteen Americans, and seriously wounding another forty to fifty victims. That's about all I told Vicky at that time because sticking with me meant exposure to a lot of unpleasantry and bad news, and I thought it best to spare her when I could. It's not that she wasn't strong, she certainly was; it's just that I recognized in less than one year I had hardened to many experiences that would have, should have sickened me, and I did not want to lose my sense of judgment in this regard.

Actually, the whole truth about the bombing was much more involved. A few minutes after the intentionally-timed dinner-hour explosion, while stunned survivors were fleeing the restaurant, a second bomb exploded along the river bank, right in their path. Now, not only the dining room but also the gangplank that connected the My Canh to the main boulevard was covered with the blood and gore of innocent men, women, and children, mostly American and Vietnamese, who just happened to be enjoying a night out at a very popular locale. These well-planned attacks were executed by Viet Cong commandos, who managed to go undetected in the aftermath. This was the fourth bombing in six months designed to inflict death and destruction and to make Saigon unsafe for Americans.

Remarkably, in 2010, the story told by one of the bombers was reported in *People's Army,* published by the Vietnamese Defense Ministry. The VC and his partner in crime planned the attack carefully. Riding bikes, they were able to easily blend into the crowd and plant their bombs without detection. Pedaling away from the scene, they heard the explosions and evaded capture. Years later, with their identities known, they were lauded as heroes to their cause, which I found absolutely revolting, but then war has a way of making heroes out of monsters.

As our taxi pulled up to the popular restaurant on Tu Do Street, I pointed out to Vicky the large sign that read, 'Floating My Canh Restaurant' and 'Warmly Welcoming our Customers' in five different languages. That sign was up at the time of the bombing, too. As we approached the canopied gangplank that would lead us to the dining room, I let my mind drift to that night's horror when Vicky quipped, "I already knew that I was with a man who lives dangerously. So, how's the food here?" If I had told her the whole truth, I'm certain she'd never cross that gangplank to the dining room. In fact, I wondered what the hell I was doing here myself. I wasn't naïve enough to think the VC were not around. I guess I just wanted to give them the finger!

"Word is, they serve the best lobster thermidor and pressed Peking duck in Saigon, and they are one of the few restaurants in Saigon to serve good French wine."

"Sam, you just survived being shot down, and then were hunted for three days in the freaking jungle, out-running, out-dodging and out-shooting the NVA. I have a feeling if anybody starts anything in the My Canh tonight, he will be sorry. Sure, let's go for it."

We sat at a table with views of the Saigon River. Vicky made me prop my feet up on an extra chair. Although the night was hot and humid, the Saigon River was not any place where I would take a dip. A fresh drink would cool me off. The food lived up to its reputation. The lobster and duck were prepared by a chef who certainly knew what he was doing, and the French wines we selected complemented our meal. For dessert, we were served a Vietnamese dish with fresh fruit and a syrupy topping, along with French roast coffee.

After dinner, we couldn't wait to get back to our air-conditioned suite, where Vicky took control and had me soaking my feet almost immediately. With proper care, my foot fungus had already started to clear up, and thank God there was no permanent damage to my feet. She applied clean bandages, then propped up several large pillows, made me lie down, and put her head next to mine. That was the setting of a very long conversation, and one I will never forget.

"So, we haven't talked about Australia much. Did you and Ed make any specific plans before you included me?"

"Yeah, as a matter of fact, we did, but you coming won't change what we have in mind. I thought I would save that as a surprise."

"Can't you at least give me a hint?"

"Nope! Sorry! Not even a hint. You'll just have to wait and see. Trust me!"

"As long as we're together. That's all that really matters. I'm sure you and Ed have something good up your sleeve. One thing I have learned about you, Sam Walker, is you are never boring! I am just curious about something that pilots are faced with and that you had to do. If you don't want to talk about it, I understand perfectly, but I would like to ask."

"Sure. Go ahead. What?"

"What's it like to eject out of an airplane? You know, making that decision and actually experiencing it."

"Well, it all starts like this: you're sitting in the comfort of your cockpit, and you know you have to get out, but you don't know what is waiting for you. You only have seconds to do it, if you want to live, because it's certain the plane is going down and taking you with it. As the Aircraft Commander, I'm responsible first for my crew; I'm the last to punch out. I had immediately given the order for them to eject, and they did as they were trained. So, now it was my turn. I felt awful that my co-pilot had just been killed, but there was nothing I could do about that, and the seconds were ticking away."

"Oh, that sounds so scary! How can you think straight at a time like that?" Vicky interjected.

"Well actually, you don't do much thinking at all. You just run on automatic because we've been so well-trained. We're fortunate that some very smart engineer types have taken care of all the decision making for us."

"What do you mean?"

"They invented something called an ejection seat, and that ain't like any other seat you'll ever sit on! Once you know you have to exit the plane, there is only one thing you must do. Just pull a lever, simple as that! That's been drummed into us in training."

"And what does that lever do?"

"It triggers the ejection within less than a second! First, you know the glass canopy overhead? Well, after you pull the lever, that canopy pops off immediately and propels away from the plane so it's out of your way. Then your seat, well, this is really something, it turns into an amusement park ride, only much better. You see, under your seat there is literally a rocket that kicks in, which shoots you right up and out of that plane; don't forget, you're already strapped into it. The whole point is to get you away from the plane, which is going down, so you need to go up, and get the hell outta' there."

"How high do you go?"

"Oh, I don't know exactly, but they got that all figured out, too. High enough to keep you clear of the plane, but low enough so you don't run into an alien spaceship."

"SAM WALKER!!!!" Vicky playfully bopped me on the head with a handy pillow and then continued, "I took some college level science classes, and I know that whatever goes up must come down! So, then what?"

"Well, after you're clear of the plane, based on a whole lot of calculations that they did so you don't have to, the seat falls away from your body, and –"

"WHAT?"

"Now don't panic, Vicky, let me finish! I survived, didn't I? When the seat separates from you, it activates your parachute! See, the parachute is part of the ejection seat, too. I told you they thought of everything. With your parachute opened, you begin to descend, ever so gently. That was my favorite part. While I was floating through the night sky, everything was so peaceful and serene. It was very dark, but when I landed, while hanging in the tree, the clouds separated and revealed a half-moon. And that moon bathed everything below it with the most glorious light, nothing like the moonlight we experience from the ground. This light was like liquid silver and glowed like shiny wet paint. It lit up everything in every direction. The jungle below was covered with all kinds of plants and trees that must have been wet with dew. When the moon glow reached that far down, it looked like a field of diamonds sparkling and winking at me. It was magical, mystical."

"WOW!"

"I have to tell you, Vicky, that I felt I was in the presence of something much bigger than me, a positive force that was watching over me. I think it was my first encounter with God. I felt such peace. I realized that I wasn't afraid, and I should have been scared out of my wits! At that moment, I felt that God was watching out for me, and I held onto that feeling my whole time in that jungle."

"That's, beautiful, Sam. So how do you feel about the experience now?"

"Good question. I know I can go back to it in my mind but never actually have that experience, again. It was something that happened outside of me, yet in me at the same time. I was in awe! Does that make sense?"

"You definitely had a spiritual experience. I'm sure the intensity of it was heightened by your circumstances. When we get to Australia,

I will find a book for you that I read years ago, *The Varieties of Religious Experience* by William James. Pretty heavy-duty stuff, but after what you just described, I think you would get a lot out of it.

"Did you know your co-pilot very well? I don't recall you ever mentioning him before."

"No. So tragic. Watson had only been in-country about three months. It was the first time I had flown with him because his assigned Aircraft Commander was on R&R. All I knew about him was that he was from Colorado. Nice enough, though! Sure feel bad for his family. And him, of course. Yeah, guess it will take a lifetime to put all of this together."

That night, we were intimate for the first time since we had been together during my recovery. It was different. The first time we made love in Saigon, and then in Hawaii, Vicky was like a tigress in bed. This time she was a kitty – very tender and gentle.

"I am going to take it easy with you, Sam. You are so beat up, my love. I could tell you were limping a little tonight. How are your feet?" she purred.

"They hurt. I hurt. I just don't want to show it. Our time is so precious together, and this is not fair to you!"

"Shh! Please don't think that for a moment. We leave for Australia day after tomorrow for ten full days. We're staying in tomorrow, and you're staying off those feet. End of subject. Got it, Sam? If we can't be here for each other in the tough times, then what good are we to each other?"

The truth and weight of that statement would be tested in our future.

***

The next morning, Vicky slipped out before I awoke. She had found a pharmacy nearby and bought more bath salts so that I wouldn't run out. She made me soak my feet again and gently towel-dried and medicated them. "OK, flyboy, let's get you out on the balcony and get those pampered feet propped up in the sunshine."

She had planned a full day of rest and recuperation for me whether I liked it or not. It was certainly clear Vicky was the boss!

"Here, put this pillow behind you. Breakfast will be delivered any minute now. So, have you made plans for when you leave Vietnam? You haven't mentioned anything about that yet."

"Well, a while back, Ed, Tex, and I had planned a trip off the grid, back-packing and hiking in the Pacific Northwest. Tex had suggested it for all of us as a good way to get our heads back on straight before trying to blend back into 'The World'. I was going to tell you about it when we got to Australia."

"I think you should do that, Sam. It would be good for you, the three of you. When do you get out, late February?"

"I arrived in the Nam on my birthday and will leave the country on my birthday, February 28."

"That works out well for me. I'll definitely be able to meet you at the airport when you arrive. What a birthday celebration that will be!"

"Oh, yeah! Then you and I could plan to reunite back in LA after our guy-trip."

"Well, since we are having this conversation, I will be brave and broach the subject. Would you like to move in with me? You know, we could live together in California."

"To tell the truth, I have never been too keen on that idea, living together. Guess I am old-fashioned that way, but then Vietnam has caused me to rethink a lot of things. Life ... freedom; the things we take for granted until they are taken away. And I have had my freedom taken away for some time now. But hey, what about your roommate?"

"Lisa's situation is changing. She's in a serious relationship and plans to move in with her boyfriend the first of the year, so we would have the cottage all to ourselves."

"Well, that gives me a lot to think about. For one thing, I'd have to get a job in California. Funny, now that I've said that, I'm not sure what I'd do out there."

"Remember I told you that my parents run their own business? Well, a big part of that is farming, and you grew up on a farm. You'd probably fit right in!"

"Gee, I don't know if I could do that."

"Why not? I thought you said–"

"Yes, I did say I grew up on a farm. A real working farm. My dad runs it, and my mom manages the household, which includes lots of canning and preserving. I worked it growing up since I was old enough to carry stuff around and follow simple orders. And I enjoyed working the land, experiencing the wonders of nature, the thrill of a great harvest."

"Then it sounds like you'd be right at home."

"That's just it, Vicky. I would not be at home. It's always been sort of understood that I'd take over my parents' farm, the house, everything. We'd always talk about that growing up. My sister really wanted to become a nurse – and she did – so she was fine with the farm going to me. It would be hard enough to tell my parents I'm not coming back and a lot more difficult to tell them I'm working somebody else's farm in California."

"Oh, I can see that now."

With that came a sharp knock on the door. Room service had arrived with our breakfast. As they moved through the motions of maneuvering the cart to set up breakfast on the balcony, we sat in silence, like the freeze-frame of a movie. Once the servers left the room, backing out politely and closing the door behind them, Vicky picked up where she left off.

"Well you know that I'm an only child, so you won't be surprised to learn that my parents want to leave the family business to me."

"Yeah, right. That's why you're working as a high-profile cocktail waitress."

"I'm gonna hurt you, Sam Walker!"

Now I was laughing. "Sorry ... sorry. OK, so that means what?"

"That means we have a unique problem or two problems, one that many people would welcome. Having your future all arranged for you. But mine is on the Pacific; yours is on the Atlantic."

I let that sink in before declaring, "Time for breakfast!"

We moved onto the balcony and started to eat, making small talk about the food. My mind was racing. I thought we were still in the getting-to-know-you-better stage, yet Vicky just asked me to move in with her and suggested I become part of the family business, something I never would have expected. That's amazing enough. I would have thought I'd jump on that. What guy wouldn't? But neither did I expect the emotions that welled up in me about not taking over MY family farm. About choosing hers over mine, about having to break the news to my family.

"Give me a minute, OK?" I took a sip of coffee, put down my cup, then reached over and poured a stiff shot of Scotch. I threw it back, followed by another. I didn't care that it was breakfast time; I needed Happy Hour! My body was still hurting pretty badly, and the Scotch really helped.

"A bit early for that. You OK?" Vicky wondered.

"Yeah ... yeah ... I'm OK. I just keep wondering when the pain will stop. But right now, I want to share my side of things, tell you where I come from. Let's see if you can follow my story."

"Alright. I'm listening."

"Just to be objective, take 'Sam Walker' out of the equation and then let me know if this sounds logical to you. Here's the scenario. You are a country kid; you grew up way out in the sticks. Both of your parents are college-educated, and your dad is a farmer, actually, a very successful planter. Your mom's domestic help has kids your age, and you grow up playing with them every day. They happen to be black, but you are color-blind. You grew up with them, and they are your friends, your real friends. When you reach school age, your parents put you in this top-notch, all-boys, private military academy, where all the other boys are rich white kids from the city. In their minds, the country kid is a dirt farmer's son. You are teased and mocked a lot. You can't understand why you don't fit in. You are hurt. You become depressed. You don't like school. That was the boy's first wake-up call, his first life lesson: Never assume others will see you as you see yourself.

"You get older. Your parents have instilled in you that you will go to college. But all you really want to do is fly airplanes. You don't really know why; you just do. You go to a great university and join a venerated fraternity. But you are nothing like your frat brothers. They love college. You don't like it at all. Once again, you don't fit in. You fly every chance you get and earn your pilot's license. Not something any of your frat brothers do. Because you don't care for college, you speed up your classes and graduate in three years instead of four. Graduating early might be considered a worthy accomplishment, but in your reality, turns out you just screwed yourself, major-league. Your early timing stinks because Uncle Sam invites you to join the war, a very unpopular war. You rationalize that you can't fight it, so you may as well join it, reasoning that if you enlist, you can become a professional pilot. Because, again, all you really want to do is fly. You wind up in this strange and dangerous place called Vietnam. In a matter of hours, your entire world changes for the worse. You realize you had no idea of what you were getting into, and now you're no longer the wet-behind-the-ears college boy. You have gone to war; not at all what you had planned. That's when you learned the second life lesson: The goal you select for yourself may lead you down the wrong road.

"While you're at war, you feel certain about one thing – that you will not meet and enjoy the company of an American girl. That would be impossible, simply because there aren't any around! But just the opposite happens! You meet the girl of your dreams – in a Saigon furniture store, no less. She's beautiful, she's intelligent, she's a wonderful person, and she's a flight attendant. All the stuff of fantasy, but for you, incredibly, it has come true. That's when you learn the third life lesson: Never assume you know what your circumstances will produce.

"Now, that last part, where boy meets girl, is already pretty far-fetched. I mean, that, alone, is the beginning and the end of a good story, right? But then she asks if you'd like to live together ... in southern California ... and work in the family business ... which just happens to be farming!

"So, Vicky, you're asking me how I'm doing? Well, I'll tell you. I'm kind of amazed and confused, happy and sad, hopeful and depressed, all at the same time. Ever since I enlisted, I've acclimated myself to taking one day at a time, not thinking ahead but staying completely focused on the here and now, because losing focus in this environment could cost you your life.

"Now here we are – here I am – contemplating what I'm going to do after the Nam. Months ahead of now; years down the road. Something I've never actually had to think about because it was all preordained! Well, guess what. I can't do it. I can't think of the future right now, especially when the present is good enough for me; in fact, it's pretty damn great!" With that, I hoisted my glass, toasted the present, emptied my glass, and poured another.

"OK, OK, OK, Sam. I get it. I really do. I'm sorry I brought it up – the future. You've explained how important it is for you to live in the present. I can see those skills kept you alive when you were shot down, and God knows how grateful I am for that. You had the wits and the skills to save yourself; now we should just focus on getting you better. We have ten days in Australia ahead, and I want us to enjoy each day as it comes."

"Yeah, let's not get ahead of ourselves."

At that point, Vicky dissolved into tears. All these days in Saigon, she had been so brave, turning herself into my private nurse, fussing with ointments, foot baths, Epsom salt, bandages. Turns out, that was her way of keeping busy, focusing on my physical wounds to avoid confronting the actual danger I had experienced in the jungle. Ointments, bandages, bath powder, these were all things she could control. The remaining days of my tour, she could not. Nobody could. I put my arms around her so she could sob into my chest. I held her close and let her get it all out. I knew it was important for both of us. When her sobbing subsided, I put my hand under her chin and tenderly tilted her face up toward mine.

"I think it's time to soak my feet again," I said with a wink.

Vicky nodded, took my hand, and led me off the porch. We did soak my feet, only after we took care of a few other important things.

Chapter 21 Australia

The InterContinental Sydney Hotel was the most luxurious lodging I had ever experienced. If it weren't for the fifty percent discount they gave to GIs on R&R, we would never have been able to stay here. I noticed that Vicky seemed right at home, but I felt more than a bit out of my league. We had regal rooms with grand balconies that overlooked Sydney Harbor. The views were expansive, especially at night with all the lights twinkling against a dark sky. I don't know what Ed did during the afternoon hours, but I know how Vicky and I spent our time.

We met in the lobby at eight and took a cab to an upscale restaurant in the White Cross district, the heart of Sydney's nightlife. We were seated at a table near the bar. After our drinks arrived, I hoisted mine and offered a toast, "To the two best people I know."

Vicky clinked glasses and added, "To two of the finest flyboys I know. Just get your asses home safe. There is only so much a girl can take."

We all laughed but were distracted, pleasantly I might add, by a stunning young woman who walked toward the bar and took a seat, only a few feet from our table. I got the distinct impression that although she was aware of every head that turned to gaze upon her as she passed, she remained unfazed about it. Quietly, Vicky urged Ed to check her out.

"Oh, trust me, I already am. She's pretty hard not to notice!"

This blonde goddess was wearing a bright yellow dress that not only flattered her figure but also accentuated her golden tan. At the bar, in heavily accented English, she ordered a bottle of Dom.

Vicky spoke up. "OK, you two, I know that other than your mamasan, I am practically the only female you have spoken to in the last several months, but for God's sake, at least close your mouths. She is almost too hot!"

My comment was a bit simpler, "Whadaya think, Ed? Hooker?"

"Yeah, that was my first thought, but a hooker wouldn't order a bottle of Dom, would she?"

"Not unless she has an arrangement with the bartender that she'd attract a man and get him to pay for it."

"You two have been in Saigon way too long. If that girl is a prostitute, I am Betty Crocker," Vicky said with a laugh.

"Ed and I both know you're better than Betty Crocker. We have been eating your cookies for the past six months."

As we continued to discuss the blonde goddess, a rather large, ruddy-faced GI who was more than a bit tipsy walked up to the bar and took a place next to her. It didn't take long before he started hitting on her.

Gracefully sipping her expensive champagne, the blonde was nobody's pushover. "Excuse me! You must go away now. I did not invite you!"

"Geez, pretty lady. I just want some company. How much do you cost? I got money!"

She drew back to put more distance between them. "You are a drunk American pig! I am not for sale! I ask you to please leave!"

"Hey! I'm in a free country, right? I just want some company. Come on. Whadaya say there, pretty lady?"

Vicky was a champ. An aspect of her character that I had not yet seen just showed up, "OK, guys, it's time to go to her rescue!" With that, Vicky rose up and inserted herself between the blonde and the bore, greeting each with a charming smile, but soon turning her back on the bore, to isolate the blonde.

Ed and I looked at each other and rose from our seats. "Let's go!"

I slipped into the gap between Vicky and the bore while Ed went on a mission. "Hey, guy, name is Sam. That's my girlfriend, Vicky."

"Yeah, so what? What do you want?" He was loud and angry.

"Well, we were sitting over there having a drink with our friend and couldn't help but notice that this young lady just wants to be left alone. There are lots of other women around that may enjoy your attention, but this one made it clear she doesn't. So, I'm just asking you to leave."

He got more belligerent. "Go screw yourself, pal. I got here first, so you just butt out."

At that moment, Ed returned with two bouncers, who were prepared to act. Each grabbed hold of one of the bore's arms, 'helped' him off his seat and guided him to the front door where they expelled him from the establishment. And off went our evening's problem.

Vicky had invited the blonde to our table, and both were chatting away as if they were close friends when Ed and I joined them. The bartender had brought over the bottle of Dom, and Adrianna requested three more glasses.

"Adrianna, this is my boyfriend, Sam, and our good friend Ed. Fellas, this is Adrianna. She's originally from Czechoslovakia but lives here now. Adrianna's mother will be joining her in Australia next month."

"Thank you for coming to my rescue. You are truly the brave Americans I have heard so much about. How can I make it up to you?" Though she spoke with a foreign accent, her English was probably better than mine.

Vicky jumped in quickly, perhaps afraid of what Ed or I might suggest. "Adrianna, if you don't have other plans tonight, why don't you join us for dinner. We'll have a nice evening and forget about that drunk. So, you'll join us for dinner?"

Adrianna broke into a radiant smile. "Thank you for the invitation, and thank you again for rescuing me! I just started a week of holiday, and now that I've met you nice people, it's off to a good start. I'd enjoy dining with you; that's perfect for me." She was definitely looking more at Ed than at Vicky and I. Not having given it any thought before, I realized that Ed was actually a nice-looking guy, though right now his mouth was open again, and so was mine.

"Perfect for you? WOW! I am starting to have Sam's luck."

"What do you mean, Sam's luck. Is he a lucky fellow?"

After Vicky told Adrianna the story of how she and I met, the four of us continued to enjoy a lively conversation for the next few hours. After dinner, we went dancing and drinking. Actually, using my feet as an excuse, I focused on drinking. At some point, Vicky and I caught a cab back while Adrianna and Ed continued to enjoy the nightlife.

***

The next morning, Vicky and I were having a late breakfast at the hotel when Ed came down and joined us. He told us they had a great evening, but in the cab, Adrianna asked to be dropped off at her place and indicated she'd join him in the morning for breakfast. She wanted to see Ed again but wasn't ready for anything else. With that, Ed bolted up and strode over to the entrance, having seen Adrianna arrive. He escorted her over to our table, in a gentlemanly manner with his hand placed lightly on her back. She looked just as stunning today as she had the previous night.

After some small talk about the previous evening, Vicky changed the subject. "Sam has been keeping the plans you guys made a surprise. It's time for one of you to talk. What's up? What are we going to do here in Australia?"

Sipping his coffee, Ed divulged our agenda. "Well, Sam and I have booked a couple of open cockpit bi-planes. We were going to either fly a few hundred miles inland across New South Wales to the Outback where we'd camp out, or fly up the Ocean Highway toward Brisbane, on the coast. What do you think?"

"You two are on R&R from flying, and you still want to go flying? Help me out here."

"We have been flying combat. This is different. This is strictly pleasure, and these are vintage planes with open cockpits, something neither of us has ever flown, making it a real adventure."

"So, you two have never flown bi-planes, and you're just taking off for a three-or four-day trip in one?" questioned Vicky, her face wrinkling with doubt.

"The fact that it's a bi-wing aircraft really has nothing do to with our ability to fly it. Both of us have flown single-engine planes with landing gear on the tail, and that's what we'll be flying here. Not a problem! You better believe the guy renting them will check us out before letting us go. Renting a plane is serious business. At any rate, we plan to spend a few days in Sydney first, relaxing and seeing the sites before exploring the countryside. That's why we booked this hotel – does it get any better than this?"

The girls agreed, and Vicky was eager to share what she had learned yesterday. "The concierge explained that this hotel is one of the world's best, and it certainly has an interesting history. It was established in 1851 as a government Treasury Building."

Whoever thought of turning it into a hotel had good instincts. The InterContinental renovation created rooms that took full advantage of the water view, with large windows and private balconies.

"So, let's spend the next two nights here and take in as much – or as little – of Sydney as desired. No pressure, no rush, no schedule. Then we'll trade in all this luxury for a vintage bi-plane and the rugged outdoors."

During the day, Ed and Adrianna would do their thing, and Vicky and I would do ours; then, we'd meet in the hotel bar for drinks before heading out for dinner and the nightlife. This arrangement suited our needs. Vicky and I were eager to spend some time by ourselves, and she continued to show concern about my recuperation and healing. Ed and Adrianna were just getting to know each other, which I figured would determine whether or not she'd want to join us on the bi-plane trip.

Dinners together were always memorable, as we sought out Sydney's best and thoroughly enjoyed the gourmet cuisine, while we could. Afterward, we typically found a nightspot for drinks and dancing. Whereas I enjoyed the drinks, I had absolutely no interest in dancing. Vicky would say that she preferred not to dance with me because Miss America was a tough act to follow and that always got a chuckle, but we all knew that she was still concerned about my feet, as was I. Who knew when Vicky would finally experience my dancing skills. My secret was safe for now.

Ed and Adrianna, on the other hand, were quite a pair on the dance floor, whether the music was fast or slow, ballroom or rock. Meeting up with Adrianna was pure luck, and both Vicky and I were happy to see them getting on so well. On our third evening, the subject of the bi-plane adventure came up, and it was obvious Adrianna was coming along. In fact, she had already moved in with Ed. Once again, Vicky and I called it a night earlier than those two and caught a cab back to the hotel.

***

In the morning, we met for breakfast and were eager to get over to the airfield and check out the bi-planes. One of the Aussies from Vung Tau, the village in Vietnam where we got seafood, had recommended Thomas Crowndale, who owns a nearby flying service in Hoxton Park. Mr. Crowndale and I exchanged letters, and he indicated he would rent a Stearman bi-plane for $50.00 per day, a special rate for American flyers. Before getting up from the table, I asked, "Are you sure you girls are up to this?"

"Sure! How many times in life do you get a chance to explore the Australian Outback in a vintage plane with an American pilot?" replied Adrianna.

In barely a half-hour, we were standing face to face with Thomas Crowndale, a crop duster in his mid-forties who also operated a small aircraft rental business.

"G'day, mates … G'day, Sheilas. I am Thomas Crowndale. What brings you out to Hoxton?"

"Good morning. I'm Sam Walker. I wrote you from Vietnam last month about renting a couple of Stearman bi-planes for a few days.

"We've been waiting for you. The aircraft are in tipper shape. Looks to me you'll be needing camping gear as well, mate."

"That's for sure."

"I got everything you need for your sojourn. You mentioned my nephew in your letter. Tell you what, you lads are fightin' in a bloody war together. Just don't feel right charging ya the goin' rate. How 'bout I charge ya a two-for-one rate for the Stearman and throw in the camping gear?"

"Mighty nice of ya, Mr. Crowndale. We're looking to use them for three days."

"So, where you headed, Mr. Walker? By the way, let's drop the formalities. Call me Tom, please."

"Yeah … and I go by Sam. We are thinking about flying either to the Darling River or up to Brisbane. What would you suggest?"

"Depends, mate! You looking to see lots of wildlife, birds, kangaroos, and such along with a lot of red desert, then fly northwest toward Bourke on the Darling. If you're looking for beautiful beaches and pretty scenery, then fly north along the coast toward Brisbane. Personally, if I had limited time, I would fly about halfway to Bourke, just on the other side of the Macquarie Marshes, camp for a night, and then fly straight due east. You should hit the coast somewhere just south of Port Macquarie. Jolly easy trip, mate, but be careful of dust storms when you fly inland. If you see one coming and you're flying, turn your arses around and fly away from it immediately, or land, secure your aircraft, and take shelter. Probably best to dig in about four feet deep and protect yourself from the wind and rain. Storms usually pass in under two hours. Bloody dust storms over here can really pack a wallop. Usually wind gusts around 100 kilometers. I'll top off the birds with petrol while you take what you want of the camping gear over there in that shed. Be sure to take two swags. They sleep two each."

"What's a swag?"

"Bloody comfortable sleeping bag, Sam. My wife made them. Heavy canvas outer shell, lined with cotton quilts. Extra padding on the bottom."

We gathered two pup tents, two swags, two short shovels, a machete, cooking equipment, and a couple of canteens that we filled with water. We were loading the equipment when Tom came over with a .22 rifle.

"Sam, take my rifle. Here is a box with about a hundred rounds. Australia has got as many poisonous snakes as southeast Asia. You never know. We also got lots of long-eared hares that are good to eat. They show themselves just before dark. Just don't shoot any of our roos!"

"Roo? What's a roo?"

"Kangaroo, mate! Guarantee you will see lots of 'um."

Now that we were sure to be taking the bi-plane trip, Vicky and Adrianna took the cab back to the hotel to pack our clothes, check out, and store the rest of our luggage until our return. In the meantime, Ed and I loaded the two Stearman with camping gear. Tom took each of us around the patch for a few touch-and-goes to check us out in the Stearman since neither of us had ever flown one. It was a real treat to be flying that old plane The Stearman models that Tom offered had been used to train pilots during WWII, and fortunately, many survived today, that is to say, both the pilots and the planes!

Back in his office, Tom went over two maps in great detail. Circling several remote airstrips along the coast, he gave us headings to fly and landmarks to follow.

"You should make the trip to the Outback in about two and half hours of flying time, at 60 percent power, 2200 rpms. After leaving the Outback, I suggest you stop for petrol in Port Macquarie, which is on your way to the coast. See here on this chart?" sliding his finger along the map, tracing our route. "The town of Newcastle to the south of Macquarie would be a great place to spend a few nights. There is a dirt airstrip that parallels the coast out on this point a few miles from the town. Mate by the name of Will Chesterton owns it. He has half a dozen nice little cabins there overlooking the beach, a few meters from the airstrip. He and his family live in a cottage on a cliff above the cabins. Easy walking distance from the airstrip. I'm sure you'll be very comfortable. Cabins only $25 each night. It would be a good stopover."

Tom was walking us back to the aircraft just as the girls returned with our things.

"I almost forgot, mates. I am placing these mooring augers in your cargo compartment. Three augers with rope for each aircraft. Be sure to use them at night to secure the planes. If you do have to endure a dust storm, and I bloody hope you don't, as a precaution, tie down these birds facing the west.

"One more thing. Very important! About an hour after takeoff, you will be flying across the southern end of the Blue Mountains. Stay above 3500 feet and you'll be safe to clear the ridge line and you'll have plenty of altitude to see any storms. They always come from the northwest. If you see a dust storm at that point, turn around and come back because for the next 100 miles or so you will be flying over the Macquarie Marshes, and there aren't too many places to land in marsh country. Plus, The Macquarie is teeming with crocs! For emergencies, I'm giving you a flare gun and six flares, two reflection mirrors, and an orange tarp. Mayday frequency is 232.0.

"I know you lads are the best flyers on the planet but don't underestimate these bloody storms. If you are within sight of the northern side of the Macquarie boundary and see a storm coming, put down and dig in. You don't want to take a chance back across the Macquarie if you got a storm breathing down your neck. After you are out of the marshes, you can put a Stearman down just about anywhere in the Outback. She is a tough old bird. I think she likes dirt landings more than asphalt or concrete, but enough of my lecture. Tally ho, mates! Have a good time, Sheilas!"

I let Ed take the lead. I took off just behind him. We circled the small airstrip and then turned northwest to a heading of 350 degrees toward Bourke on the Darling River, 340 miles away. We decided to take Tom's advice and camp out in the desert about halfway to Bourke on the northwest side of the Macquarie Marshes and return to the coast south of Port Macquarie. Ed and I had radio communication, and we had intercom communication with Vicky and Adrianna.

"Ed, how do you read?"

"Gotcha, Sam. How 'bout me?"

"Loud and clear, Ed. Let's fly a little formation. I will come up on your right side."

"Roger, Sam. I am holding steady at 350 degrees, 150 knots, and 3500 feet."

"Got it, Ed."

I flew up alongside his aircraft. We were in concert. My left wing-tip was no more than ten feet from his elevator. I couldn't see Vicky's face, but Adrianna's eyes were wide open; a look of curiosity mixed with 'What the F ...?'

"Is Adrianna okay with this?"

"She is now. I think it just startled her at first. How is Vicky?"

"Don't know. Let me check. Vicky, you okay with formation flying?"

"I have never felt such bliss, flyboy! Once again, you have amazed me."

We approached the Blue Mountains, and to their north, we could see the Australian Alps. Though these mountain ranges were small in comparison to European and American mountain ranges, they were no less majestic to behold. We pushed across the Macquarie Marshes, where we dropped down to 200 feet to see the incredible wildlife inhabitants. There were thousands of birds and several herds of water buffalo, kangaroo, wallaby, duckbill platypus, and fresh-water crocodile. From her ringside seat in the Stearman, Vicky was snapping away at the beautiful natural habitat below with her Nikon now outfitted with a 500mm telephoto lens. A long strand of her chestnut mane found its way from under her Australian Aboriginal art headscarf. Damn, she was sexy!

"Ed, whadaya say we get back up to around 3500? Looks like we pretty much have dry red desert in front of us for quite a distance."

"Yeah, Sam. Let's do it. Best we see as much of the horizon as far out as possible. Tom really got my attention about the dust storms."

"Right on! You're reading my mind."

We were approaching 1500 feet when all four of us saw it. It was unmistakable. Vicky spoke up over her intercom. "Sam, look at that red cloud off to our left. Is that a dust storm like Tom was talking about?"

"Sure looks like it. Ed, what do you think we should do?"

"That's highway 71 about five miles over to our west. The storm is still several miles from it, and I can see that the few cars and trucks on the road have their headlights on, and some have even pulled off onto the shoulder. I suggest we heed the sign of the natives. I think we need to either turn back immediately or find a place to put these birds down and dig in. Your call, Sam."

"Let's take a vote. Hands up if you want to turn around." No hands went up in either Stearman.

"OK, looks like we are in for an adventure! Prepare for a bloody dust storm!"

"Look straight ahead, Ed. That desert looks flat, not too much brush. Might be a good place to put down. Let's make a low pass over it and check it out."

"Sounds good. Go ahead of me, Sam. I will follow in behind you."

"OK, Ed, I am going to drop 20 degrees of flaps, airspeed to 60 knots, and go down to twenty feet and get a good look."

"Right behind you."

We both pulled back on power and made a slow reconnaissance of the desert below. "Looks pretty good to me. What do you think, Ed?"

"I think we better get these girls on the ground."

Once we landed, the enormity of the storm bearing down on us sunk in. The western horizon was covered with an ominous blanket of dark red and black boiling fury that commanded a new kind of respect for weather from two young pilots who thought they had seen it all.

Adrianna was nervous. "This does not look good for us. What are we to do? I am frightened."

Vicky grabbed the entrenching tools. "Come on, Adrianna. We have a big hole to dig while the guys tie down the airplanes."

The mooring augers were three feet in length but easily sliced deep into the red Australian desert. Ed and I had both aircraft headed into the oncoming storm and secured within thirty minutes. We joined the girls. I had to admit that we were pleasantly surprised at the progress they had made.

Ed threw out a sincere compliment. "WOW! You do good work."

"I'll say! Here, let us have a go at it," I said, reaching out for the tools.

Vicky and Adrianna had already dug a hole approximately three feet wide, six feet long and two feet deep. Ed and I had jumped in and were still digging when the wall of red dust, wind, and rain swooped down on us like a giant being from another planet. We jumped into our trench, now about five feet deep, and pulled the canvas from the pup tent over the top of our heads. With the girls between us, Ed and I each held down opposite ends of the tarp with a vice-like grip. Though somewhat protected from the onslaught of winds, which were in excess of 60 miles per hour, we could not evade the heavy rain and the hailstones that actually stung through the canvas and drenched the ground below us. There was no letting go of it; we clutched the edges of that tarp with all our might.

Remarkably, after two hours of relentless wind and rain, the storm left us as fast as it had arrived. We had lost all feeling in our hands, but gratefully flipped back the canvas and stood up, finding ourselves knee-deep in muddy water.

"Welcome to the Outback you bloody Yanks!" laughed Ed in his best Aussie accent.

We all looked at Ed and then at each other; four drowned rats, soaked through and through, completely covered in red slush. Adrianna started laughing first, and we all followed. Vicky ran for her camera and began snapping away as we playfully posed in ways that accentuated our filthy condition.

"So, where do we go from here flyboys?" she asked when we finally quieted down. The question was, could we take off in a rain-soaked desert? What had been hard, dry red clay on landing was now thick, wet slippery mud.

"It's after 2:00 in the afternoon. I think the chances of this desert drying out well enough for a takeoff before dark are slim to none. I say we start collecting firewood and set up camp here for tonight. The last thing we want to do is try to take off and not be able to make it."

"What do you mean, not be able to make it, Sam?" questioned Vicky.

"As we move forward, the build-up of red mud on our tires could stop us from taking off. Even worse, if we were to sink deep enough into this mud, our props could get dinged by hitting the ground, and that would spell disaster. Bottom line, it is safer to wait until morning."

Ed agreed. "Good call, Sam. I'll take off and find some firewood. Adrianna, you want to help me?"

"Let's all go, Ed," suggested Vicky. "Setting up camp won't take that long."

We walked over a quarter of a mile before we found a small dead tree covered with red muck. The limbs were about four inches in diameter, and with Ed and I both jumping on them, we were able to easily break them into smaller pieces. Then, using the machete, we hacked away the wet surface to get what we needed: dry wood.

After collecting our first load, the girls started setting up camp while Ed and I returned for more wood. For our second trip, I had slung the twenty-two rifle over my shoulder, as all we had on hand for supper was two cans of barbecued beans, and I was hoping to get lucky. We went back a third time to collect all the small branches we could carry to make a barrier between our sleeping bags and the wet ground. Heading back for camp at dusk, I spotted a large rabbit sitting next to some small shrubs. One shot nailed it. Dinner!

"Hope you girls like rabbit! Sam just shot the Easter Bunny!"

Adrianna looked bewildered. "In my country, rabbit is a delicacy. I would very much enjoy some rabbit, but what is this Easter Bunny kind of rabbit?"

"It's a rabbit that lays colorful chicken eggs," deadpanned Ed.

"You Americans! Always make with the joke! Here, I have something for everyone. And this is no joke. Will make you feel good, very good."

After rummaging through her backpack, Adrianna produced two green bottles. "How do you say, 'have someone up your sleeve'?"

Vicky laughed, "The saying is 'to have some THING up your sleeve!'"

"OK, then. I have these two bottles of Becherovka up my sleeve for you."

I reached for one of the them and admired it. "Very pretty, Adrianna. What is it?"

"It's the national drink of Czechoslovakia. How you say in English, 'will knock you on your ass!"

With that, we all burst out laughing, and then Adrianna encouraged each of us to take a big, healthy gulp. I didn't dare, preferring to take a small, exploratory sip. "I like it! What's in it?"

"It is a secret of Dr. Becherovka. It is alcohol with twenty-three herbs and spices."

I passed the bottle to Vicky.

"Wow! Nice! Really nice! Tastes like Christmas in a bottle."

By then, Ed had opened the second bottle and had already taken a gulp. We continued to pass the bottles around as we prepared dinner and set up camp. I skinned and cleaned the rabbit while Ed helped with the pup tent.

"If we want to stay dry tonight, we need to use one tent for flooring on top of the branches. The four of us can get into the two sleeping bags in the one pup tent. It will be tight, but dry and warm."

Vicky put her arm around me and squeezed. "Sounds cozy to me. Can we put the tent close to the fire?"

"Sure. Let's get it pitched while there is still some light left."

We split several pieces of wood with Tom's machete. By exposing the inner dry area, the fire started easily, and we had managed to gather enough wood to last all night. As the sun set, the desert cooled. We huddled around the campfire cooking our rabbit on a spit and heating the beans in the camp cookware. The fire dried our clothing, and the mud caked up so we could scrape most of it off with the dull side of a knife.

The Becherovka went well with rabbit and beans, and we would find out that Adrianna was right; it had pretty much knocked us on our asses. Holding on during the storm and hastily setting up camp had pretty much tired us out, and the national drink of Czechoslovakia had finished us off. Snug in our pup tent, we slept soundly under a starlit night in the Australian Outback.

***

Old habits die hard. I was up at the crack of dawn, and Ed was right there with me. The girls were still asleep. I tended the fire while Ed found the coffee and made us a pot.

"Think this clay will dry out enough for us to take off by noon?

"I think so, Sam. It's already looking pretty good. I guess we will just have to give it a go ... Oh my God, Sam! Looks like another storm coming our way!"

I had my back to the west. Turning around, I could see a wall of reddish-black sky hovering over the northwest horizon.

"Let's down this coffee, get the girls up, and get the hell out of here, Ed. We didn't come to Australia to spend R&R in the middle of the desert dodging these fuckin' storms."

"I agree. I'll start pulling up the augers and getting the planes ready. You get the girls up and the tent down."

Within thirty minutes, we were talking to each other over the radios as the aircraft engines warmed up, each of us silently praying that we would not get stuck in the mud.

"I'll go first, Sam. Then you should make a take-off run to either side of my tire tracks; otherwise, you could get stuck in my rut."

"Gotcha, Ed. Let's do it."

The Stearman was made for this type of rough terrain. Packing four hundred-fifty horsepower, nine-cylinder radial engines, the bi-plane, like a tank, had plenty of power to plow through the red Australian mud. The roll out before liftoff seemed to go on forever, but there was no shortage of desert to accommodate it. Our wheels were caked with red mud, but we weren't sinking into the mire, which had been our biggest concern. Soon we found ourselves climbing to the east to avoid another giant storm.

"Sam, let's keep highway 71 in view for a few miles and then head to Port Macquarie to refuel."

The plan was a success. Landing at Port Macquarie, we refueled, grabbed a quick lunch, and took off again. This small airport had a high-pressure hose, which we used to spray the mud off the tires, struts, and underbelly. That was a definite improvement. Flying along the Australian coast afforded views much more spectacular than I could have imagined. We dropped down to 200 feet just to take it all in. Again, Vicky put her camera to good use. Later, we landed at Newcastle's grass airstrip and found Will Chesterton waiting for us as we taxied to a full stop. We had forgotten how bedraggled we looked until we saw the look on Will's face.

"Good day, Yanks! Tom gave me a jingle and said to expect you. From the looks of ya, I imagine you had quite a night in the Outback!"

"Yeah, we got caught in a dust storm, but we got out this morning just as another was bearing down on us. One was enough! I'm Sam, by the way. I'm usually not this orange. Pleased to meet you."

"Dust storms can be a real bugger in the Outback. I have been caught in a few myself. No fun. Glad you made it out, mates. I have two cabins ready for you and your Sheilas. You'll find a stocked bar and a hot shower inside each one. Looks like you need it! There is a barbie out front, too. Wonderful to cook outside and watch the sunset. My wife, Jenny, will bring you a menu as soon as you get settled. You can choose fresh fish, steak or chicken. Just tell her what you want, and we'll deliver it to you. Jenny prepares the vegetables for ya, and they are complimentary."

We decided on fresh fish. Jenny brought us the fillets of two large barramundi, a popular fish in Australia, along with homemade marinade she prepared with ginger, lemon, and soy sauce for basting the fish over the coals. After much needed hot showers, we relaxed in front of Ed's cabin sipping cold Australian beer and watching the sunset as the grill heated up. Adrianna broke the silence. "I would never have imagined such an adventure was possible just a few days ago. There is something about you Americans that is just … well, different from the rest of the world. You … how do you say … always seem to seize the moment. I have never had such fun in my entire life as I have with you three in the last few days. Thank you so much for taking me along."

"The trip's not over yet, my lovely Czech. We have two nights to relax here, which sounds pretty good to me right now. Then, back in Sydney, we can take a train to see another wonderful part of this country. Anyone got any preferences?"

"Why not Melbourne?" Vicky suggested. "I've heard so much about it."

"Melbourne it is." Ed raised his glass, and the rest of us joined in the toast.

***

Sunshine greeted us the next morning, and we enjoyed breakfast outside, a nice change from the air-conditioned dining room at the hotel. The girls set the table while Ed and I cooked up bacon and eggs. We downed a lot of coffee, too. That day we explored Newcastle at a leisurely pace. For dinner, we opted to repeat the fish, rationalizing that it was fresh, and something we'd likely never have again anytime soon.

The next morning, after heartfelt good-byes to Will and Jenny for making our stay so comfortable, we boarded the bi-planes and headed due south to Sydney. Ed and I decided to throttle back and fly at a slow pace over the beaches to enjoy the scenery for the last time. After landing where our bi-plane adventure had begun, we thanked Tom for the experience of a lifetime. I handed him a rabbit's foot as a memento of our excursion.

Returning to the InterContinental, we asked the concierge to arrange round trip tickets for two sleepers on the overnight train to Melbourne, returning to Sydney in three days.

***

I had heard that much of modern-day Australia looked as though the clock had stopped at the turn of the century, and the train bore that out. It had the Victorian splendor of the Orient Express, right out of the Agatha Christie novel. The elegant décor included hardwood paneling accented with brass details and etched glass lighting with cut glass fringe that sparkled and tinkled as the train sped along the tracks.

We settled in our compartments before meeting in the dining car for a relaxing dinner. The dining car was rather elegant, with its white table linens, ornate china, and elegant glassware. Our waiter appeared in a crisp white dinner jacket and black bow tie and let us know, discreetly of course, that their martinis were not only among the world's best but also discounted 50 percent for American soldiers, and so, we began our meal.

As the train traveled south, we sipped martinis, nibbled on a variety of appetizers, and reminisced about our bi-plane adventure. After a delicious dinner, Vicky and Adrianna were ready to turn in. Ed and I stayed back for just one more. Vietnam seemed like another life, long ago and far away. Ed and I talked about the tug of returning to war. R&R was like finding yourself cast in a pleasant TV show, shot in full technicolor, while the film of war that awaited our sequel was dreary, bleak, and fraught with danger.

Had I known what was waiting for me, I wonder if I would have returned. On base, stories circulated of GIs who had flown to Sydney for R&R and then made their escape to Australia's Northern Territory where they faded into the fabric of a remote, new place. Others had jumped freighters going to New Guinea and beyond. A few paid thousands to someone who could make them disappear. These were men full of fear and desperation who chose to walk away from their lives, their families, and their nation, forever, rather than return to the hell that was Vietnam. Debate often ensued – were they the smart ones, or were they cowards?

All I can say is that when the end of R&R draws near, it's very unsettling, almost suffocating, or paralyzing. R&R actually has three stages. First is acclimation, when you feel strange despite the fact that you are in a nice place you know you should be able to enjoy. You're jumpy, unable to relax, and can't seem to get comfortable. The second stage is normalization; that is, you finally let your guard down and enjoy the locale with all of its sunshine and niceties. The third is dread, with a twist. You not only dread going back to war, but you also try to put a good face on things for the loved ones you're spending time with. Once this dread creeps up on you, you have to lug it wherever you go. It can really get in your way unless you can beat it back and live in the present.

Bottom line is this: it takes more guts to return to war than it does to go to war in the first place. Maybe that's why Ed and I had more martinis than the girls, many more.

***

After a night in the sleeping car and breakfast in the dining car, our train pulled into Flinders Street Station on the Yarra River, where Melbourne, the cultural capital of the continent holds old world attitudes while demonstrating a certain European air not found in other Australian cities. We had been advised to take in the railway station, both inside and out. I thought that a bit strange until I experienced it myself.

The train tracks were the busiest and longest I had ever seen; in fact, Flinders Street Station was the busiest in the southern hemisphere. In 1924, it was recognized as the busiest in the world, surpassing New York and Paris. Victorian style clocks and fixtures were everywhere. We followed the tiled walkways from the tracks to the interior of the station; it was a long walk. Vicky and Adrianna needed to visit the Ladies' Room, and they came back in awe of its size and fixtures. I would read later in a travel book that when the station opened in 1909, it was one of the first places to include public bathrooms, and the original outsized Ladies' Room mirrors remain in place today, having survived various refurbishing projects. Ed and I noticed original 'No Spitting' signs, thoughtfully preserved, that had been put in place sixty years earlier. The four of us were duly impressed with the station, and we had only seen the inside.

At the grand entrance, the interior space was awesome. The walls were lined with cut stone, and the ceiling, at least fifty feet overhead, was detailed with painted woodwork echoing the circular base of the domed top we had not yet seen. While every inch of space was adorned in some way, it did not feel overdone; I liked it. The space was flooded with light, streaming in from sizable arched windows that sat above the open glass doors. One of the most interesting features was not only practical but had become famous. A row of nine clocks, which displayed departure times, extended from the bottom of the arched window to the top of the doors. When originally installed in 1909, and for decades since, these old clocks had to be adjusted manually by a man on the ground using a very long pole. Years later, during a refurbishment, they were removed, to be replaced with a set of automatic clocks of the same size. The local public outrage was so strong, the original clocks were promptly restored to their rightful places and were later automated. A local expression, 'I'll meet you under the clocks', was universally understood and endures today.

Stepping outside, under the clocks we descended a wide staircase and crossed the street so that we could turn around and take in the exterior of Flinders Street Station. We gasped. The four-story building stretched nearly two blocks and was a confection of warm cream cut stone with contrasting red bricks. The entrance was crowned with a green metal dome, detailed with raised ribs, ornate windows, and a decorative spire. Another nine clocks back-to-back with those inside faced the street. Down at the far end of this impressive station, stood a tall clock tower crowned with its own metal dome. Elements of classical architecture that I could not name, but appreciated, caught my attention. Vicky was so impressed.

"It's times like this that I'm glad I have a Nikon," she declared as she snapped away. Then we hailed a cab to The Hotel Windsor. This old Victorian hotel was also beautiful but in need of a facelift.

After checking in, having been so impressed with the train station, we were eager to see the city and took in as many sites as we could fit into our day: the Parliament buildings, St. Patrick's Cathedral, although none of us were Catholic, King's Domain Gardens and the National Gallery of Victoria. All the while, the Melburnians extended their brand of friendliness toward strangers, especially Americans, like no one else in the world.

After a full day, we retreated to Florentino, a famous Italian restaurant with ambiance to match the cuisine, where we dined on veal shank with basil broth and black cabbage. Fully sated, we struck out to sample Melbourne nightlife and ended up on Chapel Street in the heart of the South Yarra-Prahran area, which was lined with clubs and bars. Every place we entered, someone wanted to buy a drink for the American soldiers and their Sheilas. We felt very special and appreciated, so unlike the attitudes in the States. It was pretty late when we returned to the hotel, and Ed suggested that he and I have another nightcap before turning in. Sounded good to me. Choosing a small table with an upholstered booth conducive to conversation, we ordered Scotch.

"Well, it sure seems like you and Adrianna are enjoying yourselves! This Australian adventure has worked out great for both of you. You think you'll stay in touch with her after R&R is over?"

"Yes, I agree we're very compatible. She's really quite an interesting woman. So yeah, I would like to see her again, but there's a complication." He took a long pull on his drink.

"What's that?"

"I'm married."

"WHAT? You're married?" My jaw dropped. I took a long pull then signaled for another round.

"Well, technically. I got the 'Dear John' letter a few months ago; I'm still waiting for the divorce papers."

"I never knew you were married. You never mentioned your wife."

"This all happened right before I met you. In fact, that was one of the reasons why I wanted to be your Assistant Seafood Procurement Officer. I wanted those nights at the Vung Tau beach, with all the booze and available women. I was definitely not looking for a relationship; I just needed a little help forgetting one. Well, maybe a lot of help!"

"Wow, a 'Dear John' letter. I know that happens all too often in the Nam; I'm sorry it happened to you."

"Yeah, I don't think I'll ever forget that day. When I saw the envelope, I figured it was just another letter from Rachel, you know, news from home, how she's keeping busy, how much she misses me, that kind of thing. When I started reading, I went into shock. She kept apologizing, saying she didn't want it to happen, she couldn't help herself, but that she made her decision and wanted a divorce, no hard feelings. Ha!" He took another swig.

"Do you know who the guy is?"

"No, that's another thing. She held that back. She even went so far as to say that he's really a very nice person, and if I had met him under different circumstances, I'd probably like him, too. Can you imagine?"

"Ouch!"

"Yeah. Fat chance of that! But it was clear that by the time she wrote that letter to me, they already had definite plans. Our marriage was over. She told me that I could stop sending any money her way and that she'd be vacating our apartment as soon as the lease expired. She also said she'd return the ring since that was a family heirloom. My mother had given it to me for Rachel when we got engaged; it had been my grandmother's wedding ring."

"Good to hear that about the ring, but what about all your stuff?"

"Well, a few days after I got Rachel's letter, I got one from my mother. She told me that Rachel called to come over for coffee, and when they were sitting at the table, Rachel slid the antique velvet ring box over to her. At first, my mom thought, why is she giving me this box? Then she realized the ring was no longer on Rachel's finger; it was back in the box. That's when Rachel blurted out that she was divorcing me. Mom said they both cried together, talked a bit, and then Rachel reached into her pocket and handed her the car keys. She told mom it was my car – it was – and all of my things were in it. Then she asked mom to call her a taxi and left to wait outside. My poor mom was still in shock; she said after their visit was over, she still didn't know why, when, how, or who. For a moment, she thought it hadn't really happened, but the velvet box and the car keys were sitting on the kitchen table. Then she just sat there in shock until my father got home from work. Having seen my car in the driveway, he walked into the kitchen saying, 'I see Rachel's here for a visit!' Then my mother explained it all to him. This has been very tough on my parents."

"The 'Dear John' was bad enough; thank God she didn't rip you off."

"Funny thing, Rachel was always a good planner, so efficient and pragmatic. I actually admired that about her. I used to think it would help her manage on her own while I was away. How she handled all this: clean, neat, all wrapped up, it was just like her."

"That other guy must be really something. Sounds like he has money. You don't have any idea who he is?"

"Nah, I figure someday I might find out. Still, I took it pretty hard. Those next few days were rough. Good thing I'm the Scheduling Officer; I scheduled myself for the O Club! Too much drinking, for sure. I'd sleep badly and wake up thinking it was all a bad dream, and then I'd see those fucking letters. That was proof."

"You still got 'um?"

"Hell no! Burned 'um!"

"In your hooch?"

"Not exactly. I gathered up all her letters and all my pictures of Rachel. Tore them into little pieces. Dropped them into the shitter. They got burned, all right! After that, I started to come out of it. When my head cleared, I thought it would be a good idea to become your Assistant Seafood Procurement Officer. And look how that's turned out! I wouldn't be sitting here today, with you, the guy who danced with Miss America, and with the stunning Adrianna upstairs, waiting for me."

"You going to tell her?"

"If I ever want to see her again, I guess I'd better come clean."

"If you want my opinion, after having spent time with Adrianna, she's worth it. Good luck."

"Adrianna's had an interesting life. Her parents left Czechoslovakia in the late forties when she was little. They settled in France, where her father made professional connections and found work teaching science at a university. As a kid, Adrianna attended her first ballet, and that made a strong impression. She said she walked on her toes and talked about becoming a ballerina all day long. Her mother found a ballet school run by an elderly woman, a Russian expat. I never knew much about ballet, but Adrianna explained how highly the Russians value it, and Madame Federov ran a tight ship. She always carried a riding crop, and she didn't hesitate to use it. Not to whip the students, just to 'give them a message'. If any part of your body was not where it was supposed to be, you got a slight rap on the offending part. Even if you were taking a break and Madame thought you were displaying poor posture. That's one reason Adrianna has so much poise and carries herself so well. She got the message!"

"That explains that. So, Adrianna actually grew up in France? So, she speaks Czech, French, and English. And her English is probably better than mine!"

"Ha! You're Charleston English sure is different from anything I've ever heard. Her parents still live in France, which is Adrianna's home base. She and her mother really wanted to get away from the cold winter, and her father came up with the idea of them spending some time here."

"Well, I tell you what, buddy, if you ever meet him, you better thank him!" With that, we toasted Adrianna's father, emptied our glasses, and called it a night.

***

The next morning, we slept late, thoroughly exhausted from the previous day and the late night. When Vicky and I went down for breakfast or lunch, whatever it was, we did not see Ed and Adrianna. I suggested to Vicky that we give them some space, on this, our last full day. I left a message for Ed that Vicky and I would be sight-seeing and would meet them in the lobby around seven to leave for the station.

During our stroll through Melbourne, with no specific target in mind, I knew I had to tell Vicky. If Adrianna was taking things badly, she'd turn to Vicky for consolation, and this way, Vicky would be ready. Besides, I really was preoccupied with this whole thing, and Vicky picked right up on it. I realized I'd never be able to keep a secret from her. Spotting an outdoor café, I suggested we take a coffee break; the last thing I needed was more alcohol.

"Well, flyboy, I know it's our last day of R&R, but you've been acting a bit out of sorts. If I let myself think about it, I would get depressed, too, but I don't want to spend our last glorious day, depressed. Come on, hasn't this trip been just wonderful! Think of it, we've spent our nights in a tent in the outback, in a cabin in Newcastle, on the sleeper train, and in two of the world's most beautiful hotels. We've been dressed to the nines and as drenched as drowned rats. And we've been keeping company with two very special people, Ed and Adrianna. She and I are going to keep in touch for sure. Did you know she actually lived in France for years?"

"I just found out last night. That, and something else." I proceeded to share Ed's story. Vicky was quiet throughout. When she finally spoke, she deduced that Ed must have told Adrianna, and they would have needed time to themselves. Maybe they were still in their room. She cursed Rachel and Dear John letters. She was sincerely sorry for what happened to Ed. Then her thoughts turned to Adrianna. "I know that Adrianna has really developed feelings for Ed, and she wondered if they would ever see each other again. But I have no idea how she will feel about this. I mean, in a way, he isn't really married. But why didn't he tell her? Then again, they've only known one another for nine days! How much should he have divulged? How much has she? It's complicated."

On that, we agreed. And, that it was really their business.

"You're right about something you said earlier, Vicky; this is not the time to be depressed. I am grateful for another beautiful afternoon, in a beautiful city, with the finest woman I have ever known." With that, Vicky landed a playful punch on my arm, and we set out to enjoy the remaining hours of our visit to Melbourne, but Ed and Adrianna were never far from my mind.

We enjoyed the afternoon in this welcoming city and were back in the hotel lobby close to 7 p.m. I spotted Ed sitting in a lounge chair, carelessly flipping through a magazine. Alone. No sign of Adrianna. My heart sank. Then I heard the subtle ding of the elevator, saw the door open, and Adrianna strode out with her distinctive gait towards Ed. He put down the magazine and rose from his seat. Then they embraced, and it was not just one of those greeting hugs; this one was tender. I sighed. It seemed they had weathered their storm.

Later, after having moved into our sleeper compartments, we met in the familiar dining car, for this, the last supper of our R&R. Seated at a table for four, I noticed close up that Adrianna's eyes looked a bit swollen from crying, but her spirit was buoyant and cheerful. Ed seemed relaxed, as though he had thrown off a weight he was bearing. After dinner and drinks, Vicky and Adrianna made their way back to our cars, and Ed and I remained for a nightcap.

"I think we drank all the Scotch in Melbourne last night."

"Yeah, I know what you mean. Good thing the train is well-stocked!"

Ed volunteered that he had indeed told Adrianna about his situation. Although she was shocked and hurt at first, when she understood the circumstances, she became more understanding and even compassionate. She confided with Ed that she hoped they could go forward with their relationship. In addition, Ed confided that to his surprise he finally felt purged of all the bitterness he had towards Rachel, anger he hadn't realized that he was still lugging around.

***

The next morning, Ed and Adrianna had to part at the train station in Sydney. Vicky and I said our good-byes to Adrianna and then gave them privacy while we lined up a taxi for the ride to the airport.

Returning to Vietnam this time was especially hard for me, much more difficult than from Hawaii. After all this time together, we had grown even closer; our relationship had deepened. I ached to remain in Vicky's presence. I hated being separated from her and dreaded returning to my duty. But I had to accept the fact that after boarding our flights, she and I would go our separate ways, once again, for a few more months. There was nothing anyone could do about that.

It was so unfair that a young couple could meet, fall in love, but could not just get on with living happily ever after. STOP! Fingernails on the chalkboard. I have to do what? Go fight and possibly die in an ugly, meaningless war.

On top of that, back in the real world, no one believes in this war. Worse still, people in the real world hate you for fighting in it. It was like being stuck in a nightmare from which you could not wake up. I was so ready to get this part of my life behind me. Enough was enough, yet I had three long months to go.

Now it was Ed's turn to give Vicky and me some privacy. We held each other tightly. She started to cry, and through her sobs managed to choke out, "I promised myself I wouldn't do this."

It ripped me apart to see my dear, sweet Vicky in such pain. It wasn't just about being separated; it was more about the dread. There was no denying what I was going back into. Three more months. May God watch over me. And may God give Vicky the strength and peace she would need to endure the remainder of my tour of duty.

Chapter 22 Red Alert

Last week couldn't have been any better. This week couldn't be any worse. We had returned to base camp to find that five firefights had broken out real close to our base, and Red Alert status had been declared. 'Red Alert' is as serious as it gets; it means enemy attack appears imminent. I had not yet experienced that since being in-country.

Strange to say, and nothing I'd ever admit out loud, but inexplicably, I felt relieved that our Australian trip was over. As much as we soldiers looked forward to R&R, in many ways, it was like the popular cheerleader who seductively teases the dorky, pimply-faced kid. Look, but don't touch. Too good to be true. Freedom. Normalcy ... a fleeting fantasy only to be snatched away by time; the time to return to war. From R&R to Red Alert, once again, I found myself bending my psyche to adjust from the highest of highs to the lowest of lows.

Red Alerts don't just happen. It takes a series of events to create them. During the ten days that Ed and I were away, all hell had broken loose. We had caught a chopper straight to Bear Cat, and the pilot had filled us in on the situation.

The small dirt road connecting Long Thanh and Bear Cat was less than a quarter-mile long, yet a warrant officer driving a jeep had been killed by sniper fire. It was rumored that the Cobra squadron situated at Bear Cat was pulling out. This was not good, as they were our main source of protection. The perimeter of our base camp had been breached twice by sapper attacks. Four VC killed. Two airplanes destroyed. One American soldier wounded. Highway One, the main road as we called it, ran for hundreds of miles north to south. The twenty-mile stretch between Long Thanh and Bien Hoa had seen three ambushes in one week. The first two took their toll: six south Vietnamese soldiers killed and four wounded. The third resulted in nine VC killed and two Americans wounded.

Ed and I had come back to a different place than the one we had left just ten days ago. Throughout my nine months in-country, I had never felt what you would call 'safe', but I had not felt constantly threatened or vulnerable until now. Ed knocked on my hooch door and came in. It was only 0700 hours.

"Had breakfast yet?"

"No, Ed. Guess I was trying to get up my courage to decide between SOS or greasy bacon and powdered eggs."

"Well, come on. Let's choke somethin' down. I got a favor to ask. If you say no, I'll understand."

While we ate, Ed explained. "As you know, one of my responsibilities is aviation fuel. Since the Red Alert, during my absence, no one has gone to Bien Hoa, and we are now almost out of fuel. I'm sending two tanker trucks; one officer must accompany each driver. I am going with one, and I need a second officer to go with the other."

"And you want me to go?"

"Yeah, I'm asking, but if you don't want to, I'll understand. Since we've been on Red Alert, Tipper has brought in a SEAL Team. They will be going with us, too, on the trucks. We'll also have a Special Forces Team leading us there and back. Whadaya say?"

"So why the fuck are you asking me? You know I can't say no! When do we leave?"

"As soon as we can choke down this slop."

Highway One, the main artery for the country was deserted. There was not a truck, bicycle, person, or water buffalo in sight, and usually, there were quite a few of all four. The highway had become ground zero, and my country-boy ass was riding back from Bien Hoa in a ten-thousand-gallon tanker truck full of aviation fuel. I was not surprised that the drive to Bien Hoa was uneventful; after all, there was no need for Charlie to waste any ammo ambushing empty tankers, but the return trip was a different story. *I must be out of my freakin' mind* was all I could think, sitting next to a very nervous young driver. We both wore flak vests and steel pots, and I had an M-16. There was a Navy SEAL on each running board shouldering M-60 machine guns. My mind was racing, *So, what the fuck? One RPG round in either one of these tankers would be enough to send all of us to the moon and beyond.*

Via our PRC-25s, Ed and I were in communication with the Special Forces Team in a half-track personnel carrier up ahead. The young lieutenant leading the team spoke up. "Sir, stand down. Say again, hold your position. We got movement up ahead about one-quarter klick."

Ed responded, and we stopped immediately as the lead team quietly inched forward. Then, eight men in the half-track got out. Four on each shoulder of the road about ten feet apart, moving forward, their weapons in the ready-to-fire position. In the blink of an eye, they dropped into the prone position and began firing into the jungle on full-automatic. Then, within seconds, two Cobras arrived, delivering a surgical strike that unleashed all hell onto their target below. Plumes of black smoke billowed out of the jungle. Then all went quiet, except for the sizzling and crackling burn of what used to be.

The PRC-25 clicked on, breaking our silence. "Sir, we are good to go," and with that, we were moving again.

As we rolled past the macabre scene, the Navy SEAL on my running board made a statement under his breath that I couldn't make out, but I didn't need too. Looking beyond him, a break in the smoldering trees revealed that spot in the jungle that moments ago used to be a green place with people in it. Now, the area about one-third the size of a football field, looked as though a giant egg beater running on its fiercest speed had scrambled and fried the jungle growth and everything in it, without showing any mercy.

I couldn't avert my eyes from this gruesome landscape. Pieces of bodies were strewn everywhere. Human innards hung from trees, shattered skulls were plastered against tree trunks, an AK-47 barrel was lodged into a stalk of green bananas, while pools of blood, random scraps of clothing, and pieces of violently torn flesh blanketed the killing field. Must have been at least a dozen people who found themselves in the wrong place at the wrong time that day. But of course, they had been planning to destroy us. We won this match but rode by in silence. Nothing to gloat about.

Back at base camp, Ed and I stepped out of our tanker trucks and just looked at one another. Without saying a word, we walked to the O Club where I paid Ling for an already open bottle of ice-cold vodka that she kept in a freezer for me. Got two shot glasses and sat down at a table with Ed. We finished the remains of the bottle in complete silence.

We would never speak of this experience again, but we both knew we would never forget it.

Chapter 23 Black Ops

All I had left, if I could make it, was eighty-eight days and a wake-up. I had been scheduled for a Special Covert Black Operations (SCBO) mission with Mitch, when he developed a case of dysentery, and Tex volunteered for his spot. Because these types of missions were so dangerous, a pilot had to be in-country for at least nine months before even being considered for one; the survival rate was only twenty-five percent. Generally, a pilot was limited to two per tour of duty and always had the right to decline if scheduled to fly one.

SCBO missions differed from top-secret missions in that each operation had a unique set of circumstances and objectives, for which no amount of practice could be considered adequate preparation. Actually, some regarded it as a welcomed break from the day-to-day top-secret missions we had been trained for, but thinking that way could cause you to lose perspective on its inherent danger. Despite the fact that I was in love with a wonderful woman, I was excited about being scheduled to fly an SCBO mission. Vicky would be livid if she knew about this, but I think deep down in every seasoned combat pilot, there is a hankering for the next hunt.

"OK, Tex, you and Sam listen up. This is a serious one!" said Lieutenant Young. He had a stern look on his face that I had not seen before in previous mission briefings.

"Is there any other kind?" Tex said with a chuckle.

"Even though you, Tex, are senior pilot, Sam here is going to fly first pilot in the left seat. You have the most experience, Tex, but Sam is your junior by some years, and his reflexes are just a trigger quicker, which may make an important difference. No offense intended, Tex."

"None taken, LT. The only thing that ever offended me was being called 'Sir' by a young barmaid when I was thirty."

Everyone laughed.

"You have wheels up at thirteen hundred. Direct to Tan Son Nhut. Taxi to Flight Ops and pick up General Steven Randolf and two footlockers."

"Whoa, whadaya mean, footlockers? What kind of footlockers and what's in 'um?"

"The contents are classified, Sam, but I can tell you, these are not like any footlockers you have ever seen. They do not contain any explosives or hazardous materials. They weigh five hundred pounds each."

"Five hundred pounds? What the fuck is in there ... gold?"

"You said it; I didn't."

That is exactly what it was, gold!

"You will be flying to this grid coordinate here on the map. It's in the central highlands inside Laos. Always misty, drizzling rain, and poor visibility. Pretty much a rain forest. This airstrip does not have a name. You will not find it on any map. It does not exist. Set your primary and secondary FM radios to FM 89. You will not have anyone to talk to going into the strip or leaving. Two Special Forces units, SOGs, (Special Operations Group), will cover the concealed perimeter around the airstrip. They HALO-jumped in last night. They have your ETA. They will key their mic on FM 89 with two long bursts, then wait five seconds and repeat. That means they hear you coming, and you are clear to land. Your call sign is 'Catwalk 9'. If, for any reason, the SOG units think the mission is being compromised, they will key their mic three times very quickly and then repeat. You respond, 'Catwalk 9, aborting!'

"To get across the Fence, contact Ramrod on radio seven. His call sign is 'Ghost Rider 77.' Make the call approximately ten miles from the Fence. Squawk 76868 on your transponder right after you make the call to Ghost Rider."

"What about artillery and crossing the Fence?"

"This mission is extremely secretive; you are to remain off all radios. You're going dark. You will only talk to Ghost Rider 77 on radio seven going in and coming out. As you know, no one else can hear you."

"Yeah, OK, but that still doesn't answer the question about artillery."

"All artillery along this flight path," pointing it out on the map in response, "will be down during your time to and from your grid. Tex, you ever flown in here?"

"No LT, can't say that I have."

"This is a short airstrip on the side of a mountain. It is made from Marston Mat, which characteristically stays wet and slippery. Landing on Marston can be tricky, I'm sure you both know about that."

"So I've heard," Tex exploded. "Damn CIA! Just like those assholes to put down Marston Mat in an area like this, 'cause sure as shit they don't have to land on it."

"Oh, but they do, Tex."

"No, Lieutenant, they don't. Not in our type of aircraft, they don't. They probably fly choppers or small, light planes in there. Small airstrips made of Marston were not meant for larger planes, especially Marston airstrips that are short and narrow like this piece of shit we're flying to."

Marston Mat was a 'hurry up and make me a runway' material, an industrial product inspired by Tinker toy technology, featuring snap-together metal sheets. Each rectangular panel was pierced with rows of 'lightning' holes to minimize weight, and between these rows, were U-shaped channels. The average panel was ten feet by fifteen inches and had eighty-seven holes. One edge of the long side was lined with hooks, and the other with slots so that multiple sheets could be snapped together quickly and easily installed. Marston Mat had been used extensively in WWII and was pressed into national service once again in Vietnam, but not without issues, specifically, FOD or Foreign Object Damage, a nightmare of the aircraft industry. Vegetation grew through those holes and spread across the panels, posing the threat of being sucked into certain types of aircraft with disastrous results. Another problem had to do with the climate and weather conditions. Dew and rain collected in these holes, which were formed with raised edges, causing the red clay below to soften and ooze up and out over the metal panels, creating a very slippery surface. Not the kind of surface where a ten-ton airplane hitting it at ninety miles per hour can come to a quick stop. You'd probably have a better chance landing on a ski jump.

"OK, Sam. Very important. When you are on short final to this airstrip, you will be flying over a banana grove. If you cannot feel the belly of your aircraft hitting the tops of the banana trees, execute a go-around. If you miss it the second time, abort the mission. Truth is, you might want to think about aborting even if you miss it the first time, but officially, I can't tell you that."

My concern about this mysterious airstrip heightened. "Is this place that hot, Lieutenant?"

"Yeah, Sam. It really is. Let me come off script here for a second."

That was music to Tex's ears. "Yeah, please do, LT. Look buddy, this mission sucks, and you know it. You have also known both of us for quite a while now. Let's cut through all the official bullshit. How 'bout you fill in the blanks here, pal?"

"You bet, Tex. I will tell you what I know and what Special Forces Intel thinks is happening. Remember Tex, Sam, some of this is hearsay, but under absolutely no circumstances, is what I am about to tell you to leave this room. Understand?"

"Yeah, sure," we acknowledged. Now for the good part. I leaned in.

"You will be landing on a very remote airstrip in Laos on the edge of the Truong Son Mountains, which extends through Laos, a bit of Cambodia, and Nam. Of course, you probably know the Ho Chi Min Trail cuts through that range. The gold is for the Montagnard, a name given by the French to these mountain-dwelling people indigenous to that area. They refer to themselves as 'Degar'. The French were allied with the Degar for years, but when the French left the area, they abandoned the Degar, leaving them to fend for themselves. As it was, the Vietnamese considered them inferior people – ethnic outsiders – and after having aided the French, the Degar felt particularly vulnerable to the whims of the new communist regime. They were also threatened by the North Vietnamese, who were beginning to settle in the area that had been promised to them by the French. Because of this history, Uncle Sam figured the Degar were ripe for alliance with us, so they were sought out and trained by the U.S. Special Forces, in 1961, to aid the American military. The Green Berets found the Degar loyal and friendly allies who effectively guarded our outpost against the NVA and would later prove effective when deployed to other areas.

"That is where our interest stops, but the story goes on. Another tribe of people with roots in China, known as Hmong, also lives in Laos. They, too, have managed to preserve their ethnicity distinct from the Vietnamese. They, too, were recruited and trained by us and have been very effective in stopping NVA activity along the Ho Chi Minh Trail. So, we consider both the Degar and the Hmong to be our allies as we fight against the NVA. One difference being that the Hmong are productive farmers, and opium is their premier crop. Some believe the production and distribution is all funded by others, which makes perfect sense."

"And who would the bankrollers be?" I wanted to know.

"Well, I didn't expect to get in this deep, but here goes. There is a large community of Hmong in Burma, and Burma along with Thailand and Laos, is the hub of 'The Golden Triangle', which is considered the largest producer of opium in the world. If you translate that into dollars and cents, the economic and logistical enterprise is staggering. Anything that large has a number of players involved, and they're all probably ruthless. Some believe the Chinese communists or the Soviets are the financial backbone. I've actually heard it said – and I remind you not to repeat any of this! – that the war in Laos is not being waged over communism, but rather opium – whoever stays in control or effectively plays along stands to reap a fortune. This is where things get a little more than just fuzzy, and Uncle Sam chooses to leave it that way. Because the Degar are helping us, they demand payment in gold. Gold for what, right?"

"Seems to me they would want food and medicine," I reasoned.

"Exactly. It could be that the gold goes to the Degar as a payment for their service and loyalty. But it could also be much more complicated than that. There may be a link between the Degar and the Hmong. After all, they have in common their support of the Americans and the South Vietnamese, and they are both enemies of the NVA.

"So, it's possible, though I can't say for sure, but the Degar could pass the gold to the Hmong, who, through multiple back channels, support the Golden Triangle opium trade. Then the Hmong would pass the gold to the communists as a bribe for future assurance that the communists will leave the Degar and Hmong villages alone.

"We don't know the number of Hmong in Laos, but the Degar's best estimate is about one million. Over twenty-five thousand Degar currently fight side by side with American and Aussie Special Forces. Not 'if,' but 'when' we pull out of this war, their fate may be sealed. The retribution for supporting us would be ugly. For now, we have to take care of these people.

"That is why you are flying two footlockers full of gold to a remote mountain in dangerous territory with a US Army General who is literally the delivery boy. This general, who knows the village chief, is risking his life to personally hand over the package, to give the Degar assurances that we stand behind them ... at least for now. Remember, years earlier, they fought alongside the French only to be left high and dry. They are afraid, and rightly so, that we will do the same."

My head was spinning from this tangle of geo-political history. "So, let me be sure I get this; why I am risking my life here. One, the gold is a payment to the Montagnard for fighting alongside us, or two, the gold is payment to the Hmong, through the Montagnard, to either promote the opium trade, or three, to pay off the communist Chinese and maybe the Russians to not seek retribution, which could surely mean murder, rape, village burnings, literally ending their lives in this country. Did I miss anything?"

"I would say you about got it, Sam. Though there is just one more thing, and it will be the weirdest part of this mission."

Tex threw his head back and actually started laughing. "You mean this gets even crazier?"

"Afraid so, Tex."

"Go ahead, LT. Indulge us. This is already fuckin' nuts."

"After you land, a small STOL aircraft will land behind you. It will be unpainted aluminum. It will not have a mark on it. The pilot will be a civilian, or I should say, look like a civilian. He will approach the general as the general is exiting your aircraft. The general will hand him a canvas bag, which is actually a one hundred-pound satchel of gold. They may not even speak or look at each other. The pilot will return to his plane, bag in hand, and fly off immediately."

"More gold? What the fuck!"

"Yep. You must pretend you never saw that. Do not say a word. Ever! Got it?"

"Yeah, Got it."

"OK, let's finish up, 'cause you guys need to get going. Once you land, go easy on your brakes. The airstrip will be very slick. Tap your brakes and jockey your engines if you need to, to keep from running off the runway. Two half-tracks will pull up alongside you as you taxi to get in position to be ready for takeoff. Leave your engines running. The general will be met by a truck, and four to six Special Forces guys. They will load the two footlockers and disappear into the jungle for no more than fifteen minutes. While the general is gone, be ready for an immediate short field takeoff. This is where it gets tricky."

"Yeah, like this has been normal so far!"

This time the Lieutenant chuckled. "Sam, I guarantee you have never done one of these. The runway is too short for you to become airborne. The end of the runway drops off straight down into a twenty-five-hundred-foot valley. The valley runs to the southeast. The mountains on the other side are only a half-mile away. When you leave the end of the runway, you will need to push your nose over forty degrees. You will pick up enough airspeed within twenty to thirty seconds to pull up. IMPORTANT! Be sure to turn thirty to forty degrees to the southeast, say a heading of about one hundred ten degrees, as you begin your dive off the end of the runway so you remain in the valley. Got it?"

"Oh, boy! Yeah, Lieutenant, I got it! Man, if I had wanted to join a circus, I could have joined Barnum and Bailey when I finished college. Say, LT, one quick question – actually two."

"Sure, Sam. Shoot!

"How many times have you given this briefing, and how many pilots came back without a problem?"

"Ah, this will be my third briefing for this mission, and all pilots made it back, however, not without taking fire. Two of them took aircraft hits, but no one was hurt."

"Same general every time?"

"Yep! Same general every time. By the way, I have heard he is a pretty nice fella, but he does not like to be asked questions about this mission."

"Got it. We are out of here, LT. And thanks for filling in the details."

We picked up our precious cargo: one general and two footlockers. We were airborne heading north, northwest when the general spoke up on intercom, his thick southern accent a bit different from mine.

"Say, Tex, I think we met a few years back. Were you in Da Nang in sixty-eight?"

"Yes, Sir. I remember you as well, General. Back then, I was stationed down here at Long Thanh, but I was up there for about ten days."

"How come you're not flyin' this mission?"

"I am, Sir. That is, I am flyin' it with Walker, here."

"Yeah ...yeah... got all that, but first pilot always sits left seat. Walker is left seat."

I intervened. "Excuse me, General. I just want to assure you, Sir, that I am fully qualified to be sitting here. Besides, if I screw up, Tex here will never let me forget it."

"Yeah, Walker, and neither will I. You just seem to be pretty damn young, son, that's all."

"That's because I am, General. I'm twenty-four."

Tex laughed and chimed in, "General, I can assure you that Sam here is a good pilot, or I sure as shit wouldn't be sittin' here. I trust him, especially where we're going. My ass is probably as old as yours, Sir, and frankly, I just want to get home in one piece and start enjoyin' the good life."

"Where is home, Tex?"

"Texas, Sir. Amarillo. But I will be moving to a piece of land I bought near Santa Barbara. You know, do a little huntin' and fishin'."

"Huntin' huh? What do you like to hunt?"

"Birds. You know, duck, quail, dove, pheasant."

"Yeah, me too! When are you gettin' out, Tex?"

"A few more months here, then eighteen months in DC."

"I've got fourteen months and countin'. Here's my card. It's got my home number. I'm from Baton Rouge. Perhaps we can get together and shoot a few birds when we get out. Whadaya say?"

"Sure, General, that would be great, but on two conditions!"

"OK, what?"

"I call you by your first name, and admission to my huntin' club is one bottle of rare and expensive Scotch!"

"Steve. Call me Steve startin' right now, Tex. The generals that go by 'General' got somethin' to prove. Frankly, I am tired of the ivory tower image. Scotch man, huh?"

"Yes, sir."

"Yeah, me too. Ever had Macallan? Shit is almost five hundred a bottle."

"That would be Walker's department. I drink the cheap shit. Three hundred dollars a bottle, twenty-five-year Chivas."

"Damn, Walker! You tellin' me you drinkin' Scotch that expensive? You must be from money, son. A chief warrant officer can't afford that fine stuff."

Tex jumped in. "No, he gets his supplied from U.S. Senators."

"What?"

At that exact moment, the chit chat had to end. "Tex, time to call Ramrod."

"On it. Ghost Rider 77, this is Catwalk 9, how copy?"

"Got ya, Catwalk, and your transponder squawk of 76868. You can cut it off now. Turn it back on to the same frequency on your way out. Maintain your present heading. My info says you will be back across in less than an hour. Your reciprocal heading should be good, but call us first."

"Roger, Ghost Rider. Transponder off. Talk to you in a few."

The weather was marginal; patches of ground fog in the lower valleys, misty rain conditions, but visibility was at least three miles. Tex spotted the airstrip first.

"That would be it at eleven o'clock, about three miles out."

"Got it." We went through our landing checklist.

"OK, Sam, put this sweetheart in the top of those banana trees. I am on the stick and pedals with you. Not touching anything unless I need to help."

"I know, Tex. Thanks."

I hit the tops of the banana trees just as I had been advised, but because they were soaking wet, they abruptly slowed me down a few knots, which I had not expected. I added a touch of power to compensate. When we hit the Marston, the worst of our fears came true. It was like trying to stop on a truckload of wet banana peels. It took both Tex and me, in an elaborate dance, jockeying to throttle our engines and tap-tap-tapping the brakes just so, until we finally came to a complete stop before running off the runway. Then we turned and taxied back to the other end, where we were poised for takeoff.

"Good job, men." The General was visibly nervous. "OK, I should not be gone more than fifteen minutes. When I return, I'll have the driver drop me off behind this wing so we can get out of Dodge as quickly as possible." With that, he exited the plane, having grabbed the heavy canvas bag. The small, non-descript STOL plane had landed near us. A man in plain clothes wearing dark sunglasses and khaki baseball cap moved swiftly toward the general, who planted the bag on the ground. The stranger picked it up effortlessly, turned, and hastened into his plane and immediately took off.

Then, also as planned, a two-ton Army truck appeared out of the jungle with a half dozen really bad-ass dudes all holding M-60s at the ready. In less than two minutes, four of them jumped off the truck and loaded the footlockers. I briefly wondered if they knew these footlockers were filled with gold. Then, in a flash, they disappeared back into the jungle. Two half-tracks pulled alongside our aircraft and stayed close as we positioned for takeoff at the end of the runway. Both were armed with dual M-60s. We waited in silence. It was the longest fifteen minutes of my life. Trunks of gold? Not the first time? What the fuck was going on? Some familiar lyrics came to mind from *For What It's Worth* by Buffalo Springfield:

There's something happening here
What it is ain't exactly clear
There's a man with a gun over there

Telling me I got to beware ...

GUN FIRE! Tex and I heard it at the same time. Not part of the plan. Lots of gunfire coming from the direction the truck had taken into the jungle. Suddenly, at break-neck speed, the truck came toward us. We could see that the driver was holding his shoulder. The general and four soldiers were in the truck. The general and two others had been shot.

"Sam, I am going to help get the general aboard. You be ready to get us out of here, fast."

"Yeah, no shit!"

The general was bleeding profusely. He had taken a hit in the thigh, though fortunately, the two AK rounds missed the femur and main artery, which otherwise would have been fatal. One of the Special Forces guys had applied a tourniquet above the wound. Once the general was strapped in, it was balls to the wall. On the ground, medics were tending to the injured soldiers.

I held my breath and said a quiet prayer as we literally dropped off the end of the runway. I can assure you, that's a very strange maneuver for a pilot on takeoff. Pushing your nose over goes against everything you know about flying, but miraculously, it worked. As I began pulling up, Tex yelled, "BREAK LEFT, SAM! WE'RE TAKING GROUND FIRE!"

"No can do, Tex. No room."

No sooner had I uttered those words than eight to ten rounds pierced their way through the right wing, miraculously missing the engine and the fuel tank. We were OK. We flew on.

Tex turned to me after tending to the general. "He's lost a lot of blood. Suggest you call Ghost Rider. Get us across the Fence and vectors for an emergency landing into Da Nang. I figure that's the closest place that can take care of him."

"Got it. Ghost Rider, this is Catwalk, how copy?"

"Go ahead, Catwalk. Please squawk transponder. Got you Catwalk. Turn to a heading of one one zero."

"Ghost Rider, Catwalk is declaring an emergency."

"Got you, Catwalk. Heading is good to cross over. State emergency."

"Got a wounded general on board. Please call ahead to Da Nang and tell them we are on the way. Should be there in forty-three minutes. Request straight in approach to runway zero nine zero. Need ambulance."

"Roger copy, Catwalk. Right back to you."

"Roger."

"OK, Catwalk, you are cleared for an emergency approach straight into runway zero nine zero. Ambulance standing by. Contact Da Nang on 299.89, over."

"Roger copy, Ghost Rider, 299.89. Thanks for the help."

"You bet. How is the general?"

"Lost a lot of blood, but we're hauling ass to get him to Da Nang. Thanks, Ghost Rider. Catwalk out."

"Da Nang, this is Catwalk 9, how copy?"

"We have you Catwalk 9. Understand you have a wounded general aboard."

"Affirmative, Da Nang."

"Catwalk, you are cleared for landing runway zero nine zero. All traffic is out of your way."

"Roger copy, Da Nang."

Tex spoke to me. "Good work, Sam. You're keeping your cool. One suggestion."

"Sure, what?"

"Red line these engines. Push the shit out of this plane. I'll keep my eye on the oil pressure and temp gauges. If we get critical, you can back off a little."

Tex was right. Better to have a live general and damaged aircraft than a dead general and a good airplane. Tex had the general sip a little water every few minutes. He was slipping into shock. "Hang in there, Steve. We are going into Da Nang. We'll have you on the ground in under thirty minutes. Besides, we have some duck huntin' to do."

"I hear ya. I know you're doing everything you can. I'm a tough SOB, so don't worry, I won't die on ya."

"Yeah, we appreciate that. Besides, I was already counting on that bottle of Scotch."

That reminded me of my stash, and I reached in my flight suit leg pocket. "Here, Tex. I forgot I had this. Get the general to drink some."

"Thanks, Sam. Macallan, right?"

"Yes, Sir."

My engines were beginning to show signs of overheating. Normal cruising would be at 2500 rpms. Occasionally, extra power when needed was topped at 2850 rpms. Redline began at 3000 rpms. I was at 3400 rpms.

"OK, Sam, I know we are pushing it. Engine temp and oil temp are about to max out. Back down to 2900 rpms. When the engine and oil temp drop, go back up to 3400 rpms. We should be in sight of Da Nang in the next few minutes."

"Got it, Tex. I am going in hot."

"Da Nang, this is Catwalk 9, how copy?"

"Catwalk 9, we read you. Got your landing lights in sight. You are cleared for straight in approach runway zero nine zero. Ambulance waiting at first apron."

"Da Nang, can you have ambulance move to the last apron? We are coming in hot and will land long."

"Roger, Catwalk. Ambulance moving."

When we landed, the medics were all over the general. He was conscious enough to thank us as they hurried him off to the base hospital. We had our plane's engines checked out while we waited in Flight Ops. After an hour, a doctor came out and told us the general would be okay. They would keep him awhile and then have him flown back to Saigon. We received more good news: the airplane engines survived without damage. We returned to base camp. It had been a day neither of us would ever want to repeat, nor would we ever forget. We never did find out who got all that gold. It made me wonder if we were involved in the Golden Triangle and, consequently, the drug trade. It would at least explain this crazy war; nothing else made much sense.

Chapter 24 Berm Duty

At least four or five times in a pilot's tour of duty, you got to be a grunt. We called it Berm Duty, a nightly surveillance during which officers and enlisted men pulled dusk-to-dawn shifts guarding their Base Camp. On one hand, no one would argue whether protecting ourselves against enemy attack is completely consistent with our instincts for self-preservation, but on the other, the vast majority of these dawn-to-dusk travails are tedious and uneventful; and there's the rub. While no soldier on base would deny or understate its importance, Berm Duty also fell victim to the unintended consequences of failing to inspire those engaged in doing so. Many otherwise devoted officers, when responsible for this night shift, performed their rounds in a perfunctory manner and then tended to bury themselves in an interesting book while consuming gallons of hot coffee and far too many donuts, awaiting the dawn.

Not me. Early in my tour, Laddy took the time to alert me to this phenomenon. He wisely advised me to make significant use of my rounds, pointing out that most of these soldiers were young, eighteen or nineteen, frightened about being here, and leery of officers. That last one really got to me, since many of us officers were not much older than they were. Laddy had urged me to use these shifts as an opportunity to get out and mingle with these enlisted men, to talk to them as a friend or mentor, and to make them feel valued by acknowledging their service. Showing them that you cared went a long way, he assured me.

Of course, there was another reason. All too often, some enlisted men chose to get through these shifts with a little help from their friends: alcohol or drugs, especially if they thought the officer would remain scarce. God forbid an attack on a camp with impaired guards. So, inspired by two good reasons, I conducted hourly rounds and mingled with the troops. I generally spent twenty to thirty minutes in each bunker trying to get to know the men as Laddy had suggested, and I found myself really enjoying this type of duty, despite the fact that so many pilots dreaded it.

On this particular night, while making my rounds, I entered a bunker and met a young private by the name of Teddy Swanson, who hailed from LA. While getting acquainted, we drank coffee and made small talk. Teddy was visibly nervous but eventually became comfortable enough to engage in conversation.

"Well, Teddy, I didn't know your name until now, but I'm sure I've seen your face ... in the maintenance hangar, right?"

"You noticed me there?"

"Sure did! And I appreciate ya. Believe me, every time I climb into a plane, I'm thankful for you guys for keeping those birds runnin' so well."

"Well, thanks, Sir. Just doing my job." Teddy seemed to be holding back.

"We're all just doin' our part here, 'til we can go home. Somethin' on your mind, Teddy?"

"Yeah, Mr. Walker, I guess there is. I've heard that captured pilots are tortured beyond belief. Is that true?"

"Don't really know, Teddy. There's a lot of stuff going around. Why? What did ya hear?"

"Well, I heard one thing they do is bring out this really hot chick to strip for you. You know, up close and personal. Then, once you get a boner, they slide this glass tube up your pecker and break it with a rubber hammer!"

"Shit! That would hurt. I think I would start talkin' the minute they showed me the hammer!"

"Yeah, and then there is this other thing I heard. They make you stand in a bucket of water and wrap your balls with raw electrical wire and then connect the wire to a battery!"

"Well, as long as Jerry Lee Lewis is singing 'Great Balls of Fire,' it might not be so bad."

Teddy looked at me like I was nuts, and perhaps I was, or at least well on my way. But I was really just trying to lighten him up.

"You know, Sir, that's some really scary shit! I mean really, Mr. Walker, how do you take off in that plane everyday just knowing something like that could be waiting for you?"

"Truth is, Teddy, I don't think about it. I really don't. I couldn't do my job if I let my head go there ... even for a second."

"Yes, Sir. I guess that's why all of us, you know, who don't fly, look up to you fellas. Whatever it is that you have ... well, I sure as hell know I don't have it, and neither do my buddies. Got to take some brass balls to do what you do every day."

As a pilot, I was used to finding myself on the receiving end of some hero worship, though I never really understood why.

"Well, Teddy, I tell you what."

"What's that, Sir?'

"Give yourself some credit. Take a look, buddy. Here you are sittin' in the middle of a freakin' enemy jungle behind an M-60 machine gun, ready to blow Charlie away if you have to, while your buddy back home, who somehow dodged the draft, is at the drive-in movie tryin' to cop a feel from Susie, but he's gettin' nowhere fast 'cause he doesn't have the nerve anyway, right?"

"Damn straight, Sir!"

"Well, you are pretty damn brave to me. And Susie can't wait for you to get home. As for me, just knowing you are out here lets me sleep at night, Teddy."

"Guess, I never looked at it that way. But, to be honest, Sir, I just hope I make it back alive and in one piece."

"Sure, you will. You know how well this base camp is fortified; what this Berm Duty is all about, right?"

"Yes, Sir!"

"Ok, then. Just remember that. Now let me get on over and check on your buddies in the next bunker. Just a few more hours 'til daylight. Keep sippin' on that coffee and keep a watch out. And wake up your buddy over there. He was asleep when I got here an hour ago."

"Yes, Sir, Mr. Walker, and thanks."

"Thanks for what, Teddy?"

"Just for talking with me, Sir. Just for talking with me."

"And thank you, too, for talkin' to me. I appreciate it."

I meant what I said, especially about the base camp fortifications. Long Thanh, which was divided into four quadrants, was surrounded by a ten-foot-high berm. This berm separated the camp from the jungle and formed the camp's inner perimeter. Dug into the camp-side of each berm were five bunkers along each quadrant. These bunkers were spaced every thirty yards. Twenty-foot high towers, like the type you see in old western movies guarding a fort, stood thirty yards past the first and fifth bunkers. Each bunker and tower was manned by two soldiers, one armed with an M-60 machine gun and the other holding a Starlight infra-red night scope.

Working out from the camp, forty yards in front of the berm was another defensive perimeter known as 'The Wire'. It was made of several strands of barbed wire, strung parallel three to four inches apart and about two feet in height. Just a few feet inside the barbed wire, six claymore mines per bunker were planted ten feet apart. The claymore was invented in 1952 by Norman MacLeod and named after a Scottish medieval sword, celebrated for its lethality. MacLeod's early design was continually improved, eventually yielding the M18A1, first used in Vietnam in 1966. This model, incorporating new features that triumphed over the original, is both directional and command-activated. Shaped like a curved rectangle roughly two inches thick and twelve inches long, its plastic casing contains a very powerful explosive called C4. Embedded in the C4 along the outer curve are 700 steel balls. The words FRONT TOWARD ENEMY are clearly printed to ensure they are set in the ground properly, the outer curve facing the enemy with a wire leading back to the bunker. Each mine is armed with an electrical charge that is controlled by an individual switch. These anti-personnel mines are devastating. One fateful click on a handheld switch and KABOOM! Hundreds of steel balls propel forward at such a high velocity that they can be counted on to destroy everything up to fifty yards away, spanning a 60-degree arc.

The defense perimeter includes one more important element, a warning system. One foot in front of The Wire buried a few inches deep in the ground, lies a narrow hose filled with water into which pressure sensors have been placed every few feet. Each sensor is connected by wire to a main control panel located in the Command Bunker. It takes about seven pounds of pressure to set off a sensor. When pressure is detected along the hose, a red warning light blinks on the control panel indicating the specific bunker near the alarm.

The Command Bunker is the communication hub for each berm bunker and tower emplacement and is manned by one officer and one enlisted man. The enlisted man, typically a senior sergeant, monitors the sensor board and all communication. The toughest part of his job is to stay awake and to stay focused. He can't leave his post for any reason, not even to pee. There is a urinal under his desk for that purpose. If he has to, well ... you know ... then he must have the officer relieve him or he is otherwise ordered to shit in his pants. The situation really is that critical. An open frequency to the Cobra unit at Bear Cat is maintained along with that of the Command Bunker Officer's PRC- 25, in case he is away from the Bunker when the need to communicate arises.

If a sensor light goes off, the sergeant immediately alerts the men in the appropriate bunker, and they assess the threat using the infra-red Starlight night scope. If they discover Charlie trying to come through

The Wire, the sergeant tells the officer who gives the thumbs up to detonate the claymore and open fire with the M-60 machine gun, which usually takes care of the problem. If that's not enough, the sergeant alerts the Cobras on standby. More often than not, when a sensor goes off, which gets the attention of everyone's sphincter muscle, it is usually a mongoose or very large snake.

One particular night when fifteen sensors went off within sixty seconds, everyone was convinced we were being attacked by a dozen gooks. Turned out to be a twenty-foot python.

I had made my rounds for the fourth time and was taking a break at the Command Bunker when it happened. I had been reading a copy of *The Gang That Couldn't Shoot Straight* by Jimmy Breslin, when the sergeant, speaking forcefully, got my attention.

"Mr. Walker, I think you should take a look at this. We got sensor lights on bunkers two, three, and four. No way that's a mongoose, and just ain't no snake that fuckin' long!"

"OK! Tell both towers to pop parachute flares toward two, three, and four. DO IT NOW!"

The night sky lit up, exposing a half dozen sappers determined to penetrate our perimeter. The flares caught them scurrying like cockroaches when somebody turned the light on. Now running toward the bunkers, they got hung up navigating The Wire. I immediately gave the order to detonate the claymores and open fire. The ensuing firestorm was intense and effective, but brief. A series of loud explosions signaled the firing of each claymore punctuating the rat-a-tat-tat of the M-60s.

In minutes, actually, it may have been less than one minute, all went quiet until a similar attack was launched against a quadrant on the other side of the airstrip, triggering a similar and successful response. In total, twelve enemy died an ugly death. That was a record for our base camp ... so far.

Chapter 25 Christmas

Christmastime in Vietnam was difficult for many, a real double whammy. It not only served as a stark reminder of what you were missing at home but also underscored the terms of your present condition: hopelessly trapped in a dangerous place where the odds were strong that you would either lose your life, your limbs, or just your mind. Some on-base acted to create the holiday spirit, GI-style, with make-shift Christmas trees and decorations, while others made sure that Christmas music was in the air. The brass, recognizing the importance of maintaining morale, usually outdid themselves to ensure a really memorable meal and some sense of festivity. For a base camp like ours, Tipper had Navy food sent to us from Vung Tau, and Ed and I made a seafood run. Pole was told to order seventy-five steaks and paid for them in advance from the CO's slush fund.

It was customary, on a volunteer basis during major holidays, for officers to take bunker duty to relieve the enlisted men, so Tex and I decided to take one of the towers. That particular Christmas Eve was a very long, silent night. We ate far too much Claxton fruit cake and enjoyed the homemade cookies sent by my sister, Ellen, washing it all down with boocoo coffee to stay awake. To pass the time, we talked of hunting ducks and flying planes before turning to one of our favorite topics: the trip Tex, Ed, and I had planned after leaving the Nam.

Tex kept a large World Atlas as well as other information on the Pacific Northwest back in his hooch, where over the past few months, our trip had taken shape, as the three of us spent countless hours poring over maps and planning our wilderness excursion. We yearned to be 'off the grid', although no one called it that back in those days. I don't recall how the idea initially took hold, but once we let ourselves imagine camping in the woods, hunting and fishing, free to explore these glorious parks and mountains, we could not let it go. We joked that it was difficult to imagine roaming free without fear of attack, except perhaps by a startled bear. Finally, Christmas Eve had passed, and the sun's early rays began to fill the tower.

"Well, Sam, sun's coming up. Whadaya say we pack up and get ready to celebrate Christmas?"

It was barely daylight when Tex started down the ladder with me right behind him. If we had waited another sixty seconds, neither one of us would have experienced Christmas or anything else, for that matter, ever again. Because, suddenly, without warning, an AK-47 riddled our tower from one side to the other. Bunker four called the Command Bunker, a warrant officer called in the Cobras, and they took out the sniper in a heartbeat. Seems like the North Vietnamese would have figured this out by now. Like the time shortly after my arrival to the Nam when the sniper whose round missed my head by a few feet was taken out by a Cobra in no time. It seemed to me that no one in his right mind would invite the fury of the Cobra's firepower if they understood that taking a few shots at us would bring such a deadly consequence. Our brush with certain death was disquieting, to say the least. At the top of those stairs, our heads were in the Pacific Northwest, but by the time we reached the bottom, we were reminded that we would be very lucky to get out of the Nam alive. I recalled the words of the sergeant who greeted us when I arrived in Saigon, *This is war, gentlemen, and the ugly truth is that it's all around you, all the time.*

***

I walked back to my hooch and sat down. I was shaking and shaken. Once again, almost killed by a sniper. This time it rattled me more than the first. *Killed on Christmas morning!* What a lovely message for my family and Vicky to receive. Their Christmases would never be the same. I poured two heavy shots of Scotch and kicked them back to calm my nerves. It wasn't yet 7:00 AM.

After a long hot shower, I gathered some things and headed for Tex's hooch for the Christmas breakfast we had planned with Ed, Mitch, and Tipper. A few days earlier, I had asked Nuwee for eggs, a simple request that turned into a comedic pantomime as I struggled to convey to her what I wanted without success. Finally, I squatted on the floor, flapped my folded arms, and started clucking like a chicken. When I dropped an orange from my ass, Nuwee understood. It was probably the best laugh she and I ever had together. After that, she started bringing me fresh eggs a few times a week, and I slipped her some additional cash to show my appreciation.

When I showed up, Tipper, Mitch, and Ed had not yet arrived, but Tex already had the fire going in the small grill outside his hooch. I handed him a wrapped gift.

"Merry Christmas, Tex."

"Oops! One minute." Tex disappeared and returned with a gift for me. Accepting his package, I asked him to go first.

"OK. Damn, a bottle of Chivas! Sure didn't expect this. I'll go in and get a few glasses."

"Tex, it isn't even 0700 hours!"

"Yeah, but it's Christmas. What's the matter? You driving somewhere?"

He returned with two shot glasses and ice. We poured and toasted each other. "Well, Sam, I gotta tell ya', in all my years, this is a first for me."

"What is, Tex?"

"It's the first time in my life that anyone has ever given me a really fine Christmas gift ... and it's wrapped in genuine Christmas paper. Where the hell did you get this wrapping?"

I admitted that Vicky had sent me that and some other things to be sure we had some kind of fitting celebration; then produced a box of her Christmas cookies.

"I don't know how to thank you, Sam, except to give you a little something from me."

Despite all the shit I had been through during the last ten months, I had not shown any real emotion, except for my meltdown in Tex's hooch after my first mission. Laddy had so well defined this as the 'numbness' we all developed, after having become professionals at cutting off any such displays. But at this moment, I had to look away and pretend I was tending to the coals because Tex's reaction had choked me up. I brushed away a tear before turning around to face Tex while opening the gift he had given me. Tex had noticed my emotions but didn't say anything until several months later.

"Sorry, no fancy Christmas wrapping on mine," he apologized. "A paper bag was all I could dig up."

"Gosh, man, don't worry 'bout that. So, let's see, what have you got for me? OH, WOW, Tex! I can't believe you are giving this to me. OH, MAN! Your P-51! Cadillac of the sky! I watched you build this one, Buddy. It must have taken you a month. I can't believe you would give this to me. Thank you so much, Tex."

"You bet. See! I put your call sign, real small, on the side. Now all we need to do is buy a real one when we get home."

"ONE! Shit, man, what good is one? We need to buy two!" Ultimately, that's exactly what we did, but that's a story for a later time.

After admiring the model plane a bit longer, I finally put it down and retrieved something that I brought to our breakfast.

"Here, Tex. Have one of these. Something from home called, 'Russian Rocks'. Goes real good with Scotch," I chuckled.

"Russian Rocks? What the hell is a Russian Rock? Sounds radioactive! You're messin' with me, right?"

"No way! These are really special. I've been eating Russian Rocks every Christmas since I was a kid. It's a tradition; Bessie makes them as her Christmas gift to our family. She usually makes eight or ten dozen, and this year, she sent me two dozen, so I'd have some to share with my friends. They are kinda' hard, but not like a rock ... just crunchy. Lots of good stuff in here - brown sugar, molasses, raisins, and nuts."

"OK. I'm game. As long as you swear that I won't crack a tooth! I hope this is as close as I will ever get to Russia, 'cuz I got no desire to see the place. I will lift Bessie's Russian Rock to the northeast and toast it to Mother Russia and Bessie. They can't all be communists over there. Sure, some of them celebrate Christmas. You just be sure to tell Bessie her Russian Rocks almost made it back to where they came from."

Ed, Mitch, and Tipper showed up as planned. They had brought their steaks, we had plenty of eggs, and way too much Scotch, but after all, it was Christmas. I gave Tipper, Ed, and Mitch each a quart of Chivas, and I had a bottle of Old Gran-Dad for Mitch. They thought 'The Senator' had sent it, so I didn't say anything until they had a few drinks when I explained the Scotch was really from both Vicky and me; we had bought it at the Sydney airport. There were so many bottles on hand, and so much toasting going on, we were all thoroughly trashed by noon. It was a Christmas to remember, at least those parts that we could remember.

***

Eventually, after I returned home and visited Bessie, I showed her on a world map where I had spent the past year and where Russia was, recounting what Tex had said on that Christmas morning. Since Bessie had never ventured outside of Charleston County, much less South Carolina, I realized she had no concept of distance. She was lucky in a way. Sometimes keeping one's world small can be a good thing.

***

Dear Son,

By the time you get this letter, you will have only about two months left in your tour. It is good to know that you will not be flying as much during your last months there. Just can't help but worry every day about you, Sam. Guess it's just what a mother does!

I am glad you got the two cases of canned goods I sent you for Christmas. I tried to think of the things I knew you liked and to give you as much variety as possible. Otsie said to be sure to include ALL the date nut bread she made for you. Three loaves! She must have used a whole box of aluminum foil to wrap them extra tight. I hope they were not stale. Bessie made you an early batch of Russian Rocks so we could get them in the mail on time. She and Otsie really miss you, especially during the holidays. Christmas will just not be the same without you. It will be the first one you have ever missed, but then I know it must be harder on you than it will be for us, melancholy for sure. You didn't mention anything about the Bob Hope Christmas Show that we watched on TV, so I guess it was not near your location. We were hoping, by some miracle, we'd catch a glimpse of you in the audience, so we never left the room for a minute until the show was over.

It sounds like you have met a really nice girl, Vicky. Your father and I look forward to meeting her. I can remember when the Beach Boys came out with that song, and you seemed to have a starry-eyed look about 'California Girls'. Who would have ever thought you would meet one over there?

I don't pretend to know what you young men must feel, coming home after such an ordeal, but I wish the atmosphere of this country toward our GIs were different. I have not been saying anything about this in my letters to you, but now that you'll be home soon, I feel I should tell you. Be careful, Son. Things have turned ugly over this war. I don't know if the military is making you aware of the situation back home, but it is really getting worse by the week. It seems like every night on the news there's another demonstration. In the beginning they only protested the war, but now they are blaming our brave soldiers. I must say it makes me sick.

I do understand why you and your friends plan on taking some time to just get away from it all when you get back. You always did like to camp, and I am sure there is a lot of beauty in nature in the Pacific Northwest. Be sure to take a photo of yourself next to one of those giant California redwoods. Just knowing you will be back on American soil will have to be enough for me, until you get home. Can't wait to hear your voice, so please call us on your stopover in Hawaii on your way back. Don't worry about the time difference. Just call collect whenever you can.

I have to take a break now. I completely forgot; I've got to get Bessie to the doctor for her check-up.

OK, I'm back writing. Everything's going well with Bessie; her hip is on the mend. I just saw this on the news, and I hesitated to add it, but decided I must because I know you are coming back into California. Tonight, Walter Cronkite reported that dozens of hippies were arrested for throwing rocks and eggs at soldiers leaving the Travis Air Force Base. It's a real shame you GIs are being so badly treated when you are just doing your job. Please be careful, Son. Stay clear of these people. Dad says they are full of a lot of hate, but it makes me so angry that they are taking it out on the wrong guys. I mean how stupid can they be, picking on combat soldiers! I heard your Uncle Henry and Dad talking in the den a few days ago, and Henry said that if he had been treated this way when he came home from World War II, there would be some dead people at the airport, and they wouldn't be the soldiers. Of course, you know how I am. That got me thinking. There is no sign of these young men striking back. It's not worth it, Sam. Just sure hope it doesn't come to that.

I love you, Mom

***

Dear Mom,

Thanks for the sweet letter. The food you sent is wonderful. Tell Otsie the date nut bread was delicious and not at all stale. I shared it with the guys I've told you about, Tex, Tipper, Mitch, and Ed, on Christmas morning, but selfishly kept a bit for myself. Let Bessie know that her Russian Rocks were not quite hard as a rock (HA!) but as crunchy as they were supposed to be. The guys had never heard of Russian Rocks, but now they are big fans. The Christmas cookie tin she sent them in really reminded me of home. Tell Bessie I hope her hip is doing better. I was telling one of my friends, Ed, from Maryland, about Otsie and Bessie. He is fascinated how I grew up with such sweet loving 'black mamas'. The fact that Grand Daddy brought Bessie out of a potato field to work in the house at sixteen and she is still with us at seventy-four blows even my mind. If you think about it, Mom, she raised both of us. Tell her I love her and give her a big hug for me. My friend, Tex, toasted Bessie and Russia, several hundred miles to the northeast of us, before biting into his Russian Rock!

I only have a few more missions to fly, and they are relatively safe ones, so don't worry. Plus, I have to make a seafood run next week with my commanding officer, Tipper. We're going to spend a few days on the beach. The beaches here are beautiful, and the water is clean and clear, almost aqua in some places and deep blue in others. I'm looking forward to this, for sure.

After I separate from the service in California, I will spend two weeks with Vicky and meet her family in Santa Barbara before meeting up with Ed and Tex in Portland, Oregon. Tex, Ed, and I have really planned this trip in detail. We have too much time on our hands around here, and pouring over maps and camping gear catalogs has been interesting and enjoyable. Our plan is to purchase everything we need for the 'expedition' as Tex calls it, in Portland, and then start our way hiking down the west coast and on trails along the Columbia River Gorge. Should be really nice. There are small towns along our planned trek, so I will call often. Please rest assured that this trip will be no longer than fourteen days. It will end for me in Santa Barbara where I reunite with Vicky, and then we will arrange to come out your way for a good visit. Vicky is looking forward to meeting you, Dad, Ellen, Otsie, and Bessie. Mom, you have always taught me to be outgoing, and I don't think you have ever met a stranger. I'm sure you and Dad will like Vicky.

I am glad you and Dad understand that I may want to move to the west coast with Vicky. Her parents own farmland in the Central Valley of southern California that was purchased by her grandfather some fifty-five years ago, and

I may have an opportunity there. I will have the chance to look into it while I'm out there. At any rate, don't fret. I'm not really sure what the future holds, I just wanted to let you know it's something I am thinking about. Just a different kind of farming, right Dad?

Love, Sam

Chapter 26 The Tunnel

Nuwee had become my best barometer for the local Charlie climate. Though she spoke limited, broken English, and I spoke no Vietnamese at all, we got along fine. Over time, I think she understood I both respected and appreciated her; and my trust in her grew. She was always in my hooch by six in the morning, where she swept, dusted, polished my boots and took my clothes to the laundry. She often placed fresh fruit and eggs in my refrigerator. Every Thursday, she changed and washed the sheets. On this particular Thursday morning, she entered my hooch as I was suiting up for a mission. As she was shy, she had a habit of not maintaining eye contact when she spoke, but this morning, she locked into me like a heat-seeking missile. She was really in my face.

"Sam, you must hear me. Boocoo VC in village!"

"How many, Nuwee?" I put my hands up and flipped my fingers as if I were counting. At that rate, I'd run out at ten. She put both hands up and flashed all ten fingers five or six times in rapid succession. I repeated what she had done to verify.

"Boocoo. Sam. Many VC. Be careful."

I dropped by Tipper's office on the way to my mission briefing, where he indicated that Nuwee was wrong. He had gotten a different report. There were over two-hundred-fifty VC and NVA in the village.

"Whadaya think is going on, Tipper?"

"I don't know Sam, but I don't like it. Guess you heard the Cobra unit over at Bear Cat is stepping down in a few weeks. Guarantee you Charlie has been watching them pack up. We are easy prey with them gone. Or so Charlie thinks. What they don't know is we have four Cobras coming in the day before the Cobra unit at Bear Cat leave, and these four Cobras will remain here. Newer model Cobra too. They will not be part of Bear Cat. They will be stationed right here with us, for the sole purpose of protecting us. They won't be running off to other missions."

"I like it. About time!"

"Fact is, Sam, this war is shifting. Charlie is building up, and we are stepping down. Not a good time to be here. Glad we are both getting short."

"You think Charlie would actually try to overrun us?"

"Let's hope not, Sam. I have always said, if Charlie ever figures out what we really do here, we would be in for a good fight. Neither of us has much time left, so it's natural to be a bit jumpy."

"Yeah, hope you're right, and that's all it is. Say, with all this going on, are you still going with me to Vung Tau for seafood in a few days?"

"Damn straight. Make it a two-day trip. Let's leave tomorrow morning. Want to get down there and back before the Special Forces arrive. There will be sixty of them, eight Cobra pilots, and four Cobras to take care of us in the event Charlie is up to something. We got four Chinooks bringing them in, along with all their gear, prefab latrines, field mess units, you name it. Pretty much their own traveling show. Would like to give them a really good welcome. Let's get lots of prawns and lobsters.

"Line up Ed and Tex to take the other plane we use to haul seafood. Have Ed call your Aussie buddy to contact Mr. Kim at the docks and double the order. That kind of thing will work, right?"

"Yeah, Tipper. I set it up several months ago. Works great. It saves us time, and an extra step, and they trust us to show up at the docks. The Aussies installed a walk-in cooler down there to keep their seafood and always have plenty of room for our orders. We have never let Mr. Kim down, and he always gives us their best catch. I give Mr. Kim a little extra, twenty bucks, and he not only guarantees the freshest catch but also immediately packs it in ice."

"Twenty bucks? That's a month's salary to him."

"Gotta keep him happy, Tipper."

"You're right. Sure is worth it. I got the penthouse at the main hotel down there. It takes up the entire roof. Really something."

"Damn! How much that set you back?"

"Uncle Sam is picking up the tab. Don't worry about it. I have money in a discretionary fund for important events, and we just got important. By the time the paperwork for all this reaches HQ in Saigon, my ass will be back in the world. Shit! Here I am getting ready to leave the Nam, and I've barely tapped my fund!"

"I'll tell Ed to get on it right away and let him and Tex know they are going on a little R&R. Sure there won't be any argument there."

"Let them know the penthouse is huge. Four bedrooms, two full baths, dining room, living room, kitchenette and balcony, overlooking the South China Sea. Plenty of room for all of us. My wife sent me snorkeling shit. You know, masks, a couple of pairs of flippers and two spearguns. Let's have some fun!"

"Wow! Look forward to it."

***

Up till now, despite our friendship, the four of us had never spent time together unwinding – without alcohol, that is. Several Aussies at the hotel had snorkeling equipment, so we all went together. Tex and Tipper speared a few grouper; one was the size of a small refrigerator. Ed and I went after lobster and managed to catch a few.

We invited several of the Aussie pilots to join us for a cookout on the rooftop. The luxury surroundings and stunning view of the sea stirred up feelings for Vicky. Although it was one of my more memorable evenings, I could not stop the feeling that in a place like this, I should be with Vicky. Guess falling in love does that to you. Something unnatural about having to put those feelings on hold. You can't turn love on and off like a faucet. However, just the fact that I was able to feel 'something' was comforting. I guess the numbness ebbs and flows. The sunset over the South China Sea wasn't as dramatic as Waikiki, but soon I would be watching the very same sun sink into the horizon off the coast of Santa Barbara, with Vicky. I could hardly wait.

The Aussies loved hearing about the time Ed and I spent in their country on R&R. They were impressed that we chose to fly Stearman biplanes, roared with laughter over us getting caught in a dust storm, and displayed a sense of national pride as we spoke highly of Sydney and Melbourne. But the one issue they could not get enough of was Adrianna. Several Aussies wanted to know how to find her, but Ed's lips were sealed like a bank vault.

***

We arrived back at Long Thanh on the heels of what looked like an aerial invasion but thankfully was not. Four Cobras and four Chinooks were approaching camp in a carefully orchestrated display, and the effects reminded me of the Australian dust storm I had been vividly describing only the night before. During dry season in the Nam, if you're less than six feet tall and emit a single sneeze, you could easily create a minor dust storm by agitating the loose layer of microscopic shit that is lighter than snow and covers everything in sight. No one in-the-know would deliberately trigger this phenomenon; typically, an uninitiated FNG was the source. However, on this particular day, this man-made tornado did indeed serve its intended purpose. We wanted Charlie to understand that the cavalry had arrived because we knew they would be watching; they always were.

These helicopters had been specifically developed from earlier models to meet the emerging needs of the Vietnam War, in support of our strategy to shift the battle from the ground to the air. Older helicopter models had been conceived for transport, not for battle. Modern helicopters needed to be able to attack and defend, protecting both the pilot and the gunner.

The AH-1G Cobra, note the 'AH' stands for 'Attack Helicopter' and the 'G' for Gunship, was designed for both attack and armed-escort. Its single engine powers two rotor blades, having a tip-to-tip diameter of forty-four feet. The CH-47 Chinook was built for transport; think of it as an airborne moving van. Two engines carry these big babies, one forward and one aft, each with rotating blades, which extend a diameter of sixty feet per engine. Eight of these birds hovering over the landing field, having the equivalent whirling rotor power of six-hundred forty feet, created quite an impressive cyclone. A show of such force would make Charlie think twice before messing with us ... or so we thought. As it would turn out, Charlie had other plans.

Forty pilots and sixty Special Forces men at a cookout make an impressive gathering, and Tipper was sure Charlie had a treetop view out there somewhere. Four brand new Cobras with full rocket pods had been set down on top of the berm just fifty yards from our party at the Pit. The Special Forces teams had pitched their tents right on top of the berm; they may as well have posted a sign taunting, 'OK, assholes. You want some of us? Bring it on!' We definitely sent a message. The air reeked of testosterone that night. I met one of the Special Forces team leaders chowing down on the brains of a lobster. A captain. He began speaking to me as I approached.

"Can't believe people are throwing away these lobster heads. See here ... this green part is the brain. Really sweet. The best part. Want some?" Not waiting for me to respond, he dug his index finger into the green mush and slapped it onto my paper plate. I knew better than to turn it down.

"Yeah, not bad ... not bad at all. Goes great with a cold beer. Name's Sam. Really glad you guys came in to help us out. The natives seem to be getting restless."

He wiped his sticky lobster brain-mush hand across his pant leg and extended it for a handshake.

"Everybody calls me Cowboy. Yeah, these little fuckers are up to somethin'. I can smell it. See that fella over there standing by your CO?"

"Yeah ... kinda hard to miss. He must be six-four, two seventy-five."

"Close. Six-six. Three hundred pounds of pure muscle. Buddy of mine from Mississippi. Played left tackle for Ole Miss. Goes by 'Gator'. Gator ain't never been wrong 'bout callin' out Charlie when he's 'bout to make a move."

"Oh, yeah! Well, what's Gator saying now?"

"Says, somethin' ain't right 'bout what's goin' down. Don't make no sense. Charlie ain't stupid. Intel says another hundred of 'um came into the village last night. They know we can kick their asses from here to Hanoi if they try to come across that open area from here to the edge of the jungle. No, Charlie is up to somethin' else."

"What? You don't think they are going to hit us?"

"Oh, I got to agree with Gator. They gonna hit us, OK. We just don't know how!"

***

The next day, Tipper had set up a large briefing area in one of the hangars. Everyone who was not flying was there. Tipper introduced Cowboy, the other two team leaders, and the Cobra pilots. They gave an impressive rundown of their defense strategy in the event of a ground attack, which they unanimously believed to be imminent; sometime within the next seventy-two hours. Our situation was tense.

The Special Forces teams were on twenty-four-hour alert; half stood guard, while the other half slept. The Cobra pilots were on constant standby. Same deal; four slept, while four were within fifty feet of their choppers, ready to go. Just three minutes flying time from Bien Hoa Airbase, our A-1D Skyraiders were on the same type of standby status. Each was packing enough napalm to scorch the same area of earth ten times over. Every Skyraider was also equipped with four 20mm Gatling-rotary cannons, each capable of firing 6000 rounds per minute. The truth be known, with this kind of air power lined up, Cowboy's ground troops would not have had to fire a single shot. They were like the eager kids standing on the river bank with a can of worms and cane fishing poles as a gleaming sixty-three-foot Bertram fishing boat sped by. We were confident that between the Cobras and Skyraiders, almost 300 NVA and VC would soon be massacred into grizzled body parts and barbecued to black tar in less than fifteen minutes. Still, it was hard to relax.

***

Despite a few stars, it was a black, moonless night. The flight line was always quiet, except when night missions departed and returned every three to four hours. Two men were in the control tower at all times, but once the ground crew got a mission off or secured a returning aircraft, they went back to their hooches to relax in their bunks. There was no need for anyone to remain on the flight line if nothing was going on.

At 0235 hours, an aircraft on a Black Ops mission that had been airborne for about twenty minutes disappeared into the black ink of combat on its way across the Fence and into Cambodia. Later I would wish that I had been flying that mission.

The tending ground crew had retreated to their hooches, and there were no lights on the airfield, as runway lights and taxiway lights were only on when an aircraft was in the area. Suddenly, without any warning, a series of violent explosions lit up the sky and rocked the base. Like everyone else who had been sound asleep moments earlier, I bolted straight up in bed, my mind racing to make sense of this horrific intrusion. My first thought was that an enormous plane must have crashed on the runway. Nothing else made sense, given the sound of the explosions, but within an instant, I realized that would have been impossible; our runway was too small. Having jumped out of bed and rushing to dress and grab my weapon, my second thought was that Charlie could not deliver that kind of firepower. They had mortars and rockets; not planes with bombs or 105mm Howitzers or off-shore battleships that could fire large guns at us. What the fuck was going on? How in the world could they have delivered such a crushing blow?

Within minutes, dressed in my flight suit, boots, flack vest, and steel pot, I grabbed my M-16, extra ammo, .45 pistol, a can of grenades and bolted out the hooch door headed for the bunker I was assigned to in the event of a major ground attack. I turned on my PRC-25 and heard Cowboy shouting orders.

"Listen up, men. Hold your position. Hold your fire. Say again. Hold your position. Hold your fire. Snake Eyes (Cobra pilots), stand-by. Start your engines, but do not move. Charlie is just playin' with us. Silver Bullet (Sky Raiders), hold your position, say again, hold your position."

"Roger, Cowboy, this is Silver Bullet standing by. Can be there in under three minutes."

"Roger that, Silver Bullet."

To my great shock, we learned that a dozen or so NVA, silently and successfully infiltrated our camp – not from above, but from below. They managed to place explosives under twelve of our aircraft and both fuel tanker trucks before slipping back into a tunnel they had dug months, perhaps a year, before the fireworks started. All of their timed explosive charges erupted simultaneously igniting an enormous inferno. The air traffic controllers in the tower would later report that they felt the tower shaking so hard, they thought it might collapse. Just hearing the word, 'tunnel' made my head spin. How was this possible?

But I could ill afford any attention to those questions; I had to stay focused on the present.

Other than the sound of the Cobra's turbine engines winding up and the whoop-whoop-whoop of their rotors, all was quiet. Not a peep from us. Nothing from Charlie. It was surreal. Then we noted the distant voices of the soldiers on the airfield who manned our small fire truck attempting to bring the inferno at the flight line under control. Truth is, it was not really a fire truck at all, but an Army utility vehicle loaded with a half dozen large fire extinguishers. Before this night, its sole purpose was to extinguish any fire that might have erupted on the flight line or on any aircraft returning from a mission on fire. Those things happened occasionally and had always been contained without loss of life. This thing was different, way different. As the sergeant in charge of fire containment would indicate days later, on this night, he felt his efforts were equivalent to 'pissin' on a forest fire'.

Thirty minutes, one hour, then two hours went by. Nothing. Still Cowboy was on top of Charlie's psychological game. Every fifteen minutes, he would come up on comm and only say one word, 'Wait.' At the end of two hours, he had two Cobras shut down and refuel, then the other two shutdown and refuel;,and then all started up again.

After three hours, Cowboy came up on comm. "OK, men. I have been here before. Charlie wants to scare us by blowin' up our aircraft on the flight line, hopin' we would take the bait and move to the airfield, giving them a wide berth to overrun the berm. He found out we didn't fall for it. Now he's hopin' we would tire from adrenaline subsidin' over the last three hours and that our Cobras, just sittin' there, would run low on fuel. Got news for these pricks! The Cobras have full tanks, and your adrenaline will kick back in whenever you need it, 'cause within the next hour, Charlie is comin' after us with everythin' they got. Just feel it in my bones. The SOG (Special Ops Group) team knows what to do and when to do it. You men assigned to this base camp and pilots all along the berm that are hunkered down, just hold fire. Don't panic and waste your claymores. With the firepower we got waitin' for Charlie, you may not even have to fire a shot. When the show starts, just sit tight. If Charlie gets within fifty yards of the wire, which I seriously doubt, set off your Claymores. Got to tell ya, if you have never been in one of these kinds of fights, don't let it freak you out. It ain't pretty. It's fuckin' loud and fuckin' ugly, but once it starts, it will all be over in minutes. I promise you."

Cowboy, whom I had misjudged as a bit of a hick, had his act together when it counted most. His quick assessment of what was really going on, and what to do about it, in all probability, saved everyone's ass. Cowboy earned everyone's respect that night. He was at the top of his game, and he knew it. Sick game, but somebody had to be good at it, and thankfully that somebody was on our side.

Just before dawn, Cowboy went up into a tower and scanned the area through a Starlight infra-red night scope. With his trained eye, he picked them out. Across an area three hundred yards wide, Charlie crouched along the edge of the jungle, with their weapons and evil intentions trained on us. Up to this point in the war, our work had remained a well-kept secret, and we had never been threatened by Charlie on such a large scale.

Each of the four Cobras was armed with a total of thirty-eight flechette rockets. The flechette rocket, nicknamed 'Nails', literally fires a rocket tube that explodes before it gets to its target, unleashing over two thousand nails per rocket and propelling them in all directions. Two rockets can cover an area the size of a football field, killing everything in its path. Our Cobras were coiled and ready to unleash a total of 144 flechette rockets on an area three hundred fifty yards long and three hundred yards wide, approximately six football fields. Although twelve flechettes would have been more than adequate, Saigon Command Headquarters had ordered 'overkill' and with that came the order to use twelve times as many. Not only to protect us but also to safeguard the top-secret information our compound held.

Cowboy came up on comm. "OK, everyone, listen up. I got eyes on Charlie, and believe me, there's a shit load of 'um out there. My best guess is two-fifty to three hundred of 'um. We will hit them when these pricks leave the jungle and move toward us and NOT a second sooner. Before their ground assault, they will be launchin' rockets and mortar rounds out of the jungle. As soon as we get a fix, the Cobras here and the Sky Raiders out of Bien Hoa will take them out and then come back around to take out the ground attack. Just click your mic to acknowledge. We don't need a lot of chatter right now."

Each of us made one click and waited. Of all the crap I had been through, with the exception of being shot down, this was the one thing I had hoped I would not have to face. I wasn't so much afraid of dying or even being hit by enemy fire. I was freaking out over what I was about to witness, up close and personal. Large scale death and destruction. Again.

Cowboy, still in the north tower, came up on comm. "Got movement. It's startin'! Take cover. For sure, mortar and rockets on the way. Just sit tight. Their move. Their death. Not yours. Remember that! Everybody, remember that! They got an appointment with Buddha. Our job is to get them there. We did not ask for this fight; they did."

The next five minutes went by like a slow-moving snail. I was in a bunker with Tex and two young soldiers. Tex was cool, as usual. I was afraid but hoped I didn't show it. I noticed that both young soldiers had peed in their pants. As soon as the rockets and mortar rounds started coming out of the jungle, two Cobras were all over our attackers, just like Cowboy said. By the time the Skyraiders showed up, the VC mortar and rocket emplacements had been taken out. Skyraider pilots were amazing to watch. Two pairs came over us at treetop level pushing three hundred knots and pulled straight up in a vertical climb. Because their first targets were already dead, they immediately went to a 'high perch' around three thousand feet, where they maintained a tight holding circle overhead, positioned to join the fight when needed. Cobra pilots and Skyraider pilots were recognized as a collaborative force, with an impressive history of working together to wipe out the enemy in well-orchestrated aerial assaults.

Tex spoke up in a soft voice. "You young men don't have to see this, OK. Sam and I got your position covered. We will fire your Claymores if we need to. My bet is, we don't fire a shot. With those crazy bastards overhead and a bunch of really bad-ass Special Forces fellas, this shit is going to be a bloodbath. I don't know that I can watch it either, to tell ya the truth. Sam, you bring any Scotch?"

I forced a smile as I handed him a full pint flask; I always had one stashed in my flight suit pocket; it had become part of my uniform. That feeble smile was my attempt at masking my already injured soul. I was hoping none of them would notice how broken I really was.

"Good man!" In three eager gulps, Tex downed half before handing it back to me with one hand while wiping his mouth with the other.

"Here. Polish it off. You're going to need it."

I sure did. What happened next, I would try to drown out with many, many quarts of alcohol over the years to come. These horrifying images haunt me to this day. I really wished I had sat on the floor of the bunker with the two young soldiers so I would not have seen a thing. It wasn't just the carnage, but the blood-curdling screams and the putrid smell of burning flesh, in a feeble response to the relentless, thunderous, earth-shaking rockets shot from our aircraft which unleashed the fire and fury of napalm, killing everyone and destroying everything in its path. All these ghoulish sights, sounds, and odors, shaken and mixed together like the Devil's cocktail, created a torturous scene from another world. A dastardly alien invasion. Man could not possibly be doing this to man! All these wonderful inventions, produced over time, used for destruction. From the relative safety of our bunker, we could feel the heat of napalm and smell the burning flesh hundreds of yards away. After the screams had stopped, the only sound was of hissing, crackling, and leaping flames. It was such overkill, and the entire battle seemed so senseless. After all, the NVA must have known they never stood a chance when they realized they could not draw us to the fight on the airfield. In my mind, it took a deranged commander to knowingly send his men into unavoidable slaughter, and it took a determined commander to have ordered it on such a brutal scale.

The assault stopped rather quickly because there were no NVA or VC left to vaporize. The sounds of hell fell quiet. This part of the earth was grizzled and ghostly. Nothing moved, except the large and inevitable ball of fire that crawled up over the horizon to prevail over a new day without judgment of the bleeding night. Every American soldier and every American pilot stationed in a bunker during the ordeal now stood motionless like a storefront mannequin. No one could utter a word. The scene that lay before us was from the place of the unspeakable that I had heard stories about but had hoped I would never witness. It had eluded me for eleven months, but now the definition of war that I would take home had just changed, yet again. It would be forever seared into my memory. Perhaps, up until now, I had simply rationalized to minimize the repulsive, unnatural feeling that is born in the killing of another human being. Now, I was repulsed by it.

***

The air cleared, and we were able to leave our bunker positions. Moving like zombies, we learned the incredible and unbelievable truth that triggered this deadly battle. Charlie had come through the back door, which was nothing anyone expected or could have predicted. We didn't know he had a back door until it was too late.

The Army Corp of Engineers estimated the tunnel had taken from eighteen months to two years to complete. Close to a mile long and eight feet underground, it ran from deep inside the jungle, well outside of our perimeter, to a storage area inside our largest aircraft hangar, one that was rarely used.

The enemy had literally been working under our feet, under our beds, showers, and mess hall, all the while totally undetected. Not a hint of subterfuge. What had gone so horribly wrong?

Completely undetected over that long period, the luck of these Vietcong and NVA continued the previous night when their elite soldiers, equivalent to our Special Forces or Navy SEALs, had surfaced in the hangar. Well-trained by Russians and having infiltrated their intended target, they had no intention of getting caught or shot or failing in their mission. They deftly planted timed satchel charges, each of which packed a punch equivalent to four sticks of dynamite under both of our fuel tanker trucks. Lucky again, for they could not possibly have known that one tanker was almost full and the other more than half full. This was the major source of the deafening and earth-shattering experience that had stunned us earlier. But despite the extensive damage they were able to inflict, their luck was met by our napalm. Napalm always wins.

CH-54A Skycrane helicopters brought in four bulldozers to deal with the carnage. Ravaged body parts were bulldozed into the earth and buried. Tipper had the entrance to the tunnel, now exposed, filled with a couple of hundred bags of concrete flown in by copter. It took several days of digging, but we finally found the source of the enemy's tunnel, and it was filled in as well. After that, the Army Corp of Engineers dug a trench three feet wide and ten feet deep around the camp's entire perimeter. It was unlikely, but possible, that Charlie would dig that deep in a future attempt to infiltrate our base camp with a second tunnel. For added measure of precaution, sensors were buried an additional six feet at the bottom of the trench.

***

If there was an upside to this disaster, it was that our missions had been reduced by thirty percent due to the loss of aircraft. The last thing I wanted was free time on my hands, but at least I felt somewhat safer. For like many others, I found myself spending a lot of time in the O Club, where I drank too much Scotch and ate too much red meat. Time that had been measured in days became days measured in hours. I would spend my final night in Base Camp completely awake, and I measured that time in minutes.

Although the news back home was reporting the war was all but over, the war had gotten really scary from my perspective. The entire military theater of US and Aussie presence was dwindling by the month. Although every type of military unit imaginable – infantry, artillery, helicopter units – was stepping down and going home, we continued to bring in FNGs and to replace destroyed aircraft. It didn't take a lot of smarts for the enemy to realize that we were busy doing something significant.

According to the intel out of Saigon, the NVA, the Russians, and the Chinese had caught onto our game. With American and Allied hostile ground offensive engagements reduced by almost fifty percent, while our bombing in Cambodia and Laos increased by nearly ninety percent, it wouldn't take a sleuth to figure out what pilots like me really did.

The elite group of spook pilots that I belonged to was small in number. Though we had only five squadrons in Vietnam and one in Thailand, we executed all the major bombing campaigns, especially the top-secret ones, for the entire air war. Our sorties were still very active and showed no signs of slowing down. Charlie and his 'Big Brother' buddies, Russia and China, had more time to focus on other things ... like us! But after having lost almost three hundred VC and NVA soldiers in an outsized display of our force, you couldn't expect them to simply pick up their marbles and go home.

I had a lot of trouble coming to terms with the fact that the enemy had been literally under our noses in a tunnel just a few hundred feet from our hooches. Until I zeroed out, I tossed and turned many a sleepless night. Those of us who were short-timers were completely worn out. Those who were more recent arrivals would never be able to feel secure. We had always understood there were VC moles among the mamasans. It was impossible to stop that from happening, so we were more careful about what we said and intentionally gave out misinformation, but other than that, there was not really much else you could do. Truth is, errant mamasans had not been perceived as a serious problem, that is, until now. I felt for my buddies and even more for the FNGs. Whoever had given the VC information about the vacant storage room in the hangar had to have been here awhile. Why didn't anyone notice and report seeing a mamasan out at the flight line, where she would not have had any reason to be? Other than mamasans, the only other Vietnamese at our base camp was Wai Lyn! Nah ... couldn't be.

***

We could not have known it then, but within a month, the Russians would be coming for us, intending an even larger ground assault. I was back in the world when it happened and would not hear about it for some time. Fifty Russian tanks had somehow managed to move hundreds of miles down the Ho Chi Min Trail without being detected. One of our TOs, returning from a mission out of Cambodia, just happened to pick up an unusual radio transmission, which he reported during his mission debriefing. The TO, visibly upset, strenuously insisted that during his nine months of duty and 125 missions, he had never heard anything like this. Thankfully, he was taken seriously. Ultimately, a squadron of AH-1 Cobra gunships took out fifty Russian tanks just north of our base camp.

***

Out of the blue, I received a letter from Laddy and was eager to dig into it.

Dear Sam,

Great to hear from you and glad to know you're going to make it out of there. What I have to tell you is VERY IMPORTANT. DO NOT, I repeat DO

NOT try to plunge back into the mainstream when you get home. I think it is VERY WISE that you and two of your buddies are taking some time to disappear into the woods. I wish I had. I had been home for two weeks when my father-in-law, who I am close to, showed up at my door one Sunday morning. He was driving an RV. He handed me the keys, a road atlas, his gas credit card, his AAA card, $1000 in cash, and told me to take the family and hit the road for a month. He even threw in his American Express card. Truth is, he probably saved my marriage. We needed that downtime. I suggest passing this letter along to your girlfriend if she has any reservations of how important this time away will be for you.

This war has changed the face of America, Sam. I would say it is the closest we have come to a social revolution of the youth since the American Revolution. Let's not forget, many of those guys were in their twenties as well, but that was a different fight for a just cause.

Unfortunately, the majority of Americans can't separate the forest from the trees and blame us veterans for this war. No war in the history of the world has received such day to day media coverage. The war has been a huge mistake, and everyone knows it. Walter Cronkite confirms it every evening, always ending his broadcast, 'And that's the way it is'. These simple words have sunk very deeply into the minds of Americans about Vietnam. There is more than just disdain toward us for not standing up and refusing to go. Many of them blame us directly for not seeing what was going on and refusing to participate, though I believe it would have been an even graver mistake if we as a nation had rebelled. Make no mistake, Sam, you are coming home to a broken and battered country. This nation is bitter, and unfortunately, we veterans bear the brunt of all this anger.

If there is a good side to any of this, President Nixon and Henry Kissinger are pushing for peace talks with North Vietnam to put an end to this thing, although the nightly news continues to show more B-52 bombings than ever, but then I don't have to tell you about that part.

Keep in mind, you and your buddies are coming home after winter in America. Early March, right? With your suntans and short haircuts, you may as well wear a target on your back. Start growing your hair. The best advice I can give you is to stick with the plans you've made with your buddies. Stay low, out of sight, and don't, under any circumstances, try to justify being a Vietnam Veteran.

Call me collect when you get settled. You have my number. Would love to hear from you, Laddy

Laddy's letter was both sobering and unsettling. I shared it with Tex and Ed. We all agreed we'd have to brace ourselves for an unfriendly homecoming. It was time to start thinking about what that adjustment was really going to be like, and I was having trouble wrapping my head around it.

To fear living in a combat zone is pretty damn normal. You would have to be crazy if you weren't. To be afraid to go home is not. In addition, although we knew Vietnam had changed us, we did not realize how much, nor how we would handle what was in front of us.

For the past year, my existence, my daily mindset, had been flying combat missions almost every day and never forgetting to thank God that I made it back, one more time. I had become somewhat of a 'human doing' rather than a 'human being'. My world in the Nam was very small. It was confined to a ten-foot by twelve-foot, air-conditioned hooch, filled with paperbacks and unlimited booze, and punctuated by an occasional good steak with a handful of friends. That, in one sentence, was life on the ground in Long Thanh North. Accepting such conditions as the norm is out of kilter with the rest of the world, but you don't recognize the degree of abnormality your mind has adapted to until you find yourself fighting for traction, because although you know things are about to change, you can't possibly know exactly what lies ahead of you. A soldier who had survived a year of Vietnam should never have had to consider that he would not be welcomed in the country he called home and for which he had put his life on the line ... every single day.

Chapter 27 Last Mission

On this, my last mission, I was well aware that my tour of duty was coming to an end. I was more than just SHORT! I would be going home in two weeks. All combat flyers go through the 'short jitters' before every mission. You have survived, so far. You realize you have almost made it. Your memory is riddled with the pilots who didn't; especially the guys who went down while flying short. I was about to fly mission number 187, the last combat mission of my life. For me, it was bitter-sweet. While a big part of me was relieved my tour was coming to an end, another part of me admitted that I would miss the excitement, the unknown, the next mission. I had gotten very good at an extremely dangerous game and had become addicted to the rush. My ego bathed in it. I'd been to the mountaintop; in fact, I went almost every day to that mountaintop, and I lived to tell. It's the kind of flying any 'real' pilot wants to do, and once you've lived it ... well, it stays with you. In a good way, you know, the flying part. The darker side, the killing part is different, much different. So, you deal with it. You do your job. You have seen more and experienced more than you can possibly sort out. You know that will have to wait until later ... perhaps never, so, you hold on to the good experiences as much as possible, because the bad shit doesn't want to leave you alone.

It was 1814 hours, February 14, 1972. Mission number 187. Throttles to the firewall, 115 knots down the runway, rotate 30 degrees nose up, earth falling away, gear up, flaps up. Climbing left turn to a heading of 348 degrees, level at 18,000 feet, and engage computer for update and checkpoint Z3008 Y2006. Computer readout: correct course to 356 degrees to compensate for 28-knot quarter headwind. Time to checkpoint Z3008 Y2006, nineteen minutes, and thirty-seven seconds. Fuel consumption 104.16 gallons per hour. Usable fuel remaining 685.86 gallons. I would arrive just fifteen minutes before sunset, a beautiful time of day in Southeast Asia. I had experienced flying over Z3Y2 during this time of day a few times over the last several months. Now I knew this would be my last rendezvous with Z3Y2, my favorite checkpoint, and that saddened me. Jungle parrot orange clouds on the western horizon, colored by the setting sun, caught my attention.

The shadowy veil of night is uninhibited over the jungle. There are no streetlights piercing the blanket of darkness that slides across Mother Earth below. Only God, pilots, and birds with strong wings get to experience Earth from this perspective when it is not yet night, but the day has left except for the sun still shining in their eyes because of their lofty altitude.

The sun's position at 18,000 feet gave it the appearance of being well above the horizon. It was still intense and bright from where I sat. I had to put my flight helmet sun visor down when scanning outside the cockpit into the open sky or along the horizon for other aircraft, especially MIGs. Looking toward the ground, however, I had to raise my sun visor up in order to make out earthly details. In the skyward view from the ground, only the brow of the sun touched the lip of earth, as shadows grew longer, and the inevitable darkness loomed mere minutes away.

On high cloud overcast nights, when there was neither moon nor stars to show me which way was up, the flight experience was disorienting. Flying night missions hundreds of miles from civilization, where there was no electricity to indicate human habitation on earth, added to the muddle. Without any light from above to provide equilibrium or down below to mark the way, there was only total and complete blackness in every direction and flight seemed untethered to time or space. Pilots called this dangerous condition 'flying the black hole'. In flight school, I understood I would need to depend on my instruments when flying in bad weather. It had never occurred to me that they would also become the reference point for my sanity.

Fighting my discomfort, I tried to look on the bright side of things. I was soon to behold the image of Z3Y2 one last time. I knew the circle of hooches would have their fires burning out front, lighting up the central lodge. This was a time when the families would be gathered together and their waving seemed most special because I knew they would be talking about the airplane overhead long after I had moved on. I hoped I was adding as much joy to their day as they were to mine. I would miss these people and this very special place.

I was three minutes ahead of my mission's on-target arrival time, so I put my aircraft into a gentle 360 degree turn over the hamlet and dropped down to a minimum descent altitude of 5,000 feet MSL, (mean sea level), considered safe from small arms fire. Just one more time before I went home, I wanted to soak up the magical existence of a people from a civilization thousands of years old and untouched by outside influences. This, in fact, was actually the reason I requested this, my final mission into Cambodia. Like all missions in Cambodia or Laos, this one was considered extremely dangerous, as are all night missions across the Fence. By their last month, most, if not all pilots, had stopped flying high-risk missions, and so had I, but I sought this one out. Ed thought I was nuts when I asked him to schedule me, but I could not be dissuaded.

Suddenly, when I was two minutes away from checkpoint Z3008 Y2006, it hit me like a gut punch. Something was terribly wrong! Where were the hooch fires? I double-checked my computer grid read-out. Everything looked functional and accurate. Several months ago, I had memorized the bends in the Mekong River at this location. They checked out, as well. I set up a slow descending turn over Z3Y2.

Struggling to make sense of this, my eyes began to glaze over with tears, there was a growing lump in my throat, and my stomach was doing flip-flops. By now, I had piloted my plane below the safe minimum altitude of 5000 feet. The crackle of my earphones snapped me out of it. My co-pilot alerted me that we were at 4700 feet. I told him to take over the aircraft and get us back on course, back up to flight level 18. I put my sun visor down and looked at the remaining minutes of the sunset, hiding both my tears and my grief from my flight crew.

Combat pilots can't run the risk of emotion. It's against all the rules; along with not showing or talking about fear. Fast planes, fast cars, fast women, and hard liquor. Macho prerequisites for the job. If you're not comfortable with this, then combat flying is not for you. No need to apply. A little sick? Perhaps, but when you're young, the thrill of living on the edge is either something you run towards or away from. Guess I was one of the crazy ones!

As far as I knew, Z3Y2 was encoded only in my aircraft computer. If other pilots had used it as a checkpoint, it had never come up during combat mission briefings. I had always held it too dear to give to anyone else. It had become my special oasis, and I chose not to divulge it. Sure, we shared most of our information, but this treasured place had remained sacred to me.

I reached over and zeroed the location out of the computer. Z3008 Y2006 was now gone. Gone from my computer and gone from its thousands of years of undisturbed existence. Obliterated from reality by a modern-day, high-tech war machine. The people of the hamlet never knew there was once a number assigned to them. If they had, it would not have meant anything to them anyway.

Somewhere, somehow, for some reason, someone who had the grid coordinate used it. But not in the way that I found useful. Whether through malfeasance or by miscalculation, the trigger had been pulled and grid coordinate Z3008 Y2006 was now a series of B-52 bomb craters. Nothing remained to give any hint that a beautiful hamlet and peaceful people had ever existed there.

Peaceful people, clearly not aiding or abetting the enemy. My friends. My safe harbor in the event I got shot down again in Cambodia.

Yes, I had let myself imagine what it would be like to live among them. Forever. Somehow the idea seemed OK. No, better than OK. Almost inviting. Like a lot of guys in the Nam, I felt abandoned by my own country. I wanted to go home, but the home I came to fight and die for didn't want me back. My thoughts of living in the hamlet weren't that far-fetched. I could plant rice. I could catch fish.

After completing our mission, the black hole in which we began our flight relinquished its hold on the night. The stars had come out. I was grateful to them for illuminating my way. It would have been even more difficult to deal with the excruciating emptiness I was experiencing along with the dreadful eeriness and heightened danger of flying the black hole.

That night, the stars became the hooch fires. I prayed that my hamlet friends were kept warm by them in the company of God. And I realized that it was OK for a combat pilot to cry.

***

That was my last mission. Ever. I cursed it for a long time. Why did I have to bring that particular memory home? Why couldn't I have departed Vietnam believing those gentle people were alive and well? Given all the horrors I had seen and experienced over here, Z3Y2 was the only thing that made sense, that was innocent, still good and pure, that seemed to have escaped this mess called war.

Some months later, sitting on the beach alone one night in Santa Barbara, I would find my thoughts going back not to war, which had become a daily demon, but to my friends who once lived on a farm near a riverbank. They planted rice, and they caught fish. With tears in my eyes, I looked out over the Pacific and up at the starry night. I thought of the stars as hooch fires again, for the first time since that night in February. I felt as though people were looking down at me and waving. I could not see them, of course, but I waved back . . . and my healing began.

Chapter 28 Zeroed Out

I woke up in my bunk for the last time, as excited as a five-year-old kid on Christmas morning. Day 365, and I was going home. Tears of joy unexpectedly began running down my cheeks before I even got up out of bed. Right on time, and just as usual, Nuwee came into my hooch at 0600 hours. Our ways of communicating had taken on a language of its own. She understood when I asked her to bring a chair and come sit by my bed.

"Sam, you not feel well? You sad? I see tear on face!"

"No, Nuwee, I am very happy. This is the day I go home. Remember I told you last month and again last week that this would be the day."

Nuwee dropped her head. "Nuwee glad Sam happy and get to go home. Nuwee very sad. Will miss Sam boocoo much. Maybe Sam come back soon?"

"Nuwee, look at Sam." She looked at me with her expressive black eyes. She was crying silently. I put my arms out and said, "Come to Sam. I want to give you a hug. I want to hold you a moment."

Nuwee leaned over, and we embraced for a long time. We both started to shed tears. Boy, I didn't see this one coming. After several minutes, Nuwee sat back in her chair.

"Maybe Sam can take Nuwee back to America?"

"Oh, Nuwee. If only that were possible. I wish more than anything that I could take you to my parents' farm. They have a Nuwee, too, and she would love you."

"Her name Nuwee?"

"No, her name is Otsie. She has worked with my parents since I was two years old."

"That long time, Sam. Your mamasan not need two Nuwee."

"She would make room for you, but that is not the problem." I took Nuwee by the hands and gently spoke to her humble, kind face.

"Nuwee, the war here is going to end soon. Maybe two or three more years. When that happens, it might be dangerous for you. Can you go somewhere safe?"

"Sam, Nuwee never leave South Vietnam. Not ever. Nuwee not know anywhere to go safe."

"You said you had a daughter who lives in Saigon. Her husband was fighting in the war. She lives alone with their young daughter and works as a nurse. Is that correct?"

"Yes, that correct. She would love me live with her and my granddaughter. But Sam, I make more money one-month work for your government than I make one year among my people. That why I stay here."

"OK. I understand. Please listen to me Nuwee. This is very important for you."

"What, Sam?"

"The United States is starting to send many of our soldiers home. More and more will begin to leave here. What I do as a pilot ... You know, my job, will be one of the last groups to go home. Understand?"

"I understand what you say, but I not understand why."

"That is not important. Nuwee, when you see or hear of pilots like me all going home, you know base camp will close, then you must hurry to get to your daughter. Burn everything you have in your village that is yours that shows you worked for the United States. Do not take anything to your daughter's place. I mean absolutely nothing that connects you to us."

"Sam, that not fair. What about my pictures with you and Mr. Laddy and Mr. Tex?"

"You must burn them, Nuwee. I know those pictures mean a lot to you, but when we leave Vietnam, and the NVA take over, nobody really knows how you will be treated. I don't want you to get hurt, Nuwee. You must do everything you can to show you had nothing to do with us.

"Now, I want you to take this money. The next time you go to Saigon, go to the international bank and have them give you gold coins for this cash. Then you bury the gold coins in several different places. Be sure no one sees you."

Despite the fact that we were absolutely forbidden to give the Vietnamese American money, I handed Nuwee $500.00. At this point, it didn't matter. It was more than I could afford, but then this was a woman who had taken very good care of me for one entire year. I had given her ten or twenty bucks here and there, but nothing like this. I could not bear the thought of the NVA raping, torturing, or killing her because of her association with us.

"Oh, Sam! I never see this much money. This too much for Nuwee. Here, you take four back."

"No! I want you to have it all. Remember Nuwee, very important. Take to bank and get gold coins only. Nothing else."

"Oh, Sam. I never dream of so much money. This enough for my family for three years, maybe more." Nuwee stood up, leaned over, kissed me on my cheek, and gave me a big hug.

"I go now, and later I come back and help you with your things, OK, Sam?"

"OK, Nuwee. Take your time. I don't leave until 3:00 this afternoon. No need to help me; all of my things have been shipped. The only stuff I have to carry fits into this duffle bag."

I often wished I could have brought Nuwee back home. She would have fit right in with Otsie and Bessie. Even some forty-odd years later, I continue to think of her and offer a silent prayer. Truth is, no one really knows the fate of the many peace-loving South Vietnamese people who worked for the U.S. Government. It wasn't necessarily that they were for or against anything political. It was simply that they had an unprecedented opportunity to do decent work for much higher wages than they could ever earn in their economy. The thought of the communist regime punishing or killing them under the dubious justification of 'collaboration with the enemy' was another repugnant injustice heaped on the already war-torn, suffering, and impoverished.

***

While I was packing my duffle bag and looking around my comfortable hooch for the last time, I was feeling sentimental, and that caught me by surprise. This was my first real man cave. In all the years ahead of me, I would never know such a place again. I would remember my hooch as the place where the boy became a man, and the man learned how to kill without remorse. I had experienced a slice of life that changed me forever. As my life would unfold in the future, and I looked back to consider the various slices, my year in the Nam, without a doubt, would be the most defining. I would also learn first-hand that time does not heal all wounds, and only when we accept that the wounds of war will never heal, can we learn to live with them. Back in the world, it would take a few decades to realize that I never really fit in, because returning war veterans look at life through a different filter.

I was fixing what might be my last pot of coffee here when I got a knock on the door. "Yeah, come in."

A new Warrant Officer extended his hand. "Mr. Walker, I am Mack Simowicz. I understand you are leaving, and I came to talk to you about buying into your hooch. Man, this place is really cool. It would be a sharp bachelor pad back home."

"Make it 'Sam'. Nice to meet you, Mack. So, where you from back in the world?"

"New Jersey, Sir, the Garden State!"

"Please, drop the Sir, shit. Told ya, it's Sam. Cup of coffee? Just made a pot. How do you take it back in the Garden State?"

"Black, please. So, Sam, after seeing this incredible hooch, how much for the buy in? I hear there are only three others similar to it. Owned by an instructor pilot, CW4 Tex, the CO, and the supply sergeant."

"That's right. Tex and the supply sergeant were instrumental in helping me build this little place. All handmade. Four-poster bunk beds, two large wall cabinets, stereo system cabinet, bar, desk, and chairs, with carpeting, wallpaper, 5000 BTU AC and a black light poster of Jimi Hendrix, black light included. The light alone cost over $100 to purchase and get it shipped here in one piece. Let's see, how 'bout a real deal, $3000.00?"

"$3000.00?" Mack gulped. "I mean I would have to set up some kind of six-to nine-month payment plan."

"Your FNG colors are shining through there, Mack. I was an Aircraft Commander. My job was to mission-train FNGs for three months before turning them loose. Do you know what the survival rate is for an FNG the first month he is out there on his own?"

"No idea! What?"

"Fifty-fifty. Not exactly a good credit risk."

"Why so high a casualty rate? Surely, you would know as an Aircraft Commander."

"Yeah, I do. Just finished writing a six-page report addressing that question. One of my last and few paper-pushing tasks before leaving. Listen carefully, Mack. What I am about to tell you could save your life one day."

I refreshed our coffee and took some of Nuwee's fruit salad from the fridge for us.

"Very simple reasons really. Number One: New pilots are truly afraid, but don't want to show it or talk about it. It's hard to remember or pay much attention to what you're being taught if you're trying not to shit in your flight suit. Number Two: The eighteen-hour bottle to throttle rule is ignored. A few drinks might be fine if you can handle it, but it's impossible to clear your head to fly an intense mission without hours of sleep, a hot shower, and food in your stomach. If you don't accept that, it could lead to disaster. Number Three: You find yourself agreeing with or saying yes to your AC because you don't want to appear stupid. Fact is, none of us made it this far being stupid. However, we have a stupid moment when we find ourselves going along to get along, and then one day, you find yourself flying a mission that has got you by the balls because you went along to get along instead of saying, 'Whoa! Right there! Please go back over that. I totally missed it'.

"Several months ago, several other Aircraft Commanders and I met with the top brass in Saigon. We presented these three things and asked that they be addressed with FNGs over and over, right upfront. We have flipped the casualty rate from 50/50 to 95/5. Major difference. Just can't believe it took so long for ACs to come together and address the problem.

"OK, Mack, let's get back to the hooch. It's all yours. A gift. Not a dime."

"What? What? You're kidding, right? How come?"

"Well, I look at it this way. I need to let you know you are appreciated. You matter. You've got enough monkeys on your back without additional debt. And by the way, the monkeys may leave, but the circus is always in town, and every now and then, the gorilla shows up."

"Thanks, Sam. This really means a lot, but what the heck is this gorilla thing."

"Sure. Real story. On a dark and stormy night with Charlie trying to shoot us out of the sky, we had a cockpit fire. I immediately shut down both generators to stop the wire burn from spreading to four fuel tanks. No comms. No lights. Not enough instruments to fly by instrument, but had to anyway. Couldn't talk to Ramrod to get through the Fence and around SAMs. Couldn't talk to artillery batteries, so I didn't know their fan of fire. No communication with Tactical Approach, Approach Control, or the base camp tower, and to top that off, the weather really sucked."

"Man, are you shittin' me?"

"No! Not at all. It happened to me and my crew one night over Cambodia."

"So, what did you do?"

"Had to out-think the gorilla, and there was no room for error. We had less than a ten percent chance of making it."

I gave Mack the details of what we had to do to make it home that night and then added Laddy's prophetic words, *You will find yourself doing things in an airplane that you never dreamed were possible.*

"You got another treat coming. Her name is Nuwee. The best mamasan in the squadron. Treat her with respect and kindness, or I will come back and give you a Vietnamese necktie."

"What's that?"

"Ask around. Best you find out after I leave."

"Yeah, Sam, I know you're busy packing, but I was having supper last night with a couple of guys who have been here awhile and they not only told me about your hooch, but suggested I ask you to give me the do's and don'ts around here. If you have time, that is."

"Yeah, sure, glad to. I will talk as I pack. Before I get into all that ... a few other important things. Take care of Nuwee. You know, slip her a ten or twenty every now and then. Fuck the rules on US dollars going to them. Nuwee is truly a good person, and God only knows what will happen to her when we all leave. There are a couple of prostitutes among the mamasans. One is particularly hot. Stay away from all of them. They will not only get in your pants, but will also get in your head, and they will get information. I have seen it happen to four guys in the last year."

"So, what happened to them?"

"Their wings were taken away. They were dropped one grade of rank and then shipped off God knows where."

"Out of Vietnam?"

"Hell no! That would be a reward. I understand one was put in charge of maintenance up on the DMZ. Nothing pretty up there. Trust me, Mack. We are all young and bursting with testosterone. It does get lonely over here, very lonely, and you will get horny, very horny. Wait until you get your 72-hour pass to Saigon or Vau Tau and get laid away from this base camp. Now for the other stuff." I pretty much gave Mack the same talk that Laddy and Sully had given me with some extras thrown in.

"Here, Mack, a fresh cup of coffee. Sit there at my desk. Use the legal pad and pen there. If I am talking too fast, I say something you don't understand ... whatever ... just ask me to stop and repeat. I got about five hours before I walk out of that door for the last time, and it will take a few to tell you what you need to know. None of what I am about to say is written down anywhere. You won't get it in any briefing. It is information that brings you into the brotherhood of this elite band of warriors," I said with a chuckle. "It's not information that MIGHT save your ass. It WILL save your ass. Ready?"

"Ready, Sam. What was the laugh about?"

"If you do the math, we ARE an elite group. You know, top rung of Uncle Sam's pilots. Somewhere around one percent. REALLY? So fuckin' what? We live in a shit-hole, our food is not fit to eat, and if we go down in Cambodia or Laos and a SEAL Team can't get us out ... well, we are forgotten. We don't exist. We were never here. Now I am just an old southern farm boy who learned how to fly planes when I was in my teens, and I got a college education, but damn if I can figure how the word 'elite' applies to us. Let me know if you figure that one out.

"First, what we do up there is unspeakable. No one has told you about it because they can't. You'll have to experience it. Until you have actually flown a mission, you simply can't get it. Somewhere between twenty and thirty missions, you get it all over again, except on a different level. Not trying to freak you out, Mack, but you have just arrived at hell's door. What we do is ugly. It will stay with you the rest of your years."

After telling Mack everything I could think of that would help him survive his tour, I had him read his notes back to me. Damn sharp cookie. He did not miss one thing, but I guess when you're an FNG and a few pilots with some time in-country tell you to go see Sam because he can tell you stuff that will save your life, you tend not to miss anything.

"Good job, Mack. Hope that helps a little. Oh! I left out one thing. You got the numb feeling yet?"

"Yes, how did you know?"

"'Cause we all do, and we are embarrassed that we feel it. It is the beginning of a survival mechanism that will help you deal with this separate reality. Don't fight it. Just go with it. You will keep getting numb. From what I am told, it is probably one of the most fucked up things this war does to us that we carry home."

"Shit! How do you get rid of it, Sam?"

"Don't have a clue, Mack. Not a fuckin' clue! Guess that's what I'm getting ready to find out. I'm going to have to learn to feel all over again. Whatever that means."

After Mack stood up, shook my hand, and left, something Laddy said washed over me. *Sam, the day will come when you are standing where I am and telling all this stuff to an FNG.* I just hoped Mack would make it. If he knew what he was in for, he would seriously try to get in my duffle bag. Years later, I heard from him. He had made it. He returned to New Jersey, married a girl named Denise, and became an executive with a phone company.

For the last time, I walked into the CO's office where Tipper greeted me.

"Have a seat, Sam. Let's have a farewell shot of your old Scotch before the XO and I take you to Tan Son Nhut."

We clinked glasses, raised them to the sky, and kicked them back.

"Here, Sam, a little something for the ride home. You can get it refilled in Hawaii. It's full of your good stuff." Tipper handed me a silver pint flask inscribed in old English lettering, that read:

To a pilot, a friend, a warrior I could always count on. Tipper.

"This is very nice, Tipper! For the ride home, huh? Thought that was against regs."

"It is. Just be discreet. When the flight settles down, pull a blanket over your head, and go for it. Trust me, seventy percent of the soldiers on board will have their own stash."

Tipper dropped me off in front of Flight Ops. It was an awkward moment. We could only shake hands and say 'Take care of yourself'. Truth is, I wanted to give Tipper a big bear hug and tell him how much his friendship meant to me. Just wasn't done. Military protocol.

I checked in at the counter, showed the sergeant my paperwork, and he gave me a ticket. I found a table of four, all chief warrant officers. One pulled out a chair for me. Brief acknowledgment went around. I knew they were all chopper pilots before I looked at their flight suit patches or a word was spoken. There was no doubt in my mind that these guys had it tougher than I did. Then something happened.

"Whadaya fly, Sam?"

"Fixed wing."

"What? Bird dogs, Broncos – what?"

"Neither. Spook planes." I swear you could hear a pin drop. All four pilots were now boring a hole through me until one spoke up.

"Always wanted to meet one of you types. Top-secret shit, right?"

"Yeah, right."

The waitress put another pitcher of Vietnamese beer on the table and brought me a glass. One of the pilots filled it for me. I thanked him. When he finished pouring, he said, "Cambodia and Laos, right?"

"Hey, guys. I'm sorry. I really can't talk about this, OK? I have no desire to visit Leavenworth. Maybe I should find another table."

"Tell you what, Sam, look around. There must be, what, two hundred-fifty people in this bar waiting to jump on that freedom bird in a few hours?"

"Yeah, I would say that's about right. Why?"

"Show me one ... just one pilot that has that tiger patch on his flight suit. You're an enigma, Sir. I, well, I should say, we, are honored to meet you, Sam."

Lifting their beer glasses, they toasted, "Here! Here!"

"Thanks, but I don't understand. What was that for?"

A different pilot spoke up. "Look, Sam, we will lighten up, OK? None of our damn business what you did anyway. We all made it, and we are all going home, and that's all that matters, right?"

"Yeah, right."

The same pilot continued, "I will tell you why we toasted you. You types took up a lot of our conversation. You see, Sam, none of us knows exactly what you did, but we did know that every time you flew into Cambodia and Laos, you risked becoming a POW. That is some heavy shit to deal with, Sam. If you were shot down, there was a very real possibility you would never be heard from again. Uncle Sam couldn't ask for your release because you were never there. Did you know the name all of us chopper pilots had for you?"

"No! Can't say I do."

"Ghost! Hey, buddy, you got our respect more than you know. Personally, I know for certain, I could not have done what you did."

"Well, there is something that I have to tell you. I was a door gunner for about an hour in one of your Charlie model choppers. For me, that hour was pure hell! There is no way I could do what you guys did, day after day. That takes a lot of balls! You guys risked being shot right out of the air, and crashing right into enemy territory. I am proud to be drinking a few farewell beers with the lot of ya.

"Look, I came over here a naive kid who was still wet behind the ears. I am going home a man who can get meaner than a snake in a split second if I have to.

"I remember the first morning I arrived here when a captain and sergeant entered our aircraft to 'greet' us. They may have been a few years older, but not by much. I'll never forget the impression they made just by their persona. There is no way on God's green planet I would have gone up against either one of those guys. Well, guess what? That's what we look like now."

Just then, the loudspeaker called us to the gate for our flight.

"Wow! Nice little speech there, Sam. Say, you got some hooch in your leg pocket?"

"Damn straight!"

"Good. Let's stick together on the plane. May as well continue the party until Hawaii where we can get a refill."

No in-flight movies, mediocre food, but four pleasant, rather attractive flight attendants made up for that. I had an aisle seat. Two chopper pilots to my right and two just across the aisle. The one across the aisle spoke up.

"Check out that little redheaded stew with freckles. Cute, don't you think?"

"Well, yeah. I couldn't help but notice her myself, but come on, man. Her guard is way up dealing with a plane-load of combat veterans for a ten-hour flight."

"Sam, I am sure you could tell me a few stories about making it with the ladies while you were right here in the Nam. You're a fuckin' chick magnet! It just comes naturally to you."

"Well, actually, I did dance with Miss America, and I'm dating a Pan Am flight attendant."

"Yeah, right, and I am an astronaut. Like that could really happen over here! Or even the States for that matter. Not a snowball's chance in hell. We need to do a reality check."

"Like what?"

"These planes are sittin on an ass-load of booze, but they are not allowed to serve liquor to us servicemen. Shit! It should be just the other way around! They should be giving us bottles of champagne and prime cut steaks. You know, the good stuff."

"So, what are you saying?"

"I am saying, play it up with this redhead and get us some mini bottles."

"Can't promise anything, but I'll try."

As if right on cue, here comes little Miss Sunny Brook Farm, and she stops to talk to me. "Everything OK, Mr. Walker?"

"Yeah, long flight ahead of us, but sure good to be going home to my girlfriend."

"Oh, I bet she's very special. And she's been counting the hours till you return."

"She's a Pan Am stew. I actually met her at the Caravelle Hotel in Saigon on layover at the time."

"I see where you're a pilot. The tiger stripes and wings kinda give that up right away. You're not the average flyboy. What would you be doing at the Caravelle?"

"Long story actually. Her name is Vicky Pullman."

"Oh my God! You're kidding me, right?"

"No, not at all, why?"

"Vicky and I were in the same Pan Am training class. She was smart and very friendly, but I haven't seen her since then. How's she doing?"

"Well, she must be crazy 'cause she's waiting for me!"

I leaned closer and crooked my finger to indicate I wanted to whisper something too her. Now she was close enough for me to read her name tag, and to pick up on the intoxicating scent of her subtle perfume.

"I know this is a quirky request, and if the answer is no, I understand. No offense taken. The two guys to my right and the two guys across the aisle from me are also pilots. Truth is, this is hard on all of us. Mixed emotions, glad to be going home but really conflicted about leaving buddies behind."

"Stop right there, Sam. I bet each of you has a leg flask, but that's not enough to get you to Hawaii. You want me to break the rules and slip you some extra booze?"

"Yeah ... yeah, that's what I had in mind if it's not too much to ask."

"How about a sleeve of vodka mini bottles for each of you? That will have to do. That's six mini-bottles per sleeve. We just started carrying this really good vodka, Stolichnaya, genuine Russian stuff. I will have to deliver them over the course of the next few hours. Tell your pilot buddies to put them under the blankets in their laps and make a submarine dive under the blanket to drink. When I come around to collect trash, just put them in the bag."

"WOW! You are awesome Gretchen. Write your address down. I'll take a donation from the guys so you can get a nice gift for yourself in Hawaii."

"I appreciate that Sam, but it's not necessary. You guys have already done quite enough, and sadly, it's not appreciated back home, which really ticks me off."

"Thanks, all the same, Gretchen, but you will be getting a gift."

My new-found chopper buddies were flat out amazed that the Russian vodka just kept coming. The pilot across the aisle pulled me over to whisper, "You really are seeing a Pan Am flight attendant who you met in Saigon?"

"Yep. Here is a photo of us taken on R&R in Australia."

"Who does this? What are the odds? Man, this is almost too much. I mean I know it's true because I heard Gretchen say she knew her. I guess the Miss America fantasy is not a fantasy either."

"Nope." I showed him the picture.

"Who are you, man?"

At this point, with a little too much booze under my belt, I couldn't help pouring it on. "Like Scotch?"

"Love Scotch. My favorite drink."

I produced my flask and gave him a swig. "Oh my God! Where did you get this stuff?"

"From a U.S. Senator."

"Man, if you're not kidding me, you ought to write a book!"

The fella stared at me through half-drunk eyes, which he tried and failed to focus, and then rolled over and covered his head with his blanket. Within minutes, he began to snore.

***

After landing in Hawaii for a two-hour layover, I took my place in a long line to use the payphone. Even though there was a bank of ten phones across from the bar in the terminal, it took about an hour before I finally got my hands on the phone and pumped some change into the slots. I was happy to reach Vicky and let her know my anticipated arrival time.

"Sam, it's so good to hear your voice! I can't believe you're actually coming home for good! I have to tell you, be prepared when you get to the airport. The anti-war demonstrators are growing in number. They are on the news every night."

"Thanks, Vicky, but they are the ones who need to be careful."

"Gee. Forgot who I was talking to."

"Can't wait to see you, Sweetheart. Would you please call my mom and tell her I am safe and on my way home? Tell her I'll call her when I get to California. Right now, guys are lined up behind me, and I don't want to hog the phone. Anyway, I'll be boarding soon."

"You got it. I love you, Sam Walker."

"I love you, Vicky Pullman."

Chapter 29 Back in the World

We boarded the plane in Hawaii for the last leg of our trip to Travis Air Force Base. None of the chopper pilots had anyone meeting them there, and with no reason to arrive sober, they continued to drink. I decided to take a nap and let the alcohol wear off because I didn't want to meet Vicky half crocked. Reclining my seat, I gazed out over the vast blue Pacific and allowed my thoughts to flow.

What had all of this been about? Now that I was no longer an active warrior, I wanted to let go of the anxious feelings that went along with the job, but they were always with me. Guess it was way too soon to hope for such change. After all, I was still wearing a flight suit and officially still in the service. Just two weeks earlier, one of the pilots coming through our headquarters on his way to the DMZ told us an absolutely terrifying story, and now it flooded my mind.

A group of soldiers, pilots in particular, had been heading home to process out of the military. As they were standing in line to pick up their last paycheck and have their discharge orders stamped, a high-ranking officer showed up out of nowhere and raised his hands in the universal stop sign to gain their attention.

"Sorry, gentlemen! I know this will come as a blow, but Uncle Sam still needs you in Vietnam. Due to the stand down in Nam, several squadrons have been overrun. Take your duffle bags over to the BOQ

(Bachelors Officer Quarters). Shower and change. Have a steak at the mess hall. We leave in three hours."

That had to be a mind-blowing experience, to say the least; frankly, it's unfathomable to me at this point. I had heard that several of those pilots deserted. Went AWOL. Took off for places unknown. Probably Canada or Mexico. Can't say I blamed them. If the same fate awaited me, what would I do? Go back to the Nam? Hell, no! I couldn't put Vicky through another year of waiting. The thought of it was just too much. I reached for my flask and took a serious draw of Scotch. The prospect of going back to Vietnam scared the shit out of me. Bet these chopper boys would run ... and I would go with them. So, sitting here, I realized I had to get a grip. I was hours away from clutching the piece of paper that would stipulate I was a free man.

I kept nipping at my Scotch. I had given Vicky my arrival time but told her to wait three or four hours before showing up because we had to out-process. I couldn't help but think what it must have been like for the pilots who were told they were going right back just when they had made it to the final part of the discharge process. Talk about having the rug pulled out from under your feet! How did their wives, girlfriends, and families take such horrible, unbelievable news?

My tour in Vietnam started and ended on my birthday, February 28th. I returned to Travis Air Force Base in 1972. We were kept in a restricted area, away from civilians, and were immediately shuffled through out-processing. We were given a perfunctory physical, collected lots of paperwork, and then stood in one more line to pick up our last paycheck. Finally, I faced the last and most important step – getting my discharge papers stamped. My heart was racing. This was where it could happen. Until my discharge papers were stamped, I still belonged to Uncle Sam. It was one of the longest hours of my life, right up there with any of the dreadful experiences I had in the Nam. Then, suddenly, it was over. Except for just one thing. It's always just one more thing! Although we were officially separated from military service, there was still one catch. Pilots were bound to a seven-year commitment because Uncle Sam had spent close to a million dollars training each of us. I figured they got their money's worth out of me, but I guess forty pounds of flesh wasn't enough. All pilots would be on Standby Reserve for four more years. In simple terms, that meant that if America got involved in another war, they could call us back. All that was left now was a mercifully short flight to LAX where I was to meet Vicky at baggage claim, where MPs had to dump every soldier's duffle bag and search it piece by piece. Some poor souls who had become addicted to heroin tried to smuggle some through. I was amazed at how many were caught, cuffed, and taken away right then and there. *What would happen to them?* I wondered. After what we had been through, this seemed so unfair.

Finally, I was reunited with Vicky. We embraced, holding each other tight. We could not get enough of each other, planting several kisses on lips, eyes, and cheeks. Overwhelmed, we both started to weep with joy.

"Welcome home, Sweetheart. It is finally over! You have your life back, Sam. You can look forward to a bright future. Things are going to be OK from now on."

"Yeah, Sweetheart. I know. Boy, are you a sight for sore eyes! You smell so good and feel absolutely wonderful. My head is full of the fact that it isn't just a visit this time, and that is amazing!"

"I know, Sam, but now, just walk out of here with me and straight to my car. There are probably two hundred demonstrators outside waiting for you soldiers. At least two TV stations are certain to put this on the five o'clock news."

"I will, but just give me a minute, there is something I have to do first."

I walked over to my chopper friends, who had caught a glimpse of Vicky, and made a suggestion. They said they were in, and they would spread the word down the line to the other men.

"What was that about, Sam?"

"You'll see. Just going to have a little fun with those assholes outside."

About thirty of us had gathered at the exit door to the parking lot. We all walked out at the same time to screaming hippies, calling us baby killers and psycho soldiers, and waving signs with all kinds of nasty sayings to put us down. They yelled that we don't belong here anymore. I had told the chopper pilots to go on my signal. I raised my hand with a clinched fist and brought it down fast. With that, in unison, we all yelled 'FUCK YOU!' then dropped our pants and mooned the lot of them. The crowd went berserk. Several were trying to get over the barrier and come at us. We egged them on. The local police and MPs motioned us to keep moving as they held the crowd back.

"Sam Walker, you are bad!" Vicky giggled.

"Damn right I am. And so are these soldiers. Too bad those cops can't give us ten minutes with those pukes."

"In the car, big boy. God, you have not even been out of the service one hour, and your butt is going to be on the five o'clock news!"

Our ultimate destination was Santa Barbara, but we stopped for the night when we spotted a small hotel that looked inviting. After checking in, we got reacquainted and spent the night. The next morning, back on the road, I found myself sitting in silence, staring out at the Pacific Ocean. Vicky glanced over from the driver's seat and put a hand on my knee. "Sam, you OK over there?"

I exhaled deeply. "Yeah, Baby. I'm OK. I guess it's just starting to sink in. I am out of the service. I am really home. I am with you. I made it. I just fuckin' made it ... and that's enough. That's everything! I'm completely at your disposal until the camping trip.

"I'll only be gone about ten days, two weeks tops. Truth is, I don't want to be away from you, and whatever the three of us need to get out of our systems, well, it's going to take a lot longer than two weeks. Tex, Ed, and I agreed this trip was about just getting grounded and supporting each other. Make sense?"

"Sure, Sam. That's your call. Of course, I am delighted you guys could arrange it."

"After our trip, Ed's gonna' visit his mother in Santa Fe. He doesn't know what he'll do after that, but Tex and I suggested that he consider settling in California."

"Well, tell Ed that we have a guest room, it's actually a small efficiency behind the cottage, that he can use as long as he likes. It doesn't have a full kitchen, so it can't be rented separately, but I think he'll be very comfortable there, enjoying the sea air and a bit of privacy. You'll see it later."

"That's really sweet of you, Vicky. I am sure it will give him something to look forward to. By the way, Ed took a second R&R to Australia to spend more time with Adrianna. Looks like they are serious about each other. He didn't mention marriage, but he did say he wanted to bring her to the States when he gets settled."

"That is awesome. I have to tell you, I really like Adrianna. Different breed of cat, that's for sure, but solid, honest, and tough, not to mention fun-loving and beautiful. She and I have been in touch since our amazing time in Australia, so I knew things were developing between them."

"Ed gets here in seven days. Then, when Tex arrives, Ed and I will meet him at LAX, and the three of us will fly up to Portland together. OK, now for Tex. After our camping trip, he'll be closing on his property, which is not far from your cottage."

"Remember, Sam. I met these men when they came to see you in the hospital in Saigon. I was awestruck. Got to tell ya, I will feel like your two brothers have taken up residence, which is fine with me. I grew up an only child, remember? And you didn't have any brothers, either."

"These guys are my brothers. Mitch, too. Closer than brothers really. We saw each other through some pretty tough times."

"Yeah, you did. And you will probably continue to do so. I've had a long time to think about you coming home from that war. You will not heal overnight, and I know that. I think having two of your closest friends around, who went through what you did, will be very healthy for all of us."

"Speaking of brothers, I have more good news. Mitch gets out in a couple of months and plans to settle in LA. Said after all these years in the Nam, he couldn't handle the cold in Detroit anymore. We're invited to his wedding. I look forward to meeting Sarah, too. Wow! After a year of living, surviving, day-to-day, it's great to have something pleasant to look forward to."

Then Vicky changed the conversation. "I'm reprising my role as Nurse Vicky! I want to take care of you Sam. I suggest we take it easy until Ed gets here. A few walks on the beach, some drives along the coast, see a few movies, you know, just play-time stuff. Whadaya think?"

"Hey! Twist my arm."

"First thing, when we get home: call your mom and your sister. They must be jumping out of their skin waiting to hear from you. Stay on the phone as long as you want. And speaking of family, I'm eager to show you off to my parents, Edward and Helen. As you can imagine, they are eager to meet you, but I explained it won't be until after the camping trip. Well, our family home is on the property where the farm is based, so we can talk about that too. But no pressure. It just gives you the chance to check it all out firsthand."

"Damn!"

"What, Sweetheart?"

"Oh, nothing really! It's just here it goes again. The best of times, the worst of times. Now that I'm back, and I'm not even out of the car yet, I'm beginning to see the potential for a lot of good times ahead."

I silently wished that for all of us, Vicky, Ed, Tex, Mitch, and me, but life simply doesn't work that way. You can't be both the needle and the thread, and you don't get to pick which one you will be and when.

***

After picking up Ed at LAX, we surprised him with the efficiency apartment. He loved it. A week later, when we met Tex at the airport as planned, Ed and I gave him a big bear hug. Definitely not something he was accustomed to. It was great for the three of us to be together again. In the course of catching up, I told Tex about my arrival and us mooning the protesters while the news cameras were rolling.

"Damn! Hardly back in the states for an hour, and you're into a bit of mischief! Did you recognize your ass on TV that night?" Tex prodded.

"No, I didn't, but Vicky did!"

The three of us flew to Portland, and upon arriving, Tex got the ball rolling, "Let's go get our truck and head over to a sporting goods store to get our gear so we can hit the trail."

Armed with our shopping list and several maps for our planned excursion, we hit the outdoor store and shopped for camping gear. The three of us felt like kids turned loose in a toy store, with no grown-ups around. Hiking boots, one .22 rifle, one 9mm pistol, three hatchets, and three 8" blade hunting knives were at the top of the list. Having been soldiers, we felt safer now that we had guns and knives, even though we were in the States, not in the Nam. We just had to avoid shooting or stabbing any pissed off hippies, no matter how angry they might make us. We picked up three fly rods, hunting and fishing licenses, and basic camping equipment. We stopped to get food and plenty of booze, enough to last two weeks. We were on our way.

***

About an hour before dark, we stopped at the base of a waterfall on the trail of the Columbia Valley Gorge. It was magical. The waterfall hit the Columbia River with a mellow splash, creating our background music. The mist and spray cooled the air. We could hear birds singing and the shushing sound of the wind blowing through tall spruce trees. We were a long way from the jungles of Vietnam. After we pitched camp, gathered firewood and started a fire, we sat around sipping Scotch and sharing cans of smoked oysters with crackers and apple slices, not saying a word, while fresh-caught salmon was grilling and sweet potatoes cooked in the coals. Tex broke the silence.

"Man, I've been in the Nam so long that I had forgotten what a beautiful country we live in. Just wishing I was out of the service like you two, but the thing is, I've got a great opportunity ahead of me. Eighteen months in DC where the general is going to get me certified in the Gulf Stream II; I'm being promoted to bird colonel, and then I'm out! With the property I'm buying here, and with a jet license under my belt, I should be able to make some kind of life for myself."

Funny, but Tex didn't reflect at all on his experience in the Nam. I guess he had the right not to do so. Since he grew up fending for himself, I imagined he developed the habit of looking toward the future, as opposed to dwelling in the past. And he certainly didn't feel sorry for himself. He knew his future was up to him.

"Sure sounds like it to me," Ed declared, adding, "Eighteen months flying jets while based in DC is a whole lot better than one month in the Nam! Just think: modern plumbing, decent food, beautiful American women. That's our new reality, guys."

"I'll drink to that!" I poured another round. We hoisted our glasses and took turns calling out silly toasts.

"To porcelain toilets!"

"To toilet paper!"

"To cheeseburgers!"

"To American beauties!"

"To home cooking!"

All of these things, once taken for granted, had been sorely missed. Eventually, we ran out of things to toast, stopped laughing, and grew quiet. A sullen mood had dropped over us until Ed interrupted the silence.

"I don't know. I just don't feel as happy as I should – or as happy as I thought I would feel. Here I am, discharged, in one piece, safe and back home, but I just don't feel right. Vietnam has made me realize that

I can handle a lot more than I thought I could. It taught me that I can handle 'crazy'. But now that I'm out, what I've learned in the Nam doesn't seem to have anything to do with life here back in the world. I feel like I don't fit in and don't know if I ever will. I don't have a clue about what I'll wind up doing. I want to bring Adrianna here, but I have nothing to offer her now. If it takes me too long to get settled and figure this out, I'm afraid I'll lose her. I'm lucky she's waited this long, but a fine woman like that won't wait forever." Pausing, he took a few gulps, then finished, "I guess I have a lot to sort out before I can move forward. I just don't know how to even start, and I sure don't want to blow it with Adrianna."

"Just a thought. Maybe your future is in Australia with Adrianna," Tex said.

I nodded in silent agreement, then I shared my thoughts.

"We've all flown some pretty dicey missions. Take my stay on Red Mullet Island with Mitch. From fish-whacking to napalm – the best and the worst of times. I have nightmares about having been shot down. Many nights, I wake up screaming and in a cold sweat. Poor Vicky, it scares the hell out of her. How much can she take? I thought I could handle everything that happened to me because I survived, physically. But it's what's inside, the things you can't see, that are going to get you. With Vicky in my life, I should feel a lot better, in fact, I should feel great! But the truth is, I don't. Guess what Vietnam taught me is that the best of times only last until the worst of times inevitably intrudes.

"I'm very mixed up about a lot of things, and I have no idea how to make it all right. Part of me knows it's going to take a while to feel normal, but on the other hand, maybe things will never be alright again. Like Laddy once told me, *This place will change you forever*. Truth is, and I can only say this to you two, I am afraid. I may put up a good front, but I am afraid. I feel like I have been gutted like that salmon and cast to the wind. I keep reaching out to bring pieces of me back, but can't quite get a grip on things.

"Unlike Ed, I have some options, but like Ed, I don't know where to start or how to start. It was always assumed that after the Nam, I'd go back to my family home and work the farm with my dad. One day, that farm will be mine. That's my first option. Makes sense. It's where I grew up and what I loved. I'd enjoy my work, and I could still fly small planes, but I doubt Vicky would enjoy it. The nearest airport is rather small, so she would probably have to give up flying, and having seen where she lives now, I doubt she'd give up southern California for the Low Country."

"Well," said Ed, "after just a little taste of southern California, I tend to agree with you on that point."

"Then, this prospect came right out of the blue shortly before I zeroed out. Colonel Simmons told me that Beechcraft is always looking for experienced pilots, and he could set me up with an interview and a strong recommendation. Well, I love being around planes, but I don't know what I'd actually be doing there. And Kansas? Definitely no family, no Low Country, and likely no Vicky either.

"Behind door number three, there is Vicky and her family's farm in California. I might be disappointing my parents, but I'm all grown up now, and I think they'd understand. I've mentioned this possibility in my letters to them."

"Sounds to me like you gotta go through door number three, Sam. That is, if you want a future with Vicky. What seems to be the holdup?" asked Tex.

"I'm not sure. Something inside that I can't work out. Vicky and I really love each other. She took great care of me when I was in really bad shape, so kind and so loving. But she's not looking to get married; at least not now. She wants us to live together. I don't understand why she'd be willing to live together – in fact, that was her idea – but not wanting to get married."

"You ever ask her?"

"Of course! She says that although we're very attracted to each other, and we have fallen in love, we've only spent time together in beautiful hotels in beautiful places, like on vacation. Not real life. So, we should give real life a try before making such an important commitment."

"Sounds to me like she's got a level head on her shoulders," commented Ed.

"Sounds to me like she's the pragmatist, and you're the romantic," offered Tex. "So, I'm still thinking door number three. That's the only way you'll find out if your life script has been written with Vicky in it."

"You could always check out Beechcraft just to see what they have to offer. That could help you decide. Can't overlook the fact that you love flying, and you love airplanes!" said Ed.

"But you can't cuddle up to a plane!" joked Tex, wrapping his long arms around his tall, thin body while making a goofy face.

I picked up a small branch and threw it at him, and then we all starting laughing. Tex picked up the branch and stoked the fire; Ed wandered off to relieve himself. I refilled our tin cups.

Eventually, we grew silent and sipped Scotch, while contemplating all that had been said. Light winds rustled through the trees, and the rush of the waterfall had become background music. The fire continued to crackle, and the moon's glow added to the beauty and serenity of our surroundings. This may have been the first time since back home that I felt I could actually relax. Then I was struck by a thought that was both simple and profound.

"You know what, fellas? It just hit me! WE SURVIVED! Sure, the experience has changed us forever, but we made it out of the Nam. We're home now. No doubt for the rest of our days, we got a lot to live with, but we also got a lot to live for. The best we can do is to be there for each other, without judgment, and without trying to make these awful things seem OK. They will never be OK. But we have gotta try to find what's OK for us, here, back in the world."

"I propose a toast," said Tex, hoisting his glass. "To the three of us as we are about to embark on our next mission – surviving and thriving back in the world. It will be easy for us to enjoy the good times ahead. Let's pledge to be there for each other should bad times come along, or if things go haywire, like they inevitably will. We'll have each other's backs."

We drank to that. And drank some more.

After a while, we quieted down again. I walked away to a peaceful spot and sat on a large rock. I needed to let this sink in: I, Sam Walker, survived one year in Vietnam. I survived 187 top-secret missions. I survived being shot down over Cambodia. I survived by killing the enemy face to face when not doing so would have surely resulted in my death. I witnessed horrendous overkills, but nothing that would be called a battle. Will I ever be able to excise the memory of the human ear necklace, severed heads on poles, and dismembered body parts hanging from trees? Will I ever forget the burning stench in the aftermath of napalm? Did I have to go through all of that dangerous and horrible stuff to meet the woman I would fall in love with; to forge such strong relationships with a number of good men? If so, I certainly paid a hefty price.

With a wave of optimism, I thought, *Here I am, USA, with all the bad things behind me, and the good things ahead!*

Then reality set in, and I shuddered. The bad stuff could not be left behind like an old pair of boots. I fear I'll be taking that with me wherever I go, for the rest of my days. I just hope I can carry it.

~ The End ~

Epilogue

With regard to the bombing of Cambodia, several sources disagree on specific numbers: the duration of the campaign, the tonnage of bombs dropped, and the death toll attributed to the bombing. However, the indisputable evidence of that destruction can be seen from the vantage point of the overhead skies, where the earth of Cambodia displays a scarred, cratered surface in place of a lush jungle and life that used to be. Despite differences in the numbers, it is obvious that the bombing took a catastrophic toll, ending lives, changing lives, and changing the landscape of Cambodia, both physically and politically.

The aggressive bombing campaign undertaken during the war in Vietnam contributed to the conditions under which the communist Khmer Rouge gained power. It is reported that this brutal regime, led by the ruthless dictator, Pol Pot, would go on to claim the lives of two million innocent Cambodian men, women, and children.

Sam, Tex, Ed, and other pilots with top-secret clearance performed as the conductors of an orchestra. They waved the batons that directed the B-52s that brought about the crescendo, ultimately, between the bombing and the Pol Pot genocide, leaving over 2,500,000 dead as the result of waving a baton, to orchestrate a score written by others.

These many years later, Cambodia still gives up her killing fields. Innocent children who simply went out to play, stumbled across live, undetonated ordnance just waiting like a coiled cobra to go off. The children's remains number in the thousands and continues climbing to this day. Survivors with stumps where their arms and legs used to be are living testaments to this ever-present danger.

So, if asked of these pilots, 'What did you do in the war?' their answer, 'I was a conductor in an orchestra', would not be a lie. If asked,

'What did you perform?' To answer, '*Adagio for Strings* by Samuel Barber' would be fitting.

Afterward

The incidents in this story are based on my own experiences as well as those of other real-life soldiers with whom I served in Vietnam, as a pilot flying top-secret missions. Like many war veterans, much of our post-service lifetimes have been spent battling the after-effects of war, suffering from alcoholism, drug addiction, Agent Orange exposure, cancer, cardiovascular disease, Post Traumatic Stress Disorder, and Anxiety Disorders. Far too many families have borne the brunt of failed marriages and fractured relationships due to our inability to fit 'back in the world'.

I still wonder to this day, if I had not been forced to kill human beings to save my own life, or had not been a door gunner, however briefly, but long enough to experience the need to kill or be killed, or witnessed on my last mission the extinction of a peaceful village on the Cambodian border, which I had held dear to my heart, whether I, a simple farm boy flying a little Piper Cub over tomato fields, salt marshes, and South Carolina beaches, will ever become whole again after serving my country during my tour of duty in Vietnam.

Nearly five decades later, some of my nights are laden with screaming nightmares and cold sweats, triggered by those atrocities, now forty-seven years old but as fresh as yesterday. It's as though I've stumbled into a bottomless pit of subliminal self-loathing, unforgiveness, an inability to love or to be loved, marked by train-wreck marriages, decades of alcoholism, and worst of all, strained relationships with my wonderful children.

I did not know then, I could not possibly have known, that my world would start spinning out of control soon after arriving at Tan Son Nhut Air Base and would continue to spin for almost a lifetime. I was operating at 'unusual attitudes beyond my control'. Like all good men who survive war, a part of our soul gets torn away at such a deep level, that, well … it can't be repaired. It takes God's grace to endure this life. I was willing to pay a price to perform my civic duty but never could have imagined how high that price would be. It's a price that is too high. I just hope it ends at the grave and is a pardonable sin.

Acknowledgements

Close friends, Denise and Dennis Maksimowitz, offered to help by taking on the job of editing, planning, and organizing my draft, which would still be collecting dust if not for them.

Denise Vaughn, a dear friend, just happened to come back into my life after forty-four years. During the critical months of finalizing the work, she kept me focused on the straight and narrow. As I am a disabled veteran with PTSD and Anxiety Disorder, she had her hands full. I don't think many people could have done what she did for me.

As a first-time author, I appreciate the book's endorsers, Charlie, Ron, Larry, and Bud, either pilots, combat pilots, authors or both, for connecting with my story and supporting my work.

My daughter, Holli, first read the rough draft over twelve years ago and never stopped encouraging me to finish it.

Last but certainly not least, I thank my father. If he had not supported my passion by gifting me flying lessons ... well, I might not even be here.

For all of these generous acts, I am extremely grateful.

Music List

To enhance your reading pleasure, you may find that listening to the following selections while reading the associated chapter brings you to that place in time.

Chapter 9 – First Mission - *Adagio for Strings* by Samuel Barber

Chapter 11 – Black Void - *Riders in the Storm* by the Doors

Chapter 16 – Red Mullet Island - *War* by Edwin Star

Chapter 17 – Hawaii - *When a Man loves a Woman* by Percy Sledge

Chapter 18 – Monsters - *Riders in the Storm* by the Doors

Chapter 19 – Shot Down - Soundtrack from Bat*21, *The Swanee* by Christopher Young

Chapter 24 – Berm Duty - *All Along the Watchtower* by Jimmy Hendrix

Chapter 27 – Last Mission - *Blowin' in the Wind* by Peter, Paul and Mary

Epilogue – *Adagio for Strings* by Samuel Barber

I recommend listening to this last piece in a quiet, still place. It suggests the tears of war, dripping from melodious strings.

Glossary

Agent Orange – An herbicide and defoliant chemical used to kill off thick jungle plant life to eliminate enemy advantage. Years later, major health problems, including cancer, diabetes and heart attacks, resulted from those exposed to it during the Vietnam War.
AWAC- Airborne Warning and Control – an early warning system used to detect other airborne aircraft, and most importantly, SAM sites.
Berm – In modern military engineering, a berm is a perimeter line of fortification that serves as an effective obstacle to invading sources. Typically, 10′ high, it is constructed by bulldozer pushing up mounds of dirt.
Bingo – Military slang for running out of fuel in an aircraft.
Black Void – Flying in complete, total darkness with no visual references to anything above or below.
Boocoo – Bastardized version of the French word, *beaucoup*, meaning much, many, or a lot of.
CCO – Critical Cross Over refers to the place and time it takes to cross the border, known as the Fence, into Cambodia or Laos.
Charlie – Military slang for communist forces, especially the Viet Cong and NVA.
Chopper – Helicopter.
CIA/NSA – Central Intelligence Agency/National Security Agency.
Comm – Communications.
Cowling – Removable cover of the aircraft engine.
Dead-stick - Type of forced landing when a plane loses all of its propulsive power. The stick refers to the traditional wooden propeller.
Didi –Vietnamese slang meaning *Get Lost!*
Dink- Dehumanizing racist term for Asians.

DMZ – Demilitarized Zone: an area where governments or military powers forbid military installations.
Empennage -Airplane tail assembly; a structure that provides stability.
Feet Wet- Military slang for flying over water.
Flight Ops – Short for Flight Operations.
FNG – F***ing New Guy.
Frag – short for fragmentation grenade.
G-Force – Force of gravity or force of acceleration, which can reach a lethal level for humans or aircraft.
GI – Government Issue, General Issue; or slang for a soldier because they are considered government property.
Gook – Dehumanizing racist term for Asians.
Grunt – Slang for infantryman or soldier.
HALO jump – High Altitude/Low Opening type of parachute jump into hard to reach areas used by Navy SEALs and Special Forces.
Hooch – Military or civilian, a hut or simple dwelling; typically, small and poorly constructed.
Jolly Green – Sikorsky HH-3E helicopter, primarily used for search and rescue missions, nick-named for their green body color and size.
Klick – Military slang for Kilometer, a standard measure of distance; 10 klicks = 6.2 miles.
Mamasan – Generally, a woman of authority in Asian culture; or female domestics.
Mayday – The international radio distress signal used by aircraft and naval vessels.
MP – Military Police.
MSL – Mean Sea Level.
Nuoc Cham or Nuoc Mam - Fermented fish sauce, also known as "Vietnamese ketchup".
NVA – North Vietnamese Army, the enemy.
POW – Prisoner of War.
R&R – Rest and Recreation. A soldier's short, authorized vacation from the war.

RDF (WWII RDF) – Radio Direction Finder, useful in locating the airfield tower.
RPG – Rocket Propelled Grenade.
SAM – Surface-to-Air Missile.
Sampan – A Vietnamese peasant boat.
Sapper – A Viet Cong or NVA commando, always armed with explosives, on suicide missions to kill GIs.
SOG – Special Operations Group; a code-named secret elite military unit.
Spook – Military slang for 'spy'.
Stick – Pilot slang for the airplane's hand-operated device to control and fly the aircraft.
STOL – Type of plane well-suited for Short Take Off and Landing conditions.
TO – Technical Operator.
Triple Canopy Jungle – In tropical or subtropical environments, the highest of three levels including ground, intermediate and triple canopy, characterized by dense vegetation and very tall trees.
USO – United Services Organization, a non-profit, charitable organization supporting military members and their families, known for entertaining the troops at war time.
VC – Viet Cong, the enemy.

Made in USA - North Chelmsford, MA
1062449_9781710947991
03.25.2020 1108